THEIR WILDEST SAFARI DREAM

SUZANNE MERCHANT

CINDERELLA'S SECOND CHANCE IN PARIS

MICHELE RENAE

MILLS & BOON

First published in Great Britain 2022
by Mills & Boon, an imprint of HarperCollins*Publishers* Ltd,
1 London Bridge Street, London, SE1 9GF

www.harpercollins.co.uk

HarperCollins*Publishers*
1st Floor, Watermarque Building,
Ringsend Road, Dublin 4, Ireland

Their Wildest Safari Dream © 2022 Suzanne Merchant

Cinderella's Second Chance in Paris © 2022 Michele Hauf

ISBN: 978-0-263-30232-5

12/22

This book is produced from independently certified FSC™ paper
to ensure responsible forest management.
For more information visit: www.harpercollins.co.uk/green.

Printed and Bound in Spain using 100% Renewable Electricity
at CPI Black Print, Barcelona

THEIR WILDEST
SAFARI DREAM

SUZANNE MERCHANT

MILLS & BOON

For my family

CHAPTER ONE

ELEVEN YEARS AGO she'd begged Jack to marry her, pleaded with him to make *her* the wife his father demanded he find. Until he had a 'half-decent wife', the old man had shouted, any plans Jack had to drag the Themba reserve and its two hundred square miles of African bush into the twenty-first century could go to hell.

'You, Anna?' Jack had raked his fingers through his hair, frustration and temper simmering in his slate-grey eyes. 'Are you insane? You're just a kid.'

His brutal rejection had bewildered and belittled her.

'I'm eighteen, Jack. Officially an adult, and I...'

'And you're going back to England to take your degree. It's what your mother wanted, remember?' He'd turned his back on her and walked away. 'And anyway,' he'd said, over his shoulder, 'I don't want a wife. Not ever.'

Back then, there had been no airstrip on the dusty, thorn-dry reserve. There had definitely been no such thing as a helicopter transfer from the little airport at Skukuza. It had been a lurching, rough, seven-hour journey to Johannesburg in an ancient Land Rover Defender, and Jack had taken her on it the following day, three weeks earlier than necessary.

She'd kept her head turned away from him for the entire trip, and neither of them had spoken.

Themba was the only home she'd ever known, but she'd never been back. Until today.

The helicopter dipped and banked sharply and suddenly there it was, beneath her feet: the rocky outcrop on the hilltop where the lions had used to laze in the sun, and the sandy riverbed, bone-dry at this time of year, before the summer rains came, and the dark smudge of the fever trees which had shaded the huts. She could see the rough imprint of the place she remembered, like in one of those aerial photographs of an ancient settlement, faint outlines beneath the surface on a modern map. The landscape was fixed, as old as time, but everything else had changed.

She'd been travelling for two days. She'd eaten a tiny amount of the plastic airline food, she hadn't slept at all, and nascent anxiety, in the form of that little flip of her stomach, had shown itself only a couple of hours out of San Diego. It had built with each leg of the journey. Now, it had a stranglehold on her which mocked all her attempts at controlled breathing, visualisation or mindful thought.

She gave in to it and gripped the leather tote on her knees.

The email from the institute which had dropped into her inbox, asking her to replace an injured colleague on this trip, had been urgent. There'd been no question of refusing the request. This was a work assignment, and she'd approach it with her usual stringent professionalism.

It was also, she told herself, an opportunity to get answers to her questions about her parents. Questions which tethered her to Themba and her past, however long her absence and however many miles she put between herself and the place where she'd grown up.

The pilot grinned at her from behind his aviator shades and pointed down, then held up three fingers, which she took to mean they'd be on the ground in three minutes. No doubt he interpreted her bloodless knuckles as a fear of flying.

He was right about her unease, but wrong—so absolutely wrong—about the root of it. Every muscle in her body was rigid with apprehension, and it annoyed the hell out of her. Because that impulsive, wild, eighteen-year-old, who'd suggested herself as a wife for Jack, no longer existed. She'd been obliterated in the past eleven years by three brilliant degrees and an astonishing ascent of her chosen career ladder. She could deliver a lecture to a hall full of restless students, address a conference of five hundred delegates or present a paper to a board of crusty professors of zoology with ice-cool confidence.

But the prospect of what lay ahead in the next few minutes had shredded her composure to bits.

Three minutes, and she didn't feel ready. But would she ever?

A rush of hot panic burned through her and she wondered if she could change her mind, return to Skukuza on the helicopter. She could be on a flight back to London this evening, possibly—tomorrow for sure.

Because three minutes meant she was about to come face to face with Jack.

Anna stared at the ground as it rose rapidly towards them. She glimpsed the striped dazzle of a herd of zebra, clouds of red dust billowing from beneath their hooves as they galloped away from the racing shadow of the helicopter. Then came the bump as the aircraft touched down on the baked earth.

The pilot pulled off his headset and turned in his seat. 'There you are. Safe and sound.'

If only he knew.

The door next to Anna slid open and a man in a khaki bush shirt, with the name *Themba* embroidered on the pocket, gave her a half-salute.

'Welcome to Themba, Dr Kendall.'

Jack Eliot heard the far-off thump of the approaching helicopter and swore. He glanced at his watch. They were early, dammit, and he was nowhere near ready.

He'd roared back into the camp ten minutes before, after a night of hardly any sleep and a day spent in fruitless pursuit of the poachers who'd been spotted shortly before midnight. They'd melted away into the bush in the vicinity of Crooks' Corner, as they so often did. The lie of the land would have been embedded in their souls from birth, and they'd had the choice of two borders to escape over. But at least it seemed they hadn't killed anything. Not this time. If they had, he and his tracker would have spotted the tell-tale lazy circling of vultures, homing in on their grisly meal.

He was filthy, hot and beyond exhausted. What he wanted—*needed*—was a shower and a beer and an early night. But instead he had to entertain his guests at dinner on the deck of the Marula Restaurant in two hours' time. And before that he had to welcome a representative of the Institute for Wildlife Conservation, who had arrived on the helicopter that had already touched down, judging by the slowing beat of the rotor blades. He hoped Dan was there to meet it in the Range Rover.

It was important—make that crucial—that everything went smoothly for this visit. He'd planned it, as he did everything, down to the last detail. If you had things planned, you also had them under control. The years when his life had lurched from one crisis to another were over—had been ever since his father…

He shook his head, dragging his tired brain back to the present. Now he had to hope nothing would go wrong. Although in his experience, that particular hope was rarely fulfilled. In the bush, the opportunities for disaster were legion.

In the hands of this visitor lay the power to grant him funding to extend the research centre at Themba and to train additional staff to step up the fight against poaching. Funding, although welcome, would bring with it far more than money. It would signal international recognition of the importance of the conservation work they were doing here, and worldwide interest would follow. There'd be more jobs for local people, and opportunities for education in the rural communities. The survival of the animals, many of them endangered species, depended on it.

Jack spread his hands on the surface of his desk and pushed himself upright. He grabbed a bottle of water from the fridge and took several gulps, slaking his thirst and shifting the coating of dust in his mouth and throat. He stopped short of tipping the remaining contents of the bottle over himself. The dust in his hair would turn to mud, and besides, water was a precious resource, in short supply at the dry end of winter, when the riverbeds were cracked and parched and most of the waterholes had shrunk to puddles.

So he combed his fingers through his hair instead and washed his hands. Stubble roughened his jaw, but he couldn't do anything about that now.

Ducking his head to look out of the window, he saw the dark green Range Rover with the gold Themba crest on its side cross the low bridge and bump over the cattle grid into the camp. Then he headed out of his office and across the deck.

He paused for a moment and glanced to the west, doing his habitual weather-check. The blood-red ball of the sun hovered above a clear horizon. No clouds, so no rain yet.

The Range Rover pulled up at the foot of the steps. Dan leapt from the driver's seat and strode around to the passenger side, while another staff member stepped forward to take a leather bag from the boot.

Jack narrowed his eyes as a woman appeared around the front of the four-by-four. She wasn't what he'd expected at all, because for starters he'd been expecting a man. He kicked himself mentally for his old-fashioned, oh-so-predictable mind-set. He might have hauled Themba into the twenty-first century, but was he stuck somewhere in the

Dark Ages? Doctors of zoology didn't have to be men, for God's sake. But he hadn't queried it—just assumed. They also didn't have to be grey-haired and bearded, but they didn't often come in the shape of the one who now paused at the foot of the wide, granite steps. He was certain of that because a figure like hers was one in a million.

She raised her head, and one hand moved to flatten against her chest, then it drifted across to join the other in a double-fisted grip on the strap of her shoulder bag. She placed a booted foot on the bottom step…

Anna slid out of the passenger seat before the driver had cut the ignition. Dan—her welcoming party of one—had tried to make conversation during the drive from the air-strip, and she'd tried and mostly failed to sound intelligent. Now he closed the door and followed her around the bonnet of the vehicle.

She was here, and she really, *really* needed to get this done.

At the foot of the steps she raised her eyes, tried to breathe, and tried again. Her first glimpse of Jack's six-foot-four, wide-shouldered frame had knocked the air from her lungs.

With powerful, long thighs beneath worn cargo pants, slim hips, and a chest and shoulders broad enough to block out the light, he looked harder than she remembered—and *built*. And he looked as though he'd had a hell of a day. His dark hair, cropped short at the sides and thick with dust, was untidily raked off his forehead. Shirtsleeves rolled to the elbows revealed corded, tanned forearms, and that watch which did everything was still strapped to his wrist.

She'd thought she loved him when she was eighteen, but she was over him now—right? She'd been over him for ten years and a number of days. So why had this hot rush of grown-up, X-rated desire set her heart pumping and lit a fire in her abdomen?

Anna began the slow climb up the steps towards him…

The white cotton shirt the woman wore looked crisp and clean, and it made Jack even more uncomfortable about his own straight-out-of-the-bush appearance. A narrow red leather belt was threaded through the loops of figure-hugging slim jeans, which encased long, long, wrap-around-me legs. Her lace-up leather boots were sturdy enough for the bush, and sexy as sin teamed with such a super-sleek body.

Jack jerked his thoughts back to reality. Where had that little lapse come from? He kept his distance, mentally and especially physically, from guests, staff and business associates, and kept his libido in a grip a crocodile would envy. There was no time for any involvement that didn't concern the well-being of Themba, his staff and the animals on his land. He'd fought to make Themba into what it was today, and he was damned if he'd let his purpose stray. So he instructed his brain to stamp out the annoying flame somewhere low down in his gut reminding him that he hadn't had sex since… Since he couldn't be bothered to remember when.

The thought that she might be a guest whose arrival he'd somehow overlooked dropped into his head. He'd been absent since midnight, so he might have missed something. If that was the case, he'd have words. He liked—*demanded*—to be kept informed, about everything. No exceptions.

He scanned the road to the airstrip, but it was quiet. There was no second helicopter making an approach, no cloud of dust signalling another vehicle on its way to the lodge.

As she mounted the final step onto the deck he realised she was taller than he'd thought. He studied her for a moment, something snagging at his memory. A straight nose, a wide, full, kiss-me-now mouth fixed in serious mode, and a lightly tanned complexion. She must be exhausted after a journey of twenty-four hours, so how come she looked as if she'd just stepped out of a fashion shoot?

Dan appeared at his shoulder. 'Jack? Are you okay?' He stepped forward. 'This is…'

Single pearls gleamed in her earlobes, and something about the tilt of her chin as she looked up at him disturbed a memory buried deep. Green eyes, the colour of cold sea glass, met his. His heart lurched in his chest.

He felt Dan's hand on his arm. 'Jack?'

She extended a slim hand towards him, her eyes fixed on his face. 'Hello, Jack,' she said, her voice as cool as her eyes.

'Anna?'

The word that came out of his throat was rough and harsh. It had lodged there, never to be spoken, for so long it sounded unreal—like some made up name. He tried it on his tongue again, as he closed his fingers around her hand.

'Anna…'

She left her hand in his for a moment, then withdrew it. He inhaled and tried to find some oxygen, but there didn't seem to be any in his vicinity. His head swam, and through a haze of shock he heard Dan's voice, again.

'Jack, this is Dr Kendall, who we've been expecting. Would you like me to show her to her suite?'

Jack pulled a hand over his eyes and shook his head. 'Thank you, Dan, no. I'll… I'll take it from here.'

'Okay.' Dan sounded doubtful. 'If you're sure?' He turned away, then twisted round again. 'You were out of contact, Jack. The email only came in…'

Jack sent him a look and he shrugged and backed off, turning to take the steps down to the vehicle two at a time.

She… Anna…watched him with those frosty eyes. The last time he'd seen them they'd been sparkling like emeralds with unshed tears. She'd jerked her head backwards, so the casual farewell peck he'd steeled himself to drop on her cheek had landed somewhere in the air between them.

As he'd driven off he'd watched her in the rear-view mirror and wondered if she'd let the tears fall once he'd gone. The set of her shoulders and her ramrod spine had made him think otherwise. He'd breathed a sigh of relief, even though it had felt as if a part of him had been ripped away.

He hauled his mind back to the present—to now, and how to handle this. His brain felt sluggish, as if he was watching a slow-motion movie of himself.

He hated surprises. Most of the surprises he'd had in his life had been disasters dressed up by someone else to lessen the blow. Strangely, the only good one he could remember was Anna's first arrival at Themba, as a two-year-old orphan. With the benefit of hindsight he realised that was the day when some sort of purpose had begun to emerge from the random chaos of his childhood.

'It seems you aren't expecting me, Jack.' Her brow creased.

'I… No, I wasn't.' Just in time he stopped himself from saying he'd been expecting a man. He had the feeling such an admission wouldn't go down too well with this version of Anna. 'I… I've been in the bush for almost twenty-four hours.'

He wrapped his arms across his chest and tucked his hands into his armpits to keep them out of trouble. Because his gut reaction was to wrap them around her and hold her in an embrace which would sweep them back to the time when she'd appeared, like something miraculous, from a bundle on a woman's back. To all those years when they'd been easy together, great mates who could talk about everything and anything, before she'd grown up and an inconvenient, tantalising tension had begun to crackle between them.

Her eyes warmed by one degree of frost and she tilted her head. The last horizontal rays from the setting sun caught her hair, slicking rose-pink over the blonde. Her hair—her glorious bright hair, which had used to ripple to her waist and fly out behind her in a banner of gold as she leapt from rock to rock, barefoot and agile as an antelope—was tamed and bound into a neat French plait. The end of the thick braid hung over her right shoulder, tied with a narrow length of black velvet ribbon.

Jack's brain finally kicked into gear. How had he missed this? There was something wrong—and it was her name. On the documentation he was sure it had said *Professor A. Scott*, and that wasn't her name. Was it? The awful thought that she might be married, to someone called Scott, made his stomach churn. Was she married? To someone called Scott? Surely he would have known by some process of telepathy if she'd got married?

That was ridiculous, of course, because he hadn't heard from her for eleven years, so how could he have known? But at least he wasn't going crazy. If her real name had been on the paperwork it would have hit him in the chest like a bolt from a stun gun.

And after he'd recovered from the shock? What would he have done?

Asked for someone else, probably, although that would've been pushing his luck with the institute, risking annoying them when he couldn't afford to.

'No,' he said again, forcing his voice into something like a normal register. 'Your name. It's not Scott.' He risked a glance at her left hand, which held the strap of her bag. No ring visible.

The small frown between her brows cleared. 'Oh, Alan Scott collided with a lamppost on his e-scooter and broke an ankle. I'm the last-minute substitute. Surely they let you know?'

'No, they didn't…' Jack stopped.

Links to the outside world were famously unreliable and they'd maintained radio silence since before midnight. That must be the email Dan had mentioned.

'I apologise for the mix-up,' Anna said, 'but right now…' She looked around, appearing to notice her surroundings for the first time. 'Right now, I've been travelling for forty-eight hours. I'm so tired I can barely stand, and I need a shower and something to eat—preferably in that order. Could you show me where I'm sleeping? I don't recognise anything any more.'

'Forty-eight hours? Was the flight from London delayed?'

She looked puzzled for a moment, then shook her head. 'No. But I started in San Diego.'

The door clicked shut and Anna finally—*finally*—released her stranglehold on her bag, dropped it on a low glass table and examined the room. Rough granite walls, painted white, disappeared up into the shadows of the steeply pitched thatched roof. The warm air moved to the slow beat of a ceiling fan.

She sank into one of the cream linen armchairs and exhaled, staring through floor-to-ceiling glass doors which opened onto a wide covered deck.

She'd held it together. Although fate, or something, had been on her side. The way Jack had been utterly blindsided by her arrival had helped her to hide her anxiety. Luckily, once she'd climbed up the steps—fourteen of them, she'd counted, and a fraction of the number she'd needed—she'd started to recover.

She'd seen the moment when frank interest had shifted to wariness in Jack's eyes, and then the shocked jolt of recognition.

She'd fought off the impulse to step forward and put her

arms around him. That was how it had used to be, when she'd come home from boarding school in those long-gone, carefree days.

There was a scar she didn't remember on his forehead. She'd wanted to run her fingers over it and ask him how he'd got it. But she'd kept her cool, and she'd keep it for the next week, even if it half killed her. Her professional reputation depended on it.

Fingers clumsy with fatigue, she untied the laces of her boots, and when she finally eased them off, followed by her socks, she put her feet on the cool stone floor and felt the stress drain out of her. She could have curled up right there on the chair and slept for twelve hours. But a vast bed, made up with fine embroidered cotton, with a linen cover folded at the foot, had been turned down, inviting sleep there. Misty mosquito netting, suspended from a hoop above, hung in protective drifts around it.

Anna padded into the bathroom and changed her mind about a shower. The bath was deep and long, and she turned on the taps, tipping in a good measure of bath oil from a square glass bottle which stood on a shelf alongside other luxuries. The scent of lavender rose in the steam as she peeled off the clothes she'd been wearing for two days and a night, and slid into the silky water.

Jack closed the door to the executive suite and headed for the sanctuary of his own space. His accommodation was all that remained of the original camp, and the executive suites were close to it by design. It was where official visitors stayed, and he liked to be on hand and nearby because they were always there for business reasons.

He'd have to treat Anna in the same way he treated all of them, but it would take a little time and a lot of effort to get used to the idea.

The old buildings among the fever trees had consisted

of a group of thatched huts. He and his father had occupied one each, and when Anna had been old enough she'd had her own, too. The remainder had been used by staff, and the men who'd used to come in loud, bragging groups to shoot big game.

The kitchen had been an outside affair, with a firepit and a spit at its centre. It had been the last area Jack had updated, after building the rest of the lodge. Now he had an en-suite bathroom, a proper kitchen, and covered walkways between the huts. The old kitchen had become an outdoor seating area, around a new firepit.

Here he could relax, away from the formality of the guest lodge, and be himself. Books lined the walls, and a silver-framed photograph of his mother as a young woman stood on a side table.

He strode straight through his living room and into the kitchen, where he pulled a beer from the fridge and tugged open the ring-pull. He tipped the cold liquid down his throat, swallowed and tipped some more. If he'd thought his day difficult, it had got a whole lot more complicated in the last half an hour.

Anna. He wiped the back of a hand across his mouth and walked through the sliding doors onto his deck, gazing down at the glint of one of the last remaining patches of water in the river but not seeing it. She was back, and he felt as though he'd been trampled by a charging rhino— only he was still alive.

Eleven years ago, he'd hurt her. He knew he had. And her silence had been proof, if he'd needed it, that she'd gone for good. He'd written to her, at the only address he'd had, but he'd never heard back. In the end, he'd given up.

He'd had to make sure she left for her own safety, and he wondered if he'd find a time, in the next seven days, to explain it to her in a way that might start to heal the rift between them. Only he didn't know if she'd want that.

In that split-second moment of recognition at the top of the steps he'd been catapulted back in time, to where memories churned and raged and uncertainty ruled. He drained the can and crushed it in his fist. Then he glanced at his watch.

He had an hour to calm down, take a shower, find fresh clothes and get a grip. Then he had to spend the evening making meaningful conversation with the group of nine American ecologists who were his guests this week. They were sincere, earnest and deeply interested in the work being undertaken at Themba, in conservation, education and the frontline fight against poaching. And they'd paid handsomely for the privilege of luxury accommodation, five-star treatment and his company. They deserved his undivided attention—something he knew he was going to find difficult to give this evening.

Firstly, he'd have to stop thinking about the woman who had climbed up the steps towards him and his response to her. He'd tried to kill those feelings long ago, when she was fifteen and suddenly not a child any more. He'd put up cool defences against her and she'd made a game of trying to breach them. Only today she hadn't had to try. He should have been safe after eleven years, but those carefully built defences had crumbled at the touch of her hand, at the direct cool gaze of her eyes. They'd slipped off him, leaving him exposed and unprepared. He hated the feeling.

He stripped off his dusty, sweaty clothes, lifted some weights and ran for half an hour on the treadmill. Then he decided on a cold shower. Maybe that would bring his body to heel.

The African night had fallen with its abrupt swiftness when he stepped outside again, and it was fully dark. The nocturnal sounds of the bush were ramping up, but the dry heat still lingered. Ground-level solar lanterns glowed along the edges of the paved paths which curved through the camp. He could see golden lamplight flickering through the branches of the trees which sheltered the Marula Restaurant, where he should have been five minutes ago, ready to welcome his guests.

Quiet voices drifted towards him and he quickened his pace. Then he stopped. From the angle of the path he could see a corner of Anna's deck. Soft light spilled through the open doors of her suite, silhouetting her where she leaned her elbows on the railing. The white linen fabric of a Themba bathrobe gleamed in the dimness. Her hair, released from the constraints of that tight plait, flowed over her shoulders.

He watched her for a long minute, and then she turned her head in his direction.

'I know you're there, Jack,' she said in a low voice. 'I've always known when you were there.'

CHAPTER TWO

JACK DROPPED HIS HEAD, ran a hand over the back of his neck and swore under his breath. He pulled his phone from his pocket and tapped a message to Dan.

Keep them talking. With you in ten.

The door was unlocked, but he hesitated on the threshold. Time was when he would have walked right into Anna's bedroom without a second thought, he reflected. And she into his.

'You can come in, Jack.'

She still stood on the deck, her hands buried in the pockets of the pale bathrobe. An evening breeze rustled through the trees and lifted a corner of the fine linen, exposing a long length of butterscotch-smooth thigh to Jack's hungry gaze.

He dragged his eyes away, trying to blank the thought that the robe might be all she wore. She stepped off the deck onto the slate tiles and slid the door closed behind her.

Jack moved into the centre of the room. 'Your door should be locked.' He barely recognised his own voice. He swallowed. 'It's not safe to leave it open.'

Anna lifted her chin and smiled. Her eyes gleamed with a flash of mischief. She hadn't grown out of that—or out of the dimple in the middle of her left cheek.

'So it seems,' she said.

'No. That's not…'

What was wrong with him? She had him tied in knots and he hadn't even touched her, apart from their hand-shake earlier, when his world had been shaken up and then dropped around him in a shape he didn't recognise.

He dragged air into his uncooperative lungs and shook his head. 'That's not what I meant.'

She tipped her head to one side, regarding him steadily, a hint of teasing still playing at the corners of her mouth. 'Oh?'

'It's the monkeys.' He glanced away from her, out into the dark beyond the window. 'It's okay now it's dark. But during the day they'll find their way in. They've learned to open the doors.'

He watched her walk towards him. Her bare toes were tipped in a pearly shell-pink. Since when had she ever used nail polish?

She stopped and gestured towards the crisp linen chairs. 'Won't you sit down? We should probably have a conver-sation.'

She was too close. His body had leapt into life in a way he hadn't experienced for…well, for ever. It felt like for ever since he'd walked away from her.

He caught his bottom lip between his teeth and pushed his hands into his pockets. Feeling his phone in one of them reminded him that Dan was waiting, along with the Ameri-can ecologists—waiting for him to show up for dinner and intelligent discussion.

He shook his head, relieved to have a legitimate excuse to leave. Rather than taming his wayward body and mind, the exercise and the cold shower had simply revived him. Right now, the only conversation he wanted to have with Anna would not take place on a chair…

He kept his eyes away from the gauzy mosquito netting around the bed.

'I can't stay. I'm hosting a dinner for some of the guests and I'm already late.' He shrugged. 'I'm sorry.'

'That's okay. Like I said earlier, I'm tired. And hungry.' The corners of her wide mouth lifted. 'When I've eaten and slept I'll be more like myself.'

The words that came out of Jack's mouth next weren't the ones he'd planned to say at all.

'Will that,' he asked, 'be the you I know, or this new version of yourself?'

He wished the question unasked as soon as he'd uttered it, but it was too late. He saw a flash of something like anger in the emerald depths of her eyes.

'The version of me you see is who I am now, Jack.' She pulled her hands from her pockets and curled her fingers around the edges of the robe at her throat. 'The one you thought you knew vanished…oh, years ago.' The bones of her knuckles shone white under the taut skin. 'Did you think I'd still be a naïve eighteen-year-old? Just a *kid*?'

Something hit the slate floor, stone on stone. It skittered towards him, coming to rest near his feet. Anna made a grab for it, but Jack got there first. He straightened up and examined the small heart-shaped pebble, turning it over in his fingers. A thin diagonal band of white quartz dissected it.

'What's this?' he asked, although he already knew.

Anna straightened up and lifted her chin. She hadn't grown out of that faintly defiant gesture, either. And if he'd thought she was too close before, this was approaching lethal.

'It's…nothing. Just something that was in my pocket.' She held out a hand, palm upwards. 'Can I have it? Please?'

Jack raised his eyes and his gaze collided with hers. She didn't look away.

'It's not nothing.'

Her eyes held his. 'It's…'

'It's the pebble I gave you when you were twelve.'

She didn't deny it, but her lids dropped, hiding any emotion in her eyes.

'Isn't it, Anna?'

She gave a quick nod. 'It… I found it in my wash bag and it reminded me…*reminds* me…'

Jack looked beyond her, out into the inky darkness. 'It was down there in the riverbed, where I found you that day. Do you remember?'

Anna turned her head and followed the direction of his glance. 'Yes. I remember. I was crying…'

'You were crying because you were being sent away to boarding school.' His voice gentled. 'You were afraid.'

She turned back to look at him. 'Themba was all I knew. I couldn't imagine how I would live anywhere else, with strangers.'

Her tone was forceful, but she nipped her bottom lip between her teeth and he thought it was to stop it trembling.

Then she gave a wobbly smile. 'And I'd have to wear *shoes*.'

'You were sitting on a boulder, flinging pebbles into the water, but I rescued this one.' He smoothed a finger over the small talisman in his hand. 'Can you remember what I said when I gave it to you?'

She followed the movement of his finger. 'You said that whenever I felt lonely and homesick I should hold it in my hand and I'd know you were thinking of me and I'd be back here soon.'

Jack nodded. 'Anything else?'

Her smooth brow furrowed. 'I remember the crocodile. And how cross you were.'

'It was a monster, and it could have swallowed you whole.'

There was that impish dimple again. His stomach hollowed and his chest expanded in a deep, controlling breath.

'Only they don't swallow their prey whole, Jack. You know that.'

'Do you think drowning in the jaws of a croc is any better?'

'I'd seen him. It was a safe enough distance away. And, yes…' she held up her hand as he opened his mouth to speak again '… I do know how fast they can move. I'd worked that out, too.'

'You drove me nuts with the risks you took, Anna.'

'Ah, but you were my teacher, Jack. You and Joseph. Is he still here?'

Jack nodded. 'All our current trackers have been trained by him but he's enjoying retirement now.'

'He taught me well, too. The risks I took were always informed and calculated. I only realised later it wasn't true.'

'What wasn't true? The bushcraft we taught you was impeccable.'

'Not that.' She shrugged. 'I mean, I realised you couldn't have been thinking about me every time I was homesick, because I was homesick all the time.'

'Anna…' He wanted to tell her how wrong she was.

She stretched out her hand again. 'Can I have it back now?'

Jack's fingers closed over the pebble, then he opened his fist to let it drop into her palm. Her fingers brushed against his. He knew then that he'd been right not to touch her, because the shock jolting through him made him grip her hand, pressing the little granite heart into her skin.

She inhaled, a gasp of awareness, and Jack closed the small gap between them. She was tall, but not so tall that the top of her head didn't fit perfectly under his chin.

Her lithe body, which he'd watched grow from childhood compactness into teenaged long-leggedness, felt more rounded than he'd expected. Because it wasn't as if he hadn't imagined this. He'd dreamed of holding her long before she'd left—and long after, too. All he'd ever allowed himself had been a fleeting brush of his hand on hers, a joshing shove of a shoulder over some joke, and maybe, if he was feeling strong enough, a hug when she'd come home from school or he'd returned from university or the mine.

Her naïve attempts at flirtation had stretched his self-control to the limit. But his dreams hadn't prepared him for the reality. He'd never known it would feel like this. Their palms gripped the stone between them, but he splayed his other hand across her shoulder blades. He felt them pull down under his touch as she arched closer to him. He felt her fingers rest on his waist and all the blood in his body headed south. Her breath, quick and shallow, was warm against his collarbone.

'Anna?'

'Mmm?' She turned her head and he rested his forehead against hers.

'I haven't kissed you hello.'

'You stopped doing that when I was fifteen.'

'Yes.' He'd always wondered, stupidly, if she'd noticed.

'And I didn't kiss you goodbye.'

'No. I didn't let you.'

He moved their entwined fingers to tip her chin up with his knuckles and then ran his thumb over her bottom lip. 'So that's two kisses…'

'Jack, I…'

'Don't say anything. Please.'

He let his mouth follow where his thumb had been, feathering across her lips. This wasn't the farewell kiss he'd been going to drop on her cheek, which had never found its mark. This was meant to be a cool, contained greeting between two people who hadn't seen each other in more than a decade. But it turned into a welcome of a different kind altogether.

His hand moved up her back to tangle in the mass of her honey-streaked hair and to cup the back of her head. Then his lips, no longer gentle or tentative, fused with hers, trying to make up for all the years when he wouldn't touch her and all the years when he couldn't.

Every new curve of her body seemed to fit perfectly with his. He combed his fingers through her hair, down to her waist and beyond, clamping her hard against him. Her fingers drifted up to his chest. Their tips were cool against the heated skin of his throat. Then she slipped a hand around the back of his neck and buried her fingers in his hair, pulling him down harder and opening the seam of her lips at the invitation of his tongue.

The universe shrank to this moment, this place, and he wanted it to go on for ever.

Her skin, smooth as satin, smelled of lavender and roses and she tasted… God, she tasted sweeter than honey. He devoured her mouth, trying to satisfy a hunger which had gnawed at him for ever. The little moan in her throat inflamed him even further as she ran her fingers down his spine and spread her hand across his pelvis.

Then suddenly she was pushing against his chest, shaking her head. She tore her mouth from under his and twisted her face away.

'Jack, no!'

Drowning in a whirlpool of sensation and raw desire, he held on to her, trying to claim her lips again, but she resisted.

'Anna, please…'

Her head shifted against his chest. 'No.'

Jack carefully let go of her and wrapped his arms around her, resting his cheek on her head. His breath was ragged as he tried to get his body under some sort of control. He could feel the race of her heart hammering against his ribs. When it had slowed down to something like normal, he slid his arms away from her and took a step back. She raised her hands, as if she was going to reach for him again, then let them drop to her sides.

Jack stared at her. She stared back, and he thought she looked appalled.

'I'm…sorry,' he muttered. 'I didn't mean that to happen. It was…' He stopped, not willing to explain just what she'd done to him.

'It wasn't just you, Jack,' she whispered. 'It was me, too. But this can't happen. It mustn't.' She shook her head. 'Not again.'

Jack pulled a hand over his face, trying to steady himself. She'd moved a little further away from him.

Safer, he thought. *But I don't want safe. Safe was where I was earlier, even though I'd had a terrible day. And I don't want to go back there.*

He breathed in a couple of times, watching her do the same.

'Anna…' he started, then shook his head. 'I don't know how to say this.'

She moved sideways, putting one of the armchairs between them. 'I can't help you, Jack.'

'No. Only I can say sorry for the way I hurt you…before. Before you left.'

Pain flashed in her eyes before she swept her lids down. Her hand tightened around the pebble she still held in one fist, but when she looked at him again her gaze was direct and honest.

'You did. Hurt me, I mean.'

'I know. It's been hard to forget or to forgive myself. In fact, I…'

'I've found it hard to forgive you, too, Jack. You belittled me when I'd just found the courage to lay bare my deepest feelings.'

'I know, and I'm sorry, but…'

'If you remember,' she carried on, straightening her spine and shaking that shimmering mass of spun gold down her back, 'you said I was just a kid. You asked me if I was…*insane.*'

Jack remembered. Every day he remembered. Now he nodded. 'I remember. And you *were.* Just a kid. Maybe not insane, but it was an insane suggestion.'

'I was eighteen, Jack. Legally grown up. Old enough to vote. Old enough to have sex. And to get married.'

Anger stirred and started to build in Jack's gut. Fury at his dead father, because of how he'd been forced to treat her eleven years ago, and frustration at how her memory had haunted him ever since. But his overriding emotion was shock. He might have thought of her every day and many nights since their parting, but he'd always had his emotions under control. What had taken eleven years to build had taken one kiss to be destroyed. The iron grip in which he held his feelings, his heart…his *life*…had melted in the heat of one kiss. He'd lost control of all of it, and it scared him to his soul.

'You may have been eighteen, but you definitely weren't grown-up,' he snapped. 'Your range of experience was limited to Themba, where you ran wild and often wilfully in the bush, and a cloistered girls' boarding school where you had whispered giggling conversations about boys and sex in the dorm after lights out.' He took a breath. 'You needed to get away. I couldn't let you bury yourself here for ever.'

He saw by her look of shock that his words had found their mark.

'Remember,' he went on, his voice softening, 'I also went to boarding school. And your guardian wanted you to complete your education in England.'

Her slim fingers plucked at the fabric on the back of the chair and she looked up again. 'You were right, of course,' she said. 'I did have to go. But I was afraid. I barely remembered meeting George, my unofficial guardian, when I was five and he came to Themba to check up on me. I couldn't imagine what life in London would be like. I wanted to stay here, where I felt safe.'

The irony, thought Jack, was that she'd been far from safe here. He needed to explain that to her when he felt calmer and could find the words.

'And now?' he asked, making a clumsy gesture which encompassed both of them. 'Are you punishing me for that rejection when you were eighteen?'

Confusion clouded her eyes for a moment, followed by comprehension. 'No. Not at all.' She shook her head. 'I'm here to do a job, Jack. You've applied to the institute for funding and official endorsement for Themba, and this assessment I've been sent to do is part of the deal. I have to be, and be seen to be, absolutely professional and impartial in my findings. After Professor Scott was injured I was the only person available, if you want it done now—which you do.'

Hurt twisted in Jack's gut at her words. 'So you didn't *want* to come back?'

She moved around the chair and sat down, folding up her legs and tucking her feet underneath her. 'I never wanted to leave, remember?'

'That's not…' Jack's phone vibrated. The message from Dan consisted of a row of question marks and a desperate emoji face. 'I have to go.'

He took a step towards her, but she pushed out a hand. 'Stay away, Jack.'

He stopped and put a hand up to rub his eyes. 'Okay. I'll… I'll see you tomorrow, sometime. If you need anything…'

'If I need anything I'll call Reception.' She glanced at the glossy folder which lay on the coffee table. 'I'm sure all the necessary information is in there.'

He nodded. 'Of course.'

And then, with his hand on the door handle, he turned back towards her. 'Have you eaten? Ordered food?'

'Not yet. But I will—if the lure of that bed doesn't get to me first.'

Jack swallowed. Did she *have* to mention the bed? He nodded again and pulled the door open. With a last glance at her he stepped into the night.

She'd pulled her hair over one shoulder and was weaving it into a thick plait. It gleamed like shot silk in the lamplight.

'Try to stay awake until you've had a meal. And don't forget to lock the door,' he said, as he closed it behind him.

Jack strode along the shadowy path towards the Marula Restaurant. Raucous laughter drifted through the dark and he felt a stab of guilt at having left Dan to entertain the buttoned-up ecologists. But by the sound of it some of them had relaxed in Dan's care.

He tried to order his mind, to put the importance of discussing the work they were doing at Themba before the soaring and unreasonable demands of his body. Control was something he needed in all areas of his life and at all times. He'd thought he'd mastered the art. But eleven years had dulled the memory of how Anna could test it, with her flirtatious glances and teasing games. She'd had no idea of his fierce desire for her and how he'd fought to control it. And now one touch had brought it flashing back, sharper than a hunter's knife.

He mounted the steps up to the restaurant's deck and found Dan waiting at the top.

'What's happened, mate? You look beat.' Dan frowned, his welcoming expression fading. 'Are you okay?'

Jack pinned on his best, most professional smile and hoped he'd be able to keep it in place. 'Sorry, Dan. Something came up.'

If only he knew.

It was going to be a long night. And as for the week—that hadn't even started.

In spite of her fatigue, Anna's anger simmered. Did Jack think he could pick up with her where they'd left off before she'd made that disastrous proposal? That she was still a naïve, inexperienced teenager who would hang on his every word and do as he said?

That kiss…

She drew in a sharp breath at the memory of it. She knew she was as responsible for it as he was. She'd wanted it as much as he had. Her fingers traced across her lips as she remembered the intoxicating taste of his mouth and how his scent, unchanged over the years, had swamped her with memories.

But she'd come to her senses before he had. If she hadn't pushed him away, that kiss would have gone stratospheric. Just a few more seconds and she wouldn't have been able to stop herself.

She made a determined effort to calm down, rolling her shoulders to release the tension in her neck. But before she could reach for the folder and order a meal, there was a tap on the door. When she opened it a staff member carried a tray into the suite and placed it on the low table.

'With Mr Eliot's compliments.'

Jack had remembered exactly what she liked. Before Anna removed the silver dome from the dish she could smell the buttery omelette which lay beneath it, golden and fluffy. A salad of crunchy green leaves and tender tomatoes, perfectly dressed, filled an earthenware bowl. A frosted bottle of Cape Sauvignon Blanc nestled in a bucket of ice.

Anna sipped from the glass the waiter had poured for her before gliding silently from the suite and sighed. She touched her fingers to her lips again. They were sensitive, and a little swollen, and she tipped her head back against the cushions of the chair and took another mouthful of the ice-cold wine.

Her response to Jack's kiss had shocked and shaken her. Had she honestly believed she'd forgotten how he could make her feel simply by brushing his hand against hers? He'd said she was just a kid when she was eighteen, but hadn't she grown up at all? When he'd rejected her and packed her off with undignified haste to cold, dark, wintry London, she'd gathered up her shredded pride and vowed that nobody would ever make her feel belittled, silly, *crushed*, again.

To date, nobody had.

Her desperate antidote to the unbearable longing she'd felt for the African bush, for Themba, *for Jack*, had been to plunge headlong into academic life, burying herself in work and research, and she'd come out with a set of astounding qualifications and the world of zoology as her oyster. Offers of research posts, lectureships and fellowships had filled her inbox and she'd chosen the best of them.

'What *drives* you?' a curious academic had once probed, when she'd submitted her dissertation ahead of the deadline and in immaculate order.

She'd smiled and shrugged. The truth—which she'd never reveal to anyone—was that she'd wanted to prove herself, over and over again, so that one day she could return to Themba and prove to Jack that she was no longer a kid, and definitely not insane.

And then she'd leave again. Because what she'd decided

she wanted most in the world was something very different from life at Themba with Jack.

She hadn't intended to return this way, but the visit would serve its purpose.

She just hadn't considered that it would be so gut-churningly, heart-wrenchingly difficult.

Until the first leg of her journey, when her return to Themba had become an unavoidable reality, she hadn't doubted she could handle Jack. After all, what she'd felt for him had been nothing more than a teenage crush. But somewhere in the skies over Wyoming she'd begun to wonder if she'd got that completely wrong.

By the time she'd reached the top of that flight of fourteen steps to the deck she'd known for sure she had. Because that crush had grown up along with her, and now it was hot, adult desire which flared into life the moment their hands touched. This wasn't the puffy clouds and pink hearts her teenaged self had imagined. This was hot and dangerous and unstoppable.

Every cell of her body wanted him. How could she have known they'd fit together so seamlessly? For those few brief moments in his arms she'd felt as if she'd found what she'd been searching for before she'd even known she was looking. As if she'd come home.

The omelette melted in her mouth—the perfect food for someone who was too tired to eat. After two glasses of the crisp, light wine lethargy seeped into her veins, relaxing her tired limbs and overactive brain, and the pot of smoky bush tea was the perfect calming end to the meal.

Jack's memory could not be faulted.

Anna slipped between the cool sheets and listened to the night sounds of the bush. A hippo grunted in the riverbed and another answered from further downstream. She shivered and pulled the linen sheet up around her shoulders as the high-pitched cackle of a hyena, celebrating a successful hunt curdled the air. Every sound carried a memory. Some were clear, some long buried, but they were all of Jack and those nights when they'd lain in a hammock, head to toe, outside the huts, identifying the noises and calls of the animals.

Then one holiday the hammock had gone. Jack had said it had got worn out and been thrown away, but he'd sounded unconvincing and she'd never quite believed him.

She relived their kiss for the hundredth time and shifted restlessly, turning over to reach for a sip of water. The memory of his jaw, freshly shaved, hard against her face, made her put her fingers to her cheek. To her shock, he'd smelled just as she remembered. That mix of woody citrus and intangible male had sent her head spinning and her hand pushing into his hair, dragging him closer, crushing his mouth harder against hers.

Kissing him hadn't been part of the plan. She was supposed to be going to be cool, grown-up and professional. But she'd been swamped by the power of chemistry. She hadn't expected Jack's memory to be so...*whole.*

From the day he'd given her that pebble it had stayed with her. It had been in her glittery pink pencil case at school. At university she'd kept it in a pocket in her backpack, with lip balm and make-up. When she travelled it was always in her washbag or her jewellery roll.

Jack remembered it too, and the knowledge had floored her.

Jack hadn't forgotten what she liked.

The hardest part of the coming week was going to be keeping herself out of range of his gravitational force. Her professional reputation depended on it.

CHAPTER THREE

SHORTLY AFTER DAWN the tumbling liquid call of a coucal drew Anna onto the deck, the wood cool under her bare feet.

Chattering monkeys clustered in the leafy canopy above. One, bolder than the rest, landed on the railing and eyed her, scratching an armpit. She shooed it away. It leapt onto a nearby branch and swung through the trees, protesting loudly.

Back inside, she made a cup of coffee in the state-of-the-art Italian machine, checked her inbox and found a welcoming email from the Themba research centre, with a schedule of the investigative work to be undertaken, which would form the framework of her report.

There was no sign of Jack.

Sandwiches, coffee and mineral water were delivered to her at the research centre at lunch time, and the staff there were on hand to provide her with any material she needed. She was being left to get on with her work, which suited her just fine. What had happened between her and Jack the previous night had been an aberration. Circumstances had combined with emotions, the mix resulting in an eruption of feeling that had momentarily robbed her of reason and good sense.

After a night's sleep, and with food in her tummy, she felt strong and clear-headed—which was excellent, because what she needed was to get this job done and get out of here as quickly as possible.

Hours later, Anna flipped her laptop closed. She pushed it aside and propped her elbows on the table, cupping her chin in the palm of one hand. From where she sat, in the deep shade of the research centre veranda, the view of khaki-coloured bush and wide-open sky shimmering in the afternoon heat seemed to stretch for ever.

This was not, she reflected, the best spot for concentrated work or the serious study of spreadsheets, goals and projections. Beyond the perimeter fence was a waterhole, and waterholes were the bush equivalent of the office water cooler. At some point during the day everyone turned up for refreshment and a bit of socialising. Giraffes, their legs splayed at impossible angles, stretched their necks low to drink. In the distance the outriders for a herd of elephants made their stately way towards the pool, smoky dust wreathing their feet. And skittish antelope, far more than she could count, milled about in the dun-coloured scrub, taking turns at the water.

It was easier to watch the slow drift of game than to focus on the work she should be doing. Especially when images from the past kept butting in on her train of thought. If she raised her eyes and looked to the left she could see the rocky outcrop that she and Jack had used to climb. They'd find a hidden cleft in the sun-warmed boulders and settle down to read, spot game and talk—until the day the lions had claimed it as their own personal sun lounge.

Jack had carried her up there the first time, when she was only three, giving her a piggyback ride, with her arms clasped around his neck and his elbows hooked under her bare legs and feet. It was one of her earliest memories. As a child she hadn't been able to define her emotions, but now she knew she'd felt safe and wanted. And, yes, cherished.

To Anna, the word 'home' had meant Themba. There'd

never been anywhere else she'd felt she belonged. But with a few words eleven years ago Jack had dashed her teenage dreams of staying there for ever.

It had been inevitable that someone like her, orphaned and rootless, should crave the things she'd never had—a home and family of her own that would complete her, maybe fill the hollow ache of loss she'd lived with for as long as she could remember. But Jack had made it clear she wasn't going to find what she wanted, what she needed, at Themba.

'I don't want a wife. Not ever.'

His words had cut through her heart and incinerated her youthful dreams.

She reached for the pair of binoculars she'd brought with her and raised them to her eyes.

That clean, fresh scent tickled her nostrils and the skin on the back of her neck shivered. Was it her imagination playing tricks, or had her thoughts conjured him up out of the warm air?

'What can you see?'

Her heart kicked as Jack's voice behind her made her fingers tighten. The binoculars shifted out of focus and she put them down.

Would he dare to touch her shoulder, even for a second? If he did she'd slap his hand away.

When nothing happened she released a steady breath and turned her head a fraction. In her peripheral vision she saw Jack pull out a chair and sit down at the table.

Good. Perhaps he'd taken her words on board last night.

She lifted the glass of water at her elbow and took a mouthful, slaking the dryness in her throat and delaying the moment she'd have to answer his question.

Jack took the binoculars and adjusted their focus with those long, capable fingers. She shifted on the chair as she remembered the pressure of them across her shoulder blades. And the way her body had reacted.

'I gave you these for your eighteenth birthday.'

It was a statement rather than a question and she didn't need to answer.

'There's a magnificent kudu bull coming down to the water.' He stretched an arm out to the right. 'Over there. And a couple of nyala.'

'I thought,' said Anna at last, 'I saw a sable antelope.'

Jack shook his head. 'No, it's a roan…'

Anna reached for the binoculars. 'I don't think so. If you look…'

He eased the binoculars from her grasp, but instead of raising them to his eyes he put them on the table. 'It's a long time since we played the *What animal is that?* game.'

'I'm here to work, not to play childhood games.' She kept her eyes on the view of the waterhole and her tone cool.

She wished she'd put on something more sophisticated than skinny jeans and a big linen shirt. Her hair hung over her left shoulder in a thick braid. Why hadn't she taken more care and tamed it into a grown-up knot? Because showing Jack how she'd grown up was on her list of things to achieve while she was here—along with proving to him that she wasn't insane.

He glanced at the closed laptop. 'I wouldn't want to interrupt.'

'I came here with the best intentions, but the view is distracting.'

'I came to apologise.'

Anna turned her head a little to glimpse his profile. His expression was sombre, his mouth a straight line.

'Oh?'

'Yes. Last night…'

'Was a mistake. It won't happen again.' She leaned forward, pressing her folded arms onto the table. 'It was unprofessional of me.'

'It wasn't one-sided. Seeing you again was a shock, and I was already stressed. Bit of a combustible mix, as it turned out.'

Anna shrugged, trying not to think about the touch of his fingers on her heated skin, the taste of him on her lips. She wanted it all again, and more.

'Any hint of…of emotional attachment between us would jeopardise the authenticity of my report and compromise my professional standing. I have to be completely impartial.'

'I understand.'

'Coming back was perhaps more emotional than I expected it to be.' On a scale of one to ten for accuracy, that statement scored about fifteen. 'And I was tired and on edge.'

Whoever said you learned from your mistakes was massively wrong. Kissing Jack had been one of the biggest mistakes she'd ever made, but she'd make it all over again, given the chance. And again.

Jack nodded. 'I could see you were shattered. I feel I took advantage…'

'Let's just agree we were both at fault and we won't let it happen again.' She turned her eyes back to the view. The elephants were closer, several babies trotting fast to keep up with the herd. 'Thank you for the meal. Good memory, Jack.'

'Mostly.' He stood up, pushing the chair back. 'I'll leave you to work.'

Anna tapped the slim laptop with her knuckles. 'There's a lot to get through.'

'Let me know if you need anything.'

He stretched out a hand towards her and then let it fall to his side.

'Thanks. I will.'

Except what I need right now is you...

'What I need is not to be distracted by the view.' She flipped the laptop open and stared at the screen.

Jack moved behind her, heading to the door.

'Anna?'

She swivelled her head and their eyes met across the space.

'My visitors leave tomorrow, and this evening we're taking them for farewell sundowners in the bush. Will you join us?'

Anna nipped her bottom lip between her teeth. 'Do you think that's a good idea?'

'If you want to come, yes. You'll be chaperoned by nine earnest American ecologists.'

A sunset trip into the bush was something she'd never been able to resist. Judging by Jack's powers of recall he wouldn't have forgotten that, either. She didn't want to be alone with him. Her responses to him were too unstable, too volatile. His presence switched her senses onto high alert, sending her mind to places that had been off-limits for eleven years. But if she refused to go he'd think she was afraid to be with him.

'Okay, Jackson. What time do we leave?'

Jack shut himself in his office and walked to the window. But instead of the dusty road and dried-up watercourse it was Anna he saw in his mind's eye, sitting on the veranda, her feet drawn up, her arms wrapped around her shins.

He pressed the heels of his hands into his eyes to rub away the image but it didn't help. Being close to her disturbed and electrified him all at once. The ache he'd thought he'd banished was back, bigger and more troublesome than ever.

When he'd expelled Anna from his life he'd been unprepared for the impact of the gap she'd left behind. His mother's death when he was eight had buried him in grief and guilt so intense it had bewildered him. Two years later Anna's unexpected arrival had blunted it and given him a focus as he'd vowed to keep her safe at all costs. But with her gone too the pain of loss had sharpened again, like a blade twisting in his heart.

Feeling in danger of being overwhelmed by it, he'd turned to the one thing he knew he could control. Work. He'd poured all his energy and determination into his efforts to turn Themba into a place he could be proud of, despite his father's bitter opposition. But still he'd seen the shimmer of Anna's hair in the flash of sun on water, heard her laugh on the wind and her soft footstep on the deck. It had taken weeks, months—*years*—for him to stop wondering what she was doing at any given minute of the day. But in the end he'd done it. Or he thought he had.

He'd had all night and all morning to decompress after the shock of Anna's reappearance. He'd hardly slept, in spite of his fatigue, and he'd had a hard time holding on to his temper at breakfast in the face of a trivial query from a visitor. Was the honey organic and if so could he verify that fact? Yes, and yes, but he had more pressing matters to deal with. He'd handed the query over to Dan and excused himself.

After what had happened between them last night he'd mentally armed himself against the magnetism of her allure. He'd planned their encounter at the research centre to ensure he could control their next meeting. He had to let her know, somehow, that their kiss would not be repeated. It had been difficult, but they'd drawn boundaries and he was hell-bent on sticking to them.

The fact that he hadn't dragged her into his arms, spun her round and claimed her mouth for his own he considered a good start.

He'd held back on his invitation to join the sundowners party until he'd felt confident he had himself and his reaction to Anna tied down. And then she'd swept the ground from beneath his feet and the breath from his body with the use of her old nickname for him. Nobody else in the world had the right to call him Jackson, and hearing it on Anna's lips again had rocked his universe and thrown the strength of his resolve into deep doubt.

He glanced towards the calendar on the wall. Six days to go.

The long-wheelbase vehicle with banked seating and a canvas canopy bumped off the track and across the rough scrub. Jack forced himself not to watch it.

He checked the table which had been set up under an umbrella thorn. Several staff members in Themba polo shirts stood behind it, ready to mix sundowners. The vehicle they'd arrived in, with the folding table and cold boxes of drinks and food, was tucked out of sight, behind a shrubby clump of mopane.

The site was on a promontory at a bend in the river, and three trackers stood guard at strategic points in the bush, rifles across their backs, just in case the gathering piqued the interest of any inquisitive animals. As always, their instructions were to alert him first, so the guests could be moved to safety in the vehicles.

Once, they'd had to sit it out while a herd of elephants ambled across their chosen patch. The guns were there to reassure the guests. Firing one of them would always be an absolute last resort.

He looked down the steep bank to the river. Two crocs sunbathed on the rocks, one with its mouth wide open. Jack narrowed his eyes and could just make out a tiny plover, giving the big reptile's teeth a clean. In a muddy pool the ears, eyes and nostrils of a wallowing hippo broke the mirror surface of the water. There were probably more of them, submerged, but at the moment everything was calm.

He scanned the surrounding bush, always alert. His eyes, honed by years of practice, would pick up on anything out of place.

The engine of the game-viewing vehicle died and Jack allowed himself to look across at it. Because everything was calm except for him. What if Anna had decided not to come after all? And why did he care if she'd bailed out? He wanted her to see the best of Themba in action, that was why. He needed her to write a five-star report, recommending that Themba receive all the support and endorsements he'd requested, of course.

Then he told himself to shut up and get real. He cared because he wanted her near him all the time. He felt as if he'd denied himself his favourite drink for eleven years. Now it was within reach, and his thirst for it was all-consuming. He wanted to study her clear profile and marvel at how it was the same but subtly different. Her mouth looked softer, fuller, because her jawline was more determined. High cheekbones gave her face sculpted definition. He wanted to ease her hair out of that braid, or French plait, whatever tight restriction she'd imposed on it, and thread his fingers through it again from root to tip. Mostly he wanted to gaze into the cool green pools of her eyes without feeling he should look away after five seconds. He'd always been fascinated by how they were a paler, delicate mint at the edges, transforming to unfathomable emerald depths at the centre. Depths in which he'd willingly drown.

He was in so much trouble.

'…seven, eight, nine.'

That was all the ecologists accounted for. His stomach dropped with disappointment and he walked towards the vehicle to ask Dan what had happened. Had she simply not turned up at the meeting point? Had she offered any explanation?

'Dan? Did you…?'

'Hi, Jack.'

He swung round. His eyes landed on her boots, then travelled up, and up, and…

'Anna.' He held out a hand but she jumped down from the bottom step on her own, landing next to him.

He wished he knew what that perfume was she wore. If he could find out he'd buy her a gallon. Or, better still, buy up the brand so no one but Anna could use it, ever. She had on the same slim jeans she'd worn earlier, but she'd swapped the big linen shirt for a kaftan-style top. It fell to mid-thigh and the colour of the silk exactly matched her eyes. Was it the lighter part of her eyes or the darker? He couldn't be sure. All he *could* be sure of was that he wouldn't allow himself to get close enough to find out.

'This is amazing.' She looked around, her gaze taking in the drinks table and the staff already beginning to dispense cocktails and snacks. 'A great position and well-protected, I see. A bit different from the sundowner trips we used to take in the old Defender.'

There hadn't been any guards back then. Everyone had been responsible for their own security and there'd never been an accident. Until his father…

He shut down that avenue of thought before corrosive guilt could start to gnaw at him.

He raised an eyebrow and shrugged. 'We can't have any ecologists eaten for dinner. Although it would be the ultimate example of recycling, it would also be very bad publicity.'

'Yes, I can see the headlines now.' There was that dimple. 'The Circle of Life would take on a whole new meaning.'

'The guards are all trained trackers. They can spot an

out-of-place shadow or a leaf moving when there's no breeze. We're confident we could get everyone into the vehicles before a proper problem developed.'

'Really?'

'Yeah. Come and get a drink.'

Jack forced himself to mingle among the guests, but his eyes kept straying, searching for Anna. He watched her move easily from one group to another, nodding at something that was said, contributing her own opinions. She held a glass in her fingers and took an occasional sip. She was practised at this, perfectly comfortable and confident.

The shy, leggy teenager who'd made a habit of hiding from strangers had vanished. It had been her very elusiveness that had made her so tantalising to the men who'd paid to hunt with his father. Her invisibility had put her in the greatest danger.

Realising he'd lost sight of her, Jack threaded his way through the group, needing to know where she was. His hackles rose. She'd been separated from the party by a man who was now standing too close to her for comfort. Well, for Jack's comfort anyway. He changed direction and headed towards them.

'And what brings you here...' the man, Professor Watkins, waved his glass '...to this not exactly uncivilised place? The champagne is excellent. Perhaps "isolated" would better describe it.'

Jack watched as a little frown drew Anna's brows together.

She took a small step back. 'I'm on a research trip.'

To Jack's ears her tone was neutral, but her body language said *Keep your distance*.

'Ah! An undergraduate? And what is your specialism?'

The man had his eyes fixed on her face—*who could blame him?*—and a stab of possessiveness so sharp it caught at his breath twisted in Jack's soul.

'Oh, big cats. Although all the fauna and flora at Themba deserve special attention.'

The professor proffered his hand. 'I'm Professor Watkins. Miss…?'

Driven by the need to insert himself between Anna and the other man, Jack stepped forward. 'Allow me, Professor Watkins, to introduce Anna Kendall—*Dr* Anna Kendall. She's researching the Themba model and reviewing our methods. Anna, meet Professor Watkins.'

A faint flush spread across the man's cheeks. Anna shook his hand but he drew back, his eyes flicking to Jack's face.

'Very pleased to meet you. I'll have to look you up.' He drained his glass and turned away, joining another group.

Jack watched him go before returning his attention to Anna. 'Sorry about that. He was—' The expression on her face stopped him short. Her eyes snapped with irritation.

'What did you think you were doing?'

He saw her jaw lift a fraction.

'He was harassing you. I was trying…

'*Harassing* me?' she cut in. 'Hardly, Jack. He was showing a polite interest.' Anna pushed a hand into the pocket of her jeans as tension squared her shoulders. 'And even if he *had* been harassing me, that wouldn't have been a cue for you to barge in like a hippo protecting its calf.'

'The hell it would. He was too close to you and I could see you weren't comfortable. I—'

'His sense of personal space was different from mine. That's all it was. And I'm more than capable of taking care of myself. I didn't need you to interfere, whatever your reasons.' She took a sip from her glass and eyed him over the rim. 'You embarrassed him, and if he's looking for something to complain about when he returns to the States he's going to start with you.'

Jack knew she was right. His response had been unreasonable and, worse, uncontrolled. His inner voice reasoned that he'd leapt to Anna's defence because that was what he'd always done, but he knew there was more to it than that. He'd been unable to deal with the sight of her showing even mild interest in another man—a man who probably lived in a proper house, who worked normal hours and ticked many of the boxes Anna might have lined up for herself.

Her irritation was justified, and he was wrong to have embarrassed a guest. Very wrong. He didn't recall ever having done it before. The customer was always right. Always.

Anna's eyes remained fixed on him and he knew he had to respond, but he was damned if he was going to apologise.

'I thought I was getting you out of a tricky situation,' he said, distracted by the shades of green in her steady gaze. Did her eyes go darker when she was angry? Or would another kind of passion…? He stopped that thought in its tracks. It was just the effect of the light, fading from afternoon to evening.

'I don't need rescuing, Jack. Not any more.' She dropped her eyes and swirled the wine in her glass. 'When I wanted you to look after me you sent me away to London—where I knew nobody and almost died of shock when the first blast of winter hit me outside Heathrow.'

Then she smiled, making his heart turn over.

'That,' she continued, 'was when I began to learn how to look after myself.'

'I'm sorry.' How the hell had that happened? He had sworn he wasn't going to apologise. 'I won't interfere again.' He half turned away from her. 'I need to be sociable.'

Jack walked away, seething. Anna's words stung, but he couldn't argue with her. Accepting that she no longer needed his protection would take a while to process. He felt a surge of annoyance at the group of guests, and suddenly couldn't wait for them to leave. Then perhaps he'd be able to concentrate and get things into some sort of perspective.

Until then he wasn't letting any of them near her again, however capable she thought she was.

Elongated shadows stretched over the winter-brown grass as the sun sank towards the western hills. The visitors drifted in twos and threes over to the truck for their return journey to the lodge and their farewell dinner. Jack counted them up the steps and Dan stood in the driver's footwell and double-checked with a headcount of his own.

'Nine.' He squinted down. 'We're missing one, Jack. It's Dr Kendall.'

Jack scanned the clearing. He couldn't see her and apprehension squeezed his chest, adrenaline already pumping. Had she wandered off, like she used to, sending his anxiety levels rocketing skywards and suppressed panic drying his mouth and making his hands shake?

He breathed in slowly and looked again, more carefully, and breathed out as he spotted her in animated conversation with one of the staff members behind the drinks table. The employee saw him looking and tipped her head in his direction, smiling. He heard Anna laugh, and then she turned and walked out of the shadow of the thorn tree towards him.

The staff would pack up the table and cold boxes after the guests had left, and he'd join them in the service vehicle for the short trip back. The trackers had moved in from their posts and one of them climbed onto the game-spotting seat mounted at the front of the truck, his rifle across his knees. The remaining two stood watching over the staff.

Everyone knew the role they had to play and it worked. He'd made sure of that.

'Sorry, Jack.' Anna reached the steps. 'Alice was telling me about the small business her mother has set up.'

She glanced up into the open-sided truck and Jack followed her gaze. The remaining empty seat was next to Professor Watkins.

It took a heartbeat for Jack to decide that this was unacceptable. He could suggest she ride back with him, in the service vehicle, but that would be too damn obvious. He thought fast.

'Dan?'

'Yup?'

'I'm going to walk back. There's still half an hour of light left and that's more than I need.'

'Sure.' Dan reached behind his seat and pulled another rifle from the metal box bolted to the floor. 'Here you go. Call me on the radio if you have a problem.'

Jack slung the weapon over one shoulder, keeping his hand on the canvas strap. He was aware of Anna's eyes on him as he adjusted it, and then he let himself look at her. Her face was alight with enthusiasm.

'I'd like to come with you,' she said.

Jack tried to keep his expression neutral. He was sure if he'd demanded she accompany him she'd have refused. He hesitated, then allowed faint indecision to colour his voice.

"I'm not sure…' He glanced down at her feet.

'My boots are sturdy enough, but if you don't want me to come…' She turned back towards the vehicle, placing one foot on the bottom step.

'You're welcome to walk with me if you think you're up to it.'

Anna moved her foot back to the ground. 'Is that a challenge?'

'Not at all. But you haven't been in the bush for over a decade. It's natural you'd be cautious. Or even afraid.'

'I've never been afraid.' Her steady gaze held his. 'I've missed all this.' The sweep of her arm encompassed the wide landscape and the sky. 'There may not be another chance for a walk at sunset.'

'Possibly not…' Jack raised his voice and called to Dan. 'Dr Kendall has opted to come with me.' He pushed his free hand into a pocket of his combat trousers. 'We'll take the old track, along the line of the river.'

Dan gave them a thumbs-up and gunned the motor of the big vehicle into life. It roared and then settled into a steady throb as he eased it into gear. Jack watched it pull away before strolling across to where the packing up was almost complete, to let the staff know the change of plan. Then he tilted his head towards the river.

'Let's go. Do you remember the rules?'

'Stay close, do exactly as you say and never, ever run— because anything in the bush you need to run from can run faster,' Anna recited.

Jack nodded. 'It looks as though there might be a spectacular sunset. Maybe those clouds will bring us some rain.'

The track wound through the bush, at times almost disappearing under dry grass and powder-soft dust. Thorny branches crowded in close on both sides, but the chain of pewter puddles in the riverbed could be glimpsed through them. The evening bush orchestra was tuning up, the bass grunts from the hippos a steady counterpoint to the treble calls of birds.

Jack set an easy pace, scanning the surroundings, alert for anything that might spell danger. He glanced sideways at Anna's profile. Her chin was lifted, her mouth set.

She pulled a hand from her jeans pocket and tucked a wisp of hair behind her ear. 'Walking back wasn't your original plan, Jack. Were you going to ask me to come with you?'

Jack knew he wouldn't get away with fudging this. She knew exactly what he was doing, and it was precisely what they'd already argued about.

'Yes, I was. I didn't want you sitting next to the professor.' He went on the attack. 'But you know that.'

'I think you're overreacting. And, like I said…'

'Yeah, I know—you can look after yourself. And maybe I did overreact. But I walk whenever I can. You know that, too.' He stopped and shifted the rifle on his shoulder. 'Keeping my senses honed takes constant practice and it keeps everyone safer.'

'I wouldn't have come if I hadn't wanted to. And I would have happily sat next to Professor Watkins.'

Jack smiled. 'I think I'm beginning to understand that.'

He started walking again, more quickly, and Anna skipped to keep up with his long stride.

'Slow down a bit, please.'

'Sorry.'

Jack kept his eyes on the track ahead. The senses he needed to use to keep them safe were being swamped by the way the low rays of the sun gave her hair a lick of pink and how her elusive scent reminded him of green shade and blowsy roses, a million miles from the dusty bush.

'Better?'

He glanced down at her. Was it only twenty-four hours since those lips had surrendered to his questing mouth? It felt like a lifetime. It'd be so easy to stop right here and do it again. Not another soul would see them. But they'd agreed that shouldn't happen.

He dragged his attention back to reality, berating himself for letting it wander. And when his eyes returned to the track he saw why he shouldn't have allowed himself to be distracted. A moment's inattention to their surroundings had led them both, quite literally, into the jaws of danger.

His fingers on the rifle strap clenched into a fist. His free hand grabbed Anna's upper arm and dragged her to a stop beside him.

'Jack! That hurts! What're you doing?' She tried to pull away but he tightened his grip, pulling her into his side and then sliding his arm around her shoulders to keep her there.

'Oh!'

Her shocked exclamation was too loud.

'Shh!' he hissed. 'And remember the rules.'

The big male lion which had padded out of the shadows stopped in the middle of the track. His huge head, framed in a thick, dark mane, swung in their direction and his yellow unblinking eyes fixed on them. His tufted tail flicked from side to side.

Jack tightened his arm around Anna and swore under his breath. She pressed her cheek into his shoulder and he felt a tremor of tension shake her. Her breathing became shallow as her heartbeat picked up, hammering against his ribs. She was afraid, and she needed to be, and it was his fault entirely. His attention had lapsed and now he didn't know how this would play out…or if it was going to end well for themselves or for the magnificent beast that now blocked their path, sizing them up.

The two-way radio was in his back pocket, but he couldn't let go of the gun and didn't want to let go of Anna to reach it. After such a long time away he couldn't be sure she wouldn't run, and that could tip this disastrous situation over into a catastrophe.

'Jack?' she whispered.

The tone of her voice took him spinning back down the years to when they were growing up together. She'd never doubted he'd look after her then—get them out of trouble, make things right. Her trust in him had been absolute, and sometimes ill-founded, but he'd never failed her. Until this moment.

In his mind he was back at the door of the hut, watching the women unwrap the bundle inside the patterned blanket they'd carried into the compound. Grubby little fists and feet had emerged, and then a head of blonde corkscrew curls. Intrigued, he'd crept closer. A pair of green eyes above a pert nose and a rosebud mouth had fixed on his face and the toddler had held out her arms to him.

'Up,' she'd said. 'Up!'

He'd picked her up and she'd buried her face in his neck and gripped his tee shirt with strong fingers. She'd felt like a miracle—a golden child emerging from a bundle carried on a woman's back—and he'd known he'd protect her for ever. With his life if necessary. He hadn't been able to save his mother, but he would save her.

His gaze fixed on the tawny predator twenty meters away, Jack automatically calculated how quickly the big cat could close the distance between them. Too quickly, was the answer. He felt Anna's cheek hard against his collarbone again, and knew he'd protect her whatever the danger. Taking care of her was hard-wired into him, body and soul.

Inch by inch, he eased the rifle from his shoulder, knowing that if he moved too quickly he might startle the lion into aggression, and too slowly might see it coming closer, to inspect them more carefully. Neither of those things would be a good result.

Anna's head shifted a fraction and he tightened his hold on her.

'Jack, he's so beautiful…' she breathed.

What the hell? Staring a gruesome death in the face, and she thought it was beautiful?

'Keep still,' he murmured. 'And keep very quiet.'

A few more inches and the barrel of the rifle would be in his hand.

'Don't shoot, Jack. Please. We're in his space.'

With painstaking slowness he lifted the rifle to his shoulder, squinting down the sights. He saw the lion's muscles ripple under the sleek skin, the haunches tense, ready to spring.

His finger curled, tightening around the trigger.

CHAPTER FOUR

THE CRACK OF a rifle-shot split the air, reverberating off the nearby rocky cliffs. Jack heard someone shout. A cloud of weaver birds chattered out of the trees, leaving their nests swaying over the riverbed.

Over five hundred pounds of big cat twisted in mid-spring. The animal landed on his feet with a roar and bounded into the bush. In seconds he was swallowed by the dense undergrowth.

Jack lowered the barrel of the gun and relaxed his trigger finger, keeping his narrowed eyes fixed on the spot where he'd seen the tip of the lion's tail vanish. Anna's rigid shoulders sagged a fraction inside the iron band of his arm. She inched her cheek away from his collarbone and followed the direction of his gaze.

'You missed him,' she breathed.

Was that relief he could detect beneath the shakiness of her voice?

He shook his head. 'I didn't miss. I didn't fire. I don't know who did. Whoever it was…'

A khaki-clad figure materialised out of the deep shadow of a thorny thicket. He balanced a rifle on his shoulder as he walked down the track towards them.

'It's Alex.' Jack flipped on the safety catch of his gun and slung it across his back. 'One of the trackers on the staff vehicle.'

He let the arm which still bound Anna against him slide down. She moved away from his side and he fought the urge to pull her back in. Partly to protect her, but also because the way her body fitted with his felt natural, and right, and he needed the contact.

'Jack? You okay?' Alex's voice was calm and steady, at odds with his super-alert attitude. His eyes scanned the bush, his head cocked for sounds of danger. He stopped a few paces in front of them and looked at Anna. 'And you, Dr Kendall?'

Anna nodded. 'I... I'm fine, thank you, Alex. A bit shaken but...fine.'

Jack squinted at him into the sunset. 'Where did you come from? You were supposed to be on the staff transport.'

Alex shrugged. 'That lion crossed the road in front of us. I reckoned he'd intercept this old track just about the time you were level with his path.' He gestured behind him. 'I hopped off the vehicle to track him and it seems I was right.' He pulled off his wide-brimmed hat, swiped his arm across his brow and slapped the hat back onto his head. 'Michael stayed with the vehicle so they were covered. They should be back in the camp by now.'

Jack nodded. 'Did you aim...?'

'I aimed high and I shouted to distract him. I could see you had him in your sights. I figured if my shout and high shot didn't put him off you'd still have time for a last resort shot.' He grinned. 'Just.'

'Maybe.' Jack gripped his rifle strap. 'It was close. Definitely a case for a last resort.'

'Yeah...' Alex scratched the back of his neck. 'Having to tell the institute their rep had been eaten wouldn't have done your application any good.' He flashed an apologetic smile at Anna.

'That's assuming I'd lived to tell them anything,' Jack said, emulating Alex's bantering tone.

He wasn't about to let on how he felt about failing to protect Anna. He glanced across at her, noting the pallor under her tan and the tremor in her hand as she pulled it across her forehead. She knew precisely how dangerous their situation had been, but he wondered if she'd guessed that his concentration had lapsed.

'Thanks, Alex.' He clapped the other man on the shoulder. 'Excellent foresight and quick thinking. I was…distracted for a moment.'

Alex shook his head. 'Even if you hadn't been, I don't think you'd have heard him or seen him coming. Just a case of wrong time, wrong place.'

'Maybe.' Jack half turned towards Anna. 'You okay to walk on? Or I could call up the lodge on the radio and have someone come to get us.'

He saw indecision fighting with stubbornness in her expression. She looked across the bush in the direction the lion had taken and then back at him. 'It was my choice to come. I'll be okay,' she said, her voice quiet.

Jack glanced at his watch. 'We should just make it back before dark if we don't have any more unexpected encounters. Let's go.'

Feeling nervous in the bush was an unfamiliar experience for Anna, and she didn't like it at all. If she'd thought about it, she would have assumed it would simply never be a problem for her. Her confidence, built over the years by a combination of experience and expert guidance, had always been rock-solid. Like being able to ride a bicycle or swim, it had been something she could always rely on. But now her eyes searched the scrub in the thickening dusk, her senses primed to spot the gleam of an eye or a rustle in the undergrowth.

She walked between the two men, glad to have their solid protection on either side. Her shoulder bumped against

Jack's arm and her fingers brushed his, but he made no attempt to take her hand or offer reassurance. She told herself she was relieved. She wouldn't have wanted him to discover her palm slick with the sweat of fear. She wiped her hands against the back of her jeans, and tried to keep her breath from stopping in her throat when an owl on an early-evening hunt swooped over their heads with a sudden quiet rush of wings, and a hippo snorted loudly in the riverbed below.

When the lights of the lodge flickered through the dusk as they rounded a bend in the track she breathed more easily. Within a few steps they had crossed the causeway, with its sluggish trickle of water beneath, and hopped over the cattle grid into the safety of the compound. At the foot of the steps onto the deck Jack and Alex paused. Anna kept going.

'Anna?' Jack called. 'I'll be with you in a minute. Alex and I...'

'It's okay.' She glanced back at him. 'I need to write up my notes. And anyway, the jet-lag...'

He caught up with her as she made her way along the path towards her suite. The solar lanterns were flickering into life and Venus hung, diamond-bright, in the violet sky. He fell into step beside her, walking in silence.

At her door, she dug in her pocket for the key and turned to face him. 'Jack, I'm tired and I have to work. If you don't mind...'

He raised a hand towards her but let it fall to his side. 'I put you in danger. I let my guard down, and I'm sorry. If anything had happened to you...'

Anna shook her head and looked away, avoiding his eyes. 'Like Alex said, it was a case of wrong time, wrong place. You couldn't have predicted it. It's the kind of thing that goes with the territory. I knew... I *know* that.'

'Even so, I allowed myself to be distracted and that's

unforgiveable. We were lucky to get a second chance after a mistake like that.'

'Well, I'm glad it was you and me and not one of the guests.' She slanted a look up at him. 'Although one of them *was* the reason we were there in the first place.'

Jack bit his lip. 'It seems protecting you is built into my soul, Anna. It's what I've always done.'

'Almost always, Jack. And, like I said, I'm all grown up now. I can look after myself.'

'Almost?' Jack stared at her. 'When have I ever not? Until today?'

'Sending me off to England against my will felt like the withdrawal of your protection. It was terrifying.'

Jack took a step back. 'Some time,' he growled, 'if you'll agree to listen, I'll explain to you how that was actually for your own protection.' He pushed his fingers through his hair. 'I need to go.'

He turned on his heel, but stopped and looked back at her.

Anna raised her eyebrows at him.

'Were you afraid this evening?' he asked.

Anna considered the question for no longer than a moment. 'I was. And acknowledging it was a shock, because I've never been afraid in the bush. And my fear was compounded.'

'How?' He turned back to her, intrigued.

She laughed softly. 'I was terrified the lion would attack, but I was almost more terrified that you'd shoot him. I didn't want to be the reason for a last resort shot.'

'You're still remarkable, Anna. Do you know that?'

He reached across the space between them, but she snapped her head back, out of his reach.

'You and I need to put some space between us, Jack.' She unlocked the door. 'Physical and emotional space. Goodnight.'

'Then I'll see you tomorrow,' he said, as she pulled the door closed behind her.

Jack re-joined the path and picked up his pace as he made his way to his quarters. He felt wrong-footed and dissatisfied with the way things had played out, and not only because he blamed himself for putting Anna in danger.

He rephrased that thought. He was beating himself up for allowing his possessive jealousy to put her in danger. He had no claim on her. He'd relinquished that eleven years ago. And he couldn't dictate how she spent these few short days at Themba. He needed her experience at the lodge to be as positive as possible to ensure their best shot at getting funding, he told himself. She had a job to do and he had to let her do it.

Following her through the door and kissing her senseless wasn't going to happen. Ever. Again. She'd made that crystal-clear this morning. What annoyed him—okay, *hurt* him, if he was being honest—was how she seemed to be fine with it, while his unreliable body told him he most definitely was not.

But one good thing had come out of their meeting with the big cat. If she'd been afraid perhaps she'd respect the rules of Themba and not go wandering off too far for her safety and too close to crocodiles. He rolled his shoulders and tried to relax. She'd caused him enough anxiety in the past to last him a lifetime.

Anna leaned back against the closed door and pressed her palms flat onto its surface. It felt solid and reassuring and she breathed a long sigh of relief. The encounter with the lion had shaken her, and more than anything she'd wanted to pull Jack through this door, bury her face in his broad, hard chest and feel the strength of his arms around her... hear his deep voice telling her everything was okay.

But then everything would most definitely *not* have been okay. Because it wouldn't have stopped there. She knew that, and she knew it couldn't happen.

That kiss last evening had taken her to the brink of her self-control. Her white-hot reaction to Jack had shocked and unsettled her. She'd felt in control until the moment his lips had touched hers, but after that nothing had made sense. As a love-struck teenager she'd fantasised about kissing him, being in his arms and feeling his hands caress her, but after that the picture had gone fuzzy. Her naïve imagination hadn't quite known where to go from there.

She knew where she wanted to go now. She glanced at the inviting bed.

But he hadn't followed her through the door.

She tried to quell the small curl of disappointment and pulled a bottle of iced water from the fridge. She rolled its cool contours, frosted with condensation, across her forehead and walked over to the glass doors, but she didn't open them. She felt shaky and vulnerable, and not strong enough to deal with any posturing over-confident monkeys.

She'd believed she could handle Jack. She'd never dreamed for a moment that handling herself would be so difficult. Because in eleven years she'd never met a man she couldn't walk away from. This raw, dangerous attraction which smouldered between them was outside her experience. One tiny spark of encouragement would ignite it, and once lit she knew it would consume them both in red-hot flames of need.

And then what?

It would be impossible to do her job here. She'd lose her professional credibility and the respect of her colleagues.

When a niggling voice of doubt asked her if she'd cared if that meant she could stay at Themba with Jack, she crushed it with the ruthless disdain it deserved. Once she'd wanted this life, but her aspirations had changed.

Nothing she wanted now was to be found among the dust and fever trees of Themba. A secure home, a husband, a family—those were the things she'd made her goal and they did not exist here.

And Jack had obviously been deadly serious when he'd tossed those crushing words at her over his shoulder all those years ago. *'I don't want a wife. Not ever.'* If he'd wanted one, he would have found a wife by now.

Anna cracked the seal of the bottle and swallowed three deep gulps of water. She wiped her hand across her face and rested her forehead against the cool glass of the terrace doors. Jack only needed her here to back up his application for funding, nothing more. To give in to this force that sucked them towards each other would be madness.

Her own personal reasons for being here were different. He'd dismissed her from his life, and now she'd returned to show him she didn't need him. At all.

It was just going to be a lot more complicated than she'd thought…

Showered and changed, and only five minutes late, Jack climbed the steps to the Marula Restaurant two at a time. The adrenalin from the evening's encounter had ebbed, but its effect still pulsed in his veins. He felt as if he was running on empty…running away from the searing temptation that had gripped him outside Anna's door.

She'd been afraid and he was to blame. He'd apologised, but he'd wanted to express it in more than plain words. She hadn't let him.

He paused under the arch of the entrance to the restaurant and glanced around. The visitors were all there, most of them deep in earnest discussion. He hung back for a moment, steadying himself with a deep breath and telling himself that the evening would soon be over and they'd all be gone tomorrow.

Usually he relished these visits from intelligent and committed academics. They offered an opportunity for the exchange of ideas and informed discussion about the environmental, zoological and humanitarian problems which beset the planet and how they impacted specifically on his vision for Themba. He valued outside opinion and fresh perspectives.

But Anna's arrival yesterday had felt like a bomb exploding in his life, and now he just wanted them gone. He needed to devote his energy to unravelling the tangle of emotions her sudden appearance had dragged to the surface of his consciousness. And he needed to find a way to stop the overwhelming physical need her presence had unleashed.

With sharp clarity he remembered her sliding out of the old Land Rover Defender at the beginning of the school holidays, when she was fifteen and he was twenty three. His breath had caught somewhere in his chest as those going-on-for-ever legs had appeared, followed by a lithe body and then her face, split by a delighted grin at seeing him, her slightly tilted eyes shining as she tugged the toggle off the end of her schoolgirl plait and unravelled her gold-streaked hair down to her waist.

Suddenly his perception of her had shifted slightly. To put his arms around her and give her the hug she'd expected as she'd flung herself at him felt inappropriate. So he'd dipped his head and embraced her stiffly, pulling away much too quickly.

This was Anna, and she trusted him to protect her as he'd always done. Recognising that she was growing up was difficult.

Yesterday, she had pulled away...

Dan stepped up to him. 'Everything okay?'

He nodded. 'Everything's great, thanks.'

He looked beyond Dan and saw that all faces were turned towards him and the silence was loaded with expectation.

'We heard there was a lion. Everyone heard the shot.' Dan dropped his voice. 'What happened, Jack?'

Hands shoved into his pockets, Jack stepped into the pool of light cast by the lanterns which hung in the branches above them. 'Yes, you heard right.' He made sure his voice was loud enough for everyone to hear. 'There was a lion. A fully-grown male and a beautiful specimen. I would guess he weighed upwards of five hundred and fifty pounds.' He shrugged. 'We were in his territory and he wasn't pleased to see us. But…' he paused, looking out into the darkness beyond the tables, which were set with traditionally patterned cloths, earthenware and chunky blown glass '…at Themba our policy is only ever to shoot an animal as an absolute last resort. One of our trackers, Alex, fired over the lion's head, startling him. He retreated into the safety of the ravine and we walked home.'

Dan's eyes were still on him, and the unspoken question in them had not gone away. He knew what the question was. It concerned his integrity and his ability to make a split-second decision. But he didn't know the answer to it and that annoyed the hell out of him.

'What?' he demanded.

Dan lifted his shoulders a fraction, his look unwavering. 'Nothing, Jack. Nothing at all.'

Jack pulled his hands from his pockets and stepped forward. 'Now, does everyone have a drink?'

Much later, Jack paused on the path outside Anna's suite. He was relieved to see it was in darkness. It made not knocking on the door a whole lot easier.

He imagined her asleep in the wide bed, those long legs tangled in the rumpled bedclothes, her hair spread like cloth of gold across the pillow, and he swore. Yes, she was all grown up and she no longer needed his protection, but accepting that truth was as difficult as hell. He'd been shocked rigid by a blinding realisation as he'd faced that lion. Anna remained as precious to him today as when she'd emerged from the chrysalis of that bright blanket twenty-seven years ago. That was why the question he'd seen in Dan's eyes, and which had been hammering in his brain all evening, was so scary.

If the lion hadn't been startled by Alex's shout and carefully judged shot, what would have happened? Would there have been enough time for him to squeeze the trigger, as the other man had calculated?

But that wasn't really the question... He scuffed the toe of his suede boot in the gravel. The real question was, would his shot have found its mark at all even if he had fired?

Everyone knew that the last time he'd been required to shoot an animal as a last resort he'd failed.

And the guilt of that failure would haunt him for the rest of his life.

CHAPTER FIVE

'I THOUGHT,' SAID ANNA, as Jack swung the Land Rover off the road onto a dusty patch of earth, 'we were going to visit the school.'

'We are.' He pulled up the handbrake and killed the engine.

'The sign above that door says *Clinic*.'

He looked towards the brick-built building in front of them. A group of women standing in the sun, babies on their hips, turned their heads in their direction. One of them lifted a hand in greeting.

'When we built the school five years ago I decided to incorporate a clinic. Parents bringing their children to school can see a doctor or a nurse at the same time, if necessary.' He released his seat belt and shouldered the door open. 'Some parents walk their children miles to school each day. This arrangement saves them unnecessary journeys.'

He slammed the driver's door and walked around to open Anna's.

'The clinic isn't staffed every day, but there is a fairly reliable schedule. A rota of doctors and health visitors are here three times a week. The system works…mostly.'

Anna slid out of her seat and pulled a straw hat onto her head. As they rounded the end of the building a dusty playground behind a low wall came into view. A spreading marula tree cast a wide pool of shade in the middle of it.

She stopped, getting her bearings. 'Wasn't the school under this tree?'

Jack nodded. 'It was. It's where I had my first proper lessons, and later so did you.'

She strolled to the tree and put a hand on its trunk, running her palm over the bark. 'Joseph used to walk with us, teaching us bushcraft on the way, and you always gave me a piggyback ride when I got tired. It seemed like miles, but it wasn't far at all.'

'It was too far for a five-year-old's legs.' His gaze dropped to her denim-clad thighs then flicked away. 'Come on, they're expecting us in Class One.'

Half an hour later they left a sea of waving hands and a chorus of farewells behind them. Anna shook her head as they climbed back into the vehicle. 'This is a great project, Jack. I'm very impressed.'

'Are you really?' he asked. 'And with the clinic?'

'Really. This has been achieved in…what…five years?'

'Yeah.' He nodded. 'It wasn't without its difficulties, but the payback is immense. Education is the key to so many problems. It's the route out of poverty for these rural communities.'

His tone was passionate. She looked across at him as he turned the key in the ignition. His mouth was set in a straight, strong line and his expression was sober. The engine settled into a steady rhythm and he adjusted the air-conditioning.

'This one school and clinic must have improved the lives of so many people, adults and children, and it's all thanks to you. That must feel amazing.'

'No, not amazing—although I'm pleased, obviously. It's the teachers and healthcare workers who are amazing, and the kids who walk for miles each day to come to school. I'm counting on the knock-on effects of education filtering through to a reduction in poaching. But as long as a gram of rhino horn fetches more on the market than a gram of cocaine it'll be a battle.'

'Is that really true?'

'Apparently. Although I don't know the current value of either. What I do know is that the life of these communities depends on the ecology. Without the wildlife there would be no tourism, and many livelihoods would collapse. Our aim is to provide education, so that more people can be employed locally in tourism and research. We support the establishment of small businesses, too.'

'Could we visit some of those? Last evening Alice told me about the one her mother has set up. The more positive examples of enterprise I can include in my findings, the better your chance of success in getting funds.'

'Of course. I'll arrange some meetings.'

'Some of the funding you're applying for will go towards extending the school and the research centre, right?'

'Absolutely. A bigger school means more pupils and more teachers. An enhanced research centre means more local jobs and an increased understanding of the perilous existence of some of our most endangered species, as well as finding ways their decline can be stopped, or at least slowed.'

Anna was silent for a moment. Then she bent her head and rubbed at a patch of dust on her jeans. 'This is what drives you, Jack. Isn't it?' She gestured towards the school building. 'Before, it was your work at the mine, but now it's all this.'

Jack leaned forward and rested his forearms on the top of the steering wheel, staring straight ahead. 'We all know about climate change and how we're wrecking the planet, with our plastics, our logging and extraction and burning of fossil fuels, but most of us think there's nothing we can do about it. If we all did something, however small, it would…it *will*…make a difference.' He turned his head towards her. 'In a city like London you're removed from it. Here, I can *see* it happening. The droughts and the floods, the animals disappearing… If we don't do whatever we can to stop it there are species that *your* children will never see. I cannot—*will* not—stand by and let that happen.' He straightened his arms and pushed himself back into his seat. 'These are the things I can do. It may not be enough, and it may be too late, but doing nothing is not an option.'

The determination radiating from him was so forceful that Anna almost felt intimidated. He was fixed on a difficult path and it was obvious nothing was going to distract him from his goals.

She frowned. 'What will you do if your application is turned down? Will you find another way?'

Jack beat a rhythm on the steering wheel with his fingers. 'I'll be disappointed. But it's not so much about the financial support as the recognition we'd receive if your institute endorses us. Internationally the profile of Themba and the work we're doing would be raised, and that would be much more valuable.'

'Your ambitions are admirable, Jack, and your achievements remarkable. But there is one thing that puzzles me…' She shuffled a sheaf of papers on her lap, then tucked them into her leather satchel. 'Eleven years ago, Themba was a collection of thatched huts under the fever trees. There was an outdoor school and no clinic. Most of the able-bodied men went away to work on the mines, and your father existed by entertaining parties of rich big game hunters.'

She kept her eyes on Jack's face and saw his jaw tighten. His stormy eyes bored into hers. 'Yes.'

'How has all this growth been funded?'

'The diamond mine is hugely profitable.'

Anna nodded. 'Mining is not my field, but the institute will definitely be interested in how it's run, the profit share, and any ethical practices you have in place.' She removed her hat and tossed it onto the back seat, pushing her plait over her shoulder. 'But,' she went on slowly, 'what about the hunting?'

Jack's fingers tightened over the gearstick and an inconvenient memory of those fingers pushing into her hair flared in her brain. His knuckles whitened and she dragged her eyes back up to his face. He was watching her through narrowed eyes.

'No one…*no one*…has paid to shoot an animal on Themba land since the day my father died.'

The atmosphere between them felt charged and unstable. Anna broke their locked stare first and dropped her eyes to his throat. The skin there was smooth and tanned, but a hint of dark hair showed at the neck of his blue-striped shirt. She watched the even rise and fall of his chest and wondered if he'd noticed how her own breathing had grown shallow and quick. She hoped the rapid beat of her pulse was hidden beneath the cotton scarf she wore loosely knotted around her neck.

There seemed to be far more than eleven years between them. The Jack she'd known—her lifelong companion and protector—had vanished, and the person sitting only inches from her now felt like a stranger. He was tough, and driven, and she wondered about the circumstances which had shaped him.

She felt a sudden heart-sick longing for that other time, long before he'd sent her away, when they'd been completely at ease with each other…before that treacherous spark of physical awareness had flickered to life between them. It had smouldered, unattended, for all the years they'd been apart, and now it had swelled into a flame that threatened to roar out of control.

Anna forced herself to suck in a deeper breath. 'I believe you, Jack.' Despite the cold air pumping into the vehicle through the air-conditioning vents she felt her cheeks heat under his stare. 'And…and I was sorry to hear about your father's death.' She reached out and put a hand on his shoulder but he shrugged it off.

'Thanks.' Jack nodded once. 'Not many people mourned him. And the hunters wasted no time moving on to other establishments when I banned them from Themba. My father had become a liability—a danger to himself and others.'

He stamped on the clutch and engaged the gears as if to close the subject.

'The visitors left this morning, so I'm free for a few days until the next party arrives.' He spun the wheel and turned onto the dusty road. 'Perhaps you'd like to join me for dinner this evening, so we can continue this discussion. I can provide any information you need on the mining operation.'

Jack knocked on Anna's door and waited. A breeze rustled in the trees overhead and he frowned. The flare of anxiety which had lain dormant and which he associated with looking after Anna unfurled in his chest. *Where was she?* But before his imagination could run wild, down into the riverbed amongst the crocs, or up onto the rocky outcrop where he'd heard the rasping cough of a leopard earlier, the door opened.

Each time he saw Anna he had to fight to control his response, to douse the fire which burned through his veins. The reality of her presence packed far more punch than the thought of her. And God knew his thoughts were hot enough.

Because he was sure they were clearly expressed in his eyes, he pushed his hands into the pockets of his jeans and ducked his head. But when he lifted it again his gaze tracked up her legs, and up some more…

Stop it. Now.

He took in the black skinny jeans…the loose top in a

colour which was neither blue nor green and yet the most intense hue of both. The breeze which had shivered through the treetops a moment ago swooped down to earth and unhelpfully flattened the shimmering fabric against her body, sculpting her curves in silk.

'Hi.' She threw him a cool smile. She'd freed her hair from its plait and it flowed in waves down her back from the narrow silver band on her head. 'Sorry. I was on the deck, daring the monkeys to come closer.'

'Have you…?' He stopped, reminding himself that she was a responsible adult now.

Her smile widened and his heart turned over.

'Yes, I've closed and locked the glass doors. Can monkeys look disconsolate? I'm sure they did.'

She pulled the door shut behind her and turned the key. Jack stood back as she walked down the path and turned towards the main buildings of the lodge.

'Actually,' he said, managing to pitch his voice at something above a husky growl, 'we're eating at the huts. Since there're no guests for a few days the restaurant is closed. The staff are on duty twenty-four-seven when we're hosting, so it's a chance for them to kick back and recharge a little.'

'Oh…' Anna hesitated. Doubt warred with interest in her expression. 'Okay… It'll be good to see what changes you've made. Although maybe…'

'Maybe?'

She shook her head and the little emerald studs in her ears sparkled with green fire. 'It's just maybe I'd prefer to remember it how it was.'

But she fell into step beside him on the path.

He took her straight to the main living area. She paused on the threshold and looked around, as if trying to match up the space with the one she remembered.

'I can't quite place where I am, Jack.' She shook her head. 'It's all so different.'

'I'll take you on a tour and explain.' He nodded towards a door. 'This way.'

Ten minutes later they were back in the living area. Anna slid open the glass doors and walked out across the deck.

Wooden chairs with deep rust-coloured canvas cushions furnished the space. The view over the river was dissolving in the soft evening light.

Jack watched her turn and walk towards him. He ached to turn back the clock, to an easier time when they'd been friends, and close, and life had been less complicated. But he closed down that avenue of thought with an irritated shake of his head. They'd both moved on. There could be no going back.

'Drink?' he asked.

'Yes, please. Could it be a glass of that Sauvignon Blanc I had the night I arrived?'

'It could be.'

He pulled a bottle from the small bar fridge and twisted a corkscrew into the top. When he looked up again Anna was standing in front of the framed photo of his mother. He picked up the two glasses of wine and held one out to her.

'Is this your mother, Jack?' Her fingers closed around the glass stem and she raised the goblet in a half-salute.

Jack took the time to swallow a mouthful of wine before answering. 'Yes. That was taken about a year before she died.'

Anna's eyes went back to the picture. 'She's very beautiful. I don't remember seeing that picture before.'

'After she died my father refused to have any pictures of her in the house.' He shrugged. 'That was the one I managed to save. I hid it.'

Anna's eyes filled with sympathy. 'I'm sorry. She was never a part of my life here, but you must have missed her terribly.'

Jack nodded. 'Yeah. It was a long time ago, but sometimes I still wonder…'

'What?'

He took another swallow of wine. 'How life would have been if she hadn't died. But it's no use speculating.'

'I'm glad you saved her picture. I wish I had one of my parents. I have no idea what either of them looked like. George knew my grandparents, and apparently they were so upset when my mother gave up her life in London to follow my father to Africa they cut all ties with her and destroyed all the family pictures.' She shook her head. 'Seems a bit extreme, don't you think?'

'That depends. I destroyed a lot of family mementoes when my father died.' He kept his back to her. 'But they were mostly hunting trophies and pictures of macho men standing on the animals they'd shot for sport. I'd always hated them.'

'The men or the pictures?'

'Both.'

'I hated them too, once I was old enough to understand who they were and what they did. And the photos…they were awful.'

Jack inclined his head towards the glass doors and Anna followed him onto the deck.

'There,' she said, 'is where the hammock used to be.'

He nodded. 'I had the deck built around the trunks of those two trees. They give excellent shade in the afternoon.' He steered the conversation away from the hammock. 'Burning all those photographs was one of the first things I did after my father died.'

They settled into chairs, facing the river and the darkening hills beyond it. Anna slipped her feet out of her flat pumps and tucked her legs underneath her. Jack swallowed and gripped the stem of his wine glass between his fingers. He'd caught a glimpse of her smooth thigh beneath her bathrobe two nights ago, and the memory of it snagged at him repeatedly. How would that satin skin feel under his slightly roughened fingertips? And how would he feel if he could trace a path further up, towards her forbidden and secret places?

He leaned forward and propped his elbows on his knees.

'But he was your father, Jack. Surely you took time to grieve for him?'

'My grief was for the man he should have been. The one my mother must have thought she married. By the time he died alcohol was his only pleasure, and I don't think that even took the edge off the guilt he felt. He was tormented by her loss, and the part he'd played in it.'

He'd kept his eyes trained on the horizon, but he knew Anna's were fixed on him.

'You never talked about her, Jack.'

'No. After she died no one was allowed to mention her name, and after a while not talking about her became the norm. My father tried to erase all evidence of her existence from Themba—and he succeeded to a certain degree. But I suspect it wasn't so easy to wipe his memory.'

'You told me once that your mother died of a cerebral haemorrhage while your father was away…' Anna wrapped her arms around her shins and rested her chin on her knees. 'But you never wanted to talk about it.'

'No,' Jack repeated.

He put his glass down on the deck and folded his arms across his chest. The familiar sense of panic threatened to impede his breath as his heart rate picked up. But he'd learned to control it years ago, like he controlled everything else in his life. By sheer will power. The guilt was a different thing altogether. It could hit him when he least expected it, and it felt like being kicked in the chest by a buffalo. It made him gasp for air.

'I never have talked about it because the guilt is…crippling.'

'Guilt? But it wasn't your fault. Not any of it.'

'When my father left that day to go hunting he told me to look after my mother. I felt proud that he thought I was old enough. Afterwards I knew it was because he felt guilty about leaving her when she was ill. She had a terrible headache and begged him not to go. I couldn't save her. I failed. She was my responsibility and I let her down—and my father, too.'

He dragged his eyes from where they'd been scanning the darkness beyond and found her steady gaze fixed on him. When she spoke her voice was gentle, and more like the voice he remembered.

'It must have been terrifying for you. I'm so sorry.' She extended a hand towards him, but then dropped it into her lap.

He shook his head and wiped a hand across his face. 'It was how my father behaved when he returned that was frightening. He smashed things up and threatened the people who'd tried to help her. Then he went on a bender. And when he eventually sobered up, days later, he was like a different person. Hunted instead of hunter.'

'It wasn't your fault,' Anna repeated.

The night had fallen swiftly, but the glow of the solar lanterns on the deck kept the dark at bay. Jack pushed himself back in his chair and tipped his head to look at the emerging stars. His logical brain told him that Anna was right. He knew there was nothing his eight-year-old self could have done. But as a child he hadn't understood that.

And then there was that other guilt, which he could never reveal to her.

It was true that he'd feared for her safety at the hands of the rough groups of men who'd come to Themba to hunt.

He could tell her that. But had he used them as a convenient excuse?

Because the real reason he'd sent her away had been his fear of his own feelings. He'd feared that the hot surge of desire that took over his body every time he saw her would be the one thing he wouldn't be able to control. It made him vulnerable to hurt. And he'd decided a long time before that nobody would ever hurt him again. So he'd hurt Anna, instead.

Jack closed his eyes briefly, then stood up. 'Let's go in. I'll get the food.'

Anna sat still, mulling over Jack's words.

Perhaps now she could understand a little of his father's behaviour. As she'd grown up she'd wondered what had made him assume responsibility for an orphaned two-year-old.

She knew it had taken him months to establish that the people who'd died in the plane crash were her parents, Aidan Jones and Rebecca Kendall. The flight appeared to have had no origin and no destination and it was many more months before accident investigation officials let him know its probable point of departure. By then the state, further north, where they'd lived, was in the grip of a vicious civil war and many government buildings had been destroyed. Public records had been burned and no wills or birth certificates had survived. He registered Anna's existence and address with the Consul in Cape Town and let her stay at Themba.

And then, when she was five, a letter had arrived from Dr George Lane. Although he did not expect to hear from Rebecca often, he wrote, when she'd been silent for almost three years he'd grown concerned. He'd written to several Consuls to ask for help tracing her. The one in Cape Town had given him his answer.

All George had was a letter from Rebecca telling him of Anna's birth and asking him to look after her if necessary. She hoped she could grow up in Africa but would like her to complete her education in England.

Once, in an attempt to engage with him, Anna had asked Jack's father why he'd allowed her to remain at Themba. He'd stared at her for a long time, and then switched his gaze to the massive baobab tree in a far corner of the compound.

'I had to make atonement.' His voice had roughened. 'I'm afraid of failing another human being.'

Now she walked back into the open-plan living area, where a lamplit table had been set with a bowl of pasta smothered in a creamy sauce, a salad of green leaves and places for two.

'Mmm… Smells delicious. Thank you.'

Jack topped up her wine glass as she sat down.

'At last,' she said, 'I think I understand your father's motivation.'

'For what?'

'I asked him once why he'd let me stay and he said he had to make atonement. That he was afraid of failing another human being.'

Jack propped his forearms on the table and looked across at her. 'Who do you believe he was afraid of failing?' He frowned. 'You or me?'

'Well…at the time I didn't understand him. I didn't know what atonement meant. But now I think he meant me. He'd failed your mother, but he'd taken me in. Perhaps somehow in his mind he thought he'd balanced the scales.'

'He also knew that you'd become very important to me—very quickly. Giving you up would have meant him taking you from me, when I'd already lost my mother.'

Anna nodded slowly. 'Perhaps it was for both of us, then. I hadn't considered that.'

'I was always desperately afraid that something would happen to you, or you'd be taken away.' Jack leaned back and folded his arms. 'I made keeping you safe my purpose in life. I hadn't been able to save my mother, and my father had become a distant, isolated figure, but I was determined to stop anything bad from happening to you. Ever.' His eyelids dropped briefly. 'That's why, when you were eighteen…' He shook his head and then brought a fist down onto the table—hard. 'God, I hated those men.'

Anna jumped, startled. 'What men? You're not making sense, Jack.'

'The men who made me send you away.'

'It was *you* who sent me away, Jack. Three weeks early. You said you'd explain why, and that it was for my own safety, if I'd listen.' She cupped a hand under her chin. 'Maybe now's the time?'

'Well, it wasn't because I thought you'd become over-confident in the bush—although you'd caused me to panic more than once.'

'I thought it was because I'd asked…okay, *begged* you to marry me, Jack. Your father wanted you to find a wife and I saw myself as the obvious solution. The thought of leaving Themba terrified me. Everything I knew was here. Everything I…loved.' She picked up her glass and swirled the pale wine. 'Even though I knew it was my mother's wish, the pain has never quite gone away.'

Jack looked exhausted, and sad, and Anna wanted nothing more than to walk around the table and put her arms around his shoulders, rest her cheek on his head. But she had a good idea of where that would lead, and she wasn't going there. She was here to do a job and she'd do it professionally, as well as she could. And then she'd walk away. Show Jack that she'd grown out of him and into a much bigger life, where she could fulfil her dream of having a home and a family of her own.

Any physical contact between them, even a simple gesture of comfort, would be the quickest route to crossing the boundaries they'd set. His comment earlier in the day about her future children—he obviously never planned to have any—and now seeing his home was all the proof she needed that Jack had no plans to allow a woman into his life.

From the leather furniture to the dark wooden shelves packed with books and the slate-tiled floors, this house was a private male sanctuary. The wide bed in his bedroom, with its pale grey linen and quilt, had pillows on one side only. The chrome and grey marble wet room had a glass door onto a secluded part of the deck where he'd installed an outdoor shower.

As she'd walked back into the living room, its single note of femininity had hit her between the eyes. The picture of his mother. It was in stark contrast to the ambience of virile masculinity surrounding it.

'I know I hurt you, but I had to make you leave,' he said now.

'I figured that much out, but I thought it was because my marriage proposal had embarrassed you. Was there some other reason?'

'I had to make you leave because of the discussion a party of hunters had had around the firepit a couple of nights before. It concerned you—although I'd rather not go into the details of their observations. Then they started placing bets on which one of them could get you into bed first. From their language it was obvious they didn't have romantic seduction in mind, and that it wouldn't matter if no actual bed was involved.'

Anna felt as if the air had thickened and something heavy was compressing her chest. How naïve had she been? As Jack had pointed out, her experience of life had been bounded by Themba and a girls' boarding school. The possibility that any of those blustering, sweaty old men would consider her as anything other than a girl wouldn't have occurred to her in a million years.

She felt slightly sick.

'I was always uncomfortable around those men. I tried to keep out of sight as much as possible. I... I didn't think they'd even noticed me.'

'I think that was part of it,' Jack said. 'Your elusiveness made the chase more exciting.'

'So,' Anna said, 'when you said I had to leave it wasn't to save me from a rogue elephant or a bad-tempered rhino.' She swallowed. 'Or marriage to you.'

'It wasn't. And I don't want a wife.'

'Yes, I remember.' She nodded. 'Not ever. Why was your father so insistent that you find one?'

Jack laid his fork on the side of his plate. 'He was goading me. We were arguing about everything by then. I wanted the hunting to stop, so we could turn Themba into a model game reserve where important research could be undertaken. I wanted to be at the forefront of the fight against poaching.' In a gesture of frustration he raked his fingers through his hair. 'I told him I'd never marry after I'd seen the sort of life a wife could expect at Themba, and his response was that he'd consider some of the reforms if I found a wife.'

'I would have thought you were crazy if you'd tried to explain to me about those men,' said Anna.

'I did write to you to explain. Several times.'

'I destroyed your letters without opening them. I was hurt and humiliated, and for a long time I told myself I'd never come back.'

Anna remembered the arrival of each letter. Every time George had left one on her desk its presence had stolen her attention and sapped her concentration until she had picked it up between thumb and forefinger, carried it downstairs and dropped it into the drawing room fire. Luckily the letters had stopped by the time spring came and the fire was no longer lit.

'But you did come back. And I'm glad. Because there's something I need to show you.'

Jack pulled the battered backpack from a high shelf in his dressing room. He wiped some of the dust off it with his sleeve, then carried it into the living room and dumped it on the glass coffee table.

'That's your school backpack.'

Anna had come to stand next to him, but he sat down on the leather sofa and patted the space beside him.

'Yeah, it is. Sit down, Anna.'

She perched on the edge of the seat and he noticed the healthy gap she'd left between them. She wasn't crossing boundaries, either.

He tugged at the zipper of the bag and pulled out a bundle wrapped in a blanket, its pattern dulled with age. He unrolled it on the table.

'You were wearing these when you were brought to Themba.'

The tee shirt had faded to the palest pink, and all that remained of the elephant on the front was a faint outline. Anna stared at it and he saw her throat tighten.

'That was mine?'

He nodded. 'Yes. And these.'

The colours of the candy-striped dungarees had lasted better. They had a pocket in the bib and two slanting pockets at the sides. The brass buttons and buckles still had a dull shine.

She put out a hand and fingered the fabric. 'And I was wearing them… My mother must have chosen these clothes to dress me in on that last morning.'

He saw her teeth fasten on her bottom lip as a tremor ran through her.

'You were bundled up in this blanket and the women un-wrapped you like a parcel on what passed for our kitchen table.' He tipped his head. 'Out there—beyond where the kitchen is now. To me it seemed like a miracle as this fairy child with candyfloss hair and eyes the colour of my favourite green marble emerged from the folds of a rough blanket. They undressed you to give you a wash.'

Anna picked up the tee shirt and spread it on her knees, tracing around the outline of the elephant. 'I can't believe I was ever this tiny.' She laughed, but the sound caught in her throat.

'You didn't want to be washed. You demanded that I pick you up and then you hung on to me like a meerkat. They had to prise you out of my arms.'

'But where have these clothes been all this time?'

'When I began renovating the huts I found them at the back of a cupboard. What was in the pockets was more interesting, though.'

Jack undid the buckle which fastened a flap over an outside pouch of the backpack and pulled out a cloth bag. The contents rattled as he tipped them onto the table.

There was a long, charged silence. Anna left the tee shirt on her knees and leaned forward, peering at the chunks of rock. She ran a finger over their four-sided shapes. They looked like pale lumps of glass.

'Rough diamonds…' He could barely hear her voice.

'They were sewn into the pockets of your dungarees. Evidently in the excitement of your arrival nobody noticed your clothes were heavier than they should have been.'

He picked up one of the stones and rolled it around in his palm.

Anna's breathing was quick in the quiet room. She lifted her eyes to meet his and then looked back at the stones.

'I don't know what to do with them. Is it even legal to own them? And where did they come from?'

He held up a hand. 'Slow down, Anna. What you do with them is your decision. They could be worth a lot of money, but they might be difficult to sell because there's no Kimberley Process Certificate to prove they were ethically mined—I'm guessing they were not. As for where they came from…it could probably be established, but the answer might not be what you want to hear.'

'What do you mean?'

'I've done some research and found out a bit about your father.'

Anna's hand shot out and her fingers circled Jack's wrist. 'What have you discovered?'

'It's not much.' He took her hand and placed it on the sofa between them. 'The plane you were in wasn't his. It had been stolen a couple of weeks earlier from somewhere north of here. There's no evidence pointing to your father as the thief, but he was probably working for the man who was. There was a story circulating that your father and his accomplice had found a valuable seam of diamond rock and kept its location a secret. He was probably taking some of the gems—these diamonds—as proof of the find, to show to someone they hoped would finance an illicit mining operation.'

Jack watched a series of emotions flit across Anna's features. She wiped at her cheeks with the heel of her hand and crossed her arms across her body. The sleek academic who had climbed those steps two days earlier and extended her cool hand towards him had vanished. She looked shaken, and vulnerable, and suddenly very young, and at last Jack recognised something of the Anna he remembered.

He ached to take her in his arms to comfort her, but he didn't dare. It would be far too dangerous.

Anna twisted to face him. 'This is the closest…the *nearest* I've ever been able to get to my parents or to who I am, Jack.' She glanced down at the faded clothes and the diamonds. 'It means more to me than I can say that you kept these.'

She bit her lip and balled her fists in her lap.

'Don't do that.'

'What?'

Jack raised a hand and ran his thumb along her bottom lip. 'Don't bite your lip. You'll hurt yourself.'

'Oh…' She turned her face into his palm. 'I didn't realise. There's too much to think about and it's overwhelming.'

Jack took a steadying breath as his fingers came into contact with the soft skin of her cheek. His hand slid around the back of her head and their eyes locked.

'Anna…' he said on a breath.

'Mmm…'

He lost the battle with his willpower as she dropped her forehead to his shoulder and he pulled her into a hug. He thought of how it had felt to have her pressed against him while he squinted down the barrel of the rifle at the lion. He remembered the question in Dan's eyes and wondered how he could have doubted he would have pulled the trigger in time.

There was no lion this time. No gun. Just the two of them. Alone in his house, where nobody would find them and her research report would not be compromised. She was shaken, and her emotions were running high, and he'd never take advantage of that, but he had to comfort her. Nothing more.

For a brief second he rested his cheek on the crown of her head, and then he settled her into his arms.

'I wish,' he said, 'that I could tell you more.'

He felt the slight movement of her head against his shoulder as she tipped her face up towards him. A convulsive shiver shook her and he tightened his arms around her.

'You've given me a link to them,' she said. 'Something

tangible. I didn't come back expecting to unearth much information about my past. I came…' She shook her head. 'But now I'm thirsty for more—even though there's probably no more to discover. I suppose I've never really come to terms with what happened.'

'I'm so sorry. But if there was more I think I would have found it. Memories have faded, and people are unwilling to talk about anything that might incriminate them even after such a long time.'

Anna rested a hand on his chest and he covered it with his own, rubbing his thumb across her knuckles.

'Seeing these things…suddenly finding a connection to my past…has shaken me. I've wanted to find something… anything…for so long, but it's not only that…'

'What, then?'

'Those men.' She swallowed, her fingers curling and gripping the fabric of his shirt. 'You protected me from them.'

Jack clenched his jaw. 'That was never going to be okay. I knew I couldn't always be here to keep you safe, and I couldn't leave you here, for them…'

As he said the words his conscience wrung his heart and shame tasted bitter in his mouth. He was not being honest with her. He'd fought for weeks to resist Anna's naïve flirtations, and hearing the hunters discuss her had been the push he'd needed to send her to England.

If he hadn't, he was afraid he'd have given in. And that would have made him no better than one of them.

He looked down. She'd squeezed her eyes shut but a tear had escaped and trickled across her cheek. Her body shook with a series of violent tremors. Somehow, somewhere, he had to find the strength to resist the tug of his desire.

'You're shocked, Anna. I should have been more careful about what I told you. You've had an information overload.'

'Maybe. But I needed to know. I'm all grown up, Jack.'

That is my biggest problem.

'I just need time to process it,' she went on.

'I'll get you a hot drink. It'll help to calm you down.' He eased himself away from her. 'Redbush tea?'

Anna nodded. 'Thank you.'

Jack stood up.

And a double whisky for myself, with a cold shower on the side.

Anna pressed her knuckles into her eye sockets and counted through a couple of breaths. *In and out.* Then she pushed herself off the sofa, testing the reliability of her shaking knees before taking a step through the open glass doors onto the deck.

The temperature had fallen and the cool night air wafted across her face like a balm. Her eyes felt swollen and hot, and an uncontrollable shivering had sapped her energy.

She leaned her elbows on the timber rail and dipped her head. From the fever trees across the narrow river came the distinctive call of an eagle owl. Something mysterious plopped into the sparse water. A mouse, running for cover, scampered through the pool of light thrown by one of the solar lanterns and vanished under the safety of the deck.

She wrestled with her thoughts. Eleven years ago Jack had protected her from the attentions of a lecherous group of men by sending her away. Had he really wanted her to stay? If they could have spent those remaining three weeks together would things have been different between them?

But this evening he'd said those words again. *'I don't want a wife.'*

Pretending it might have been different was a waste of time and emotional energy. Whatever she'd felt for him then had been based on familiarity and the fear of change.

His series of revelations this evening had stripped back her emotions until she felt raw and ragged.

Her mind raced. The ghosts of her parents, of whom she had no memories, no pictures, felt tantalisingly close. Her mother had seemed to speak to her through the small faded garments spread out on the coffee table, and her father through the uncut diamonds. What hopes and dreams, even illegal ones, were bound up in that little collection?

As a child she'd fantasised that their disappearance from her life had all been a mistake and that they'd turn up one day. Perhaps they'd survived, fled the scene of the crash for some reason known only to themselves, and would come back for her so they could be a proper family. In her dreams they'd been strong and good, their flight that fateful day a mercy dash to help someone in need. Even in adulthood she'd clung to the idea that their deaths had been a noble sacrifice.

But now that dream had crumbled like burnt wood into dry ashes. Her childhood clothes looked forlorn, and the illicit diamonds which had led her mother and father to their deaths seemed to radiate a dull malevolence.

She needed time and space to come to terms with this, to recalibrate all of her life up until now. But the effort required seemed too great, and the new narrative she was likely to come up with too painful to confront.

Jack's footsteps sounded on the deck, but she kept her head bowed. He put a mug of tea and a glass on the wide wooden rail beside her, and she stiffened as she felt his hands on her shoulders, easing her round to face him. She'd thought he was going to kiss her again while he'd held her, and she knew she would have let him, but he'd opted to make tea instead.

'Here you are.' Relief laced his voice.

'Where did you expect me to be?' She raised her head.

His thumbs described small circles on her shoulders

and he shrugged. Anna caught the gleam of silver in his eyes as he smiled.

'Going on past experience, you could be half a mile away by now, dancing in the moonlight or climbing a tree, so nothing would surprise me.'

'I gave up moonlight dancing and tree-climbing when I left Themba, and I have a healthier respect for the bush now than I did before.'

He nodded. 'Good.' He ran his hands down her arms and linked his fingers with hers. 'How many more days,' he asked, looking over her head into the darkness, 'will it take you to finish your research?'

The beat of her heart seemed to pause, and then it lurched into a quicker, more urgent pattern. She tried not to let her breath stutter. She lifted her chin and turned her head to one side, attempting to think. Her brain was over-worked and tired. Too tired to cope with this blindsiding question.

He wanted her gone.

What else could it mean?

He'd told her all he could. Shown her the small collection of her childhood belongings and cleared his conscience. An over-emotional woman trying to make sense of her dubious past would create inconvenient ripples in the smooth fabric of his life and work and take his attention away from the important issues. He needed her to do her research, recommend the funding and then get out of his way.

She was meant to be here for a week, but if she worked long hours she could reduce that time. At least one extra day had been built into the schedule in case of problems, but so far there'd been none. Jack had Themba so well organised and controlled that it had all been straightforward.

One thing was certain, though. Hell would freeze over before she allowed him to tell her she had to leave. She'd go, but she would make it look as if she was going in her own sweet time.

'Um…' She feigned nonchalance, pretending to do a mental calculation. 'I should be leaving on Monday, but everything is so well-documented I can probably complete my investigations before that.'

To her ears her tone sounded a little forced but she hoped Jack wouldn't pick up on it.

'So?'

'So probably two more days? If nothing unexpected turns up I could be gone…' she swallowed '… I could leave on Saturday morning. Friday evening at a push. If there's a daytime flight to Heathrow on Saturday I could catch that.'

'Perfect.' Jack nodded.

He let go of her hands and turned, propping his hips against the railing next to her. Anna caught the smoky whiff of whisky as he lifted a glass containing a hefty measure of amber spirit.

'I'll be able to tell you for sure in the morning.' She cradled the warm mug of tea against her breastbone and bent her head, inhaling the fragrant steam.

'Okay.' Jack sipped at his drink. 'Because the next party of visitors doesn't arrive until Monday, and I'd like to get away for the weekend.'

'Oh?' Anna raised her head and stared straight ahead. 'In that case I'll make sure I'm gone by Friday evening. If you can organise the helicopter pick-up, I'll book into one of the airport hotels.'

'That won't be necessary.'

From the corner of her eye Anna saw him lift the glass to his mouth and swallow.

'I'd like you to come with me.'

Her fingers went rigid and a splash of hot tea sloshed

over the rim of her mug. Her head jerked round and she stared at his impassive profile.

'*Why?*'

'Because I've had an idea. If you agree… If you think it might help you to find closure… I could take you to the site of the plane crash.'

CHAPTER SIX

'ARE YOU OKAY with camping?'

Jack was waiting for her on the deck, at the top of the granite steps. He reached out and gripped the straps of the backpack Anna carried over one shoulder and slid it down her arm.

The question stopped her in her tracks. She'd expected *Did you sleep well?* or *You must be exhausted by the long hours you've worked over the past two days.* Had she really changed that much? Did she look like someone who was not okay with camping?

She considered her reply. In his eyes, she supposed she was a completely different person from the eighteen-year-old he'd dropped at Johannesburg International eleven years ago. He hadn't recognised her when she'd arrived, but she was sure he'd been expecting a man. Not that he'd ever admit to making such a blatantly sexist assumption.

Today, she'd shed her professional academic persona. The slim jeans and white shirt had made way for khaki cargo pants and a *Save the Whales* tee shirt underneath a two-sizes-too-big hoodie. She'd wound an Indian patterned cotton scarf around her neck—mostly for sun protection.

She tucked her hands into the pouch at the front of the hoodie. It was her favourite garment for travelling. On long-haul flights she would pull the hood up, snuggle into it and feel safe and comforted.

Jack had looked away, towards the east, where the sun had recently risen—an orange ball in a wash of soft yellows and pinks, lighting up the few clouds which studded the pale sky. Now she felt his eyes back on her.

For a moment she wondered if she'd spoken the question out loud. *Had* she changed that much? But she saw he was still waiting for an answer.

'I'm fine...absolutely fine with camping, Jack.' She rolled her shoulders and pulled a pair of sunglasses from the pouch. 'I assumed we might not make it there and back in a day, so I'm prepared for a night away.' She glanced at the backpack which Jack had adjusted on his shoulders. 'Perhaps you can show me where we're headed on a map.' She pushed the shades onto the top of her head. 'I like to know where I'm going.'

'Good.' Jack nodded. 'Just thought I'd check because you...' His eyes raked over her and she felt her cheeks warming. 'You're... I thought perhaps camping wouldn't be your thing any more.'

'I may look different, Jack, but I'm the same person underneath.' She looked down at her boots and scuffed the toe of one of them on the wooden deck. She knew that wasn't true. She wasn't the same person at all. 'A grown-up version of the same person,' she amended.

She hadn't camped for years. Okay, not since leaving Themba. But Jack didn't need to know that. All her conservation research and work was connected with the role urban zoos could play in saving critically endangered species. But she wasn't telling Jack that, either. If he really cared he could look her up on the internet and find out for himself in seconds. He probably had.

At the foot of the steps a Land Rover Discovery was parked, painted in camouflage. Anna glanced up at the capsule fitted to the roof.

Jack followed the direction of her gaze as he opened the

tailgate and pushed her backpack in, fitting it amongst the camping equipment.

'It's a pop-up tent.' He slammed the door. 'So we don't have to sleep on the ground with one of us waking every couple of hours to stoke the fire to keep nosy animals at bay.'

Anna's mouth dried and she made a conscious effort to stop her jaw from hitting her boots. 'Do we *both* sleep up there? Or will one of us be in the back?'

'There's not a lot of room in the back, unless you sleep curled up. The tent is very comfortable. There's a good mattress. Even I can stretch out on it.'

Was he kidding her?

His expression was serious, his mouth in a straight line, and there was no hint of laughter in his eyes, so she didn't think he was teasing.

Curled up next to him on his sofa two nights ago, and then standing on the deck with her fingers linked in his, all she'd wanted was for him to kiss her. She'd expected it; waited for it. *Ached* for it. But it hadn't happened. He'd been kind and solicitous, making her a cup of tea when the comfort she really sought, the oblivion from the thoughts which caused her head to spin, would have been found in his arms and beneath his mouth. Even though she knew she shouldn't, it was what she'd wanted above all else.

That breath-stealing, body-melting kiss they'd shared the night she arrived had to be a one-off. They'd agreed on that, and Jack was leading the way in sticking to their decision. The avalanche of emotion, memories and regrets it had unleashed had knocked her sideways, because she'd believed she had them firmly under control. Yet all it had taken was one brush of his lips on hers for that control to be swept away.

Now, sharing a tent with Jack in the bush, miles from anywhere, was going to be the ultimate test for her. But from the look on his face he had no such concerns. Was this trip to be his final deed in wrapping up the problem that was Anna? On Monday he would see her onto the helicopter, breathe a sigh of relief and have forget about her by the time he returned to his office. Another problem solved and filed away.

And yet his memory of their shared past was forensic in its detail. As she climbed into the passenger seat and Jack slammed the door she thought she was more surprised by that than anything else.

Jack unfolded a battered map and spread it out over the console between them. He traced their route with an index finger.

That finger—tapered, strong—and that hand—bronzed and powerful... God, she had to stop fantasising about his palm moving over the contours of her body, those fingers burying themselves in her hair... She dragged her attention back to what he was saying, nailing down a brief fantasy about his mouth along the way.

'We'll leave the made-up road here.' His finger stopped. 'And then follow this track to the north-east. Somewhere around here...' he pointed again '...is a border post, but it won't be manned. It's just a painted sign on a boulder at the side of the track.' He made a circular movement with his fingertip. 'From about here the going will be rough, and the track will disappear completely after a while, but this village—' he tapped the worn print '—is where we're headed. The people who brought you to Themba came from there.'

Anna nodded and snapped the buckle of her seatbelt into place. 'Do you know why?'

'Why?'

'Yes. Why Themba? It's a long way.'

'Yup. Three days' walk back then. There were even fewer roads and tracks than there are now, and a lot more wildlife. But the answer is that they believed there were people at Themba who would know what to do with you. It was the closest, safest option when there wasn't much choice.'

Five hours later, when the gravel road climbed around the shoulder of a hill scattered with giant boulders, Jack pulled the Land Rover over to the side, into the shade of an umbrella thorn, and cut the ignition. Silence settled around them, punctuated by the tick of the cooling motor as the dust drifted away. On the plain below Anna could see a herd of elephant moving through the bush, creating their own small dust cloud.

Jack jumped out of the vehicle and Anna watched him survey their surroundings, studying the rocky slopes above and below and listening intently, before opening the rear door and pulling out a cold box.

'Lunch,' he said. 'I think it's safe to get out.'

Anna swallowed the last mouthful of grilled chicken salad and then bit into the creamy flesh of a peach. Jack twisted the cap off a bottle of water and balanced it on the front bumper between them.

'I thought,' she said, wiping peach juice from her chin, 'the restaurant staff were off duty.'

'They are. I put this together.'

She pushed up the brim of her straw hat and studied his profile. It was achingly familiar, in spite of the years they'd spent apart. Yet it was also subtly different. The serious mouth was bracketed by faint lines. Similar lines radiated from the outer corners of his eyes. Most people would have labelled them laughter lines, but she knew they resulted from years of narrowing his gaze as he squinted into the distance, or the sun.

He tipped his head back and took several deep pulls of water from the bottle in his hand. She watched the smooth bronzed skin of his throat move as he swallowed. The previous version of Jack had scarcely ever set foot in the kitchen. Meals—sometimes at irregular intervals, always plain—had just appeared and been eaten. She'd never given much thought to how they'd got there.

Jack had produced a perfect meal three nights ago and a gourmet picnic today. He was harder, more rugged, but he'd developed skills in the kitchen. And there was that scar…

He turned to face her. 'Have you found what you're looking for?'

Anna swallowed the last mouthful of peach. How did he know she was looking for anything? He'd be the last person she'd share her dreams with. They'd wither and die in the blast of a single one of his scorching glances. She'd learned that the hard way.

'What do you mean?' she managed, when she'd forced some air into her lungs. 'I'm not looking for anything. I'm just…'

'You're staring so hard that I wondered. That's all.'

Ah… She'd been so absorbed in his nearness, in the reality of him, trying to puzzle him out, that she'd read far too much into the question.

'I'm thinking how you're the same yet different,' she said.

'How different?' He raised his eyebrows.

'You're tougher.' She looked away and pressed her hands to the bumper on either side of her hips. 'More…ruthless, somehow.' She smiled, trying to lighten her words. 'Mean and lean.'

'You're right. I am.' He screwed the cap back onto the bottle, tightening it hard. 'I have to be. Getting to where we are now has been a struggle, and the struggle will go on. It's a harsh environment and it's tough. Running the mine and Themba take up all…*all*…my time.'

'Then it's exceptionally kind of you to take time out for this trip. I'm very grateful.' She settled her hat firmly on her head so it shaded her eyes again. 'But you seem to have a reliable team in place. Are you not happy to leave Themba in their hands while you're away?'

'They're an excellent team, but I prefer to be there. I'm involved in every detail of both operations. I expect to be kept informed about everything and anything, and I don't ask my staff to do anything I wouldn't or couldn't do myself.'

Anna gestured towards the cold box. 'So you've learned to cook?'

She'd intended it to be a light-hearted comment, but Jack simply nodded.

'That's a good example. The restaurant serves world-class meals—sometimes from a surprising collection of ingredients when food deliveries or power supplies have been disrupted. I respect staff who can turn their hands to anything and see adversity as just another challenge. And I know their roles as well as, or better than, they do themselves.'

'Even on the mine?'

'I have an excellent team there, too, headed up by an exceptional manager, but I fly up at least once a fortnight—or immediately if there's a problem. There are not many diamond mines left in private ownership, and it's up to me to see that the highest standards are met all the time.'

'Have you ever considered selling out to one of the big conglomerates? It would make your life a lot easier.'

Jack tossed the half-empty water bottle from one hand to the other, then dropped it into the cold box at their feet.

'There've been offers, but none of them have come with a guarantee to maintain the level of staff welfare and profit-sharing that I've put in place. And, yes, the profit share I take *does* finance Themba, but the diamonds are ethically mined at no human cost. So at the moment selling out is not something I'm considering. An easier life would not necessarily be a better one,' he said slowly. 'As a child I was powerless to prevent some of the bad things that happened at Themba—my mother's death, my father's drinking, the hunting…' He wiped his forehead with the back of one hand. 'I made the decision, a long time ago, never to be powerless again.'

Anna considered the workload he'd taken upon himself and remembered the pallor of exhaustion she'd noticed under his suntan.

'I can understand why your patience would wear thin with trivial requests from annoying guests.'

'Mmm… If you mean Professor Watkins…?' One corner of his mouth lifted in a teasing smile. 'And don't tell me again that you're grown up. I've worked that out.'

Anna ignored the gentle provocation. She wasn't prepared to put her Jack resistance to the test right now. She'd need it all tonight, in that tent on the roof. She glanced up at it and saw him register her look. She thought fast, needing to stamp on that spark of awareness that arced between them, bright and dangerous.

'It must be exhausting, this life you've built for yourself.'

Get back to reality. Extinguish the spark before it becomes a flame.

'Maybe. But this way I have control. The alternative… Well, I've seen that and it's not an option.'

He leaned forward and flipped the lid of the cold box closed. Then he handed her the bottle of water he'd put between them.

'You need to keep hydrated, Anna. I'm sorry—that sounds patronising. I'm sure you remember that this dry heat can be deceptive.'

Anna took the bottle, careful to avoid contact with his fingers. She took a sip.

'What do you mean, Jack? And I don't mean about the heat. I *do* know about that.' She loosened her cotton scarf, marvelling at the fact that it had been cool enough earlier for her to wear her hoodie. 'I mean about the alternative.'

Jack stood up and took two paces away, keeping his back to her. His hands were rammed into his pockets and she saw tension ripple through the muscles across his wide shoulders. His back expanded as he drew in a breath.

'The chaos I inherited is what I mean. My father had lost control of his life—of *everything*. He was mired in a pit of alcohol and guilt and he was powerless to escape the clutches of either of them. It made him furious, and most of that fury was directed at me.'

His voice was so low Anna could barely hear him, but the bitterness in his tone jumped out at her. She sat very still.

'I believe he wanted to die that day. Maybe that's why it happened like it did.'

She allowed a beat of silence to pass before she spoke. 'What happened, Jack?'

Jack turned to face her. Lines of stress etched a frown between his eyes. 'You don't know?'

'I know your father died not long after I left. So what *don't* I know?'

Jack rocked back on his heels.

'I thought everyone knew,' he said, almost to himself. 'It feels as though everyone knows…'

Heat radiated off the surrounding boulders, sending the temperature to furnace levels. Anna felt its oppressive weight pressing onto her head, into her lungs as she tried to keep her breathing even and quiet.

'Knows what, Jack?'

'That I didn't pull the trigger in time to save him.'

The midday silence was absolute, and then Anna gulped in some air, filling her lungs, giving up the attempt to keep her breathing regular. In her mind's eye she saw again that muscled lion crouching on the track ahead of them. The rifle thrown against Jack's shoulder. She almost felt the imprint of his collarbone on her cheek. Even in the face of extreme, primitive danger she'd felt safe with him.

She stood up and closed the distance between them, holding out a hand. 'Let's get out of the sun.'

They climbed into the vehicle and Jack gunned the engine, but Anna put a hand on his arm.

'It's okay, Anna. We're not going anywhere just yet. I'll just run it for a couple of minutes to cool us down.'

He adjusted the air-conditioning controls and a blast of air hit Anna's face. She turned sideways in her seat.

Jack flipped his head back against the headrest and closed his eyes. They felt gritty with dust and fatigue. He massaged his eye sockets with his knuckles and then crossed his arms again. Someone had once told him it was a defensive gesture, and that was just fine.

'You don't have to tell me—' said Anna.

He interrupted her. 'I do. Because if I don't someone else will.' He stared straight ahead, fixing his gaze on the far horizon. 'My mother died when I was supposed to be looking after her. That was a huge thing for me to deal with— even though I know it was a burden no child should have had to bear. But as if I could make up for it I promised myself that I'd always protect *you*. Keep you safe. You should have been safe with me on Tuesday evening, but the thing is I don't know if you were.' He paused, searching for the right words. 'The hunting business my father ran appalled me. We argued bitterly about it, but I couldn't make him change. After he died I swore no animals would be shot on Themba land ever again unless it was to protect human life or to end a sick or injured animal's suffering if there was no alternative. But I could always see the doubt in the eyes of the trackers. That doubt is the reason Alex tracked the lion we encountered. They just can't be sure of what

I'd do. After all, if I didn't shoot to save my father's life, who *would* I save?'

He turned to look at her and found her cool gaze returning his questioning one.

She folded her hands in her lap. 'Please, Jack, start at the beginning and tell me what happened.'

He marvelled at her calmness. Did she suspect he was about to destroy any illusions she still had about him? That he wasn't the man she believed him to be at all. He was conflicted, and confused, and he had to work every minute of every day and frequently a lot of every night to stay sane. Because if he stopped he'd have to confront his demons and answer the question that plagued him.

He hadn't been able to save his mother, and he'd seen his father die because he hadn't squeezed the trigger of his rifle in time. And when he had pulled it, the hopelessly late shot had gone wide anyway. Now, added to all that, he was tormented by the thought that he wouldn't have saved Anna, either.

Sitting here in the midday heat, looking at her, he knew she was the most precious thing in the world to him. His unforgivable lapse in concentration had put her in terrible danger and now he couldn't trust himself to protect her. If anything happened to her he would not be able to live with the unbearable burden of guilt.

Bringing her on this trip, even if it might well turn out to be a disappointing wild goose chase, was the least he could do by way of compensation. If he could help her to put her past to rest he'd have done a good thing. And the next good thing he could do for her would be to put her on that helicopter on Monday morning and wave her goodbye—before he screwed up her life completely.

'Jack?'

'Yeah. Okay.' He gripped the bridge of his nose between his thumb and forefinger and shook his head. 'It was an elephant. The same tusker he'd been hunting for years. Only by then he and the bull were both old, and they were both angry, and one of them was reckless.'

She still didn't look shocked. Those ocean-green eyes hadn't widened. She hadn't gasped…put a hand to her mouth.

'My father went out on his own. When Frank—one of the trackers—suggested going along with him he received a torrent of abuse. Do you remember it was one of the rules…?'

'Never go into the bush alone.' Anna nodded. 'I didn't always comply.'

'No, you didn't.' Jack felt again the jolt of anxiety he associated with her and her alone. 'God, Anna, you kept me in a constant state of high alert, and there were times when I thought I'd lost you…'

'I'm sorry. I should have been more considerate. I think I am now…'

Jack let his eyelids drop and wondered if he'd ever be able to relax if Anna wasn't in his sights. It felt impossible.

'He'd taken the old Land Rover and Frank and I went after him in the Jeep. Shooting that elephant had become an obsession with him. He'd been hunting him when my mother died, and by some process of twisted logic I think he'd come to blame the elephant for what happened to her.'

'It must have been so difficult for you, Jack…'

Jack remembered with horrible clarity the details of that day. The heat and drought through a long summer had been relentless, and the pale dust which had coated the landscape would only be dispersed by rain. A sense of impending catastrophe had overcome him as he'd raced through the crackling dry bush, trying to reach his father in time.

'I had a good idea of where the old bull was spending most of his days, but by the time we found my father he'd left the vehicle and was staggering towards him, shouting and waving his rifle. He was one of the biggest elephants we've ever had on Themba land. He eyed my father for a few seconds, and I could tell from his elephant body language he wasn't faking it, like they sometimes do. He was about to charge for real. His ears were pinned flat against his head and he'd curled his trunk inwards. He went from nought to full speed in the space of a breath. I'd stopped behind a clump of scrub and got out of the Jeep and I had time to aim. But I was shaking. My usual cool head had deserted me. Watching the disaster unroll felt like a slow-motion movie. It still does.'

'And your father? Did he…?'

Jack shook his head again, frowning. Even after ten years he found it difficult to make sense of what had happened.

'He threw his gun down and stood there with his arms stretched out. Frank yelled at me to shoot. I remember it so clearly. But I didn't. And then my father was gone, under those enormous feet, in a billow of dust. That's when I fired—way too late—and the elephant kept going, right past us. My shot had gone wide. He was so close I could see the expression in his eyes, feel the rush of air whip against my skin.' He put his fingers up to the scar on his forehead. 'A stone flew up from under his feet and cut my face. I only realised later, when blood dripped into my eyes, that I'd been injured. Frank and I ran to my father but he was… gone. His body was crushed and broken, his life snuffed out. It felt…extraordinary. Because seconds earlier he'd been living and breathing. We took him back to Themba and buried him next to my mother, under the baobab tree.'

'Jack…' Anna laid a hand on his shoulder. 'It sounds as if he really was intent on dying. Perhaps he simply couldn't live with his pain any longer. Maybe, somewhere deep down, you knew that you needed to help him let go of it. What good would shooting the elephant have done? It might still have trampled him—and you and Frank, too.'

'Possibly. But the thing is, Frank knew I hadn't acted quickly enough to save him. Now it's what everyone believes. And it's the truth.'

She was quiet for a while, and Jack waited to hear her say she was sure that wasn't the case. That everyone knew he was brave, resolute. Utterly dependable. Instead, her next words were unexpected.

'This may not be the correct thing to say, Jack, but my gut reaction is that I'm *glad* you didn't shoot the elephant. Like I'm glad you didn't shoot the lion.'

She rubbed his shoulder. Jack stared at her, then shook his head.

'I haven't been able to see it that way. I don't think anyone else has, either. I see the questions in their eyes. I see them wondering what sort of man I really am.'

'Has it occurred to you they may simply be concerned for you? They may not be judging you, but you're judging yourself—and harshly. Have you talked about it to anyone? A therapist?'

'Get real, Anna.' His fists gripped the steering wheel. 'Can you see me talking to a therapist?'

His voice dropped as Anna's hand ran down his arm and covered his whitened knuckles. He felt drained and suddenly tired of maintaining this façade of impenetrable strength.

'I haven't had the courage to talk to anybody. Until today.'

'So that's about ten years of internalising the trauma. I don't know how you've kept going, Jack. And you didn't really grieve for your father.'

'Like I said, I could only grieve for the man he might have once been. I felt no sense of loss. All I felt for him was a real, deep anger.'

'That,' said Anna quietly, 'is all part of the process.'

'You sound very sure of your theories.'

'Remember that I lost my parents too, Jack. I have no memories of them, but that doesn't make it easier. In a way it raises even bigger questions. And from what you've told me I'm never going to find any more answers now.'

'I'm sorry if I've destroyed any dreams you had about them. My intention was to help you find some closure, but perhaps this trip was a bad idea. It might make things worse for you.'

'It might, in the short term, but I'm prepared to risk that. I hope it'll help me to draw a line under the past, if nothing else.'

'Is that what you want? To forget the past and move on?'

Regret and sadness wrapped around his heart, but he refused to express those feelings to Anna. Moving on was exactly what he needed her to do.

'Yes, it is.' Her gaze was unwavering. 'And I think that's what you need to do, too.'

Jack didn't know how he could leave his past behind when it had suddenly reappeared, all grown up, back in the centre of his life. Anna was the woman he'd driven himself wild imagining, but his imagination had fallen short of the reality she'd become. Her kind, thoughtful opinion of his actions surrounding his father's death had floored him. He'd been ready to be defensive—aggressive, even—but she'd taken away the need, leaving him unsure how to react.

But he felt strangely better—as if a coiled spring wound tightly inside him had been released and had spent its energy, leaving a calm space where there'd once been turmoil and anger.

All that separated them was the console between the two seats. The heavy gold braid of her hair lay across her shoulder. Jack wanted to lift it out of the way and bury his face in her neck, to breathe in that tantalising perfume. He still hadn't asked what it was. She had bent up one of her endless legs, propping her knee against the gearstick, and he wanted to run his palm up her long thigh and see what his touch would do to her. It would only take a second to reach out and pull her onto his lap…

How would it feel to hold someone in his arms who he cared about? Someone who accepted him for what he was, without reservations or conditions attached? Who wasn't there simply for a luxury weekend at Themba and a couple of nights of great sex.

He realised, with a jolt of regret, that he had absolutely no idea, and wondered why he'd even had the thought. He wasn't in the market for caring. Hell, no. Caring for someone meant you lost them, sooner or later, whether they died or you sent them away.

He wanted to tell Anna how amazing she was, with her compassion and her gentle sympathy, but he couldn't trust himself to frame the words. He'd wanted to kiss her again, on his sofa and then on his deck, but he'd dug deep into his resolve to stop it from happening. That he'd succeeded still surprised him, because he craved the oblivion he knew he'd find if he gave in to those innermost desires. But Anna deserved better than someone using her to forget his guilt for a few moments.

Any affection she showed him now would be the result of pity, and he wouldn't accept that. Sympathy and understanding he could just about deal with. Pity would undo him completely.

He twisted round to straighten up in his seat and fasten his seatbelt. He glanced at his watch. 'We need to get going. At the foot of this hill the track—if we can find it—gets rough, and it'll take us another two hours, at least.'

Out of the corner of his eye he saw Anna nod, and he heard the metallic click as she fastened her own seatbelt. He exhaled a long breath and shoved the gearstick into low gear. Her calm acceptance of his story, the total lack of judgement in her response, had shaken him. He felt as if the wall he'd constructed between himself and the rest of the world had been quietly breached, exposing his vulnerability, threatening his control.

And that scared him more than anything he'd ever encountered in the wild.

CHAPTER SEVEN

MORE THAN TWO bone-shaking hours later, Jack pulled the Land Rover to a stop. Anna eased the death grip she had on the handle above the door and tried to rub some life back into her cramped hands. As the engine shuddered into silence she saw a group of people watching them from the shade of a grove of fever trees.

She glanced across at Jack. 'Are they expecting us?'

'They are.'

Anna raised her eyebrows. 'How come?'

'I sent a message to the mine. I don't know the details of the route it took from there to here, but I knew it would reach the right people. Almost everyone has a phone these days, even if the signal is unreliable. Communications can be dodgy, but something usually works.'

The group consisted of an elderly man who leaned on a tall stick, two middle-aged women, and a young mother with a baby cocooned on her back. As Jack climbed out of the driver's door they moved from the shadows into the sun, towards him.

Jack addressed the man in a dialect Anna didn't recognise. The women studied her with open curiosity, exclaiming to each other and clapping their hands. When Jack spoke to them they nodded, and then one of them gestured towards Anna's face, talking fast.

'They say they remember your eyes, Anna.'

A shiver raised the hairs along Anna's forearms. 'Do you mean these are the people who found me?'

Jack spoke again and they nodded, wide smiles lighting their faces. 'Yes,' he said. 'This man and these two women found you after you'd been flung from the plane as it crashed. This younger woman is the daughter of one of them, and the baby is their granddaughter.'

Emotion and gratitude swelled in Anna's chest as she tried to speak. Had her mother thrown her from the wreckage in a desperate bid to save her before the plane turned into a fireball? Or had her survival simply been luck?

She reached out and squeezed the women's hands in hers as a lump clogged her throat. She looked to Jack for help, and he must have read the plea in her eyes because he spoke again and then translated for her.

'I've told them that you thank them and will be filled with gratitude for their actions for ever. At least I hope that's what I've said. I'm not fluent in the dialect.'

The elderly man began to walk up the track and beckoned them to follow. Jack fell in beside him, listening as he talked.

'Their village is on that hill.' He pointed. 'He says there was a fierce thunderstorm that afternoon, with a strong wind. The plane came down low, out of the clouds, and then disappeared beyond the trees. There was a loud noise, like more thunder, and flames and thick smoke. Many people ran from the village to help, but the fire was too intense to get close.'

Jack dropped back a pace to walk next to Anna.

'One theory was that they had cans of extra fuel on board. They probably planned to land somewhere remote and refuel. It's why the fire was so intense.''

Anna clamped a hand over her mouth to try to hide her distress. She stopped and bent forward, her hands on her knees. 'This is…hard for me to hear.'

He dropped a hand onto her shoulder. 'I'm sorry. Of course it is. Do you want to turn back?'

She straightened up and shook her head. 'No. I must go on. I must see the place.'

Jack nodded once. 'Okay. Just say if it gets too much.' He strode forward again.

Their progress through the dense bushland was slow. Vicious thorns snagged at their clothes and insects buzzed in their faces, but eventually they reached the edge of what had evidently once been a clearing. The bushes looked stubby, and the few trees were spindly and half-grown.

Their guide made a sweeping gesture and turned to Jack again.

'He says nothing grew for many years on the burned place, but one day soon all the evidence of a crashed plane will be gone, swallowed up by nature.'

Anna looked around. 'And...me?' Her voice shook. 'Where did they find me?'

The women took her hands and led her to a place on the far side of the space, where young trees grew. They pointed at her, and at the ground, and patted her arms.

Anna stared at the patch of brown dried grass and leaves and wondered how she was supposed to feel. She searched herself for some sort of emotion, however slight. Hearing about the crash and the burning plane had been harrowing, but now all she found in herself was a hollowed-out dark void. She'd imagined this place all her remembered life, and thought about the people who'd carried her to safety. But now that she was here she felt drained and numb.

Nausea churned in her stomach, and she was horribly afraid that she was about to be sick. She wondered why she'd agreed to come. She could have been boarding a flight to Heathrow about now, if she'd chosen the sensible option.

She sensed Jack behind her, felt his hand cup her elbow. 'Do you need a moment on your own?'

She was grateful for his touch, because the warmth of his hand reassured her that she could actually *feel* something. She wanted to lean back and be supported by his broad, solid chest, with his arm gripping her waist to hold her close. If she could tuck her head into his shoulder and feel his cheek on her hair perhaps she'd feel human. Perhaps this would all feel real.

But she lifted her chin and straightened her spine, staying rigidly upright. 'No, thank you. I'll be fine. It just feels weird.' She took a shuddering breath. 'I expected a huge rush of emotion, or some sort of feeling of connection to this place. It's where my parents died, where I only survived by a chance twist of fate, but I don't feel anything apart from sick.'

She turned to look at him, to see if he understood.

'I can't sense anything of them here. Anything at all.'

They made their way back to the Land Rover, the silence broken only by their feet swishing through the grass and the young mother crooning a song to her baby.

Anna folded her arms across her stomach and turned to Jack. 'Please will you thank them again? I'm very grateful.' She lifted her shoulders. 'What can I possibly say to the people who literally saved my life?'

Jack nodded and translated her words, and they all raised their hands in farewell. The villagers turned away and Jack opened the car door for her. She stared straight ahead as he started the engine and turned the vehicle.

'I'm sorry, Anna.' Jack twisted his head to look at her. 'I underestimated how traumatic this would be for you. I think it was a bad idea.'

She shook her head. 'No. It was the right thing to do.' She pushed the seatbelt buckle into its slot with more force than necessary. 'I'll always be grateful to you for bringing me here, but I won't need to come again. And I don't want the diamonds, but I don't know what to do with them.'

Jack found a place for their overnight camp on a bluff overlooking an almost dry riverbed, where the view to the west stretched on for ever. He made a fire and boiled water for tea, then pulled a can of beer from the cold box.

He watched Anna, where she sat with her legs dangling out of the passenger side of the vehicle. Her gaze appeared to be fixed on the horizon, but he suspected it was really turned inwards, doing some soul-searching.

Since leaving the village she hadn't uttered a word. Her silence didn't surprise him. It had been a stressful, emotional day, and he thought she was probably suffering from the slump that often followed an adrenaline overload.

He handed her a mug of tea and propped himself against the side of the vehicle, rolling the can of beer between his palms. 'Want to talk?'

'Not about this afternoon.' She took the mug of tea and sipped. 'The sunset is spectacular.'

'Mmm… Possibly too spectacular.' He flipped up the ring-pull on the can and peeled it back. The beer hissed and foamed. 'Those storm clouds are some distance away, but they look as if they mean business.'

Mountainous thunderheads were heaped on the western horizon. Arrows of red and pink, fired by the sinking sun, radiated from behind the bright gold which traced their edges.

'Do you think it'll rain? Tonight?' she asked.

Jack lifted a shoulder. 'Maybe. But I hope we'll make it back to Themba before there's a deluge.' He tipped back his head and took several swallows of beer. 'We want the rain, but not while we're out here.' He drummed his fingers against the can. 'You know how ferocious early summer storms can be. We should get an early night and be away at first light. After we've eaten I'll sort out the tent, and you can get settled while I clear up down here.'

'Okay.' She peered over her shoulder into the back of the vehicle. 'But are you sure it wouldn't be…better if I slept in there?'

Jack emptied the rest of the beer down his throat and crumpled the can in his fist. The hell she'd sleep in the boot. Wherever she slept, it was going to be with him, so that he knew she wasn't wandering off in the night to paddle in what was left of the river with the hippos and the crocs. He wanted her where he could feel her breathing next to him…where he could reach out and put his arm around her waist to keep her there if he had to.

He knew he had to stop treating her like a child and start accepting her as the responsible adult she'd become, but he told himself she'd been traumatised. She needed watching. He could keep her safe for these last few days.

And if that felt like an excuse he could live with it.

At some point that icy composure was going to shatter, and he needed to be there to keep the pieces of Anna together when it happened. That was all, he told himself. There was no other reason. He'd proved he could resist her, after all.

He hoped the shake of his head as he answered was convincingly dismissive.

'No. I can see you're worn out. Today has been long and emotional, and the drive wasn't easy, either. Besides…' he threw her a half-smile '… I need you where I can keep an eye on you. You don't have the best record for staying where you're meant to be.'

He thought she'd laugh, or at least smile and acknowledge that he was right, but she just shrugged, shaking out the dregs of tea from the mug.

'Okay.'

They sat on folding canvas stools, and he was pleased

to see her eat one of the hot dogs he assembled. He hoped the glass of red wine she'd swallowed in three gulps would relax her enough for sleep.

When she shivered he unrolled a blanket and dropped it over her shoulders. 'I'll build up the fire. You'll sleep better if you go to bed warm.'

'Thanks.'

'I can make you some hot chocolate, if you like.'

She shook her head. 'I'm fine.'

He knew she was far from fine. It felt as if the air between them crackled with unspoken words and half-formed thoughts. But he also knew better than to probe. He remembered how he'd felt in the aftermath of his father's violent death. How it had taken him years to process it and he still had not come to terms with it. The death of Anna's parents had also been horrifying, and she was still only just beginning the process of grieving all these years later.

He picked up the bottle of wine and held it out to her, then topped up his own glass when she declined.

She stood up and bundled the blanket into the boot. 'I'll...go to bed. If that's okay.'

She'd managed the whole evening without once looking directly at him.

'Sure,' he said easily. 'I'll see you in the morning. If we make an early start we'll beat the storm, if it's coming our way. You'll be able to sleep in your own bed tomorrow night.'

'My own bed,' she said over her shoulder, 'is a long way from Themba.'

He heard her sluice water from the big plastic bottle over her face and neck, and brush her teeth, and then she climbed up the ladder and disappeared into the tent. The battery lantern he'd left burning cast her flickering shadow against the canvas sides. When the movements stopped he assumed she'd settled down to sleep.

He took his time packing up, then added more wood to the fire and watched it burn down while he tuned in to the night sounds. When he'd suggested identifying what they could hear earlier Anna had said she was too tired. The temperature had fallen sharply with the fading light, and now a sneaky breeze curled up from the riverbed, raising a shiver along his arms. Finally, when he'd run out of reasons not to, he closed the tailgate as softly as possible, kicked over the embers of the fire and climbed up into the tent.

Anna slept curled up in her sleeping bag, her knees wedged against the side of the tent. She'd pulled the hood of her top up over her head. Jack moved carefully, stowing his boots next to hers near the zipped-up entrance and sliding, fully clothed, into his own sleeping bag. He stretched out, flicked off the lantern and tucked a folded arm behind his head.

He stared into the darkness, listening to the measured rise and fall of Anna's breathing, and ran the events of the day through his head once more. He'd never verbalised how he'd watched his father die to anyone, and while he recognised that talking had been cathartic, it had drained him emotionally. He felt raw and exposed. And on top of that he'd watched Anna go through all kinds of hell this afternoon, although she'd insisted she was fine. She might feel nothing now, but that protective numbness would wear off and then her emotional reaction might be unexpected in its ferocity.

He wished she'd confide in him…spill the thoughts he was sure were churning behind those opaque evergreen eyes. He wished he could close the small space between them and spoon her so that when she woke she wouldn't feel so alone.

He wasn't expecting to fall asleep any time soon. It might have been a long day, but it was going to be a very long night.

Jack went from sleep to full-on alert in the time it took him to open his eyes in the absolute darkness of the tent. He lay motionless, every muscle tensed, every nerve-ending tuned in to the silence.

Something was wrong, and that something was the silence.

He knew without stretching out his arm to find her, without straining to hear her quiet breathing, that he was alone.

Anna had gone.

He swore and pushed himself upright, struggling to kick his way out of the sleeping bag and find the lantern at the same time. How had she done this? Only inches separated them. The zip of the tent's entrance was not quiet. When had he ever slept through even the slightest disturbance?

He swore again as his groping hand knocked the lantern over and it rolled out of reach. He cursed himself for not having his powerful torch in bed with him. What use was it stowed in the vehicle? His fingers, clumsy with shock and hurry, fumbled for the zipper. Finally locating the metal tab, he tugged at it, ripping it upwards and pushing the flaps aside.

His hands made contact with something soft, blocking his way out.

'Jack?'

Her voice, even though it was barely a whisper in the dark, felt like a punch in the chest, relieving his lungs of oxygen. The air rasped in his throat as he dragged it back.

'*Anna?* I thought...' His searching hands found her shoulders, the long braid of her hair, the curve of her neck. 'I thought you'd gone.' His heart slammed against his ribs and his breath was quick. 'What the hell are you *doing*?'

Her narrow shoulders, swamped by the hoodie, shifted under his hands. 'I woke up. I needed some air. Some space.'

Jack closed his eyes and sent a prayer of thanks to whoever might be listening out here in the wild. The vivid scenario which had flashed through his mind fully formed, of having to try to find her before something bigger and hungrier beat him to it, faded. He tried to control the tremor which seized him, and he closed his hands around her upper arms.

'You scared me stupid, Anna. It's… Are you okay?'

A translucent slice of moon hung low in the sky, no competition for the light from the stars. They glimmered like splinters of crystal flung by some giant hand across black velvet. He felt that lift of her shoulders again and she angled her head towards him.

'I feel…lost.'

He caught the gleam of dampness on her cheek.

'I don't want to know anything more about my past. It doesn't sound good. And the future I thought I wanted seems…out of reach.'

'Hey…' Jack bent his knees and put his arms around her ribcage, shuffling her backwards until she leant against him. He tried to ignore the perfect fit of her thighs between his, the snug contact with his groin. 'Yesterday was all a bit of an overload. Things will feel more manageable in daylight. They always do.'

He thought he felt her body grow a fraction heavier as she relaxed. Her breathing settled, her ribs expanding and then flattening against his abdomen.

'Look up, Anna. The stars are incredible.' He needed the distraction as much as she did.

'Mmm… They are. I'd forgotten how bright they are out here. No light pollution.'

'None at all.'

'It's like being inside an upside-down bowl of stars. They shine all the way down to the horizon.'

Jack raised a hand, smoothing her hair back from her forehead and settling her head into his shoulder. This was Anna, he reminded himself, and he needed to look after her and make her feel better.

'Do you remember the story of how the Milky Way was formed?' he asked.

He felt her head move as she searched for the dense pathway of millions of stars which wove its way across the night sky.

'There was a girl who wanted to provide light so that her people could find their way home...' Anna wriggled her shoulders, settling further into the crook of his arm. 'She flung the ashes from her mother's fire into the air and the ashes became the stars of the Milky Way.'

Jack nodded, his cheek rubbing against her hair. 'That was one of the first stories I told you. When the sun rises tomorrow you'll feel different. You'll know what you want.'

'I've always known what I want, Jack.'

He thought he knew what she wanted: a proper home and family, to make up for never having had one of her own. A real bricks and mortar house, not a collection of thatched huts. A husband. And two point four children.

During her school holidays she used to return to Themba and describe to him the details of her visits to schoolfriends' homes. She'd been intrigued by the workings and dynamics of those 'normal' families.

He could give her his protection, but he could never give her that kind of stifling security. He'd seen the havoc a reckless, selfish man could wreak on his family, and he was never, ever going to risk seeing history repeat itself through him. He'd vowed years ago to stay away from commitment, family and anything resembling...*love*. He had trouble forcing himself even to form the word as a thought.

His mother must have loved his father to put up with the years of hardship and neglect she'd suffered, and look what had happened to her. He could never risk putting any woman through that. The only love he'd witnessed had been destructive, and it had ultimately led to loss. It wasn't something he was willing to experience ever again.

He shifted a little, remembering the way he'd shattered Anna's dreams eleven years ago. He'd laid the blame for sending her away at the feet of those men, circling her like hyenas closing in on a defenceless gazelle. But he hadn't been able to trust himself, either—although it had taken him a long time to admit that. He'd had to get her away. He'd meant it when he'd said he never wanted a wife. That didn't mean he hadn't wanted *her*.

Now he wanted her grown-up self even more, and that made the situation they were in perilous.

Her seductive perfume invaded his senses, playing havoc with his responses, and her hair slid like silk against his sensitised skin. Beneath the bulky hoodie the curves which had developed from her teenager's skinny frame filled his arms perfectly. He tried to ease himself away from her, alarmed at the sudden urgency of the sensations building in his body. He'd resisted them before. He could do it again.

He sucked the cool night air into his lungs and raised his head. 'Can I get you something that'll help you sleep, Anna? Is there anything you need?'

Her head fell back revealing the sweep of her cheek, her full lower lip, the starlight reflected in her eyes.

'What I really need, Jack, is for you to kiss me.'

Jack felt as if the universe had paused along with his breathing. He could do the sensible thing—put space between them and tell her he didn't want to kiss her. Or he could abandon sense completely and do what they both wanted, what they desperately needed, more than anything else.

Inches separated their lips. Her eyes were just a gleam in the dark, her face a pale oval. He raised one hand and cupped her cheek in his palm, running an unsteady thumb across her cheekbone.

'Anna…'

'Please, Jack.'

He dropped his head a fraction and rested his forehead against hers.

'Anna, I don't know…'

Her hand drifted up and cupped the back of his head, her fingers tunnelling into his hair.

'Jack, I know we shouldn't. I know you're trying to be sensible. But I just…need you. Now.'

She lifted her head and he felt the feather-light brush of her lips along his jaw, pausing at the corner of his mouth.

Jack sighed out a breath and his lips found hers. They tasted of sweet peppermint, and he could swear a hint of that peach she'd eaten earlier still lingered on them, but perhaps he was confusing it with her scent.

He fought to keep the kiss gentle and light, barely touching her. There would still be a way back from that. But she reached for more, pulling his head down and sealing their lips together.

Her soft sweetness melted under his mouth as molten desire poured through his body, unstoppable as hot lava. He heard her moan in her throat as he deepened the kiss and he thought it was a muttered 'yes'. His tongue traced the join of her lips, parting them with its tip, allowing himself to go further, to invade her warm mouth.

They'd shared one hot kiss, but this was becoming off-the-scale scorching. He probed deep, his tongue tangling with hers, then withdrew to take her bottom lip in his mouth to suck on it. Anna gasped, responding with thrusts of her own tongue. She twisted towards him, flattening her body against his, as if she needed to obliterate any gaps that remained between them.

Jack hauled her across his lap. Her arms wrapped around his neck, clamping him against her body so he could feel the push of her breasts against his chest. He rested a hand on her waist, then found the edge of the ridiculously big hoodie and the hem of her tee shirt. He felt her stomach muscles contract, making space for his hand to move under her clothes, and then heard the sharp intake of her breath as his exploring fingers found her smooth, hot skin. Her breathing turned quick and shallow as he moved his hand upwards, finally cupping the silk-covered mound of her breast before his thumb drifted across the puckered nipple.

'Oh, Jack…'

'Do you want me to stop, Anna? If you do…'

Her answer was to pick up his hand in hers. He didn't know where he'd find the self-control, but if that was what she wanted, he would listen. But she guided his hand down, to the inside of her thigh. Her legs shifted and he realised what she wanted. His fingers stroked upwards, increasing their pressure until he felt her damp heat through the cotton of her clothes. She lifted her hips towards him and cried out against his mouth as her whole body tensed. Then she relaxed, limp in his arms.

Jack gathered her against him as she shuddered twice. He listened as her rapid breathing slowed into a deeper rhythm and felt her heartbeat begin to steady. Frustration welled up in him but he fought it, denying his own need. Anna was relaxed at last. She seemed to be deeply asleep.

He dropped a kiss on her cheek. To hold her was enough.

He inched back into the tent, pulling her with him, then slid her from his arms onto the mattress, putting a pillow under her head. She sighed and turned onto her side, drawing her knees up. Jack unzipped his sleeping bag and unfolded it. Then he lay down next to her, spreading it over them and putting an arm across her waist. He closed his hand around her slender fingers and tucked her head under his chin.

She wouldn't be able to move an inch without him knowing about it.

Anna woke slowly, dragging herself out of a deep, dreamless sleep, and it took her a few moments to work out where she was. Heavy lethargy weighted her body. And then she realised something had pinned her down. She raised her eyelids and saw that it was an arm, clad in a checked cotton shirt, and that the hand belonging to it had her own hand loosely clasped in long, strong fingers.

Jack. Her brain engaged with reluctance, and then the memories of the night began to unroll. He must have put her back to bed after… Her cheeks heated as she remembered what they'd done…what *she'd* done. But even as embarrassment made her want to squirm, pleasure at the memory, intense and undeniable, spiked through her, kicking up the beat of her heart and sending arrows of renewed desire deep into her body.

His breathing altered a fraction and she knew he'd woken.

'Anna?'

'Mmm…?'

He shifted behind her, inching away, but not before she felt the hard imprint of him against the small of her back.

She felt him move, propping himself on one elbow. She turned her head. His dark hair, tousled from sleep, flopped over his forehead and rough stubble shadowed his jaw. Eyes, iron-grey and serious, regarded her. Need pierced her and she wanted to turn into his arms and lose herself again under the sweet magic of his skilled mouth, the stroke of his tongue and the caress of his clever fingers.

But sex with Jack was not part of her plan. Her plan was to be cool and professional. To prove to him that she could come back to Africa, to Themba…okay, to *him*…and handle it all with the control worthy of an ice queen. And then she'd turn her back and return to her life. The real, proper life that she'd begun to build for herself with painful care. Which was what she wanted—what she told herself she'd always wanted.

Last night had been a blip…the consequence of a traumatic, tiring and in the end shattering, day. She'd needed something, someone, to hijack her thoughts…to stop the endless churning of *if onlys* and *what ifs* in her head. It had been Jack who'd delivered her to sweet oblivion. But it could have been anyone. Couldn't it?

She caught her lip between her teeth and dragged her eyes away from the face that constantly got in the way of her determination to live life on her own terms. She looked beyond him, over his shoulder, to distract herself.

'Are you okay?' His voice was gravelly, sexy as sin.

'Are you?' she asked.

'Frustrated as all hell and short of sleep.'

Anna blinked, surprised by his candour. 'I'm…sorry, Jack.' She turned onto her back. 'I shouldn't have done that. I just needed to…to forget for a while. Perhaps it's selfish, but I don't think we should continue…'

There was a beat of silence and then Jack rolled over and sat up, his back to her. The tension across his wide shoulders screamed for her to stretch out her hands and massage those muscles until they relaxed.

'Of course we shouldn't. So let's forget it.' He pushed a hand through his hair. 'Anyway, it's late. We need to go.'

CHAPTER EIGHT

DESPITE THE BLAST of cold air from the air conditioning unit, the atmosphere inside the vehicle felt as sultry and threatening as the day outside. They'd packed up in near-silence and Anna had refused any breakfast. Contrary to Jack's promise of the night before, nothing looked better in the morning. For starters, the sun hadn't come out. Also she was confused, and sad, and she wanted him with an ache that shocked her. No amount of silent, sensible reasoning would soothe that.

A leaden sky hung above them. The air felt sluggish and thick, and the land seemed to crouch, sullen, beneath its weight, holding its breath. Jack looked to the west as he swung himself into the driver's seat.

'It's already raining in the mountains. We don't have much time.'

Anna wanted to ask how much time they didn't have. And what would happen when it ran out. But Jack's set jaw and the lines around his straight mouth, the frown of concentration between his brows, stopped her. She'd find out soon enough, and right now she had to concentrate on holding on to the handle above the door as Jack depressed the accelerator and the Land Rover lurched over rocks and the mounds of ant hills.

When they reached the track he put on more speed, and she felt relieved that talking had become impossible.

Did he resent what had happened last night? Had he expected her to take it further this morning? To ask him to make love to her? Or for her to take control and make love to him? She'd wanted to. God, how much she'd wanted to. But that wasn't how things were going to be between them.

She had her own path to follow and it led her away from Themba. He had his, too, and she knew it was nowhere near wide enough for her to be at his side. Once she would have been grateful to follow behind him, hoping he'd occasionally turn around and include her in some aspect of his life. That was no longer an option.

She kept her head turned away and stared out of the window at the bush racing past. She thought about the email which had dropped into her inbox two days ago. It contained a permanent job offer from the zoo in San Diego, to head up their big cat conservation project. It was everything she'd ever wanted since that long-ago day when she'd accepted there'd never be a place for her at Themba, with Jack.

She wondered why she hadn't accepted it immediately.

She thought of Brett, a sexy doctor of marine biology, and the message he'd pinged to her phone earlier in the week.

I miss my beach buddy. When are you coming back?

Brett spent his working life under the ocean and most of his leisure time on its surface, surfing or swimming. His laid-back Californian approach to life was sharply at odds with her driven determination.

'Come to the beach with me,' he'd say, appearing at her desk in board shorts and flip-flops, and she'd be charmed away from her research by his slow smile and warm brown eyes.

She knew beach buddies could easily become bed buddies. And then what?

She frowned, because her imagination always stalled on that thought.

Her attention bounced back to the present as the vehicle slewed to a stop and Jack pushed open his door.

'Hear that?'

For a moment Anna thought a part of her mind had remained in Southern California. The distant rumble sounded like the big rollers of the Pacific, powering ashore. But as it echoed off the rocky cliffs on the far side of the riverbed they were following she nodded, fully present.

'That's the storm breaking. We need to get out of the valley. There'll be a flash flood, for sure.'

He slammed the door and gravel spat from under the wheels as the vehicle accelerated.

A twinge of anxiety snagged at Anna and she twisted to look at him.

'What time will we get back?' She had to shout above the roar of the engine.

'Mid-afternoon…' His attention was fixed on the winding track. 'If we can keep going at this pace.'

He swerved around a boulder and Anna was flung sideways, her shoulder hitting the door.

'We should have left at first light. I could smell the rain coming last night.'

She slapped away a twinge of guilt. It was her fault they'd overslept, but if they'd made love this morning, as she knew he'd wanted to, they'd have been even later.

The track climbed up out of the valley to higher ground and Anna felt her tension ease. They'd be safe from a flash flood now. She counted the hours to when she could sink into a steaming hot bath in her suite and allow all the sadness and confusion of the past two days to dissolve. She'd think about the job offer. Ask for more details.

Mentally, she began to compose a reply to Brett.

Hunger gnawed at her, and she wished she'd had breakfast after all, but Jack's grim expression and reluctance to talk had tied her stomach into a tight knot. Now she decided to try to re-establish something of the rapport they'd tentatively begun to build.

'Can we stop for something to eat?'

He threw a glance at her and then returned his eyes to the road.

'We need to keep going.'

'But we're out of the valley. We're safe from the flood— if it even happens.'

She kept her eyes away from his fingers as he gripped the gearstick and changed down to power up a steep incline.

'It'll happen. And we're on the wrong side of the river, Anna. Remember the ford yesterday morning? We need to get back across that before it's submerged.'

Anna remembered the low concrete causeway. It had no railings at the sides and crouched low over the riverbed. A few muddy puddles dotted the area around it. An eight-foot Nile crocodile had been sunning itself on a sandbank.

'But the river was almost dry, Jack, and it's not raining.'

'It's been raining in the west since the early hours of the morning. That thunder is the storm getting going. The flood will be on its way. We just have to beat it to the causeway.' He swore under his breath. 'It's my fault. I was awake until dawn and then I overslept.'

'That was my fault,' Anna said, staring straight ahead.

Jack removed a hand from the steering wheel and furrowed his fingers through his hair. 'No. It's my responsibility to keep us...*you*...safe.'

A jagged fork of white lightning split the purple sky, followed a second later by the crack of thunder. A sudden splatter of fat raindrops hit the windscreen, joining up to create rivulets of mud on the dust-caked glass.

'*Damn.*' Jack slammed the heel of one hand against the

steering wheel. 'We're not going to make it.' He braked hard and the big four-by-four skidded to a halt. 'Come and look.'

Anna slid out of her seat and joined Jack where he stood on the shoulder of the dirt road.

'Watch the bend in the river.'

As she fixed her eyes on the spot he'd indicated Anna became aware of a distant dull roar, separate from the thunder. The noise built with every second and it triggered a memory.

She'd been standing on top of the rocky outcrop behind Themba, her arms stretched wide, her head tipped back. A storm had been raging around her, the wind whipping her hair into a tangle and rain bouncing off the rocks. Then a figure had burst from the huts below. It had been Jack, shouting at her to come down, that it was dangerous to be on the rocks during a storm because the ironstone attracted lightning strikes.

She'd been mesmerised by the spectacle nature was staging for her, and Jack had had to climb the boulders and drag her, protesting, to safety. But she'd seen the wall of water, several feet high, roaring through the valley, engulfing the low bridge and spreading a brown, choppy blanket out across the dry bush. Back under cover, Jack had shouted at her, white-faced and shaking, about disappearing on her own and getting hurt.

She'd glared at him, puzzled. 'But I'm not hurt. And *you're* not the boss of me.' She'd stamped a foot.

'I am,' Jack had said, his chest heaving. 'Because if I'm not, who is?'

'Nobody! I'm the boss of myself!'

She'd stomped off to her hut.

Now Anna watched a repeat of that flood on a much bigger scale. The wall of water thundering around the bend in the river was higher, wider and moving much more quickly. It lapped against the foot of the cliffs below the place where they stood, and on the far side it spread inexorably outwards, dislodging rocks, uprooting bushes and shunting logs in front of it. The wave roared past them, leaving an expanse of muddy water churning in its wake.

Jack turned to her. 'I'm sorry.'

'Sorry?' She shrugged. 'It's not your fault, Jack. I know you control everything at Themba, but not even you can control the weather.'

'No, but I can… I *should* be able to control my own behaviour. Things went wrong last night and I overslept this morning. It was a misjudgement, and now I've put you in danger.'

Anna stared at him. 'I think, Jack, that it was *I* who should have had more control last night. But you know what? I'm *not* sorry. I'm also *not* your responsibility. Not any more. You have to change your thinking.'

Jack shook his head, his eyes fixed on hers. 'I can't. I've tried, and I can't. I promised I'd always look after you. What if something happened to you? I'd…'

Another flash of white light ripped through the inky sky and thunder crackled sharply overhead. In a few seconds the rain changed from single heavy drops exploding in the dust at their feet into saturating sheets of what felt like solid water.

Jack threw an arm across Anna's shoulders and bent to shout in her ear. 'Get under cover!'

He hustled her to the passenger door and she scrambled in, but she was already wet. She swiped water out of her eyes as he leapt into the driver's seat.

'What now, Jack? Do we sit it out here? For how long?'

He shook his head, flicking his hair off his forehead. 'We must keep going, before the roads are all knee-deep in mud. I'll see if I can get Themba on the radio. We might be within range.'

'Are we on Themba land?'

'Yeah. Just. And there's one option…'

He picked up the radio handset and flicked switches. Static crackled and then she heard a voice.

Deafened by successive claps of thunder, Anna couldn't make a lot of sense of Jack's half of the conversation, but when he'd finished he turned to her. His eyes held relief, but she could sense apprehension in him, too.

'If we can make it to the treehouse we'll be okay.'

'The *treehouse*?'

The shaky platform they'd visited as children, miles from the main camp, hardly merited the title. It had consisted of a few planks, barely held together by old rope, wedged in the canopy of a massive ebony tree which grew on the edge of a deep ravine. Jack's father had used it as a game-spotting platform.

'Would that be the same treehouse…?'

'Yeah. But it's undergone a renovation. A couple in the party arriving tomorrow have booked it for two nights, so it's all stocked and ready.'

'But we can't use it, Jack, if your guests need it.'

Jack revved the engine and inched the wheels back onto the slick surface of the road, switching the wipers to their fastest speed. He raised his voice so he could be heard above the drumming of the downpour on the roof.

'They're coming by road from another reserve. They won't make it tomorrow. It's going to be days before anyone can get in or out of Themba.'

'My flight…'

'No chance.'

'But what about the helicopter? Why can't…?'

'The helicopters will be busy lifting food and medical supplies to communities cut off by the floods. Perhaps you've been away too long to remember this is Africa, Anna. The land of wild and fierce extremes, where nothing is predictable.'

Mud churned beneath the wheels and twice the vehicle lurched dangerously towards the edge of the track. More than once Jack had to stop, reverse, and try a different way.

The storm raged without let-up, ear-splitting and ferocious, pouring torrents of rain from the swollen clouds.

When it seemed at its most intense Jack swung the wheel and took a smaller track which had become little more than a gushing stream. The water rushed past them at wheel-arch-height and Anna expected it to seep through the doors and swamp her feet at any moment. Then they stopped. Jack cut the engine and peered through the windscreen.

'It's not far from here. We'll have to run. Just don't let go of my hand.'

Anna was soaked to the skin as soon as she left the shelter of the vehicle. Water swirled around her legs. She tugged her hood over her head and gripped Jack's hand. Then they ran, splashing through the water, slipping on the mud. She stumbled, but Jack yanked her to her feet and kept going uphill, through the hammering rain. She was half dragged up a flight of wooden steps, and then Jack paused and pulled keys from a box beside a solid wooden door. He pushed her ahead of him, out of the rain.

The door slammed, shutting out the storm. Above them the thatch muffled the sound of the rain and the thunder seemed more distant. Their breathing sounded loud and ragged in the relative quiet. Anna's shoulders heaved and her lungs burned while her racing heart tried to play catch-up. She glanced around, and in the gloom could make out the massive tree trunk which rose through the centre of the space. A polished wooden floor stretched around it, and folding glass doors, sealed against the weather, let in pale light, filtered through the leaves.

Jack stood in front of her, pushing his dripping hair off his forehead, water pooling at his feet. His plaid shirt was plastered across his broad chest and his rain-darkened cargo pants clung to his braced thighs. His eyes, grey as the spring storm outside, were lit with silver flames.

He took a step towards her. 'Welcome to Ebony Tree Lodge.'

'Thank you.'

She felt suddenly awkward. A rivulet of water trickled its way down her plait and discharged itself in a tiny cascade to the floor. Jack raised a hand and took hold of the end of her pigtail and squeezed some of the water out of it. Their eyes locked. The magnetism of the connection between them felt too powerful for Anna to break. She swayed on her feet and saw concern flicker across his face. He moved closer, sliding his hand from her hair to her shoulder.

'Jack…?' Her voice sounded distant. 'I…'

He was so close she could feel the warmth from his body, but she shivered.

'You're cold, Anna. We need to get you warm.' His voice was soft, almost a murmur, as he eased the hood away from her face and pushed it back.

'Not cold. But…' Her breath shallowed and she pressed a hand to her chest to try and still her heartbeat. Jack's fingers drifted across her jaw and dropped to the place at her throat where she knew her pulse was thudding out of control. As he watched her his clean scent swirled through her senses, making her feel dizzy, and his eyes became her one fixed point of reference.

She heard the rain on the thatch, the wind lashing the branches of the tree above and around them, and she felt utterly safe, cocooned in this space with him, disconnected from everything in the world except each other.

She put a palm against Jack's chest and felt his powerful heartbeat through the wet cotton, his pecs solid under the fabric. Her hand flattened against the hard bead of a nipple.

His breath stuttered in his chest and he raised his head. 'Anna. Are you sure?'

She nodded, not trusting her voice. Sex with Jack was not what she'd planned, but it was what she'd wanted for what felt like for ever, with every clamouring cell in her body. She could still be cool. Still walk away afterwards, back to the life she was meant to lead, she told herself. What could be more grown-up than that?

His hands closed around her upper arms and he pulled her towards him, wrapping her tightly and burying his face in her damp hair. Then he tipped her head back and rested his forehead against hers.

'You'll never know how much I've wanted you,' he muttered against her mouth. 'You've invaded my very soul.'

And as their lips met it felt to Anna as if they were in the eye of their own private storm as it broke around them inside the treehouse.

Jack interrupted the intensely erotic kiss only long enough to pull the wet hoodie up and over her head. He tossed it aside and then his fingers tangled with the buttons of the shirt she'd put on this morning, in place of the *Save the Whales* tee shirt. Impatience seethed through him and he gripped the edges and ripped them apart, sending pearly shell buttons skittering across the floor. His big hands circled her ribcage, then he moved them up to cup her breasts, feathering his thumbs over their iron-hard peaks.

'Anna.' He kissed her hard. 'I want to look at you, but I can't wait.'

He squatted and pulled off her boots, and his own, then reached up and helped her with the zipper of her cargo pants. He hooked his fingers into the waistband and began to ease them over her hips with her briefs, tugging at the saturated fabric where it stuck to her wet skin and then lifting first one of her feet and then the other away. He straightened up, holding her pelvis steady and running his mouth from the vee where her thighs joined up over her tummy to the groove between her breasts.

He felt her fingers tug at the buckle of his belt. Somehow he helped her to drag his wet clothes off, and then he walked her backwards until her spine rested against the tree trunk. As he lifted her she coiled her legs around him and rocked her hips. He gasped, trying to slow down.

She was experienced, he could tell, and wild with the need which had simmered between them for years. Jealousy arced through him at the thought of any other man touching her, making love to her.

Get a grip, Eliot. Did you expect her to save herself for you?

He took several deep breaths, trying to hold her still. 'Anna, wait…'

Supporting her, although it was clear she didn't want to wait, he carried her through the open-plan living area, shouldered a screen aside and pulled back the mosquito netting which hung around a wide bed. Then he eased himself down onto the white linen cover, taking her with him. She clung to his shoulders and protested when he tried to move away, so he stretched out one hand to find what he needed in the bedside cabinet.

His fingers located the foil packet and he breathed a quick sigh of relief. The treehouse was, indeed, equipped down to the last detail.

As he slid into her warm, ready body she arched her back and he drew a rosy nipple into his mouth. The silk which covered it created an unbearably erotic friction between his tongue and her skin. He heard her cry out, and then he was flying, carrying her with him in his arms.

He cradled the back of Anna's head in one hand and buried his face against her shoulder. She sighed on an unsteady breath and he raised his head to look at her. Long lashes lay against her flushed cheeks. Her heart thundered against his ribs. When he shifted his position a little her thighs tightened around his hips.

He reached down and grabbed the soft throw which

lay folded at the foot of the bed and pulled it over them. Her body, lying under his, felt utterly relaxed. His fingers stroked tendrils of her hair off her forehead, making space for him to place his lips on her dewy skin. Then he couldn't stop himself from brushing a thumb across her cheek. He wanted to keep her here, like this, for ever.

She opened her eyes. 'That was…'

'It was.'

'Can we do it again?'

She pulled a hand from under the blanket and folded it in his. He felt the tightening begin in his groin again.

'Since this is the only bed, and we're stuck in this tree, I think the answer to that is definitely a yes. But first I'm going to run a bath for you. Or for us, if you prefer. And then…'

'A bath? In a treehouse?'

'No luxury has been spared.' He wound his fingers through a strand of her hair. 'And then we'll eat whatever delicious food has been left for the poor guests who are missing out on this incredible experience.'

'Should I feel guilty?'

'Not on their behalf. They can come later in the week— if they can get here. And if you feel guilty about anything else…?'

'Nothing.'

He studied her face, believing she was being honest. So there was nobody else in her life at the moment, then.

Shut those thoughts down, Eliot. Anyone else in her life is nothing to do with you. Nothing at all.

Should he hope there was someone else? So there was no chance of her wanting to stay, asking him for what he couldn't give? He wouldn't think about it. He had her here—they had each other here—for two days, max, while the floodwaters drained away. Then they'd return to Themba, and she to London and California, to the proper life she wanted.

He shifted a little and her eyelids fluttered to her cheeks again. He eased himself away from her and bent his head to kiss her mouth.

'Don't go, Jack.'

'I'll come back…and then I'll carry you to the bathroom. The view from the bath is stunning, but it's too dark to see now. We'll have to have another bath tomorrow.'

He padded from the room and found matches in the kitchen area, so he could light the oil lamps. The solar power had done its work during the day and the bathwater was hot. He tipped a generous slug of lemon-scented bath oil into it. White linen bathrobes hung on hooks. He slung a towel around his hips, carried a robe to the bedroom and lit more lamps…warm globes of light blossoming in the dusk.

'It's still raining heavily, but I think we'll find everything we need here. Tomorrow I can get anything you want from the Land Rover.' He held up the robe. 'Until your clothes are dry you can wear this.'

Anna had propped a mound of pillows behind her and pulled the throw up around her shoulders. She'd undone her hair and it shone like dark gold brocade across the white linen. She stretched out a hand and circled his wrist, tugging at it until he sat down on the edge of the bed. The cashmere throw clung to the curves of her body beneath it…curves which he wanted to explore, slowly and in great detail, with his hands and his mouth.

'I don't think my shirt is fit for purpose any more—wet or dry. And although this treehouse is equipped down to the last detail, I don't think that includes a kit for sewing on buttons.'

Anna shrugged and the throw slipped a little. A dimple showed in her cheek.

'Contraceptives but no sewing kit. Who dictated those priorities?'

'I'll let you guess.'

Her skin glowed creamy in the lamplight and he couldn't drag his eyes away from the exposed curve of her breast, covered in lacy silk, still damp from his mouth.

'I might decide to go topless. I'm guessing nobody can see in.'

'Then we won't be leaving the bed, so having no clothes won't matter. At. All.' He made himself breathe. 'Now, come on—the bath's waiting.'

He swept her up in his arms and hugged her against him, their skin-to-skin contact feeling completely natural.

Anna scooped up her hair into a messy knot on top of her head as Jack lowered her into the steaming water. He stepped in behind her, putting his hands on her waist and drawing her backwards between his spread thighs to lean against his chest.

'So decadent, Jack. A lemony bath in a treehouse.'

'They don't have baths in Californian treehouses?' He kissed the vulnerable-looking hollow at the nape of her neck. 'You surprise me. But we need to get rid of this…'

He tried to distract himself with the practical business of unclipping her bra, but the catch was quickly dealt with. He pulled the garment away and dropped it onto the floor, then put his arms around her and rested his chin on her shoulder. He felt her heartbeat quicken as her ribcage expanded into his hands.

He needed to make the time they had perfect, because these memories would have to last him for ever.

CHAPTER NINE

IN A SHADY corner of the deck a wide canvas hammock hung between a post which supported the thatch and a stout branch of the ebony tree. The dizzying drop into the gorge on three sides of the treehouse kept it safe from predators. The only access was up the wooden steps and through the solid door, the way they'd come when they'd taken refuge from the storm the previous day.

An afternoon breeze stirred the leaves against a rinsed cloudless sky. It was almost impossible to believe that twenty-four hours earlier that expanse of blue had been filled with roiling black clouds and riven by lightning. The storm had abated in the early hours of the morning, and with the dawn calm had emerged from the maelstrom of rain, thunder and lightning. The only reminder of the tempest was the gurgle of streams, dry for months, now tipping over the edge of the ravine to plunge into the river. Far below, the watercourse still raged, the torrent of muddy water overflowing its banks, carrying ripped-up trees and other victims of nature's fury on the long journey to the sea.

Anna stretched out a leg and nudged the wooden rail with her toes, setting the hammock into gentle motion again. She lay in the crook of Jack's arm while his fingers twined through her hair. Her linen robe slipped open and she relished the feel of the warm air brushing her skin. She wondered if contentment could be any deeper or the sense of place any more complete.

'Jack?'

'Mmm…?'

His response rumbled in his chest and she placed her palm on his sternum, loving the feel of the hot silk of his skin beneath her hand. He wore a pair of shorts, low on his hips, and she trailed her fingers, barely touching him, down his body to the edge of the waistband.

'Hey.'

'Hey, what?'

'Any more of that and I won't be responsible for what happens next. I don't think sex in a hammock is a safe or sensible idea, but…'

'I never cared much about safety…'

She looked up at him. Grey eyes regarded her from under dropped lids. He inclined his head to brush his mouth across her temple. Her hand flattened against his abdomen.

'Anna…' His chest rose on a rough inhalation. He slid his fingers from her hair and curled them over her hand, lifting it back up to his chest, then pulled the robe across her.

'What happened to the hammock at Themba?' she asked. 'You said it had broken.'

'You remember that?'

'Most of the details of my life at Themba are engraved on my memory, Jack.'

He tucked her in closer against his side. She half turned, placing a bent knee across his thighs. The hammock tilted and swayed.

'Do you remember how excited you always were to come home for the holidays?'

'Of course. I lived for the holidays…for being back at Themba. Back with you…'

'That last time when you flung yourself into my arms

for your usual welcome home hug I simply wanted to keep on holding you. But you were innocent and naïve and I couldn't bear the thought of spoiling that. I never wanted you to change.' He smoothed the cool linen over her hips. 'I really didn't want to mess up, and I was trying to limit my exposure to temptation. So I made the hammock disappear.'

'I made it difficult for you. I hadn't a clue what I was doing.'

'Your girlish attempts at flirtation almost drove me wild.'

'And now? Now I'm grown up?'

'Now? You're clever and skilled and incredibly…sexy.'

He paused and she felt his chest rise on a big breath.

'Have there been many…?'

She bit her lip, wondering how to answer him. She'd had lovers, but she'd never loved any of them. And none of her experiences had come anywhere close to what she'd felt in Jack's arms last night and this morning. Again and again he had taken her to peaks of passion and fulfilment beyond what she'd dreamed possible.

'Many lovers? Hmm… A few, but it's never felt like this.'

'How *does* this feel?'

It was difficult to describe. Thrilling? Satiating? Passionate? There were no words to express her depth of feeling, the sense of rightness that permeated deep into her soul.

'Complete,' she said, the word escaping her lips before she could stop it. 'It feels complete.'

'Do you mean it was inevitable?'

'Not at all. This…' she kissed him just beneath the collarbone '…is not what I came back for. But it's happened…'

Anna twisted round and looked out over the ravine, down to the river and the wild land beyond it, keeping her expression hidden from Jack. She didn't want this precious time to be spoiled by questions and confessions. She wanted it to be perfect and…complete. When it was over she wanted to look back on it without regret and without wishing she'd done anything differently.

'Why *did* you come back?'

His question took her by surprise. 'The institute asked me to. You know that.'

'Couldn't they have found someone else?'

'The professor they appointed had an accident and broke his ankle. He should probably never have been riding an e-scooter. If the report had been delayed any longer your application would have missed the deadline and you'd have had to wait another year.'

'And you wanted to help?'

'I was simply doing my job. I'd planned to return one day, and this seemed like a good opportunity.'

Anna tried to keep her tone light. He didn't need to know that she'd thought the short notice meant there'd be no time for her to overthink things and pull out. She'd imagined returning to Themba countless times. Imagined showing Jack just how much she'd grown and achieved, and how little she'd ever really needed him. Her teenage crush had dissolved very quickly, she'd imply, from a cool, professional distance. She'd moved on, formulated a plan for the life she wanted—which didn't include Themba or Jack.

But her careful plan had been derailed. How had she gone from the cool academic who'd stepped off that helicopter to the woman whose wild lovemaking had made her come apart in his arms last night? She'd never realised how much Africa held her in thrall, or how soul-shatteringly emotional returning to Themba would be. As for seeing Jack again… From the moment she'd set eyes on his tall silhouette at the top of the steps last week she'd known she'd massively under-calculated the misgivings which had surfaced during her journey. That teenage crush had vanished, for sure, but proper grown-up lust had replaced it.

'I've always been curious to explore who I am, and I thought seeing Themba from an adult perspective would help me come to a degree of acceptance about my past. Perhaps it's time to move on from that.'

'And that's what you do? Move on?'

'So far, yes.'

'From relationships?'

'Mmm…'

'So if you've never given your heart to anyone you've never had it broken.'

Anna remembered the searing agony of his rejection. How she'd begged him to let her stay with him and his cruel dismissal. He might have been protecting her from his father's clients but it had felt utterly personal and belittling, and she never intended to feel that way again. It might only have been a teenage crush, but having it destroyed had torn her heart to shreds.

Just once, she wanted to say, *eleven years ago*.

But she shook her head. 'No,' she said. He hadn't just broken her heart. Something broken could be mended. He'd destroyed it. 'Never. How about you?'

'Nothing has changed for me, Anna. Themba is all I need.'

'And this?' Her question was soft. She put a hand against his cheek and turned his face towards her. 'Don't you need this? Sometimes?'

'This,' he said, stroking his thumb across her bottom lip, evading the question, 'is something I'm enjoying, very much.'

Anna watched his eyes darken as she took his thumb into her mouth and sucked it.

'God, Anna,' he muttered, 'everything about you drives me crazy. I can't believe this is you I'm holding in my arms. I don't know you any more. At all.'

She let his thumb slide out of her mouth and gripped his hand in her fist.

'I hoped I'd know more about myself after coming back, and I do. Only I'm not who I thought I was. I'd woven a stupidly romantic and idealistic narrative around my parents…' She felt the pressure of his cheek against her hair. 'But now I know my father was a criminal, dealing in illegal blood diamonds, and my mother… How did she come to be with him?' She looked up at him. 'How, Jack?'

He shook his head. 'There's no way of knowing. She must have loved…him… Hasn't George shed any light on the past?'

Anna nodded against his shoulder. 'He's been able to tell me about my mother. They worked together on research projects. She was a hugely admired doctor, respected in the field of tropical diseases, and she treated rare illnesses successfully. But she gave up everything for love. My father Aidan was a patient. A year after he recovered and returned to Africa she followed him, with no idea of what life with him would be like. She walked away from her career, and her family disowned her in fury and disappointment. But obviously her love for my father overrode all that. It's not something I understand.'

'Mmm… I know it took my father a while to unravel the mystery of that crash,' said Jack. 'They were flying under the radar in every sense. But the names that came up were Aidan Jones and Rebecca Kendall—as you know.' He stroked a finger across her cheek. 'They weren't married.'

Anna nodded, running her thumb across his knuckles. 'My mother wrote to George to tell him about me and asked him to look after me if anything happened to them. He couldn't become my legal guardian because there were no wills, no birth certificate. All official documents had been destroyed.'

'She must have known life with your father would be

unpredictable and dangerous. Writing to George meant she cared about what would happen to you if things went wrong.'

'I'd like to believe she cared…'

'She cared enough to choose George.'

Anna felt Jack's arm tighten around her shoulders.

'I remember the day he arrived at Themba to check up on your well-being, when you were five. I was terrified you were going to be taken away.'

'Were you?' She squeezed his hand. George told me he was happy knowing I was growing up in Africa, as my mother had wanted, as long as I got an education. And he also told me it was my mother's wish for me to go to university in England.'

'He must be wise and generous. It could have been so different. And if I'd lost you…'

Anna felt his body tense beside her.

'During those years I felt like you were my whole reason for living. And even though he couldn't be your official guardian, he's been kind to you?'

'He's the kindest, most thoughtful person. I was frightened when I landed at Heathrow that winter, knowing nobody. He did his best to make things easier.'

'I'm sorry, Anna.'

'Some days I felt as if I couldn't breathe in the cold under those leaden skies.'

She waited for him to say it had been hard for him, too. That he'd lain awake at night longing for her.

But he pulled her into his side in silence, his arm banding around her shoulders, then eased himself on top of her, parting the edges of the linen robe. He dropped his head, resting his forehead against her shoulder. She felt his body stir.

'You said sex in a hammock was unsafe…'

He raised his head, his lips seeking hers, and then he smiled against her mouth. 'If you keep very, very still…'

Her fingers drifted down his spine.

He took a ragged breath and arched his back.

'Not happening, Jackson.'

Pearly light was beginning to sift through the mosquito netting when Jack woke. He slanted a look down at Anna, where she slept curled against him, her back to his chest, an arm crooked under her cheek. If he obeyed the demands of his body he'd wake her gently and make love to her again before the sun rose. But a feeling of unease made him shift away from her and roll onto his back. She stirred in her sleep before her breathing settled into its rhythmic pattern again.

Jack raised himself up on one elbow and watched her. During the past two nights, and some of the day in between, the ecstasy he'd found with her had gone soul-deep. Her responses to him were generous and passionate, and she'd given him more than he had ever expected in his wildest imaginings. In return, he'd broken his own unwritten rule and given her all of himself.

Now, if he laid a hand on her thigh or dropped a kiss on her temple, he knew she'd wake and turn to him, opening her arms. But something held him back.

It had taken only two brief nights for the sight of her in his bed to become one he wanted to hold on to for ever. Two nights for their bodies to become perfectly attuned to each other.

It was the one thing he'd sworn he'd never want.

It was terribly dangerous.

Last evening on the radio Dan had confirmed what Jack already knew. The level of the river was falling. The causeway would be clear by the morning and they'd be able to go back.

He should be pleased, because without his finger on the pulse of Themba he felt untethered and uncertain. He needed to make sure everything was fine, even though Dan had assured him, several times, that there were no problems. For the past eleven years Themba had been his reason to be. His drive and willpower had shaped it into the place it was today, and the idea that it could operate without him, even in a crisis, rattled him.

But, gazing down at Anna's sleeping form, he found the thought of wrenching them from this remote place, insulated from the world, was impossible. It was inconceivable that tomorrow she'd walk out of his life again and this time it would probably be for ever. The perfect life she'd set her heart on wasn't ever going to be here, in the bush and dust of Themba with him. It couldn't be. Because nothing about him was perfect.

Finally, with a jolt that stopped the breath in his throat, he identified the source of his disquiet. During the night, as she'd clung to him, she'd whispered something.

'Jack, don't let me go. Please don't let me go.'

Was she going to wake in a few minutes and beg him to marry her again? Ask him to let her stay?

He sat up and swung his feet to the floor. Grabbing a towel to tuck around his hips, he walked through the door they'd left open so they could make love in the soft night breeze and moved across the deck to lean on the railing.

Anxiety crawled up his spine as he watched the sky lighten in the east. He had to stop this from happening. But he knew it was too late. He'd found the answer to the question he'd asked himself. *This* was how it felt to make love to someone he really cared about and who cared about him.

All the times he'd convinced himself that she was his responsibility, that he had to keep her safe, he had simply been avoiding the scary truth. He'd been too afraid to acknowledge it, but now it was here, staring him in the face, and he had nowhere to hide any more.

He loved Anna.

He'd loved her when she'd emerged from a bundled blanket with her shock of white-gold curls and mesmerising eyes.

But this love was something entirely different.

And tomorrow he would summon the helicopter and send her away again, even though it would rip his heart apart. Even though at her most vulnerable, having given everything of herself to him, she'd asked him not to let her go.

He had everything he wanted and needed here, under his control. Nothing happened that he didn't know about or approve of. The risks he took were calculated. There were few shocks or surprises he didn't anticipate.

He'd learned long ago that he couldn't protect those he loved, and he had no intention of having that proved to him again. Love was more dangerous than anything he'd ever had to face, because losing it left pain that couldn't be controlled. He'd first learned that when his mother had died. Loving someone meant losing control of your emotions, your body, your *soul*.

A tide of fear rose through him at the thought.

'Jack?'

He turned slowly, keeping his white-knuckle grip on the rail. Anna stood in the doorway, her hair messy, the flush of sleep on her cheeks. She had pulled on his spare shirt, which he'd retrieved from the Land Rover yesterday. The sleeves were rolled up to her wrists and the hem hung down to mid-thigh. She was the sexiest thing he'd ever seen.

'Jack?' she repeated, pushing her hands through her tousled curls. 'Come back to bed. It's early.'

She took a couple of steps towards him. He fought for an expression of indifference and she faltered, uncertainty flickering in her eyes.

'Jack, is something wrong?'

He pushed himself upright, looking away from her, down into the valley, where morning mist wreathed the river.

'The river has dropped. I need to get back. There're things to do...'

He saw the hurt flash across her face before she lifted her chin and wiped her expression. His heart lurched.

'Can't they wait a few more hours? Or has everything gone wrong in your absence?'

'No. But I don't like being away. You know that.'

'If that's how you feel I'm sorry we made the trip at all.' She shifted from one foot to the other, obviously confused. 'I thought you were enjoying being with me, but perhaps it was a bad idea in the end.'

Jack shrugged. 'We had sex. Great sex. Now I need to get on with running Themba and you need to get on with finding your perfect life.'

It was as if someone had hurled a brick at her stomach. Anna gasped. She felt her heart crushed in a tight fist of hurt, and with every cruel, cold word it squeezed tighter. How could he be like this after the exquisite tenderness, the sweet words they'd shared just a few hours before?

She fought for breath, trying to push her numbed brain into finding some logical reason for his behaviour. Could this be the same Jack who had cradled her so tightly against him, his arms around her like bands of iron but his lips and hands achingly gentle?

'Is that all it was to you, Jack?' she finally managed to ask. 'Sex? Okay, *great* sex. Thanks for that.' Her voice rose as panic welled up inside her. 'Because it actually felt like something different. To me it didn't feel like we were just having sex. It felt like we were making love.'

She gulped in a breath. All her instincts for self-preservation, which had been dangerously dormant, surged back.

She would not let him see how much he'd hurt her and the only thing she could hide behind was anger.

'But obviously,' she flung at him, 'I misread the signals. *Massively.*'

Jack hardened his expression as he looked across the space which divided them. The look she gave him was level, and then she turned on her heel and walked away.

'We'll leave in half an hour,' he said to her retreating back.

'Fine.' She spun round and took two steps towards him. 'Only I don't think that's long enough for me to say what you need to hear.'

She folded her arms and the shirt—*his* shirt—rose a little higher up her thighs. Her eyes, blurred with sleep a moment before, were suddenly wide, flashing angry green fire. As she advanced across the deck towards him her cheeks glowed, but no longer with the flush of sleep. Anger blazed across her face.

'There's nothing to be said, Anna.'

Jack held up a hand, intending to stop her, but she ignored it. She didn't stop until she was an arm's length from him. He could reach for her, pull her against his body, bury his face in her hair. But he knew that would be perilous.

'*You* may have nothing to say, Jack.' She pointed a finger at his chest. 'But I have enough for both of us.'

Jack gripped the rail behind him with both hands. This was Anna as he'd never seen her, and he had no idea what to do.

Anna had seen the shutters come down over Jack's face when she'd stepped onto the deck. But she wasn't going to let him off the hook again. It was time he realised she was older, experienced and she didn't need him any more. Most of all, he couldn't manipulate her. *No one* could.

'You're not doing this to me, Jack. Not again.' Her voice shook with fury.

'Doing what? You need to calm down…'

'You know exactly what you're doing—only this time I know, too. And don't patronise me.'

'I don't know what you mean, Anna. All I said was that I need to get back.'

'The *hell* you don't know what I mean… But I'll explain anyway. I've been kind to you, Jack. Patient. I understand why you have a problem with emotions. Awful things have happened in your life. But you've fought for what you wanted and got it—mostly. And that's admirable.'

She took a deep breath and pushed her hair off her face with the back of her hand.

'What's not so admirable, however, is believing you can treat me like you did last time. Haven't you learnt *anything* in the past eleven years? Or even the past *week*?'

The words caught in her throat and she swallowed, suddenly feeling horribly close to tears. But if there was one thing she would never, ever do again, it was cry in front of him.

'Don't cry, Anna, please…'

'I'm not crying. And even if I were, why would it matter? You've decided to shut me out, so why would you care? Last night I went to sleep in your arms. This morning I think it was reasonable for me to expect to wake up in them—not to find you out here, stony-faced, telling me we have to leave before the sun has barely risen. How dare you? How *dare* you behave like this?'

'I… Last night, Anna, you said…'

'Ahh… So *that's* it.' She nodded. 'Well, forgive me for saying something in the heat of the moment, after sex, when I might not have been in perfect control. I don't recall *you* exercising much control last night, either. Perhaps I was thinking back to an earlier time when I actually *wanted* to stay with you.'

'It's…' He pulled his hands down over his face. 'It's… I need to protect you, Anna.'

She shook her head. 'No, Jack, you don't. What you need is to control me—like you control everything else. Losing control makes you panic, and I think over the past week something has…slipped from your grasp. And the only way you can see to get it back is to get me out of your life.'

She looked beyond him, across to the craggy cliffs where the sunrise was steadily shrinking the shadows.

'I've loved being back here, and I'll cherish these memories, but I'm leaving, Jack—in my own time. And, believe me, this time it *is* what I want.'

She took a step back, afraid that his nearness would shake her resolve.

'There's no reason for me to stay. You've made that very clear.'

Her eyes met his and she saw stubborn anger in their grey depths. He didn't like what she'd said, and he was going to like her next words even less.

'All this time I don't think you've been protecting me at all. You've been protecting yourself.'

Anna turned and walked away from him, anger keeping her head high and her limbs moving.

CHAPTER TEN

ANNA WRAPPED BOTH her hands around the grab handle as Jack accelerated through a section of flooded track. The vehicle lurched as a wheel hit a pothole hidden beneath the water. She twisted her head to look at him.

His frown of grim concentration had deepened. He engaged a low gear and the engine growled as the wheels dug into the mud. His fingers curled around the steering wheel in a white-knuckle grip.

Anna pressed her face to the window beside her and squeezed her eyes shut.

You will not cry.

Returning to Themba had been a huge mistake. It had taken a week—okay, make that about five seconds—for her to fall under Jack's spell again. Or rather for her to recognise that his spell had never been broken. Those years spent searching for the perfect conventional life had been a total waste of time. All she wanted—all she'd *ever* wanted—was right here.

The suburban house with a tiled roof and a neat garden where children could play in safety could all go to hell—along with the boring husband with a nine-to-five job she'd conjured up for herself. She wanted Themba—*and Jack.* Because the two were inseparable. And she wanted all the danger and raw wildness that came with both of them.

But he absolutely did not want her.

She had to do something to distract herself, so she pulled her uncharged phone from the side pocket of the door and plugged it into the lead Jack kept connected in the central console.

'I'll need my phone to make travel plans as soon as we reach the lodge.'

Her teeth had begun to chatter, and she clenched her jaw to hide the symptoms of shock. Then, to disguise her shaking hands, she gripped the seatbelt that crossed her chest.

His face was devoid of expression. 'As you wish. The helicopter is doing a run bringing in supplies this afternoon. I'll see if they can fit you in on the way back.'

'Actually, it'll have to be tomorrow. I've thought of a couple of points I need to verify at the research centre.'

With desperate determination Jack focussed his attention on the road. He risked a sideways glance at Anna, but her face was turned away. Anger at the things she'd said flared inside him again.

As he powered the Land Rover, too fast, down the final slope towards the causeway in front of the lodge Anna's phone pinged. In a reflexive movement his eyes flicked sideways to where it lay between them.

The message was from someone called Brett, and the words he saw included 'beach' and 'with you'.

His foot hit the brake and the wheels locked in a violent slither of mud and gravel. He hauled on the steering wheel to correct the skid, realising with a shock that he'd been close to losing control again.

And not just of the car.

Anna released one hand and snatched up her phone. 'Be careful or we'll land upside down in the river, Jack.'

He was damned if he was going to apologise.

So that was why she'd been so keen to charge her phone. She'd been waiting for a message from *Brett*. Whoever he was, he hated him already. Was he a contender for providing Anna's perfect forever home? The two-point-four children?

Fuelled by an anger intense enough to scare him, he accelerated across the low bridge at a dangerous speed and the big vehicle bounced as it hit the cattle grid.

He knew he'd been looking for a hook to hang his behaviour on, and now he pretended he'd found it. There was another man in her life. Probably some slick blond Californian. That explained her even honey-coloured suntan, some of which, he suspected, had been acquired topless. There was someone else who kissed her, held her, made her scream like he'd done.

It was an unbearable thought.

He punched the brake and swung the Land Rover to a gravel-biting stop at the foot of the granite steps. Before the quiet settled around them Anna had released her seatbelt and had her hand on the doorhandle. Jack eased the stranglehold he had on the wheel and flexed his aching fingers. He stared straight ahead, through the filthy windscreen.

'Who the hell,' he grated, unable to help himself, 'is *Brett*?'

Anna's feet hit the ground and she whirled round to face him. Some icebergs must be green, he thought distractedly. He was sure they were the exact colour of her eyes now as they bored into his.

'He's a…a friend. In California.' She began to turn away. 'Not that it has anything at all to do with you. Open the rear door, please, so I can get my backpack.'

Jack didn't mean her to hear his next remark, but he mistimed it. 'A friend with benefits?'

'Yeah. *Great* benefits.' She slammed the door.

Anna dropped the backpack on the slate floor of her suite and doubled over, pressing her forearms into her abdomen.

Real pain clawed at her, and she thought she might be sick or pass out. She tried to breathe rather than gasp, but the tight band around her chest made it almost impossible.

After a minute she found her way to the armchair. Pulling her knees up to her chest, she curled into a ball and released the scorching tears that she'd been aching to shed for hours.

How had she not realised this visit was a terrible idea? She should have known it was a fast-track route to heartbreak. *Renewed* heartbreak. Dismissing her feelings for Jack as a teenage crush had simply been an attempt to protect her pride and restore her own self-confidence.

Now, with the dubious advantage of experience and maturity, she faced the stark truth. Nothing and no one could ever replace Jack in her heart, but he had no space in his life for her. He'd told her that truth eleven years ago and nothing had changed except the fact they'd had sex. Mind-blowing, incredible sex, which she'd stupidly thought meant something more than simply satisfying their own desires.

Her body shuddered with the sobs which rose from somewhere so deep inside her she couldn't believe they'd ever stop. It frightened her to be so out of control, at the mercy of such raw, destructive emotion. She pushed her knuckles into her mouth and bit on them, hoping if she concentrated on the pain she'd be able to bring her panic under control.

It felt like hours before the crying began to subside and the tears slowed. She scrubbed at her eyes with the backs of her hands and then stumbled to the bathroom to splash cold water on her face. Her throat ached and her eyes burned.

Bracing herself against the hard edge of the handbasin, she stared at her reflection in the mirror. She looked a total mess, but she was beyond caring. What mattered was that she'd *allowed* this to happen. And as she peeled off her clothes and stepped under the shower, she vowed she would never, ever expose herself to such vulnerability again.

With her washed and dried hair bound in its neat braid, some make-up applied and dressed in jeans, white shirt and jacket, layer by layer Anna restored her outward professional appearance. Her carry-on bag took only moments to pack, and then she sat cross-legged on the floor and wrote a note on a sheet of the Themba stationery.

She placed the folded paper under the heart-shaped pebble on the coffee table. When Jack had given it to her he'd promised that every time she held it she would know he was thinking of her.

She had no plans to hold it ever again.

As she picked up the phone to speak to Reception she heard the approaching beat of the helicopter...

Jack turned from his office window as Dan came into the room. He kept his hands bunched in his pockets because they still shook with anger. He couldn't switch off the sound of Anna's voice, and the more he thought about what she'd said, the angrier he felt. He had to get his thoughts in order—and then he'd confront her and tell her just how wrong she was about him.

'You okay, Jack?' Dan sounded uncertain.

Jack unclenched his jaw. 'I'm fine.' He faced Dan across the desk but did not sit down. 'Tell me what I need to know.'

Dan shrugged. 'Not a lot. Everything's okay. We were more worried about you and Dr Kendall than about anything here.'

Jack frowned and rolled his shoulders. 'Nothing happened to us. The treehouse was a good suggestion.' A sense of disbelief coloured his next words. 'Are you sure nothing went wrong while I was away? It was a ferocious storm.'

'There was some damage to the perimeter fence. We've repaired it and checked the rest of the boundary for weak spots. Mud washed into the swimming pool, but we've sorted that.'

'Anything else?'

'The power went down for a few hours, but the generators kicked in on cue, so that wasn't a problem.'

'Is that all?'

'Pretty much, Jack. We coped.'

Jack realised he didn't want to hear that. It made him feel superfluous, a little aimless, and his anger deepened.

'Right,' he bit out. 'That's good. I'll see you later.'

He threw a belated 'thank you' at Dan's back as the other man left the room.

He had to see Anna now. Make her listen to him and understand his point of view. His childhood experiences meant that her safety had become his prime concern. For her to suggest he'd always had his own interests at heart was ungrateful and cruel, and he was going to tell her exactly how wrong she was. It was the only way he could defuse this rage.

He followed Dan out of the office, slamming the door behind him.

She wasn't at the research centre, and when there was no answer to his knock at her suite he tried the door.

'Anna?' He stopped in the middle of the room, glancing towards the bathroom. 'Anna…?'

He slid back the glass doors and scanned the deck and the bush beyond the rail. He went back inside and his eyes fell on a folded sheet of thick Themba writing paper on the coffee table, weighed down by a stone in a shape he recognised.

His stomach dropped as realisation hit him and panic detonated in his chest.

The room was empty, and not just of Anna and her possessions. Her essence, which had enveloped him ever since she'd arrived, had gone with her.

The space where she'd been felt more than empty. It felt desolate and abandoned. And what hurt so much that he gasped was that she'd left behind that little pebble, and all it meant.

Jack sat on the edge of the armchair and picked it up, closing his fingers around the cool stone. Then he spread the paper out on the glass tabletop. She'd gone, she said, on her own terms, in her own time. Could he, she asked—and there was cool politeness in every neat, cursive word—dispose of the diamonds and make sure the people who'd found her after the accident benefited in some way from the proceeds? And, lastly, would he please not contact her? Ever.

He smoothed a finger around the edge of the little heart, rubbing it with his thumb as if he could magic Anna back like a genie from a lamp, so he could explain to her why he'd had to make her leave. Why they could never be together. She made him lose control, and he couldn't live with that because it terrified him. His mouth dried and his stomach lurched at the thought.

But she'd gone. For good. And her manner of leaving had demonstrated, if he needed to be shown, that he no longer held any sway over her. He knew his behaviour had shattered and hurt her, but she hadn't collapsed or crumbled. Her strength of will and confidence shocked him once more.

He glanced at his watch and a spark of desperate hope fired in his brain. There might still be time to stop her, so he could explain…

But as he stepped outside he heard the accelerating throb of the helicopter and saw it lift into the air beyond the trees. It dipped to the left before levelling out and heading south, diminishing with every second until it disappeared into the afternoon haze. His heart echoed its beat long after he could no longer hear it.

Jack tried to breathe. Anna was gone and she'd never

come back. He'd never hold her again, feel her hair beneath his cheek or hear the little sound she made when he kissed her. He'd lost the most precious thing in the world and he was entirely to blame. The only person he could direct his anger towards now was himself.

CHAPTER ELEVEN

GEORGE WAS SEATED at his favourite table in the corner. Anna knew he liked admiring the gardens from the shelter of the Orangery Restaurant, and so he'd have his back to her as she approached.

She threaded her way through the restaurant, slipping out of her jacket and shaking her hair free of her beanie hat. Summer had given way to early autumn during the time she'd been back in London, and the leaves of the trees in Kensington Gardens were gilded with gold.

'George!'

He turned and his face cracked into a wide smile. He stood and drew her into a hug and then kept his hands on her shoulders for a little longer than usual. When he'd kissed her on both cheeks and taken her jacket and bag to dump on a spare chair, she was aware of his close scrutiny. She'd learned early on in their relationship that while he might appear laid back and lost in thought a lot of the time, not much escaped his keen notice.

She was fine with that. She didn't intend to hide anything from him. But she didn't plan to tell all, either.

When they'd ordered their food and drinks, and she'd stopped arranging her bag, checking her messages, tucking her phone away and basically exhausted her supply of delaying tactics, George propped his folded arms on the table and leaned in towards her.

'So, Anna. Tell me all about it.'

Anna met his penetrating blue gaze, slightly magnified by his black-rimmed glasses, and dropped her eyes to her hands, where they tangled together on the starched tablecloth.

'Where do you want me to start? The job? The trip? I'm negotiating terms for the job, but…'

'Oh, the job…' He waved an expressive hand. 'The job can wait. I want to hear about the trip.' He inclined his head. 'It must have been emotional, going back.'

Anna talked her way through her serving of crisp fish and chips, and George listened as he ate his poached salmon, nodding occasionally, sipping from his glass of wine.

'I'm pleased to see you eating well,' he remarked, as Anna picked up a chip with her fingers and dipped it in ketchup. 'You look a little thin. Or is that the result of a couple of months of Californian clean eating?'

'Mmm… Maybe.' The truth was she hadn't eaten much since she'd left Themba. Everything tasted like sawdust and eating was way too much trouble.

George's arched eyebrow expressed his scepticism. 'Have you submitted your report?'

'Yes, last week. They asked for a meeting. There were a few points that needed clarification.'

'Such as?'

'Oh. Um… Questions about my previous connection to Themba and how much I'd interacted with…the team.'

George signalled to the waiter and requested coffee, glancing at Anna for confirmation. Then he looked out at the gardens. A breeze had picked up and it rustled through the trees, bringing a flurry of leaves drifting to the ground.

'You've told me the *work* story, Anna,' he said. 'Now tell me the story of the shadows in those green eyes. What really happened?'

Anna shifted on her chair. Their coffees arrived and she stirred hers for longer than necessary before sipping it while it was still too hot. She sat back and released a long breath.

'I thought I could use the visit to find out more about my parents. I wanted to feel some kind of connection to them. I hoped I might get a sense of who I really am, now that I'm an adult and able to ask the right questions.'

'And that didn't happen?'

'Well, yes… And then no. At first I was excited. J-Jack showed me some clothes he'd found after I left. The ones I was wearing when the plane crashed. Dungarees and a tee shirt with an elephant…' She shook her head. 'Sorry, George, you don't need to know this. It's boring for you.'

'Not at all. I'm really very interested. Go on.' He kept his eyes on her face as he raised his coffee cup.

'Seeing—*touching* the clothes was…surreal. The thought that my mother had dressed me in them, on that last day… It was the closest I've ever felt to her. But then Jack showed me a stash of uncut diamonds that had been sewn into the pockets. That was shocking.'

George's expression sharpened. 'Ah. So things got a bit complicated.'

'Well, yes. It seems, from rumour and supposition, that my parents were smuggling diamonds when their plane crashed. It explains why there was no record of the flight, no destination logged.' She shrugged. 'Suddenly my whole existence felt…*tainted*. The romantic vision I'd created of my parents was utterly wrong.'

'I'm sorry Anna. That must have been extremely upsetting. But, you know, even though it ended in tragedy, their story *was* a romantic one.' George gripped his hands together and rested them on the table.

Anna stared into her now cold coffee. George summoned the waiter and asked for a fresh cup for her. She bit her lip. Then she looked at him again.

'I get that it was a romantic story. You've always impressed that on me. But I don't understand… I just *don't*.' She shrugged. 'My mother was intelligent, highly qualified, respected. How did she fall in love with someone who was nothing more than a criminal, dealing in blood diamonds, whose dishonesty and greed ultimately killed them both and almost killed me?' She shook her head. 'Whoever I am, I'm half of that person.'

'Is that it? What's bothering you?'

'Oh, that's not the end of the story. Jack took me to the site of the crash, to meet the people who rescued me. I thought I'd feel something incredible at the place where they died, where I'd last been with them, but I didn't. I felt empty and pointless. I just wanted to leave. And then I think Jack felt sorry for me. And…'

George scrunched up his napkin in a fist and then released it onto the table. He sipped from his water glass.

'Anna.' He leaned forward again. 'There's something I need to tell you. I've had news from Themba.'

CHAPTER TWELVE

JACK TOLD HIMSELF he'd soon feel better. He'd coped without her before. He'd do it again. But her final words hammered in his skull, tormenting him, and as the days passed and his anger cooled, allowing him space for rational thought, he began to believe she was right.

When she was eighteen he'd sent her away earlier than necessary. It was true that he'd been protecting her from his father's guests, but his far greater fear was that if she stayed any longer he'd lose control of his emotions, leaving him open to renewed pain and loss when she left to study in England.

He'd had his emotions in an iron grip for most of his life. His mother's death, dealing with his father, losing Anna... all had taught him how to maintain it. Only Anna had come close to breaking it. He would never let that happen—could never take the risk of loving again.

He'd poured all his energy, all his passion, into improving and running Themba, making it the place he wanted it to be and the place where he wanted to be—because that was where he felt safe. *In control.*

Had he always been simply protecting himself? He resented the fact that Anna had left without giving him the chance to refute her words and explain his motivation. That he'd never have the opportunity to do it was driving him crazy.

And then he received a message, via a complicated chain of communications. The elderly man who had been part of the group they'd met at the crash site wanted to see him again.

Telling Dan he'd be out of touch for a few days, he headed north, following the route he and Anna had taken two and a half weeks before.

His relief at escaping the place where everything—*everything*—now reminded him of her did not last. The route was littered with memories of their trip: the place where she'd exclaimed over a bossy family of warthogs, trotting across the road, the particularly rough bit of track where she'd hung on with both hands, her laugh of delight as he'd slammed on the brakes, allowing a tortoise to complete its stately amble across the track in safety.

And the place where they'd stopped and he'd told her about his father's death.

Wherever he could, Jack floored the accelerator, determined not to linger over either the memories or the places. He knew he was driving recklessly, but it kept his mind focussed on the present, not mired somewhere in the regret of the past, or untethered in the bleak, shapeless future.

When he arrived, the old man invited Jack to sit in the sun in front of his home and offered him sweet bush tea. Then he bent and pulled what looked like a metal strongbox from under his chair. It was battered, scorched, and the lock had been forced.

'I should have given this to you the day you came with the girl.' He pushed it across the earth towards Jack.

'I have been afraid of it for many years and hid it from my sight. But that day I saw you are a good man. You tried to help her. And at the mine they say you are fair. That you care for your workers.' He nodded towards the box. 'You will know what to do.'

Jack bent forwards, fingering the broken catch and pad-lock. 'Where did you get this?'

His host shrugged. 'You can see it is damaged and burnt, as if from an accident.'

The hinges were rusted, and they creaked as Jack prised the lid open. He sucked in a quick breath of shock. No wonder it was heavy. It was filled to the brim with rough diamonds. He ran his fingers over them and then raised his eyes to meet the old man's calm gaze.

'What do you think I should do with it?'

The man sipped from his mug of tea. 'Whatever is right. We heard that they were involved in…bad things…illegal diamond dealing.' He glanced at the box. 'After I found it I did not know who I should tell. Nobody came to investigate the crash for many months. It was as if the plane, and the people in it, had brought bad magic. Everyone feared it. I was afraid for the child, so we took her away to Themba, where she would be safe. And I buried the box. I did not want it to be mine because I knew it would bring trouble, but I did not want to pass on trouble to anyone else.'

Jack picked up one of the pearly lumps of rock. 'So why have you changed your mind?'

'Ah…' He smiled. 'This will not bring trouble to you, because you will know what to do. Also, I wish to die in peace. I do not want my spirit disturbed by an old tin in the ground.'

'Do you expect to die soon?'

Their eyes met over the rims of their mugs.

'Who knows? But it is best to be prepared.'

Jack propped his elbows on the railing of the treehouse deck and cupped his chin in his hands. Stubble scraped his palms. It felt as if he'd been on the road for a week, but it had been only three days.

He could have headed straight back to Themba, but he'd

needed the headspace and the silence in which to explore and confront himself, and now he knew what he would do.

He had something that would make Anna very happy, but he had to do more than that for her. He needed to show her how he meant to change and how he wanted to at least try and allow himself to love her. She might reject him—he wouldn't blame her for a second if she did—but he had this one shot at true happiness and fulfilment and he had to stop trying to protect himself from hurt and go for it.

The thought scared the hell out of him, but the idea of not trying, of never knowing, scared him more.

The irony was that the old man had thought the diamonds were the valuable part of the box, but he'd been wrong. Because half an hour ago, when Jack had tipped its dusty contents onto the deck, he'd found something far more precious underneath them.

CHAPTER THIRTEEN

ANNA'S FINGERS GRIPPED her coffee cup, her shoulders rigid.

'*You've* heard from Themba?' Cold foreboding rolled through her. 'Why? What's happened?' She shook her head, feeling confused. 'I haven't heard anything… Is it Jack? Has he…? Has there been an accident?'

Images of the lion crouching on the track, the elephant charging Jack's father, the huge crocodile near the causeway, all flashed across her mind.

George reached out and covered her hands with his. 'I'm sorry. I should have been more specific. I've had news from Jack, to be precise, and he's fine.'

Relief swamped her as the adrenaline rush ebbed. Only George's firm grip kept her hands from shaking. 'Then what…? Why has he contacted you?'

'It's an interesting story, and one which you'll hear in full when the time is right. But the most interesting part of it is this.' George's gaze was unwavering. 'Jack has found your birth certificate.'

'*What?*' A fresh wave of adrenalin pumped through Anna's veins. She half stood, but George's hand anchored her forearm and pressed her gently down again. 'How is that possible? Where did he find it?'

'All those questions will be answered in good time.'

Anna heard the strain in George's voice, and she thought

she saw pain in his eyes. 'What is it, George? What's wrong?'

'Nothing's wrong, but there is something else I need to tell you.' He propped his elbows on the table, tension straining his shoulders. 'Your mother Rebecca and I were research partners. But to me she was more…much more… than that. I loved her deeply, but it wasn't enough. I couldn't compete with Aidan's dashing romanticism.'

'Oh, George…' Anna tried to take a sip of coffee but her hand still shook. The cup rattled against the saucer. 'She broke your heart, and yet you've been amazingly kind to me.' She sniffed. 'You might have resented me.'

'As you know, I was pleased and touched when she wrote to tell me of your birth. And when I finally found you, living happily at Themba, the relief was immense. I've always taken my unofficial guardianship of you seriously, and I'm extremely proud of what you've achieved. How could I possibly resent someone who has brought so much joy to my life?'

Anna attempted a smile, but her lips felt wobbly and wouldn't co-operate. 'Thank you. You've been my rock, George. You always will be. I'd never have achieved any of it without your love and encouragement.'

'Whatever your thoughts about your father, remember that Rebecca loved him enough to give up everything for him. And you must believe that Rebecca loved you very, very much, too.'

Anna nodded. 'I'll try to see it that way, and to believe she loved Aidan.'

'What I remember most about Aidan is his air of fierce determination.' A corner of his mouth lifted in a half-smile. 'I think you inherited that determination from him.'

Anna managed to smile back. 'But when did you hear from Jack?'

'Yesterday. He called me.'

'And he asked you to tell me he'd found my birth certificate?'

'He thought you'd be happy to know it has come to light. But he also said you'd asked him not to contact you, so…'

'That's true. I was angry and hurt… Did he tell you anything else?'

'I think Jack would like to tell you the story himself, if you'll let him. But perhaps you should tell me about what happened with him first?'

Anna pushed her fingers into her hair and massaged her scalp. 'There's nothing to tell. Not now. I left. I said I didn't want to hear from him. I…'

'Why?'

'I…misread the situation. I thought what we had was something more than…what it was. Jack can't do emotion or love. He does control and management. You know me. I want it all. The house, the husband, the family. The stuff I missed out on.'

Even to her own ears she sounded unconvincing.

'That "stuff", as you call it, is meaningless if there isn't true love and steadfast commitment at the core of it. You were happy at Themba. You loved your life and you didn't want to leave it. How do you know you'd love your version of perfection?'

Anna hesitated, tapping the side of her china cup. 'I don't. I suppose I look at other people's lives and see the stability and consistency I never had and think it's desirable. Some people I met at university had families who'd lived in the same houses for generations. That intrigued me. Because when they asked where I was from, how did it sound when my answer had to be *I don't know*?'

'To them it probably sounded impossibly exotic and romantic,' said George. 'But what about Jack? What does *he* want?'

'Nothing. He wants nothing more than he already has—

although when we were…together…it felt as if he wanted…
me. But for his own complicated reasons he can't trust himself enough to allow himself to love.'

'Do you love him?'

George's blunt question was a shock. Anna felt tears
threatening again and she forced them back.

'Yes. I do.' It was difficult to shape the words. 'Very
much. Enough to give up my dreams of the perfect home
and husband and family. Enough to make my life with him,
whatever that means.'

'Have you told him that?'

'No. Why would I subject myself to another rejection?'

'What if he knew that what he has at Themba is what
you want, too?'

But she knew it was too late. She'd walked away without saying goodbye—again. She'd left her precious talisman pebble behind. When he found it he'd know without
doubt that she'd wiped him out of her life.

She'd truly burned all her bridges. She'd achieved what
she'd set out to accomplish and proved to Jack that she
didn't need him.

She'd never let him know the truth.

Picking up her bag and jacket, she stood.

George sat back and watched her. 'Where are you
going?'

'Where I always go when I need solace.'

'The Natural History Museum?'

She nodded, then bent to drop a kiss on his cheek. 'I'll
let you know what I decide about the job.'

When she turned at the door to wave he was looking
at his phone.

Crowds swarmed along the pavement below, but there was
only one face Jack was looking for. His heart thumped
against his ribs as a lithe figure peeled away and began to

run up the shallow steps. Every muscle in his body tensed. Would she pass him without a sideways glance? Would she see him and turn away, refuse to talk to him?

He curled his fingers into his palms, fighting to stay calm.

But Anna stopped three steps below him. Slim blue jeans encased her long, long legs, and a loose-fitting black jumper brushed her thighs. An index finger hooked her jacket over one shoulder. Her hair shimmered, rose-gold, in the soft autumn sunshine.

He wanted to tell her he preferred her hair loose, and wanted to close the distance between them and ease his fingers into that French plait and tease it out, so that he could bury his face in the matchless silky ripple of it. But he stood and stared, drinking in her image, feeling his tired body fire up with all kinds of need.

'Jack?'

She climbed another two steps towards him and he caught her perfume on the air, saw her knuckles turn white around the strap of her bag.

'Anna.'

'*Jack?* How on earth…?' She shook her head. 'You're supposed to be at Themba.'

'I was—yesterday morning.'

She mounted the final step and he caught her in his arms, breathing her in, wanting every inch of her against his body. Her heartbeat was as loud as his own and just as quick. He slid his fingers to the nape of her neck and pushed them into her hair, tipping her face up.

'I just want to look at you.'

He pressed his forehead to hers and then, unable to resist her, dropped his lips to her mouth. She tasted sweeter than in all his memories, and pure, hot desire mainlined around his body. He shifted his thighs, slid a hand down her spine and clamped her against him, feeling her mouth driving him frantic.

But her response was to press her palms against his chest and push him away. With her forest-dark eyes, her lips rosy from kissing and her flushed cheeks, she was more beautiful than he remembered. He tried to pull her back in, but she resisted.

'No.' Her breathless voice was throaty. 'I'm not doing this.' She shook her head. 'I can't.'

Anna leaned against the cushions in the corner of her sofa as Jack sat down in the chair opposite. They'd walked in silence through the South Kensington streets, and she'd led him to her flat because she needed to be in a place where she felt in control and safe.

She cradled a mug of tea in her hands, tucked up her feet and studied him. His grey eyes, dark as a storm cloud, ranged over her. The lines etched between his straight brows deepened as he placed his own mug on the table between them.

'What are you doing here, Jack?'

His eyes interrupted their tour of her body and returned to her face. 'I'm here now, but I've been to all nine circles of hell since you left.'

It was an unexpected response. She felt uncertain of his mood.

'I needed to get away and you wanted me gone.' She sipped her tea. 'You were quite clear about that.'

'Yeah, but that doesn't mean it wasn't hard as hell. I thought I'd never see you again.'

'And that bothered you?'

'More than I could ever express. But I needed time to think, to work things out. I hadn't realised how difficult that would be when everything…everything reminded me of you.'

Anna put down her mug and gripped the end of her plait in her fingers. 'What things have you worked out?'

He took a few moments to reply. 'I've decided to step back. I want to appoint Dan as general manager of Themba, freeing me to concentrate on conservation and development. I'll oversee the extending and commissioning of the research centre and the school and find new staff.'

'My report…'

Jack held up a hand. 'Wait. If I…*we*…don't get the funding, I'll sell some shares in the mine. While I'd like the recognition the institute can give us, finances won't be a problem.'

'Are you sure you can do this?' Anna watched his face. 'Giving up total control of Themba and the mine are two massive steps.'

Jack pulled a hand over the back of his neck. 'No. I'm not at all sure. I like—I *need*—to be in control. That's no secret. Handing over to someone else, however capable they are, will be hugely difficult. But I've got a great team and I need to cut them some slack. Start trusting them. I believe it's the best way forward for Themba. Ultimately my plan is to turn it into a co-operative, but I haven't worked out the details yet.'

'Have you discussed this plan with your team? Or is it something you're going to implement without their input?'

'Not yet. But obviously—okay, *not* obviously, given my track record—I *will* listen to their opinions. I have to get myself out of the middle of things. God, Anna, after you left I had to find space to *think*. I haven't done that… I haven't *allowed* myself that…since I don't know when. So when I got a message from the old man who found you, it was the opportunity I needed to get away.'

Anxiety fluttered in Anna's stomach and she threaded her plait through her fingers. 'Did *he* have my birth certificate?'

'In a way, yes.'

'I... I had lunch with George today. In Kensington Gardens. He told me you'd found it.'

Jack nodded. 'I know.'

'You *know*? How?'

The corners of Jack's mouth lifted in the ghost of a smile. 'George told me where to find you, obviously.'

'You were waiting to hear from him?'

'Mmm...' Jack reached into an inside pocket of his jacket and pulled out a brown envelope and a folded piece of paper. He held the paper out to Anna.

Anna's fingers trembled as she unfolded the document. 'I'd given up hope of ever seeing this.' She looked up at Jack, finding his gaze steady. 'It feels odd. As if I now have a proper beginning on which to build the rest of my life. I didn't *want* my father to be a crook, but George has made me realise how much my mother loved him. I want to respect that.' She reached out to take the envelope from Jack's hand. Two battered passports slid onto her lap, followed by a faded photograph of a young couple. The man stared at the camera and Anna could see the blaze of determination in his eyes. The woman's soft gaze was turned to the baby she held in her lap. Tears blurred Anna's vision. 'Thank you, Jack.' She wiped tears from her cheeks. 'For as long as I can remember I've wished for a photograph of my parents. In a way, with this and my birth certificate, I feel as if I can start afresh.'

'In California?'

'Perhaps.' Anna put the documents on the coffee table but kept the photograph in her hands 'Now, you've described your plan for Themba. But what about you?'

'What about me? I'll be working harder than ever. Conservation is the ethos at the heart of what Themba stands for, and that's what I'm passionate about. I'll be able to make a bigger difference if I don't have to spend time entertaining ecologists and professors. Dan's very good at that side of things and he loves it.'

'What you mean is you'll be setting yourself impossible standards and continuing to beat yourself up about things over which you have no control.'

'Anna, every time poachers kill a rhino or an elephant I have failed in my duty of protection. I can work to prevent that.'

'For over two decades you've blamed yourself for your mother's death, then you added your father's to that burden of guilt. You've made yourself responsible for every living thing, animal and human, on Themba land, and that's amazing. But you can't keep them all safe, Jack. Stuff happens. Sometimes it's bad stuff. It might happen less, but it'll happen, and if you isolate yourself…if you won't allow anyone to support you through the bad times and rejoice with you in the good ones…you're going to…'

'Drive myself crazy. Yeah. So that's why I'm here.' Jack leaned forward and propped his elbows on his knees, pushing the heels of his hands into his eyes. 'I loved my mother. And my father. In different ways.'

He pulled his hands away and his look was so bleak it cracked her heart. 'Jack, I…'

'It may shock you that I loved my father, in spite of how he was. But I loved the man he had been…and the one he should have been.'

Anna's stomach clenched. When she'd lain in Jack's arms she'd allowed herself to imagine that he might love her, but he'd dashed that thought with a few words. She tried to steady herself before she spoke again.

'But Jack…' She took a deep breath, steeling herself. 'When you and I… What we felt…'

'When you asked me not to let you go, I realised something that terrified me. I couldn't let you stay even if I wanted to.'

'*Why*, Jack?'

'What if I asked you to stay, but you left me? Life at Themba isn't what you want. What if I ended up losing you, too?'

Anna wrapped her arms around her shins, wanting to put out a hand and comfort him but afraid she'd drive him further away.

'It wasn't your fault, Jack,' she whispered. 'You were eight years old. None of it was your fault.'

He looked at her as if he didn't understand. 'My love has never been enough. I'm afraid it never will be.' He stood up and walked to the window, keeping his back to her. 'But, Anna, I have to try. Because I've realised that the worst possible thing would be not at least *trying* to love you. All those years when I took care of you, protected you, had you in my life, it wasn't responsibility I felt. It was love. I've loved you from the first moment I set eyes on that little girl with the platinum curls and emerald eyes, wrapped in a blanket. For years our friendship was innocent, and I hated it when it changed. I wanted it to always be the same. But I couldn't deny that I wanted you. I tried. God, I tried. I had to get rid of the hammock. I had to force myself to stop hugging you when you came home from school. When I made you leave it wasn't only because I couldn't protect you from the predatory men my father insisted on entertaining. It was to protect you from me.' He dropped his head. 'You had to go to London. It was your mother's wish. But if I'd let you stay another three days, never mind three weeks, I'd have given in to your naïve attempts at seduction. It was all I wanted to do. But it would have been absolutely wrong.'

Anna stood and followed Jack to the window. She wrapped her arms around his waist and laid her cheek against his shoulder blades. Tears burned in her eyes.

'I don't need to be protected from you, Jack. All I need is for you to love me.'

He went very still. When he spoke his voice was quiet. 'Themba is unbearable without you, Anna.' He turned in her arms and took her hands in his. 'Everything—absolutely everything—reminds me of you. I buried our memories for years, but when you came back I found they were all there, in bright Technicolor, haunting me every moment of the day and most of the night. And now there are new ones. But the life I lead isn't the life you want. I know that.'

Anna raised a hand and stroked his cheek, longing to feel the roughness of his unshaven skin against her body instead of just her palm. She placed a finger on his lips.

'I planned to prove I didn't need you, but I hadn't counted on my heart telling me that I always will.' She pressed her forehead against his chest, breathing in the scent that was just uniquely...*his*...and kissed the knuckles of the hand which gripped hers. She raised her chin to look at him. 'My mother had a successful career as a specialist in tropical diseases, but she gave it all up to follow Aidan to Africa, to an uncertain life full of challenges and danger. She gave it all up for *love*, Jack, because love was—*is*—more important than all the material trappings in the world. And it turns out I'm very like my mother. Your love means more to me than all my dreams of a conventional life. All the things I thought would make me happy would be meaningless without you.'

She turned her cheek into the warm cotton of his shirt, listening to his heartbeat and to his breath hitch in his chest.

'Africa is my birthplace, Themba is where I grew up, and I love them both. I think you know that. But most of all I love you, Jack, with every fibre of my being and with all my heart and soul. I've always loved you. I want to share in the tough times and help you celebrate the successes. I want to care for you as you have always cared for me. I want to help you to love me.'

She couldn't wait another second to taste his mouth

again, so she slipped a hand round the back of his neck and buried her fingers in his thick hair, pulling his head down until their lips met.

Jack's powerful arms encircled her, sealing her against his hard body as his mouth and tongue plundered hers. He groaned, cupping the back of her head in one hand while the other traced a path down her spine, making her arch into him.

When he tore his mouth away and rested his cheek on her hair they both gasped for air, their hands entwining again.

'Anna, I've dreamed of this—of having you in my arms, in my bed and in my heart—but the fear of losing you has stopped me from believing it could ever happen. I might drive you insane with my over-protectiveness while I get used to it.'

Anna smiled up at him. 'I'm strong and tough, Jack. You made me that way, teaching me how to live in a place like Themba. I think I can tolerate anything—even your over-protectiveness—if it means being loved by you. Together we'll be stronger than we could ever be apart.'

Jack's mouth took hers in another long, deep kiss. He slid his fingers to the nape of her neck, where she felt them nudging into her hair, loosening her plait. So she tugged at the ribbon and teased the strands free.

'That's better,' he murmured.

She felt the brush of his mouth on the top of her head. Then he lifted her off her feet and cradled her against his chest, his lips feathering across her temple.

'I'm never, ever, letting you go again, Anna. You're the missing piece that completes me. With you I feel strong enough to face my fears.'

He carried her over to the sofa and eased himself down, settling her across his lap.

'We'll build a new house at Themba. Dan can move into the huts. If he'd like to.'

Anna frowned. 'As long as it has a thatched roof and a deck with a hammock, I'm in.'

Jack pushed a hand into a pocket of his chinos and withdrew it with his fist clenched. 'You left something behind, Anna. Hold out your hand.'

Anna flattened her palm and felt Jack release the cool, familiar shape of the pebble into it. Hot tears brimmed in her eyes. 'I told myself I no longer wanted it, but I missed it so much. Almost as much as I missed you...'

Later, as darkness crept across the windows, Anna lay in the crook of Jack's arm, her fingers entwined with his.

'So the diamonds that were sewn into my pockets were just the beginning? There were far more of them?'

He nodded. 'I think those in your clothes were the ones that wouldn't fit into the box. It was crammed with them. If I hadn't tipped them out I would never have found what was underneath them.'

'What will you do with them?'

'We can add them to the ones we already have and then they can be analysed. We can probably discover where they originated. That means certificates can be issued for them and they can be legitimately sold. And since the people who found you also technically found the diamonds, the proceeds can go to them. I think our elderly friend will see to it that the money is carefully spent for the benefit of everyone in the village. He's anxious to leave a good legacy and to be untroubled in the afterlife.'

'That's what I'd like to happen, if possible.'

'Are you sure? You could keep the proceeds yourself, you know. How about a cottage in the country? A really fancy watch? Or...?'

Anna turned and punched him gently in the ribs. 'Stop it. You know that's not what I want.'

'Oh? Would *this* be more to your liking?'

He smoothed the palm of his hand over her hip. She turned her head into his shoulder.

Jack's eyes darkened as her body began to thrum under his long, exploring fingers. Her breathing stuttered when his mouth found the super-sensitive place under her collarbone. She loved that he'd remembered it.

Holding her gaze, he lifted a lock of hair from her forehead and stroked it behind the curve of her ear. 'I love you, Anna. I *need* you. Please say you'll stay with me for ever.'

As her focus narrowed, and her awareness contracted until it was concentrated solely on the man she loved, Anna curled her fingers around his hard biceps.

'That, Jack, will be the realisation of my wildest dream.'

EPILOGUE

ANNA AND JACK were married in a ceremony on the deck as the summer heat softened and the shadows grew long. The wedding celebrations began immediately afterwards in the boma—a traditional, circular enclosure of thorn branches around a fire pit. It was a new addition to Themba, built in three months for the wedding, and the new events manager had plans to make it available for other exclusive celebrations, offering guests a taste of Themba hospitality alongside the opportunity to engage with the latest conservation initiatives.

A log cracked and a column of sparks wreathed in smoke hissed upwards into the night sky. The insistent beat of traditional drums swelled, growing louder and quicker, underpinning the ululating chant of the women who swirled and clapped, bare feet stamping in the dust.

Firelight flickered over the hundred guests who had gathered to witness the marriage and celebrate far into the night. Every branch held a sparkling lantern, and garlands of fairy lights were looped through the trees and across the tables where dinner had been served.

Anna and Jack could hear the festivities from where they stood under the ancient baobab tree in a corner of the compound. The graves of Jack's parents had been tidied and planted with indigenous flowers, and a headstone had been erected to mark them.

Anna knelt to place her wedding bouquet beneath it. Jack drew her to her feet, clasping her hands to his chest and running his thumb over the square-cut emerald ring and the gold wedding band on her finger.

'Thank you,' he murmured, pulling her against him. 'Since I allowed myself to love you and to accept your love in return I've been able to remember my parents with love instead of with anger and guilt. For the first time I feel they're at peace.'

Anna reached up to kiss him. 'We'll always remember them, Jack.' She squeezed his hands. 'I promise.'

The celebrations had reached fever-pitch and a great cheer went up as they appeared in the arched opening in the stockade. Anna's oyster silk vintage dress, embellished with a delicate tracery of pearls and jewels, gleamed in the firelight, her hair rippling over her shoulders from beneath a wreath of cream roses.

As they paused Anna's gaze travelled over the assembled guests and tears pricked her eyes at the number of familiar beloved faces she recognised.

George, who had walked her across the deck, kissed her cheek and then placed her hand in Jack's, smiled, his eyes bright.

Brett, who had come all the way from California, took a brief moment out of the sensuous dance he was enjoying with her bridesmaid Emma to blow her a kiss.

Emma, an old school friend, had flown up from Cape Town, where she worked in the university's Oceanography department.

Dan, whose awesome organisation skills had solved every problem in the lead-up to this day, lifted a hand in a half-salute.

Joseph, who'd given her invaluable bushcraft lessons, had come out of retirement to see them married.

And two colleagues from the institute, who had arrived

with the news that Jack's application had been successful, were engaged in a furiously energetic drumming lesson.

Jack slid an arm around her waist and bent his head.

'How many of these buttons are there, Anna?' His fingers traced a heated path down her spine. 'And how long is it going to take me to undo them?'

His hand came to rest in the small of her back. Anna slanted a look up at him. 'As long as you don't rip them off...'

Her breath caught as his slow smile sent heat racing through her.

'Not promising, Anna,' he murmured, 'but perhaps it's time to go and make a start?'

Accompanied by a surging tide of well-wishers, they made their way on lamplit paths to where the Range Rover waited. As they rattled over the cattle grid and crossed the causeway Anna looked back at the cheering crowd. The sight of the boma, glowing in a halo of golden light under the starry sky, and the fading sounds of drumming and singing raised goosebumps across her skin.

She reached out to rest a hand on Jack's thigh. 'I think the party's just beginning,' she said.

The glance he threw her was intense. 'You bet.'

It was after midnight when they reached the Ebony Tree Lodge. The steps were strewn with summer bush flowers and a bunch of aromatic herbs had been fixed to the door. Jack put an arm around Anna's shoulders and the other behind her knees and swept her up. He shouldered the door open and carried her through the treehouse onto the deck.

The feel of the voluptuous silk moving over her skin as he let her slide down his body almost shredded his control. His hands cupped her face and his thumbs brushed her cheekbones. The moonlight filtering through the leaves bathed everything in a wash of silver, but her eyes, holding his, shone like the emerald on her finger.

'Anna…'

'Mmm…?'

His mouth dropped to take hers in a gentle kiss, but then she made that sound in her throat that drove him wild. The grip he'd been forced to exercise on his desire since he'd turned and seen her on George's arm, walking towards him across the deck, finally slipped.

As their kiss soared out of control, he slid a hand to the back of her neck and began to undo the little silk-covered buttons…one by one.

* * * * *

CINDERELLA'S SECOND CHANCE IN PARIS

MICHELE RENAE

MILLS & BOON

This story is for anyone who has ever wondered
if they can begin again.
Yes. You can.

CHAPTER ONE

Paris

VIVIANE WESTBERG DIVIDED her attention between the luscious chocolate pastries behind the glass display counter and the equally snackable man standing to her right. He also perused the delightful offerings, for which any kid would shove aside their toys to eat on Christmas Morning.

A waft of spicy cologne teased Viv's nostrils more so than the sweets. The man oozed a subtle pheromone that demanded her attention. Tall, his figure was straight, clad in black trousers and a fitted white business shirt that jealously hugged his biceps and pecs. Diamond cufflinks flashed. He was clearly unafraid to flaunt his obvious wealth.

Dark stubble peppered his square jaw. Rich black hair, tousled but not messy, tickled the starched shirt collar. A few strands of silver woven into the black made her smile. Sexy and seasoned?

Rolling her eyes, and forcing her attention back on the pastries, Viv inwardly laughed at her thoughts. She had been in Paris three days and already she was eyeing up dating prospects?

Well. Diving back into the dating pool *was* on her short-list. A woman could only survive so long without some companionship. And physical connection. That was on her list, along with kickstarting her new business. Exterior landscaping had been her gig the last two decades. Now she wanted to move it inside. Plans for her interior garden business had been on paper for a decade. And right now, in Paris, she planned to nurture that paper dream into a beautiful blossom.

As for dating? Her husband had passed away three years ago. She had loved Brian dearly. And yet this adventure across the ocean was all about Taking the Next Step. Yes, in capital letters. And, while she understood less than a percentage point of French, the melody of the language could seduce her into a swoon. If Monsieur Sexy of the diamond cufflinks acknowledged her with a glance, she might melt like the chocolate glaze gleaming in the morning sunlight.

Startled to realize the clerk behind the counter had prompted her for her order, Viv apologized—*pardon* was easy enough—and then pointed to the one Opera cake remaining on a mirrored platter. Coffee and buttercream? Yes, please!

Deploying her worst French, she said, *"Un, s'il vous plait."*

"Non, madame. Monsieur has already chosen that one." The clerk gestured to the sexy mystery man. "You select another."

"Oh, but I…"

As the pastry she'd wanted was drawn out and placed in a pink-and-cream-striped bag, Viv glanced to the man she had been drooling over. His broad shoulders rose in an apologetic shrug. Mercy, were his eyes really that blue? The corner of his mouth tilted up before blossoming into a full-on smile.

Viv's heart fluttered. Her neck heated.

"Sorry," he offered in English. "Might I suggest the *cerise gâteau*? It is a cherry cake. Delicious. You must try."

Oh, that voice. Deep and a little rough, as if he'd just woken. It brushed against her skin in a subtle tease. Promised kisses to swoon for. Anything he offered—she was up for.

Viv arrested her lusty thoughts before they swerved toward heavy breathing and bared body parts. "Cherry cake, then."

The clerk retrieved one of the small cakes.

The man turned to Viv and offered his hand to shake. "Rezin Ricard. I'm staying in the neighborhood for a few days and remembered how much I enjoy this shop's Opera cakes. You must be vacationing?"

Slipping her hand into his felt as if she'd entered a new realm. Was being led across a mysterious threshold into something bright and intriguing. He held her hand for a moment that felt like a lifetime. A sure, strong squeeze, and then he released her.

Feeling like a teenager who had been touched by her crush, Viv prayed her blush wouldn't flush her cheeks too brightly. Flustered, she made the save.

"I'm here for a few weeks," she offered. "For work, actually. I'm reviving an ill-cared-for indoor garden. It's down the street. I've been taking morning walks, and this bakery has become my reward for all those steps."

Oh, Viv! Too much information! Heck, she'd forgotten how small talk worked. It had been a long time since she'd engaged in such a thing with a man who was not her husband.

Body completely facing hers, and head slightly bowed to focus on her—as if she were the most important thing to him—he said, "Tell me what you've discovered about our city that surprised you."

"Oh…"

An intriguing question. And he seemed genuinely interested. Refreshing, especially after the cold shoulders she'd received from the locals and shop clerks who had to endure her ridiculous attempts at the language.

"The Tuileries is beautiful this early, with the dew on the ground. I think I made friends with a duck." Viv laughed nervously.

Really? A duck? Way to make a first impression with the stunningly sexy Frenchman.

"I do love the royal garden."

The man—Rezin—was prompted by the clerk. He spoke to her in rapid French that completely exceeded Viv's comprehension, then handed her a black credit card. Then he turned back to her. "If this is your morning routine, then perhaps I can hope to see you tomorrow around this time?"

Viv's jaw dropped open. Was he asking her for a date? No. It was just a polite comment. Maybe? That glint in his eyes certainly teased something. Was it, *I dare you*? Now she felt a flush of heat at her temples and trickling down the back of her neck.

Please let it be a pesky hot flash, and not a noticeable blush!

"I work on the Champs-élysées," he added. "So I drive by here daily."

The Champs-élysées was the famous elite street that featured luxury retailers that attracted celebrities and tourists in droves. However, Viv had counted a McDonalds and a few cell phone stores in the mix, even a Starbucks.

Rezin collected his credit card and the pastry bag, then winked at her. Winked!

"See you tomorrow," he said. "Uh…what is your name?"

"Viviane," she said on a breathy whisper.

"Au revoir, Viviane." He turned and walked out of the shop.

Mouth gaping again, Viv followed his strides until he was out of sight. A handsome Frenchman had suggested he wanted to see her again. Score! Maybe? Oh, heck, she'd take it.

When someone cleared their throat behind her, she had

to force herself to turn around and resume normal Viv mode. As in your average American widow who had traveled to Paris to forge a new path in life. And, yes, to indulge in her fantasies about meeting a handsome Frenchman. Even though she knew they would remain fantasies. Because, really, she was not the sort of woman who could simply snag a French lover with a glance.

"Monsieur Ricard is very kind," the clerk said as she handed over Viv's bag to her. "No charge."

"What?" She shoved her hand in her back pocket, where she kept a ten-euro bill for snacks to fuel her morning explorations.

"Monsieur Ricard paid for yours. And…" the clerk gestured "…look inside."

Stunned and impressed at the man's generous move, Viv opened the bag. Inside sat the Opera cake.

"He asked me to do a swap." The clerk twirled her finger to emphasize the sneaky switch.

"Thanks," Viv said, and then corrected herself. *"Merci."*

Outside the shop, her smile exploded. She gripped the folded bag top with both hands. Precious cargo, gifted by a fantasy man. An inhalation lifted her chest as high as her spirits. That encounter would see her flying for the entire day. And, since the rest of the day involved battling a nasty overgrowth of thorned and desiccated foliage, she would ride it for all it was worth.

The fifteen-minute stroll from Le Beau Boutique to the mansion nestled at the river's edge of the Eighth Arrondissement was a good way to shake the stress from his body.

Rezin Ricard had not called his driver to pick him up after work today. Because of the scarring on Rez's left leg, from the car accident, the muscles there tended to seize and make him limp. More so after a long day of sitting. To counter that, he found walking helped. He hadn't gone to physical therapy in over a year. No time.

He had been thankful this morning to walk away from a beautiful woman without showing signs of his limp. Sacrificing his favorite Opera cake for the sight of a pair of pretty green eyes? What an ego boost. And he did hope to see her tomorrow morning. If only to experience more of her difference. Viviane hadn't been like the locals, with their subtle yet precise style. Not like the tourists, with their souvenir tee shirts and gawking gazes. And not like…

Her.

Shoving aside a rise of memory that might lure him to brooding, Rez entered the digital code and walked through the narrow courtyard to his three-story eighteenth-century mansion. Pausing before the main doors, he tilted back his head to take in the June sunshine.

Work demanded he give a hundred and ten per cent—or risk losing it all. And lately, that extra ten per cent was trying him. He did need a break, but as owner and CEO of his jewelry business, Le Beau, he was not ready to retire. Nor could he conceive of his son, Jean-Louis, taking over and steering the company in the direction *he* desired—which involved celebrity endorsements and "focusing on the bling" as Jean-Louis put it.

Le Beau had been founded one hundred years ago, by Rez's great-grandfather. They designed and curated classic rare jewels and commissioned pieces. Glamorous, sumptuous, and elegant. In the worldwide realm of jewelers they were highly respected. And Rez had no intention of re-branding to focus on the bling.

Rez hadn't stood within these cool limestone and marble walls in years. For good reason. But his penthouse in the Sixth was being renovated. The herringbone wood floors were being refinished, the cabinets refaced, the wall between the kitchen and the living area he'd always wanted knocked out was finally coming down, and there would be many other refurbishments. And instead of staying at the Ritz, or Hotel Regina, he'd decided that this empty mansion would serve.

As well, it would give him time to let go of the memories of his wife that haunted him. This mansion had been Colette's folly…her *tanière*—her lair, as she'd called it. Much as she'd thrived in the spotlight—she'd modeled in her twenties and thirties—even she had needed to recharge on occasion.

Two black leather suitcases sat in the foyer. His driver, Henri, in possession of the entrance code, had delivered them hours earlier. The place was kept in order, with a monthly visit from a cleaning service. But food was not stocked. Easy enough to order in meals. He'd be fine here while he waited out the penthouse reconstruction.

As long as he didn't wander into the Victorian-style indoor greenhouse at the back of the mansion. There, Colette had fussed over her roses and her painting projects.

Following Colette's death two years ago, his mother-in-law, Coral, had insisted he keep this place. Rez had wanted to sell immediately. But Coral, a world traveler who did not intend to stop trotting across the globe until her bones ceased to move and her body simply gave up, used the mansion a few months out of the year, whenever her adventures returned her to France. As well, Jean-Louis had once mentioned he used it on occasion.

Marriage issues already? Rez didn't want to get involved. Not with the tenuous relationship he and his son currently held.

It was after eight p.m., and the light that he'd absorbed outside drifted through the kitchen windows to glimmer across the pristine marble countertops. Rez eyed the gleaming coffee maker. No. He wanted restful sleep tonight. Tomorrow promised a meeting with a new client, to design a wedding set for his fiancée. A prince of some Scandinavian country...

Rez couldn't remember the country's name. He hated it that little things slipped his mind. Since the accident, in which he'd suffered a concussion resulting in traumatic brain injury, his short-term memory played tricks with him.

A new name could slip his hold before the handshake had even separated. The fact that he'd pushed back his chair when standing would evaporate and he'd then sit down—to land on the floor. Add to that, the dizziness. He was getting better at anticipating when a dizzy spell would attack, and now he could prop his shoulder against a wall or grab the back of a chair to ride it out. Yet that physical malady was difficult to hide from his coworkers...and his son.

Tonight he wouldn't think about Jean-Louis's intentions to rebrand Le Beau. Not when his leg urged him to sit and relax. Some days he even used a cane. But that felt wrong. Thriving at fifty-five, he was fit, healthy, and shouldn't need to use a cane like a geriatric.

With a sigh, Rez opened the fridge. He was surprised to see bottles of water and juice, as well as fresh fruit and charcuterie. His driver must have left the provisions for him. Henri, who had been with the family two decades, was good to take care of him like that.

Grabbing a bottle of water, Rez glanced down the foyer toward the spiral staircase. He'd sleep in the second-floor guest room that faced the Eiffel Tower. Not the large bedroom that mastered the third floor and faced the Arc de Triomphe. *Their* bedroom.

He couldn't bring himself to even peek inside. He guessed that Coral must use it when she stayed, because she'd once mentioned that the size of the closet could fit all her worldly belongings. The mansion was huge—a Paris gem worth forty million. Should Rez list it, it would sell immediately.

And that was his intention.

But first he needed to say *au revoir*. It was the least he could do for the wife he had loved for thirty years. Even if he suspected she had not returned that love in the latter part of their marriage.

A crashing noise toward the back of the house alerted him. Rez limped down to the open foyer, beneath the massive crystal chandelier. Who was in the house? Had he hit on a day when the maid stopped in? Wasn't it a little late to be cleaning? Unless the crash had been someone breaking in? No, the exterior security system was top of the line.

Wincing at the pain in his leg, he neared the conservatory. The property was backed by a solid limestone wall, but it was easily climbable. Break one of the greenhouse windows, and—

Though the noise hadn't sounded like shattering glass.

The double doors to the conservatory were open and the inner light was on. Rez cautiously approached the room. Overgrown foliage frosted the windows and walls. Most of it was green, spots here and there wilting and brown. The two-story room looked like a jungle that defied tidying.

Calling out, he walked inside. "Who's in here?"

"What? Who's here?" a woman's voice called in English.

Green fronds jiggled to Rez's left, and out popped a blonde head. The woman was on her knees, which were stained with dirt, and she wielded a gardener's spade.

"It's okay. I bumped into the utility cart. I didn't know anyone else was here— Oh."

Her mouth dropped open.

Rez's anger softened from tight fists to utter confusion. It was the woman from the *pâtisserie*. He didn't understand why she was here, on her knees, looking as though she had a purpose and a reason to be in his home.

"*Madame*, you must explain yourself."

"Please." She held up a palm. "I don't understand French. Can you speak English?"

The audacity!

"You have no right," he said tightly in French. "This was her—"

He squeezed a fist near his thigh and coached his rising blood pressure into a simmer. Very well, if he wanted to get his point across he must use English.

"Get out. I don't know why you're here, but you must leave. Now."

Using the toppled cart to pull herself up to stand, the woman tugged down her dirt-smeared tee shirt and stomped her feet, which settled her rumpled pants. After a sweep of her hand over her messy ponytail, she propped her hands akimbo.

"Rezin Ricard, right?" she asked.

Untidy copper-blonde strands poked out around her hairline. She was a nymph emerged from a forest, little concerned that she'd been disturbed from her natural habitat.

"What are you doing in my home?" he insisted, unwilling to allow her tattered beauty to dissuade him from his righteous anger.

"I'm staying here. And it's not your home. It belongs to a woman. Coral... I don't recall her last name, but I have it in my phone..." She glanced toward an array of spilled gardening tools and piles of dead foliage.

"Coral Desauliers," Rez said. "She is my mother-in-law. She doesn't own this mansion."

"Oh? *Oh...*"

Her pale lips distracted Rez from his fury. Burnished rose, her mouth, and seemingly soft... Had she enjoyed the pastry as much as he'd enjoyed making sure it was hers?

"I'm sorry. Coral hired me to revive the garden. She said I could stay here while I work. A month, if needed, though I anticipate only two weeks. Mother-in-law? You're...married?"

A confused tilt of her head emphasized the streak of dirt on her cheek. Rez wanted to brush it away. Was her skin as soft and pale as it appeared? The nymph had been playing in the dirt…

But then he found his anger. "What does my marital status have to do with a stranger squatting in my home?"

Her mouth dropped open.

Really? She was getting angry at *him*? Everything about this situation put her in the wrong and him in the right. And he would not tolerate another woman treading his wife's *tanière*.

"First." She put up a finger. "I am not squatting. I signed a contract with Madame Desauliers. Second. And this is off the topic, but strangely very key," she iterated with a stab of her forefinger. "If you're married, then why the flirtation at the bakery this morning?"

About to spew a protest at her, Rez calmed his need to be right. It was work, and stress—and, damn it, his struggles with Jean-Louis. This woman did not deserve his fury. Not until he found out what was actually going on.

"First," he said, and put up a finger as well. "It's not a bakery. It is a *pâtisserie*."

The way her eyebrow arched in challenge teased him to smile, but Rez snatched back his waning righteousness.

"And second," he resumed, "I am no longer married."

It hurt to say it out loud. It had been two years. Removing his wedding band a year ago had been the hardest step he'd taken on this miserable journey called grief.

"Oh." Her shoulders dropped. She sighed. "Sorry. Divorce?"

He shook his head.

"Oh." She nodded. "I get it. I'm a widow, too."

He softened his stance at that confession.

"It's tough. Some days it's not so tough. Other days you think it can't get any worse." She pressed her lips together and lifted her shoulders. "Right. No need to state the obvious. Anyway, Monsieur, I'm sorry if you weren't informed about my working here, but I insist on staying. I don't have anywhere else to go. And I do have a contract with Coral. And— Well, what are you doing here? I wasn't told that anyone occupied the place. I've been here three days."

Three days she had been in his home? Touching his wife's precious garden?

He took in what once could have been called a garden. It hadn't been properly cared for since Colette's death. The monthly cleaning service had made him aware they were not gardeners, but they did water occasionally. The room was in desperate need of care.

Rez's gaze landed on the overgrown rose bushes. They stretched almost as high as his chest but did not look healthy. No blossoms, and the leaves were curled and dry. Those had been Colette's pride and joy. No one must ever touch them.

"Monsieur?"

How strange that he'd met this woman that morning and had thrilled over their light banter. He'd even felt a boyish embarrassment should his limp be revealed to her. She was beautiful, and she'd seemed so normal, down-to-earth and welcoming, in the *pâtisserie*. A difference he'd wanted to embrace and hold and, he'd been looking forward to seeing her again.

Yet now that he did stand before her…

Rez cleared his throat. "This can't happen. Not now. I'm…" *Not prepared to allow another person to tread my wife's territory.* "I will call Coral and get this straightened out."

He turned to leave the room, but she rushed around him and blocked the open doorway.

"Please, I need this job," she said. "I used to be an exterior landscaper and then, when my husband died— Well.

This is my pivot. I'm starting over. Designing and refurbishing indoor greenhouses is my new business. I'm calling it Glass Houses. Or maybe The Plant Whisperer. Haven't decided which is more marketable yet. I've got a plan. It's all in my notebook."

She gestured to the mess of tools on the floor. An oversized red leatherbound journal lay amongst the scattered objects.

"This project is my maiden voyage. I can bring life back to this garden."

"Who said it needs life?" Rez hissed.

With that, he pushed around her and marched to the kitchen. He called Coral. The connection forwarded him to messages, where her recorded voice stated that she was on a cell-free sabbatical for the next four days.

Slamming the phone onto the counter, Rez hung his head. Was life not content to take away his wife, leave him mentally and physically scarred, and pit his only son against him? Now it had tossed a new twist into the mix. A beautiful woman with green eyes and a magnetic pull that demanded he not ignore her. A woman who intended to pull up the most precious memories he had of his wife.

CHAPTER TWO

UNSURE WHAT TO do after that unsettling exchange, Viv brushed the dirt from her chinos and tossed aside her gardening gloves. He couldn't kick her out. Well, he *could*, but she wouldn't allow it. This garden needed her help. And her future depended on her finishing the job so she could use it as an example to attract more clients. This was the testing ground for Glass Houses. Or The Plant Whisperer.

She really needed to decide on the name of her business. Harley Monroe, her assistant, who worked remotely from Minnesota and was currently "reviving her socials," had insisted she decide. And fast.

After showing her friend Kiara Kirk, a jet-setting international Realtor who sold luxury homes, her plans for an indoor garden rescue business, Kiara had been the one to hook her up with Coral and this home. Now here she was in Paris! Doing what she loved. And doing it well.

For over a decade she'd tried to convince her husband, Brian, to move indoors from exterior landscapes, but he had always refused. He'd been an outdoorsman, had loved the massive scale they'd worked with, and couldn't be bothered with some of the more delicate indoor work. Still, she'd never given up hope that someday her dreams of a more intimate, focused garden service would come to fruition. Using her experience with wholesalers, construction crews, botanists, spreadsheets, and even architectural design, she'd drawn up a detailed plan. And while she'd been dreaming, she'd included the European element. She'd always wanted to travel, to visit foreign gardens, to immerse herself in new worlds.

The couple of hundred thousand dollars she'd received from Brian's life insurance was enough to get her started. But from that she'd have to set something aside for living. Her social security benefits didn't kick in for another eight years.

Viv had started to believe that—with a lot of hard work—she had a future as an independent woman who could take care of herself.

Until Rezin had yelled at her, pummeling her confidence. He'd been so kind and charming in the bakery. For a few precious seconds he'd made her feel like a teenager swooning over a sexy guy.

Of course, if he hadn't known she was staying here then he had every right to be upset. Why had his mother-in-law offered Viv this job and the free stay if she didn't even own the place? While she'd not actually spoken to Coral, the woman had talked with Kiara, who had forwarded to Viv a one-page list of what was expected. Restore the garden, all expenses would be covered, and she could stay in a room at the mansion.

Yes, she'd signed an e-contract, but whether or not the contract was legal…

Viv knew she'd do whatever she could to stay. Sure, she could purchase a return flight and head back to the States. But what was there for her in small-town Minnesota? She had no intention of keeping a base for her business there. Harley worked from wherever she tended to roam. And Viv could to do the same.

Since her husband's death she'd taken up gig work— delivering groceries, dropping off fast food on people's doorsteps. A means to pay the bills and eat, since their

landscape business had lost all its clients during that final
year when they'd had to shut it down so she could care for
Brian. The chemotherapy and radiation had robbed him
of his strength, motivation and dignity. He'd suffered so
much. It had almost been a blessing when he'd said his final
"I love you" to her.

Almost. The loss of the man she had loved for decades
would never leave her soul. Her heart would always bear
that scar. Brian was no longer here. That was her new reality. And he would insist she did not wallow in grief and
moved on. And she was. Viv was even ready to start dating. And had thought she'd snagged that first date earlier
this morning.

Not really a date. More like another chance meeting.
But planned. Less chance and more… Heck. She shook
her head. That chance was obliterated now.

She wandered toward the greenhouse doors. Too bad
he was a jerk. A handsome angry jerk. Who had also lost
his partner.

Poor guy. She would cut him some slack. But this was
not over. She had only just begun to manifest her dream
job. Viv was not prepared to go down without a fight.

With a glance over her shoulder to the climbing monstera
that had stretched its nearly two-foot-long yellow and white
leaves to the glass ceiling in a quest to take over the room,
she knew exactly which card she would play. Steeling her
determination, she aimed toward the foyer.

Monsieur Ricard strode out from the kitchen as Viviane
neared. He was taller than her by a head, and she stepped
back from his overwhelming presence. He was no longer
in a rage, but she could sense he was still off. She felt horrible for intruding on his—

No. Stick to the plan, Viv. You must keep this job.

"Coral is incommunicado," he offered with a splay of
his hand. Then he jabbed it at his hip, which shoved back

the suit coat. Businessman, for sure, Viv decided. And in need of relaxation. A quiet evening to shrug off the day's challenges. Not a battle with a stranger.

But…

"I can't abandon my work," Viv blurted out. "The plant that is climbing the south exterior wall needs to be removed immediately or it could cause structural damage. There's already a crack in one of the ceiling windowpanes."

After looking ready to protest, Rezin suddenly shifted from evident anger to genuine concern. "Really?"

Sensing him waver, Viv eased in further. "I called a rental place earlier. They will deliver a tall ladder tomorrow. I really shouldn't cancel. There's no telling how quickly that crack will spread and then you'll need to replace the entire glass pane. Who knows? The entire ceiling could come down."

A bit dramatic—the ceiling was well-supported with an iron framework—but it felt like a deal-closer.

Rezin rubbed his jaw, where the dark stubble was thicker this evening than it had been this morning. It gave the suited businessman a rebel look. Like he was all business during the day, but after he stepped out of the office… Watch out! Viv had always been a sucker for rebels. Brian, who had grown up on a dairy farm, had been as straight and narrow as men were forged. *Marry for stability, save fantasies for just that.*

"Fine," he finally said. "Remove that one plant. And take photographs of the damage for me."

"I will do that. If you text me your details I'll send you photos as soon as I take them."

He gave her his number and she entered it in her contacts. Yes! She'd won that battle.

"You have until I can reach Coral," he said. "Where are you sleeping?"

Now he wanted to know her sleeping arrangements? How quickly the man's interests swerved. Rebel, indeed.

"Viviane?" he prompted.

Tugged from a delightful foray into imagining sleeping with a sexy Frenchman, Viv straightened. "Uh... Down the hall." She pointed over a shoulder. "Where Coral said I should stay."

"*Bien*. The servants' quarters."

"It is? Oh. It's such a beautiful room. With a large attached bathroom." Soaking in the bathtub with a goblet of wine in hand... She had already been working the Parisian lifestyle. "But if this is your home, I'd hate to impose. I suppose I could find a hotel room—" She didn't have the budget for a hotel room. *Pivot, Viv!* "But I promise I won't be in your way, Monsieur Ricard. Coral really didn't mention you living here."

"I don't live here. I need a place to crash while my penthouse is being renovated."

"Well, I'm sure you'll stay in one of the many bedrooms on the second or third floor. Not that I've been snooping, but I did look around when I first arrived. It's a beautiful mansion. Luxurious. And the garden can be restored to its natural lush, yet tamed, state. It's actually in much better condition—"

Rez thrust up his palm. "Just remove the problem you mentioned, then cease all other work in the conservatory. I don't require such work. I'll get it straightened out with Coral. You will be properly compensated for the inconvenience. Understand?"

"I do." Darn! She was not prepared to walk away from this job. "But it might take a few days to carefully remove the monstera and clean up. I want to save as much of the plant as possible. It's remarkably hardy and can be propagated—" The man's growing sneer stifled her rambling. "But, like I said, I won't get in your way."

He huffed and checked his phone, perhaps scrolling to Coral's number and texting, because he'd started typing something in.

"I'll…uh…" Viv gestured toward the kitchen. "Grab something to eat and go to my room for the night. I head out in the mornings for a walk— Oh."

He tilted his head, giving her his complete attention. They were both thinking about their encounter. Or she hoped his memory had been jogged and he was feeling a modicum of guilt for being so hard-headed right now. On the other hand, she couldn't read his oh-so-blue eyes and suspected he was still seething but controlled it well. Yes, he seemed like a control freak to her.

"Guess the date is off, eh?" she tried. Her wince was quickly hidden with a bow of her head.

"The date?"

"Tomorrow morning at the *pâtisserie*? I mean, another chance meeting."

Oh, heck… When would she learn to keep her mouth shut?

"Ah. That."

Viv's heart raced as she waited for him to say *No worries…it was all a misunderstanding. Let's make up for it over Opera cakes and coffee.*

"Right. I have a lot of work in the morning," he said. *"Bonsoir, madame."*

He turned and headed toward the stairway.

Madame… Was that the French form of address for a widow? Or did she revert back to *mademoiselle* after losing her husband?

Viv hated being called a widow. The word was always delivered with a sad face. She was still young, alive, and had half her life ahead of her. She intended to live to one hundred. She was determined not to wither, play bingo on Tuesday nights, and grow a cat collection.

A new journey had begun in this Parisian mansion owned by this gruff yet handsome man. Viv was going to take that journey.

And be successful at it.

The next morning Rez leaned over his desk, fingers curling into fists. His son, Jean-Louis, whom he'd not expected to see in the office today, stood on the other side of the Louis XV desk that had been in the family since the inception of Le Beau.

Jean-Louis was going on about how he wanted Rez to go for a check-up with a doctor. What he wasn't saying, but had certainly implied, was that the doctor he wanted his dad to see was a psychiatrist.

His son had been suggesting he seek further medical help since the day Rez had left the hospital, but within the last few months his son's dedication to that concern had annoyingly veered toward Rez's mental health. Of course, he knew Jean-Louis had his best interests in mind, but he wasn't crazy!

"It's been a rough couple of years." Jean-Louis smoothed a palm down his lapel. He'd inherited his father's zeal for a fitted suit and diamonds at his cuffs. "You never take a break from work, Papa."

"I am perfectly capable. Especially here." Rez tapped his temple.

Why must they even have this absurd conversation? He was not mentally unsound. The memory loss episodes he experienced were few and far between.

"I have been CEO of Le Beau since I was twenty-eight. I know every aspect of the business from the acquisition of gemstones and fine metals to the design and marketing. I know each client by name and family. And I've been invited to more weddings than is believable. I *am* Le Beau.

You will get your chance to sit in this chair in time, Jean-Louis. I promise you that."

Jean-Louis scoffed. "You think I want to steal the company out from under you? It's not like that. Papa, I am worried about your mental health. You forget things."

"You know that's a result of my brain injury."

"Yes—not your fault. But it must be watched. You require regular medical check-ups. And what about your dizzy spells? You collided with Penelope last week."

He'd not *collided* with Penelope, their receptionist/personal assistant. Caught by a sudden wave of dizziness, Rez had simply stepped wrong, and Penelope had been near him. He'd steadied himself by grasping her forearm. Not a big concern.

"Are you spying on me?" he asked.

"*Papa!* I'm in the office often. Penelope and I are great friends."

Jean-Louis was the principal buyer for Le Beau. Three-quarters of the year he traveled the world. The majority of his flights landed him in Amsterdam, the city of diamonds, and the key diamond center any successful jeweler must navigate like the back of his hand. When Rez had been hospitalized for two months following the accident that had taken his wife's life, it had been Jean-Louis who had overseen Le Beau.

His son had suggested Penelope for the assistant position, and Rez had been grateful to gain such a smart, efficient employee. She also brought in homemade croissants brushed with honey butter. Often.

"You don't know *me*," Rez said. He settled in the chair and shoved his hands over his hair. "I'm not ready to retire."

"Ready has nothing to do with this, Papa. *Uff!*" Jean-Louis checked his watch. "The client is due in moments."

"Yes, I do know that," Rez said defensively. "I've had the meeting scheduled for weeks." His watch sent him a reminder an hour before all important meetings. Without that crutch, he might not remember. "If you will leave us to discuss the design they want for their wedding set…?"

"I'm going to sit in on this consultation." Jean-Louis leaned against the brick wall, arms crossed over his chest. The Picasso painting hung on the wall next to him had been purchased by Rez's father in the sixties. "The client has requested I do so."

Rez's jaw dropped open. Had the client requested his son's presence out of the blue? Or had Jean-Louis encouraged the client to include him? At the very least, Penelope should have alerted him to his addition to the meeting.

"I am perfectly capable—" Rez started.

"Today's meeting has nothing to do with your mental capacity," Jean-Louis said. "And I would never say as much to any of the clientele. You can trust that our family secrets are safe, Papa."

Family secrets? They had no secrets. They were a family of father and son, grieving over a lost mother and wife. Very well, Rez did not want his condition to be known. He'd not told Penelope about his memory loss or dizzy spells, but he suspected Jean-Louis might have done so. His limp was an obvious fact; he couldn't hide that.

"This client wants innovative ideas," Jean-Louis added. "The Prince is marrying an American hip-hop singer. So…"

Inwardly, Rez rolled his eyes. Why had they come to Le Beau if they wanted bling? *Ugh.* He hated that word. He despised the hideous creations that hung around necks on red carpets and in music videos. Thick, gold, and massive amounts of diamonds.

Rationally, he knew it would be a relevant step for Le Beau to make. To add celebrity endorsements. To offer "bling." To appeal to the younger generation. But, as well, Rez felt sure his great-grandfather would turn over in his grave should such a travesty manifest itself.

The intercom buzzed, and Penelope announced she would show in the clients.

Rez stood abruptly and winced, catching his palm on the desk to maintain balance. He'd had pins in his thigh to hold the bones together while they mended for six months. Now what remained was a thick scar from hip to knee. Never knowing if his leg would support him made him feel incapable. But he was not. A man did not need two good legs to run a billion-dollar jewelry empire. And he still wielded the mental capacity to control and run the business that meant everything to him.

Most days he did, anyway.

Rez tightened his jaw. The thought of losing control of the company was terrifying. It was all he had left.

"Papa?" His son had seen his reaction to the pain.

"I'm fine. Let's do this, then."

Viv dumped the can of whole yellow tomatoes into a bowl. Sliding her hands into the cool goo, she broke up the tomatoes with her fingers. She had forgotten how the sensual art of cooking made her feel. Connected to something that she could create. Reawakened by scents, textures, and flavors. Almost like her gardening, but creating sustenance. And love. Food, she'd realized early in her marriage, was her love language.

Since Brian's death she rarely cooked for herself. Yes, she'd not shown herself proper love. Food came from a box, frozen, or was picked up in the drive-through. Not the healthiest way to eat, but she'd let nutrition slip from her self-care ritual. Along with many things, such as dressing up and wearing make-up, reading a thick historical novel, going for walks, even the occasional weekend of binge-watching a TV series.

That she was cooking for the handsome, yet prickly owner of this fabulous mansion brightened her smile. Was she plying her seductive culinary skills on him? Hardly. This was a simple lasagna.

With the tomatoes sufficiently crushed, she rinsed her hands, then seasoned the sauce and mixed in the sautéed onions, along with finely diced zucchini and mushrooms. No meat. She wasn't a vegetarian, but she didn't know if Rezin was a meat-eater. Now to layer it with the cooked noodles, along with lots of fresh mozzarella and ricotta. The cheese shop down the street was remarkable. She would never buy pre-packaged cheese again.

Admiring the assembled dish, she tried to remember when she'd last made lasagna for Brian. He had eaten anything and everything she'd made. Always complimented her on it. Most hard-working men were thankful for a home-cooked meal after a long day.

A wistful heaviness landed in her heart. The feeling was strange. Almost as if she were cheating on the ghost of her marriage with tomato sauce and hand-torn cheese.

"Oh, don't be silly," she quietly admonished herself out loud.

And yet a tear blossomed. Sniffling, she closed her eyes. How odd…the things that tugged at her grief. Lasagna, of all things. She certainly hoped she'd be able to sit across the table from Rezin and eat it without shedding a tear.

That was *if* he accepted her meal as a peace offering. She had no idea when he would return to the mansion this evening. And likely he preferred fancy French cuisine.

Placing the pan in the oven, she set a timer on her phone.

Now to do some sweeping.

Viv was determined to make the conservatory ready for when she won the approval to work on its entirety. Because no matter what, she must win it.

Rez stormed over the mansion's threshold and slammed the door behind him. He had been muttering to himself during the entire ride from work to home. Now, away from the office, he was free to let loose.

He swore. Punched the air. "Jean-Louis had no right! Trying to make me seem feeble… And that ridiculous design!"

The Scandinavian Prince had settled on a rose gold setting with extremely large diamonds. Too many of them for taste and elegance. And the fussy Asscher cut he'd requested—reminiscent of the Art Deco style—did not properly suit the contemporary setting.

When had he lost connection with his son so that—? *Hell.*

Rez blew out his breath.

He and Jean-Louis had never been close. Colette had been his son's best friend. Rez was his father—a kind one, but also an exacting teacher who had always demanded the best as Jean-Louis navigated his way into the company. Emotionally, he might never embrace his son, or even think to pat him on the back. It wasn't what the Ricard men did. They provided for their families. They were respected community members. They showed their love with action, not emotion.

And they never disrespected their fathers by trying to shove them out of the company.

Swearing again, Rez limped toward the kitchen, but his anger got the better of him again as he recalled his living situation.

"Can't even get comfortable in my own home. Have to stay in this…memory trap. Of all places! And with that strange woman in the garden."

"I am not strange."

The words came out defensively from behind him.

CHAPTER THREE

REZ SPUN TOWARD THE VOICE. A spritely face peered between a broom handle and a bundle of long bamboo spikes. Emerald eyes beamed from between lush lashes. A perfectly kissable mouth, held in tight concern, teased at his need to soften it. Yet capping the sweet face was a mess of tangled hair, struck through with a few of the spikes. And the dirt smeared on her cheeks further added to her strangeness quotient.

"Strange is…debatable." Rez gestured to her face.

That moment of taking her in had swept him down from his tirade. Since the accident, anger tended to strike without warning.

He breathed out.

Calm, Rez. You're not angry at her. You're angry at Coral for not telling you she would be here. Touching Colette's plants. Treading on your memories.

With his next deep, surrendering inhalation Rez caught a whiff of something delicious. "What is that?"

"Lasagna," she replied. "I thought the least I could do was to feed you, since you're putting up with me staying here when you hadn't expected a guest."

It did smell delicious after a long day at work. During which he'd only bothered to drink coffee and down a *pain au chocolat* for lunch.

And yet… He would not be so easily distracted. "Was

the ladder delivered? Did you complete the one task I allowed you?"

"The ladder was not delivered, so I wasn't able to attack the climbing menace. Tomorrow for sure. They promised. Maybe. That's what I understood from their blend of French and English."

"I doubt talking to them is how the dirt got on your face. I meant it when I forbade you from working in the garden."

"My work does involve dirt, *monsieur*. Sorry. No way around that one. I had to clear an area for the ladder."

He cleared his throat. Made a huffing dissatisfied noise. Again, Rez reminded himself not to take out his anger on this innocent American woman. That messy hair was appealing, in an odd, can-I-tidy-you-a-bit? way. The urge to reach over and brush the hair from her lashes twitched his fingers. And what was that about? Was he attracted to her? Could he be angry with her and want her at the same time?

Want her? Now he was thinking foolish thoughts.

No, he was a man! She was an attractive woman. Of course he entertained *ideas* about her.

"We'll discuss any concerns you may still have over dinner," she said, and walked away, swinging the broom at her side.

A bit too confident for a guest in his home. However, Rez rather liked it that she had not balked at his tirade. Yet he would not soften simply because he could imagine kissing her soft rose lips and raking his fingers through her messy hair.

Certainly not.

Very well. A discussion they would have. Over lasagna. He did enjoy Italian cuisine.

"Très bien," Rez said as he dished a second helping of lasagna onto his plate.

Viv beamed. She was pretty sure that meant very good.

The compliment felt like a much-needed hug. Perhaps he understood her love language?

She did long for physical connection. With a man. But she should not fall into the fantasy of Rezin's sexiness again. Was it possible her menopausal hormones had somehow reverted to teenager level? It certainly felt like it. She almost sighed when she was gazing into his bluer-than-blue eyes.

"It is tasty, isn't it?" She made the save before embarrassing herself with the kind of lovey-dovey sigh that should only come out of the mouth of a schoolgirl. "I looked up the recipe on Pinterest."

Rez flashed her a look over his fork.

She shrugged. "My recipe book is at home in Minnesota. Lasagna is my go-to dish. I gathered the ingredients this morning on my walk. That little market a couple blocks away is awesome. I got fresh blueberries as well. Organic, even! I'm thinking about making syrup for pancakes in the morning."

"Crêpes?" Rez offered.

"Yes, of course. When in France, eh?"

She winked at him. Actually winked!

Viv quickly looked at her plate, forking up the noodles and tomato sauce. Had she really done such a thing? This flirting stuff was nerve-racking.

Was that what this was? Flirting? Oh, mercy. She was not ready for this.

But, yes—yes, she was. Maybe? Could she channel a teenager long enough to figure out how this stuff worked nowadays? It had been nearly thirty years since she'd flirted with a stranger. That made her feel ancient. But she was not!

"The dinner is lovely," Rez said.

Whew! Saved from her mental dive into decrepitude by a smoldering French baritone.

"The fact you're still working in my garden is not."

Viv set down her fork. She'd prepared for this argument while weeding through the desiccated undergrowth that edged the conservatory walls.

"You said you were going to talk to Coral about it?" she asked.

"She's still incommunicado. Coral does that. Goes off on soul-searching adventures for days, sometimes weeks."

"That sounds wonderful. This trip for me is a bit of a soul-searching mission."

She noticed his wince even though he tried to hide it behind a bite of food. They were not any sort of confidantes, and he could probably care little what her soul desired. Right. *Stay on task, Viv.*

"You should know that I've inspected the greenhouse and all the foliage over the past few days. Assessed what needs to get cleared out, what can be salvaged—"

"It will all remain untouched," he interrupted firmly. "You Americans have difficulty with the word *no*."

"I take offense on behalf of all Americans," Viv said, but added a light tone. "Still, that plant must come down."

Rez leaned his elbows on the table. The man must be some kind of corporate raider, because he wielded the solemn stare and conviction that Viv imagined such a job required.

"The monstera," he said. "Is that what you called it?"

"Yes." It was a common plant, but it impressed her that he'd remembered.

"I had no idea plants could be so destructive."

"Well, they don't do it on purpose," she defended. "That particular plant can become a bit of a weed if it isn't tended often. And it's a weighty thing."

"As I've said, when that job is complete, so is your gardening refurbishment."

"If you say so."

But if—when—she got her way, things would go much differently.

Slow and easy, Viv. Don't spook the man.

She propped an elbow on the table and caught her cheek against her palm. "Are you okay?"

Setting down the wine goblet, he tilted his head. "Why would you ask such a thing?"

"You seemed upset when you arrived earlier. I know I can be a little strange. I have an affinity for tucking crystals in my bra, I'm distracted by cats and will hold complete conversations with them, and I also cry easily— Oh. Sorry. I also tend to ramble about odd things no one ever wants to hear. Anyway…" She tried a smile and got the tiniest curve of his mouth in return. "If it's me staying here that's upsetting you…"

"You have nothing to do with my earlier outburst. I do apologize for that. Sometimes I have to hold things in until I get home. I don't like to rage at the office. It's not that I rage. It's just…"

She could sense his need to change the subject. Who would want to talk about something like their anger?

"What *is* the office, actually?" She knew he was a jeweler; the pastry shop clerk had told her as much.

"I own Le Beau. The jewelers. We've been in business for a century."

"That's impressive. Is that the company I've heard about that caters to the rich and famous?"

"We cater to a certain elite clientele, *oui*. I am the CEO. I spend a lot of time on video chat with various vendors, and approving paperwork and contracts, but my favorite part of the job is designing."

"Really? You make fabulous necklaces and bracelets?"

"And rings and earrings and brooches. From the sketch on the page, to obtaining the fine gemstones and metals, to putting it all together. I am unique in this business, in that I like to immerse myself in the entire process. Unlike the CEOs of most jewelry companies, who send out all the work beyond the design, I don't hand off my creations to the cutters and setters. My reward is seeing my work adorn a woman's graceful neck or fingers."

"You must have designed for celebrities?"

"Many."

"Like who?"

"Some princes, an opera singer, royalty..." he casually offered.

"How is it that jewelry can make a man so furious? I mean, when you came in earlier..."

He clasped his hands before his chin and eyed her carefully. Blue eyes and daydreams teased Viv to lean forward, resting her chin on the back of her hand.

"My son arouses the fury in me," Rez said. "He has... certain ideas about the direction Le Beau should move in to stay relevant."

"You don't want to stay relevant?"

"We already are. That's all I'll say about that."

"Fair enough." Interfering in a family matter was not something she cared to do. And she cared little about celebrities and their quest for sparkly things. "More wine?"

"I'm good. But I'm also curious."

Something lightened in his expression; it changed his entire face. So much so, Viv felt herself lighten.

"Crystals in your bra?"

She'd *said* that? *Oh, Viv!*

"It's a thing. I love crystals. Minerals. Pretty stones. And a garnet worn against your heart invites warmth and love."

"I...don't know what to say to that."

"Well, you believe much the same, without even knowing it."

His eyebrow quirked. The man was too delicious. She could stare at him all evening.

"You design jewelry with precious stones. You may not be aware of the qualities each stone attracts, but they do."

"So, garnets for love? I'll remember that," Rez said. "Thank you for the meal. Now I should retire. I've some notes to make for work tomorrow." He rose and smoothed a hand down his tie. *"Bonsoir, madame."*

Rez left the room, his hand gliding along the wall as he did so. As if for balance?

"Goodnight!" she called. "I promise to only touch the monstera tomorrow."

Her line of vision followed him to the stairwell, where he slapped a palm on the newel post and paused. Was that a wince? The man really did allow his anger to get to him. That was not good for anyone's health. Poor guy. He needed a hug.

But she couldn't simply walk up and hug him. That was intrusive. And, as a certified introvert with only brief moments of regretful extroversion, not her thing. Rez was still a stranger. And, apparently, she was strange.

I'll take that. She smiled. Better to be strange and still have a job than be kicked out on her keister.

From the pocket of her chinos she dug out the small crystal she'd purchased while on her morning walk. Moonstone. The creamy white stone blinked bright blue when she tilted it. Flashy, yet hiding so many more secrets. It reminded her of Paris.

And, yes, the garnet in her bra was for love. But also it was a very sexy stone. She *did* want to get her sexy on. And boy, oh, boy, she knew of an eligible bachelor who would help her.

Leaning back on the chair and crossing her legs, she eyed the lasagna. When Rez had disappeared from her sight, she dished up another helping.

In his room, Rez slipped off his coat, shoes, loosened his tie, and sat on the end of the king-sized bed.

Relevant. Had he actually used that word? Of course Le Beau was relevant. And Jean-Louis would never convince him otherwise.

He tossed his dark tie onto the light counterpane. Everything in this room, from walls to furnishings and fabrics, was a soft cream color. Plain. He liked color when he could control the combinations, the moods. Setting colored gemstones was one of his favorite things to do. It was a fine art.

He was aware that gemstones had been assigned certain qualities, attributes, and even emotional resonance. Bunch of nonsense, that stuff. But garnet for warmth and love?

"More than warmth and love," he muttered. "It's sexy and passionate."

Stretching his arms over his head, he tilted his head from side to side. That had been a delicious meal. Certainly beat frozen dinners from the supermarket.

And Viviane was not so difficult to converse with. Even if she did seem snoopy. He would not normally reveal anything about his family troubles to a stranger.

If structural damage could be caused by that overgrown plant then he certainly wanted that taken care of—and quickly. So she'd be around another day or two.

He'd survive the intrusion. After all, she was a beautiful woman. She'd cleaned up nicely for dinner. Not a dirt smudge to be seen. Her hair was a certain shade he couldn't decide on. Rose-blonde? Pale copper? It was bright… gleaming. It framed her heart-shaped face. And her curiosity didn't offend him so much as intrigue him. She was simple, down-to-earth—quite literally—and…

And the complete opposite to Colette. Not at all fussy or self-aware to a fault, as his wife had been. He'd loved Colette, even when she'd selfishly demanded his constant reassurance of her beauty, her agelessness, her appeal.

Rez glanced at his reflection in the mirror across the room. He'd learned to make those assurances by rote. They had grown to mean little to him. A woman needn't cater to anyone to gain acceptance. All women were beautiful in their own way. And now, with a splash of fresh air in the form of a strange gardener, his interest had been piqued.

"I could get to know her," he said aloud, his mood daring to lighten.

He was a single man. And a man had needs. Like touch, conversation, and sex. And Viviane was staying in his home. So close. Sexy and passionate…just like the gemstone.

Was he ready to have another go at dating? Simply get closer to a woman? And, if so, might he have a fling with the gardener?

The fact he was considering it proved his broken heart wasn't completely shattered. He was a living, breathing, wanting man. And it was about time he started acting like one.

CHAPTER FOUR

THE LADDER WAS to be delivered before noon. Viv decided to take a quick walk around the neighborhood, starting with her favorite *pâtisserie*. She'd stepped outside the mansion and turned to pull the door shut when Rez appeared and walked out.

A nice surprise to see him. But she crushed a few proverbial eggshells while they strolled to the main sidewalk. What sort of mood was he in? They'd come to terms over her working on the one plant, but he was still adamant that was all she'd touch. And he'd dismissed her when she'd sort of suggested they do the bakery date.

"Are you off to work?" she asked gaily. "Designing jewelry?"

"Yes. I've a long day ahead of me."

He opened the wrought-iron gate and she walked through. The sunlight glowed like fire. It caught in Rez's eyes and glinted. Like some kind of fairytale prince.

Silly, Viv.

And yet they were both here. And her destination was close.

"Want to change your mind about walking to the *pâtisserie* with me?" she asked. "My treat. I'm sure they've a good supply of Opera cakes this early in the morning."

Rez winced and glanced to the street. Only then did Viv notice the black limousine parked there. Oh. His driver?

"While I'd love to walk with you," he said, and his tone sounded genuine, "as I've said…work."

"Oh, of course."

What did she know about the rich and obviously entitled? He probably took a chauffeur everywhere. And his stylish leather dress shoes certainly were not walk-wear.

Suddenly Rez leaned in and bussed one of her cheeks. A kiss? So soon? Should she turn her head into it or—? Oh. Viv realized the man was doing the French thing. When he moved to her opposite cheek she fought the urge to tilt her head and bring their mouths closer and let the common French means of saying farewell happen.

The brisk contact thrilled her. Perhaps he didn't completely hate her?

"I woke up wondering something," he said with a touch of lightness.

"Good dreams, eh? What were you wondering?"

He chuckled. "What sort of crystal you might have tucked in your bra today."

When she tried to meet his gaze he looked to the side. Embarrassed? He'd woken up with *that* on his mind? Viviane tugged in the corner of her lower lip.

"Sorry, that was forward…" he said.

"Moonstone," she rushed out. "It's a piece I picked up from a shop in the Louvre the second day I was here. It reminds me of Paris."

"Is that so? Moonstone…" He considered it, then nodded. "Appropriate. *Au revoir, madame,*" he said. "The ladder arrives today?"

"Yes—er…*oui.* Don't worry, I promise only to do the necessary work. You have a good day."

Viv watched the limo pull away from the curb. She smoothed her cheek where the heat of his touch lingered. Burnished to a rosy warmth by the brush of his stubble.

"Nice…" she whispered.

Ten minutes later she had selected the Opera cake, and also a half-dozen *macarons*. When she dug out cash to pay, the clerk—the same one who had served her yesterday morning—waved her hand.

"*Non, madame.* Monsieur Ricard has covered it."

"What?"

The clerk nodded enthusiastically. "All your purchases are paid for. Always."

Tapping the ten-euro note against her lower lip, Viv took that in. What a nice gesture. Rezin Ricard was a gentleman. Who had almost…sort of…kissed her out front of the mansion.

She knew it hadn't been a kiss in the romantic aspect, but she was going with it for as long as his heat remained on her skin. And, yes, she could still feel him there…so close.

"*Madame?*"

Right. No place to daydream.

Viv took the bag of pastries and walked outside. Could an American woman, out of place in her life, and precariously balancing a line to a new path, dare to dream about getting closer to a handsome Frenchman who might also be walking the emotion-laden line that grief and loss tended to draw?

"Why not?" she muttered aloud, and then walked toward the Tuileries Garden, her steps much bouncier than usual.

Sitting in the back of his limo, Rez massaged his leg. Today the pain in his leg pierced him as if with a steel poker. He'd had to grit his teeth while talking to Viviane.

When he'd bussed her cheeks it had been a means to hide his wince. But in those seconds he'd drawn in her scent. Sweet, with a hint of green. Like foliage and candy. Subtle, yet delicious. Naturally erotic.

Thinking about the luscious aroma rising from her skin averted the pain. The utter freshness of Viviane was a unique and refreshing swerve from Colette's uptight perfectionism.

More than anything, he would have loved to stroll alongside Viv. Chat. Get to know her better. Thank her again for the delicious supper.

But although little things slipped his mind, he never forgot to check his calendar. And this morning it had reminded him of a video call with Sven Stellian, to go over the next few months of mining projects. Sven was the mastermind behind Le Beau's precious metals. He appreciated decades-old whiskey from Scotland. Rez made sure the man received a good supply every Christmas.

Hours later, Rez signed off with Sven. He closed the mining file on his computer and—the entire screen went blank. What the hell…? With a flutter, the screen blinked back to life and showed the open page where the mining file had been but was not anymore.

Gritting his jaw, Rez tapped a few keys. The file had been there. He wasn't computer illiterate. He knew how to find and open files and save backups and…

He swore. He must have hit delete. It was the only explanation for the missing file. With a sigh, he slouched into his chair. Were Jean-Louis's concerns true? *Was* he losing it mentally? Even to consider it made Rez's stomach lurch. His brain had been damaged in the accident. The doctors had said he'd have to live with this new normal. But they'd not said he'd get worse.

"Monsieur Ricard?" Penelope peeked in the open doorway of his office. Her bright red hair was coiled into a forties-style updo. "How did the meeting go?"

Rez exhaled. "Penelope, I need your help."

Fifteen minutes later the file was restored, and the changes Rez had made during his conversation with Sven remained.

"*Merci*, Penelope. You just…" *Saved my ass.* "Made my day."

"Not a problem. Thanks to the linked computer system, I do backups of all your files. Please don't think I'm overstepping."

"Absolutely not. You are a valuable employee. Some days I would be lost without you."

She shrugged, and then paused on her way out from his office. "If you don't mind my saying… I care for you like a father, Monsieur Ricard. You mustn't think Jean-Louis is out to get you."

He'd not realized that Jean-Louis and Penelope shared such intimate details. But perhaps she was just perceptive. The woman did have a way of always knowing when he'd need coffee, or arriving with files for a project minutes before he thought to ask for them.

He knew Jean-Louis was not out to get him. Rez just liked to maintain control. And control over Le Beau was one of very few things he actually could still manage.

"Your perspective is different than mine, Penelope. But I do thank you for your concern."

She should not concern herself with his personal life. But he wouldn't say that. She meant well.

"Shall I bring you some croissants for lunch?" she asked. "I made them this morning."

"With honey butter?"

She nodded enthusiastically. "I'll be right back."

Croissants would see him through an afternoon of paperwork. Yet the idea of returning to the mansion prodded at him. An intriguing woman occupied his home. Her scent still teased at him with the crook of a finger and a quirky smile.

She'd be gone soon enough. And then he would be alone.

And, since Viviane had crashed into his life, being alone no longer appealed to Rez.

CHAPTER FIVE

ANOTHER FAVORITE DISH of Viviane's was quiche. Baked until the crispy pale brown crust ruffled at the edges. Bits of ham and Emmental cheese added a savory touch. Her mother had passed along the recipe to her.

Raised by a single mom who'd never had a desire to marry, Viviane had garnered independence and necessary life skills by observing and following her mother's actions. When she'd passed away eight years ago from old age—her mother hadn't had Viv until she was forty—it had felt natural, blessed, and like she was moving on to something bigger and better.

Violet Westberg had lived her life exactly as she'd desired and had regretted nothing. Viv believed her mom would be proud of her setting off on this new life adventure.

"You don't have to cook for me every night." Rez sat down before the table. "Although…"

Viv sat across from him. "Although?"

"My next thought was that I hope you don't take that statement seriously. This smells *incroyable*."

The look on his face told her she'd scored another win. While cooking to seduce wasn't part of her master plan to keep her job here, it wasn't a terrible side hustle in winning the man's trust.

"I don't mind cooking for two," she said. "I have to make something for myself. I might as well double it for you. As long as you don't mind me tooling around in your kitchen? I know you'd rather not have me in your home at all."

"On the contrary. It's the garden."

"So, you don't mind me traipsing about the rest of the place?"

"Traipsing?"

"You know… Floundering. Meandering. Generally wandering."

He chuckled. "Until I can reach Coral you are welcome here."

"And when you do reach her? Then I'm out on my behind?"

He didn't answer, instead sipped his wine.

"I'm voting for Coral to win the struggle," Viv said. "I've already lost my heart to the garden. There are half a dozen varieties of fern, most still very salvageable. And the hostas! Anyway, I want to start at the top and work on the monstera and take propagatable shoots when I can. I climbed to the top of the ladder before you arrived, while the delivery man was still here. I was able to get some good shots of the cracked glass pane while I was up there."

"Can you send them to me?"

"I already did. Check your texts after we eat."

He patted his jacket pocket but didn't take out his cell phone. Good call.

"Do you feel safe climbing the ladder with no one around?" he asked.

His genuine concern buoyed her. "Yes, it's very sturdy. And the delivery man did me a favor by anchoring it midclimb to a supporting beam on the outer conservatory wall. As well, he included a safety harness."

"Your profession seems quite specific. Refurbishing indoor gardens? Do you get a lot of work?"

"As I've explained, it's a new business model I'm creating. I'm an award-winning horticulturist, so I've got the skills. I also worked in landscaping for the last two decades, so I do know the lay of the land, so to speak. I published a book ten years ago, titled *The Plant Whisperer*."

He wrinkled a brow. "You…whisper to plants?"

She chuckled. "Sometimes. Talking to plants releases humidity into the air and they thrive on that. Anyway, I was even on *Good Morning America* to promote the book. It was fun. But I suspect my fifteen minutes of fame never made it across the ocean to France."

"Why is it that you are here in France and not America?"

"That's all part of the plan. I want to work in Europe. Travel. Experience the world while making a living. I can create an entire garden from scratch in a pre-existing space, or revive an ill-cared-for garden. I think I mentioned I want to call it either Glass Houses or The Plant Whisperer? What do you think when you hear those titles?"

"'Glass Houses' sounds too narrow. You want to be able to work with clients who may not have their garden under glass. There are a lot of terrace gardens in Paris and other European cities."

"You're right. I'll let Harley know. The Plant Whisperer it is. Harley is my marketing pro, who works with me remotely. She's currently reviving my social media and I send her photos daily. She's very good at what she does. I plan to employ only women. We *are* the nurturers, growers and keepers, after all."

"Bold…"

Viv eyed the man over her wine goblet. He met her gaze with those gorgeous blues. The connection felt electric. Longer than a glance, for sure. Was she interpreting it correctly—that he was interested in her—or had it simply been too long since she'd made simple eye contact with a man?

Reading a man's thoughts had never been her forte, even while she was married.

"I like a woman who goes for what she wants," Rez said. "Strength is attractive."

Now she blushed.

Oh, Viv, there's no sign of strength in flushed cheeks.

She glanced aside. Why was it so difficult to accept a compliment from this man without reading more into it? Did he find her attractive? Like, enough for dating? A real kiss? Romance?

No, it was a figure of speech, obviously. Maybe… Oh, God, *could* he be attracted to her?

"Thank you," she finally said. "Are you finished? I'll wash up the dishes."

"I'll help. I like talking to you," Rez said. "And this will extend the conversation."

"I like talking to you, too. You're my first Frenchman."

"Is that so? First in what way?"

She caught his husky intonation. Mercy, if the man knew that the mere sound of a French accent made her melt.

"In every way. Talking to. Cooking for. Living with. We are, in a manner, living together."

"So we are. You…have a thing for Frenchmen?"

"Honestly?"

Did she dare? Why not? She was a grown woman. The time to couch her sentiments with care and be wary of putting her truth out there was in the past. This was her new life. Viviane Westberg would not shrink from adventure.

"How could any woman not? The French language is melodious, and so sexy. And you've got this voice…" She handed him a plate and, with no more dishes to wash, turned her hip against the sink to watch him.

"This voice?" He set the plate on the counter.

"It touches me. My skin," she added. Since it didn't seem to be freaking her out, she settled into the flirtation. "But I bet you get that all the time. When you walk down the street all the women swoon, right?"

Rez chuckled deeply—and there was that resonant tone that glided across her skin like a lover's touch.

He suddenly paused and gave her a look. "Seriously?" he asked.

Caught! She shrugged. "It's the truth."

"I don't walk down the street very often. Not lately, with my leg acting up."

"I noticed you favor it. Have you been in an accident?"

Rez turned his hip toward the sink to face her. "Yes. The injury is a couple of years old." He eased a hand down his thigh.

"Does it hurt all the time?" she asked.

"Some days I don't even notice it. Other days it's always there. Not excruciating, but enough to distract me."

"Do you take medication for it?"

"Painkillers?" He shook his head. "Not into drugs. The neighbor who lives on the ground floor of my building in the Sixth brings me teas that she's concocted from her garden. I have no idea what herbs are in them. Some of them taste awful. But they do alleviate the pain."

He sat on the chair before the table and stretched out his leg. He probably didn't want her to see his wince, but she did.

Viv walked over and touched his hair, then bowed to kiss his forehead. A real kiss. Not a genial bussing of the cheeks in a farewell kiss.

"I know that won't make it better, but it's something my mother always did for me. I was thinking about her as I was cooking. She was so nurturing." Viv pulled her fingers from his oh-so-soft hair. "Sorry. That was— I shouldn't have… I sort of just reacted with that kiss." It had been something she'd always done for her husband, too.

Rez closed his eyes. "React all you like. I think that kiss may have been as restorative as herbal tea. Why don't you try another here?" He tapped his cheek.

Really? Their light flirtation had taken on a suggestive tone. Her muscles loosened and her jaw softened. Butter-flies invaded her heart. Nerves? When was the last time she'd stood so close to a man who was not her husband? And had him suggest she kiss him?

Too long. Pre-marriage long. It would only hurt to start counting by decades.

But she wanted this. Felt sure she was ready to take this step. Diving back into the dating pool was on her shortlist. It was now or never.

She bent to kiss Rez's cheek. Leather and wine scented his aura. Solid and sure. His presence silently reassured while also teasing her closer. The brush of her lips against his stubble startled her.

In the next moment she kissed his cheek quickly, then pulled back and met his gaze. A kiss to take away the pain? Or something so much more? "Better?"

"I think so. I… Uh…"

Viv swallowed. Something in his gaze grasped her, held her, but gently, and with a seeking innocence.

"Do you want to give me another?" He tapped his lips. "Here?"

Oh, did she! And yet….

Tilting her head, Viv did not move away from him, but she did not kiss him. Because her heartbeats thundered. Because his gaze still challenged her to make the next move. Because…

"I'm not sure I remember *how* to kiss a man." The words spilled off her tongue. The truth. A silly confession. "It's been so long."

"A person doesn't forget how to kiss."

"I think I may have."

"The one to my forehead and cheek felt right."

Yes, and logically if she kissed his mouth it would re-quire the same movement and bravery. Truthfully, she'd not forgotten the mechanics of such an intimate act. But she couldn't tell him that. And she really did want to feel his mouth…

Closing her eyes, Viv leaned in, taking her time. Nervous anticipation made her fingers shake and her breaths shallow.

Yes, you remember. You can do this.

Rez's scent subtly spiced the air. His soft breaths lured her. Should she tilt her head? Definitely keep her eyes closed. But part her lips slightly? Or keep a closed mouth? She couldn't remember the rules of a first kiss!

Viv, just…react.

Heartbeats pounding a path toward a cliff, she made contact. Soft, warm mouths. Breaths entwining. A gentle connection. She hadn't missed the target.

Stop thinking about what can go wrong.

Pressing more firmly, Viv moved into the kiss. Rez's hand slid up her back, reassuring, holding her there. His heat surprised her, while also melting her inhibitions.

Yes, this was okay.

It was more than okay. It felt different. New. Yet not so new. She'd done this a thousand times before. Muscle memory took over. Actually, it felt right. Nothing wrong with this. She was a woman kissing a man. A man who had asked her to kiss him.

Take some more if you dare.

So she did dare.

Stubble tickled her chin. A brisk brush of masculinity. Viv deepened the kiss, taking what she had craved for so long, but hadn't been aware she was missing. This, she needed. This abandon. This sharing of desire. This feeling of being wanted. Tasted. Touched.

He kissed her in return. No signs of pulling away. He wanted it as much as she did. Both his hands held her—

one at her back, the other clutching her hip. He did not demand. He accepted. And gave back.

The soft wet heat of their mingling tongues sent shivers down her spine and tingled across her skin. Butterflies swirled in her core. She slid a hand along his stubble-roughened jaw and threaded her fingers into his soft, dark hair. Holding him. Telling him what she wanted with her mouth. Taking whatever he would give her.

And when she felt him pull away, his gemstone blue eyes searched hers. A smile quirked his mouth. And this time he kissed her. She slid a leg along his hip and sat on his lap. He bracketed her head with his strong, powerful hands. Kissing her deeply, lingering, tasting her. Finding her.

He moaned. A deep, throaty resonance that vibrated in her core.

And then something changed.

Viv sat back, tugging in her lip with a tooth. The sound of his pleasure had inexplicably slammed on the brake. She touched her mouth. A tiny "Oh!" escaped. And then… "I…uh…"

She stood and pressed her hands over her pounding heart. The hard outline of the moonstone and her nipple rubbed her palm. The kiss had been okay. It had to be. Right?

And yet… Guilt rose. What had she just done? She had sat on the man's lap! And he wasn't even her husband!

"I need to be away… Right now. Because…uh…" She fumbled to explain her conflicting thoughts. And then gave up.

Viv rushed out of the kitchen, aiming for the quiet room in which she was being allowed to stay. Closing the door behind her, she ran to the bed and slumped down on the floor before it, her back hitting the mattress and wood frame. Catching her head in her hands, she tried to fend off tears, but it was too late.

She swore softly. Closed her eyes and shook her head.
What are you doing, Viv?
Maybe she wasn't as ready to dive in as she'd thought.

Rez tilted back his head and closed his eyes. The taste of
Viviane lingered in his mouth. Wine and quiche. And the
sexy surprise of her settling onto his lap and forgetting
herself in that incredible kiss. She had not forgotten how
to do it, that was for sure. And, holding her in his arms, he
had felt the pain slip away. So had the grief.

In that moment he'd shared intimacy with Viv, he'd not
thought about Colette. And he hadn't been struck by lightning or been wailed at by a disgruntled spirit.

It was all right to move onward, to invite a new woman
into his life. It would never be easy. He would always bear
the guilt. And he could relate to that look Viv had given
him when she'd pulled away. That moment of uncertainty.
Of wondering if it was truly right to move forward. Begin
again.

He didn't fault her for running away. And he wouldn't
chase after her. He couldn't.

When would it get easier? He wanted to be comfortable
kissing a woman again, touching her body, having sex. He
needed that contact. Craved it. And he desired Viv. But he
didn't want to scare her away or tread on any tender threads
that still tethered her to her husband. Because he could relate to that emotional bondage.

The only way this could work— Well, he hadn't a clue.
But he didn't want to give up. Not this time. Something
about Viv made him want to try.

But was it possible right now, with his life the way it
was? He had enough to contend with, dodging Jean-Louis's
demands he see a psychiatrist.

Viv was a life buoy that he wanted to grasp, but it felt
as if the tides were pushing him further away from safety.

CHAPTER SIX

THE NEXT MORNING Viv did not head for the kitchen, where she heard Rez brewing coffee. After last night's kiss, she wasn't sure where she stood with him. And first thing in the morning was not her best time for confrontations.

So she veered toward the conservatory and took a few more photos. She forwarded those to Harley, her "Mistress of Marketing."

Harley had given herself that title. They'd been friends for a decade, and she was a master of social media, creating and maintaining websites, and pinpointing marketing angles. Viv was only one of her many clients. At the moment she lived in Viv's apartment. After breaking up with a boyfriend, Harley had had to move fast, and the timing had worked perfectly for her to take up the rent on Viv's place.

After a sign-off to Harley, Viv then climbed up the ladder, garden clippers hooked at her utility belt, to begin the heavy pruning. It was all she could do with the short rein Rez had given her regarding work. It would take a few days if she took her time and was careful.

She'd fallen asleep last night after a long shower. Her dramatic escape following The Kiss had been just that. Drama. She was over it now. Mostly. Pulled in two directions, her heart was not so much having a difficult time with the introduction of a love interest, but rather taking its time adjusting. *Was* Rez a love interest? Or had it merely been flirtation? A moment when they'd both dropped their guard?

She didn't know how to label it. Nor how to label that moment of panic when she'd realized she was sitting on a man's lap.

It had been nearly thirty years since she had kissed a man who was not her husband. And even before marrying, when she'd dated in high school, she'd had all of two boyfriends. Both of them short-term. So her kissing skills, while exercised and honed, had not been practiced on a variety of subjects. As well, those flirtation skills she might have once been proud of had not been utilized in any serious manner lately.

Last night's dive into the heady waters of pleasure had been delicious. Rez's mouth… She sighed to recall their kiss. And his hands moving over her body… So strong and holding her with such surety. She'd climbed onto his lap! No, she wasn't brazen. She'd just got lost in the moment, taking what she'd wanted.

Had he tugged open her shirt and glided his hand over her breasts she would have let it happen. Or would she? Who knew? She'd fled before it could go any further.

If he had been Brian she would have pushed him down and torn off his shirt. Because she'd been comfortable with her husband.

She wanted to do the same to Rez. She wanted…

What *did* she want to happen with Rez? Wild sex? Sure! But a relationship? Was she ready for all that *being a couple* entailed? What if something happened to him? She couldn't go through losing another man. Grief was not easy. And, much as she felt she had moved beyond it, she knew her heart was still fragile. Was it worth the risk of starting something with Rez when she couldn't know what that would bring?

"I'm not sure," she muttered aloud as she dropped a

heavy leaf to the floor below. "Maybe I just need to let it happen. Right?"

Right. She was an adult. She could kiss a man if she wanted to. She could have sex with a man if she wanted to. Well, not on a first date. But she didn't need approval or permission from anyone. Not even her dead husband.

But she did need permission from herself.

"You have it," she told herself.

Now to really believe it.

It was six-thirty when Viv set aside the pruning shears for the day. The monstera had been removed from the ceiling and the wall. It had attached its aerial roots to the iron support frame, wedging itself between glass and metal. This species of plant was hardy, and determined, sometimes even attaching itself to smooth indoor walls to climb. Had it been cared for monthly it never would have grown of control. A small crack in one glass pane would have to be restored by a glazier, but there had been no damage to the metal frame.

Stepping back from the piles of cuttings she'd sorted, for disposal or repotting, she noticed her stomach growl. She hadn't even realized how hungry she was until now.

I need to head out for groceries.

Stopping in her room, she combed her shoulder-length hair and touched up her blush, then switched her tee shirt for a floral blouse. Back out in the foyer she met Rez, who was walking down the staircase. She hadn't realized he was home.

When he neared the bottom step he stumbled, and his palm slapped the newel post for support. Viv rushed over to him.

He thrust up a placating hand. "I missed the step," he said. "Wasn't paying attention."

"Oh." She ran her fingers up the back of her neck. The steps were wide, marble, and sturdy. Seemed pretty safe.

And easily walkable. Hard to really miss a step because you weren't paying attention.

"I was distracted by a beautiful woman," he suddenly added.

"Oh?" Viv glanced around. "Where?"

She saw Rez's jaw fall open.

"Me?" Taking delight in her innocent ruse, she said, "I'd hate to be the reason for sending you head over heels."

"Really? Isn't that supposed to be a good thing?"

The subtle flirtation burned at the base of her neck.

"That it is," she said. "I was going out to find something for supper. Are you hungry?"

"I am, and we have the same goal. We can walk together."

"I'd like that. If you feel up for walking?"

"I am perfectly capable."

He gestured toward the door, where the coat rack held his suit jacket—and something she'd not noticed before. A cane.

"If you don't mind walking alongside a man with his cane?"

"If it helps you stay steady, I don't mind at all."

She followed him out the door and onto the sidewalk that led down the street to the smaller grocery and shops.

Noticing Rez glance around as if he were being watched, she said, "It's kind of sexy, actually. Your cane."

He chuckled. "You don't need to say that, Viv. I'm not an old man. This cane feels wrong. But I do need it."

"Of course you're not an old man. Nor am I an old woman."

"Far from it."

That statement was issued with a husky tone that swept her skin into a sensual awareness. "Then let's both agree not to worry about what others think. We are young, sexy, and—"

Rez glanced at her. "Did you call me sexy?"

"I did."

He looked ahead, but she caught the grin curling his mouth. "I'll take it."

Offering his free arm to hook with Viv's, he walked slowly. The cobbled street was punctuated with bollards at each end so no cars could drive it. The shops were old, cozy, and their displays invited browsing. But while Rez set the pace with a slow perusal of the shop windows, a needy impatience rose in Viv. She couldn't let things remain as they were.

"So," she said. "About last night."

How to tell him she was sorry about running off? But not sorry for kissing him. But in that moment she'd had to dash. Her crazy heart had reacted. A heart she'd thought had healed following her husband's death apparently still had a few cracks in it.

"I felt the same way." Rez turned his back to a display of chocolate bonbons. "About the kiss," he said.

"Yes, but—" Just what was *the same* to him?

"It was awesome."

"It was," she quickly said.

Whew! He hadn't felt she'd been awkward. Score one for the out-of-practice kisser.

"But you rushing off like that…"

Oh, no, here it comes.

"You needed to do that," he said. "And, honestly, I needed that distance myself. *Oui?*"

"*Oui.* It wasn't because I didn't like the kiss, or us, or—"

"I know," he said. "No need to explain. Or apologize. And, so you know, I'd like to kiss you again. Whenever you want it to happen."

"Oh. Well."

Yes! Every nerve ending in Viv's body suddenly glittered. Her inner bouncy teenager surfaced.

"I feel the same. I…uh… Well, it's my silly heart."

"Your heart is silly?"

"It is when I think I've come to terms with something but it decides I have not. This is new to me, Rez. I mean, being intimate with someone who isn't—"

She didn't want to bring her husband into this conversation. She didn't need Brian's memory as a shield. Did she?

"Same," Rez said. He held out his hand to her. "Let's see what happens."

Viv put her hand in his. The invitation felt immense and open to so much. "I'm all in."

CHAPTER SEVEN

REZ SUGGESTED THEY eat in a restaurant so Viviane wouldn't have to cook. Not that she *had* to cook, he quickly added.

"I love to cook. But I won't refuse a dinner date." She squeezed his hand. "Can we call this a date? It would be my first in decades. What about you? Have you dated since—well...?"

He sensed she was nervous. He felt those fluttery wings in his gut as well. One thing he'd learned since his wife's passing: people never knew how to speak about his loss. Awkward questions abounded. And that sad look of forced concern was growing tired. Yet he was comfortable with Viv, because she understood and had probably experienced much the same.

"I have tried to date," he said as they walked. "Twice, actually. Never made it to that first kiss, though. Didn't feel right to me."

"Yes, it's weird. I mean, our actual kiss wasn't weird. It's the getting close to a new person part of it that's sort of...you know...weird."

"Exactly. And you are not weird."

"Just strange?"

He laughed. "A little. So... It's a date."

Her cheeks pinkened. Simplicity and ease, this woman. Completely the opposite of Colette, who had been high maintenance. Maintenance he had not minded.

Rez had lavished his wife with clothing, shoes, jewels—anything she'd wanted. He couldn't imagine Viv being comfortable in a crystal-laden ball gown or walking in stilettos. The dark pants and slightly rumpled blouse suited her. And he wouldn't tell her about the dirt smudge on her knee.

He veered them toward his favorite restaurant, a four-star establishment that required reservations months in advance. He'd yet to need one. The owner's wife had an account with Le Beau and used it often.

He gestured toward the front door, where the liveried hostess checked her iPad and spoke to guests, and as he did so he felt Viv's resistance in her tug at their clasped hands.

"What is it?"

"This place looks a little too fancy for how I'm dressed," she said. "I don't know…"

"You look lovely. They don't judge attire here, only taste."

"But it looks busy."

"I'm sure it is. Come along, *ma chérie*. You've been walking every morning, talking to ducks, taking in Paris from the ground level. Now I want you to see my city from a different perspective."

With a nervous tug to her lower lip with her teeth—she did that often, and it gave him shivers…the good kind—she nodded and allowed him to lead her onward.

The hostess, with impeccable make-up and sleek black hair, smiled as Rez approached. "Monsieur Ricard! Your usual table?"

"Oui, merci."

She spun around the podium and smiled warmly at Viv, which Rez appreciated. Viv noticeably relaxed as she followed the hostess. Rez took up behind her, his cane still supporting his steps. That Viv hadn't blinked at his using it made it a little less humiliating.

Traversing the curling steel staircase upward, they landed in the roof dining area. Only three tables up here. Hundreds of potted plants framed the rooftop, forming a thick hedge but not blocking the view of the city. Sparkling fairy lights were strung across the latticed canopy. And a soft tango sounded through speakers hidden within the foliage.

"Champagne?" the hostess asked as she showed them to the farthest table, which was canopied by climbing greenery.

"Let's start with wine," he said. "Whatever the sommelier recommends."

The hostess left them. Viviane ran her fingers across a frothy plant that Rez thought might be a fern, but really he had no clue. Sounds of marvel gasped from her lips as she found her way to the stone balustrade at the corner of the roof. On tiptoes, she took in the view, panning the cityscape.

"Amazing, isn't it?" Rez walked up behind her.

"This is incredible. There's the Eiffel Tower. And I can see the Ferris wheel in the Tuileries. And over there is the Arc du Triomphe! Wow. When you said you wanted to give me a different perspective of the city you weren't kidding. And..." she turned and took in the rooftop "...we're the only ones up here. Just how rich do you have to be to be able to sashay in like we did?"

"Very." He pulled out a chair for her before the table. "I hope you don't mind a surprise meal. It's chef's choice when you're seated up here. I've never been disappointed."

The sommelier arrived with wine. They exchanged a quick conversation in French about the engagement ring Rez had designed for his son's fiancée. And then, after he'd tasted the Bordeaux and assured the man it was plush and darkly sweet, they were again left alone.

Viv sipped the wine. Her eyes brightened. "This is… I don't even have words for this wine. It tastes like…plums?"

"It's from near the Gironde estuary. Their terroir is impeccable. It's a bit sweet, but smooth."

"I love sweet wine. Well, I just love wine. But not too much. I'm not a lush."

With a nervous laugh, she looked at the lights strung across the rooftop. Rez noticed the freckles dancing across her nose and cheeks. More proof she was indeed a garden nymph.

"It's like a fantasy world up here," she said.

"I'm glad you like it. I haven't been here in years. I'm surprised they even remember me."

"I suspect the owner of Le Beau is difficult to forget. And you are handsome. Remarkable."

"Says the prettiest woman in the place."

Her laughter was forced, but he suspected the blush was not. He really did enjoy her blushes.

"I'll take that. It's been a while since I've felt pretty."

"Why?" He leaned forward. "You are a natural beauty. I imagine you tumble from bed and you're ready to go."

She shrugged. "You don't want to hear my beauty routine. But it's nice to get a compliment. To tell you the truth…" She toyed with the silverware, her mood growing more solemn. "I've thought about such things since my husband's death. After being married for so long, we often forget to tell our loved one simple things, like *You are handsome* or *You make me happy.* Am I right?"

He nodded. He didn't want the conversation to turn to their lost loves. He wasn't sure he could talk about Colette so casually with another woman. Yet. But she was right. He'd complimented Colette often. Yet had she ever called him handsome, as Viv just had? Made him feel…worthy? That was an odd thing to realize. His bank account proved his worth was billions. His reputation was impeccable. But to be admired by someone like Viv, who seemed so genuine and open, superseded that material status.

"I'm sorry. I forget that not everyone is on the same acceptance level with their grief as I am. We don't have to talk about our spouses," she offered. "I'm still learning how to be this thing called 'widow.'" She made a face, nose scrunched. "Being referred to as a widow feels so dismissive. And it's always accompanied by a sad moue. Yes, I lost my husband. But you know…life goes on. I didn't crumble and you don't have to treat me with kid gloves."

"Kid gloves?"

"It's a way of saying to take excessive care or concern with someone. I'm sure you must have gotten the same treatment."

"I did, and still do. But do you have children? How have they managed the loss?"

"We never had kids. Both of us loved them, but not so much that we wanted to grow our family. Brian and I enjoyed working together and that was what worked best for us. How is your son with his mom's absence?"

"It is difficult for Jean-Louis. He and his mother were close. He…"

It had been Jean-Louis who had stepped in for Rez when he'd been recuperating in the hospital after the accident. His son had handled the reins of Le Beau without issues. At a time when he should have focused on his grief.

"My son has lost a lot. Sometimes I forget that I'm not the only one affected by my wife's death. I agree with you. We've survived a painful experience and we're still here. On to the next adventure?"

"You don't sound so sure about that."

She'd guessed exactly right. There were days when he was ready to dash forward and begin a whole new chapter. Other days he wanted to reread his favorite parts and cling to those memories. And why hadn't he talked to Jean-Louis about his grief? Le Beau was their common interest; they'd never been close beyond that.

But he couldn't pull the mopey act now. Because Viviane intrigued him. And whatever was happening between the two of them… He wanted it to happen.

"What's more sure than sitting across the table from a beautiful woman on a date?"

She beamed at him. "If it is an official date, that means I'll get another kiss out of the deal."

"Of course you will."

But just as he considered leaning over to kiss her, the waiter arrived with their first course. And a new wine.

"How do you like the red?" Rez asked, after Viviane had tried it.

"It's quite special. You do love your wine. Is that a French thing?"

"Could be. And I own a vineyard."

"Wow. Where is it?"

"In the Rhône Valley. It's southeast of Paris. If you'd like a tour, I'd be happy to take you there."

"Really? I would like that. I usually take the weekends off. Unless you want me to work. You are the boss."

"That I am," he said, and the second course was served.

After cheese, salads, a tiny concoction of lamb and what had been described as an onion mousse, the dessert plate was delivered. Four small *bonbons* gleamed under the fairy lights. Viv cut one in half on her plate and cooed at the layered filling.

She was not self-aware, he thought, and would laugh without a care. And those freckles highlighted by the golden glow… They fascinated him. He must make a freckle count on her soon. She was so easy to be with. Rez wanted to learn all he could about her.

"What was the last good book you read?" he asked.

"Really? You want to know what I read?"

"Of course. I read all the time. I prefer adventure fantasy stuff, like Jim Butcher."

Viv almost choked on her bite of dessert. "Seriously? You like Butcher? I love the Harry Dresden series. Bob is my favorite."

"A talking skull? You have to love that."

Viv sighed. "Wow. You just got infinitely sexier."

Rez quirked a brow. "I thought I was already sexy?"

"Oh, yes. But you got more sexy." She dramatically fanned her face. "Whew! Give me the lift of a brow any day and I'm happy."

Rez laughed. "If that's all you want, then you're easy."

"Oh, men!" Viv declared dramatically. "I'm never easy. My material wants are few, but my emotional wants are great."

"Let me guess. Companionship, trust, and love?"

"I'm impressed. You got it on the first try."

"I think everyone wants those things, Viv."

"Especially people who have loved and lost?"

Rez slid his hand across the table to touch hers. Because he couldn't *not* make such a move. She compelled him.

"Even us," Rez said. "We're not different from anyone else walking the streets, are we?"

"Most definitely not. Though I will confess that knowledge struck me hard a few months after Brian died."

"How so?"

"I was in a store one day, randomly wandering the aisles. I'd just spent five minutes in the car, bawling over an AC/DC song. That was his favorite band. I only heard that song at specific times following his death. It was him speaking to me—I know it."

"I can understand that." He'd not had any signs from Colette—not that he had noticed—but he could relate to specific things dredging up memories. Like roses…

"Anyway, I wiped the tears away and went inside to

find some cereal and fruit. I saw a child crying, and his mother muttered to me that he'd lost his dog earlier that morning. I know now that it doesn't matter if you've lost a dog, a friend, or a spouse of decades. You can't know what the person standing in line next to you is going through. If they're happy. If they've lost someone. Grief is universal. We have to learn to move with it. Take it as life gives it to you. And for some reason that allowed me to rise up from the tearful days and move onward."

"No more tears at all?"

"Oh, dear… I cry at everything. Especially movies. But I don't cry when I hear AC/DC now, because I take a moment to remember. And those memories make me happy."

Rez clasped his hands before his face, blowing out a breath. He wished his memories were the same. But the accident had changed his memory. Made it difficult to keep hold of some things. Obliterated other memories. He sensed some memories about Colette had been stolen, because when he thought about their marriage, their life together, there were spaces—blocks he couldn't recall. Had they been a happy couple? Most of the time… Colette had been a model. He had been the husband standing in her shadow, little bothered by the shade. But there had been times he'd wondered if he was making her happy. On an emotional level.

Well, it didn't matter anymore, did it?

"You have memories?" she asked.

"I do. And I don't. The accident knocked my brain hard. It's called traumatic brain injury. I have trouble with short-term stuff, like appointments and what I went into the kitchen to look for. But, as well, I can't remember anything about the night of the accident. Only a feeling of terror as the car swerved off the road. And then I woke in the hospital and was told my wife was dead."

Viviane threaded her fingers through his. "I can't imagine losing a spouse in an instant like that. At the very least I had three years to say goodbye as Brian struggled with cancer. You woke to a life without your wife. I'm sorry."

"Thank you," he whispered. "I…don't talk about this with anyone."

"I don't want to intrude on your grief," she said.

"You're not. Being with you…another soul who has been through what I have…makes it easier. I won't make the mistake of calling you easy again, but you are…comfortable to be around, Viv."

And then he found his moment. The tableware might glisten like gold in the city lights, but it was Viv's face that truly blossomed in this golden moment.

"Six," he said.

"What?"

"Six freckles on that cheek. And on the other…" He bowed his head to make a count. "Six. If there are six on your nose…"

"No one has ever done a freckle-count on me before. I warn you, I have some on my shoulders. A lot."

"Six on your nose," he announced. "And I look forward to exploring your shoulders."

She gave his hand a squeeze. "Is it all right if we sit here for a bit?"

The city breathed around them. The night air was perfumed with flowers, softening Rez's anxiety over his missing memories. And Viv's presence coaxed him away from dire thoughts. She was so fascinating in her quirky manner, and a little strange. Talking to cats and crystals…? He smirked.

"What?"

"I was just wondering what sort of stone you have in your bra this evening."

Viv laughed. "It's the moonstone."

"Can I see it?"

She looked to each side. No people on the roof besides them. She tucked her finger under her neckline and mined the stone from her bra. It flashed under the hanging lights. She handed it to him.

"It's warm."

"It was just tucked against the girls."

He snickered. He wouldn't mind being tucked in the same spot.

He held up the stone and studied the flash. "That's called chatoyancy, the flash."

"Really? Cool. I love the piece. I've been carrying it with me every day since I've been in Paris."

"Doesn't it ever…fall out?"

"Sometimes I do forget I've tucked a crystal in there, and when I get undressed at night it'll fall to the floor. Broke a perfectly good fluorite once."

"You know, there is an easier way to keep a precious stone close. Can I set this for you?"

"Oh. Well, I'd love that, but I'm sure I can't afford your work."

"Nonsense." Rez shook the stone on his palm. "Consider it part of the payment for your work. A bonus. *Oui?*"

She nodded.

He tucked the moonstone in a pocket. "Let's walk."

CHAPTER EIGHT

REZ SCROLLED TO Coral's number in his phone. His finger hovered over "call." His brows furrowed. The cup of morning coffee sitting on the kitchen counter steamed near his hip. From the hallway, he heard footsteps approaching the kitchen.

Quickly, he tried to summon one reason why he needed to expel Viviane from his home. While the usual argument was obvious, it didn't rise as necessarily urgent. Her work in the garden had saved him from a disaster. The whole ceiling could have been pulled down from the weight of the overgrown foliage. A touch-up on the conservatory would also increase the sale price on the mansion.

And, if he was honest, he enjoyed Viviane's company. And counting her freckles. And kissing her. He reached into his trouser pocket and pulled out the moonstone cabochon. Nestled against her breasts all day? What a place to be.

"Good morning. Or is that *bonjour*?"

She wandered into the bright sunlight. Hair gathered into a messy chignon and leather garden gloves on, she clasped her hands before her and waited for him to reply.

Rez was still lost in the sparkle of her eyes. The utter freshness of her standing next to him. It was as if she carried in new air along with her. He inhaled, gathering as much of her as he could. Green, vibrant, airy.

"Rez?"

"*Bonjour?* You've got it correct," he said. "Though I think the spunkier *salut* might fit you as well."

"You think I'm spunky?"

"You project a certain bouncy appeal."

"I can do bouncy." She waggled her shoulders in example.

Rez slid a finger over the home screen, then tucked the phone inside his suit pocket. Coral could wait.

"There's coffee."

"I can smell that. How's the leg feeling this morning?"

"Tight, but Henri is waiting outside for me. I see you've already dug into the garden?"

She splayed a gloved hand. "Just bagging up the last of the debris. According to a schedule I found in the supply room, garbage pick-up is this afternoon, so I want to get that out."

"I can help you." He'd seen five or six large paper bags filled with foliage nestled by the back door. "Before I leave."

"Are you sure?" She slid a glance down to his leg.

Rez straightened, taking offense at the unspoken cut. It was emasculating enough having to use the cane on occasion. "I'm not feeble."

"I know you're not."

But did she?

"Let's do it now so Henri isn't kept too long."

He headed for the refuse bags. When the final bag had been hauled out, Rez leaned against the limestone wall that backed up his property. Viv had carried out two bags to his four.

"I appreciate the help," she said, swiping aside a strand of hair from her face. "Gardening is a lot of heavy lifting. I can manage this particular job on my own, but I'll have to hire local muscle on future jobs. You available?"

Rez chuckled. "If it's in Paris, sure."

He reached to wipe a dirt smudge from her forehead. It

was stubborn. He licked his thumb, but when he got close to her face she dodged.

"Is that a mother thing?" she asked.

He looked at his thumb. "I suppose... Sorry."

"It's okay." She laughed, and crossed her eyes in an attempt to look up at her forehead.

Mon Dieu, did he love her laughter.

When she licked her own thumb and tried to swipe at the smudge, he clasped her wrist to direct her to the right spot. That sheen of dirt was stubborn; he decided he'd let her get it all later. But he didn't drop her hand.

"Is it gone?" she asked.

"Most of it. I like you rumpled."

"You...*like* me?"

He made show of wobbling his head, as if giving it some thought, but really he could have answered much faster. "I've decided I enjoy having some 'strange' in my life. You've grown on me—much like that crazy plant you took down in the conservatory."

"That plant almost cost you a big repair bill."

"The money doesn't matter."

"I suppose not."

The next seconds were silent as their gazes spoke more loudly than words. Hope and kindness beamed in Viviane's green eyes. He wondered if she could see the need to trust in his. He had been hurt emotionally, but in ways he still struggled to pinpoint.

"I suppose Henri is wondering what's taking you so long," she prompted.

He'd forgotten about his waiting driver. And about the fact that he did have a job which required him to leave this house, this woman.

This woman. She had altered his perspective in ways he wasn't even aware of. He just knew he liked what Viviane did to him.

He nodded, but still he held her hand. "Now that you've finished that project, you may go ahead with the refurbishment in the rest of the garden. With the exception of the roses on the north side."

Her jaw dropped open.

"I still can't make contact with Coral," he lied. "And now that I've seen what you can do, I know sprucing up the conservatory will be worthwhile."

"Oh, I can do that! Thank you, Rez—er... Monsieur Ricard."

Not liking being addressed by her that way, Rez reacted. He bent to kiss her. Quickly. But their lips connected as if designed for one another. They knew their place, marked it, and then parted.

"It's Rez," he said, and pressed his forehead to hers. "I think we've moved beyond formalities."

"Rez. But...uh...you *are* officially my employer. Do the French always kiss the hired help?"

"Not always." Rez stood back and adjusted his tie. He winked at her and decided that a parting smile was all she required as explanation for that.

"If you tell me when you'll be home," she called as he strolled away, "I'll have a meal ready."

"Early," he decided, even as his brain told him that was very un-Rez-like. "Five."

"I'll see you then!"

As he headed toward the foyer an irrepressible smile curled his mouth. He even ignored the cane hanging on the coat rack as he exited the mansion.

Viviane lay on the tiled conservatory floor. She had won over the staunch owner! In more ways than one. What an interesting way of advancing her employment. Smooching the owner. She wondered what he would do if she slept with him?

"Never say never," she said with a smile.

The room's humidity was rising. She'd adjusted the temperature controls that morning. Now she could look to salvaging the entire garden. There was much to do, according to the plan she'd detailed in her notebook. Today she would work on the lower vegetation. It all needed trimming and new mulch around the roots. A soft moss base would be perfect. As for those ratty white wicker chairs set in the back circle of the room…

They would go. And in their place? Something elegant, but cozy. A place where a person could relax and forget the world. Stretch out, curl up with a fantasy book.

She pushed her fingers through her hair, closing her eyes to the bright sunlight that beamed through the glass roof. Lying here, in a multi-million-dollar mansion—in Paris— was beyond fantasy. It was incredible. An amazing gift. And she did not take it lightly. Top it off with a handsome millionaire who had actually showed interest in her, and who was an incredible kisser, and she might be walking in a dream. Was she sleeping?

She snapped a finger against her temple. *Ouch.* This was not a dream.

Despite the fact that she had come to terms with being single, and now actually enjoyed it, she did crave companionship, sharing conversation… The connection. Heck, touching another human body….

Yes, she wanted to have sex with Rez. Was she ready to make that dive? She had been married for twenty-five years. Including college boyfriends, she'd only ever had three sexual partners. And one had been a constant for two and a half decades. Could she really open herself to intimacy with a new man?

"Yes," she whispered aloud.

But it felt daunting. When they were married, a person got used to routine. It hadn't been a big thing to undress before her husband, to walk around in holey underwear, to be seen tugging her bra out from her shirtsleeve after a long day at work. Heck, even to fart in his presence. And to admit to all the things that should never be spoken out loud.

Rez was… Well, he was the homecoming king who made her feel giddy and blush whenever he looked her way. And she knew they were not hot flashes. How to go beyond kisses with him? Did *he* want that? She'd not forgotten how to have sex—had she? Maybe. No! It was a natural thing. Just like kissing. New partners always provoked nervousness and a lack of confidence. Right?

Viv blew out a breath. She was overthinking this. If sex was on the table, she'd go with it. But she sensed that until Rez completely trusted her they would never get past making out, as they had briefly following their meal in the restaurant last night. A kiss goodnight once they'd walked inside the mansion. Oh, so lovely. But he still grieved his wife. And Viv didn't want to push him. He might grieve for Colette the rest of his life. Never incorporate that grief into his life in a manner which didn't prevent new relationships from blossoming.

The thought of Brian sometimes made Viv smile, sometimes cry. Some days she didn't think of him at all. Other days, seeing a perfectly round boxwood shrub could reduce her to tears. But she was coping. And she did not feel she was cheating on Brian with Rez. She had a right to move forward.

Rolling onto her stomach, she propped her chin on her fists and eyed the thorny rose bushes. This project could not be a success unless she was granted permission to prune them. If they had been his wife's favorites then he should *want* them tamed, able to grow and provide him with wonderful memories year after year. All Viv had to do was trim them way back and…

Ah, heck.

She finally got it.

Tonight's meal was a mix of charcuterie and cheeses, along with crispy baguettes and macarons. Viviane had gathered the spread during her afternoon walk. The wine was sweet, the cheese remarkable, and the man across the table from her was gorgeous. But she'd been troubled since figuring out those rose bushes earlier. And she'd never been adept at ignoring her curiosity.

With a long sip of wine to fortify her courage, Viv said, "I'm sorry, Rez. I finally understand about the roses. The whole garden. You think I'm destroying your wife's memory."

The man set down his baguette slice and rubbed his palms along his thighs. She thought the look he gave her said a lot. *Oh, you...the American woman who likes to constantly challenge me. Not giving me a moment to enjoy this meal?*

Ready to apologize for her apology, Viv lifted her chin—and then silenced that worry. They were adults. They could talk about the tough stuff. They had last night at the restaurant.

"It's not that you're destroying her memory," Rez said. "The garden is *my* memory."

"I get that. And the more I rearrange and trim in the garden the more I tramp on the things your wife cherished. I get it, Rez. And I'm so sorry I didn't make the connection sooner. If I touch those roses, I'm touching something only your wife touched. I'm changing them. And then your memory is changed."

He pushed back on his chair, head bowed. Viv could feel his anger—no, it wasn't that. It was...sorrow?

"I don't want to step on her memory," Viv said softly. "And I know you're tired of me arguing about this with you, but please hear me out."

Crossing his arms, he kept his head bowed. A partial agreement to listen. That was better than him storming out.

"Those roses were once beautiful. Perhaps they remind you of your wife's beauty. But they've gone wild and are in desperate need of pruning. I'm surprised they haven't died." She swallowed. Not the best word-choice, but she had to be honest. "They won't survive much longer. But if you'll allow me to trim them back—and I warn you, it would be extreme, leaving them as stubs for the rest of this growing season—then I promise the results will be stunning. And I don't wish to make any presumptions on behalf of..." she winced "...her..."

"Then don't," he said roughly.

"But, Rez, I think if your wife loved those roses she would be utterly torn to see them in the condition they are now. She would want them restored. Flourishing."

"You're right," he said, and stood abruptly, plucking the wine bottle from the table. "You shouldn't presume anything."

With that, he marched out of the kitchen.

Viv leaned over the table and caught her forehead in hand. She'd had to try...

CHAPTER NINE

THE NEXT EVENING, Henri pulled the limo up before the mansion. Sitting in the back, Rez felt his thoughts turn toward the woman in his conservatory.

Colette's conservatory.

His wife had been thrilled to find the mansion up for sale only months after they'd married. She'd attended a wild party there in her teens, and had told him about the garden in which she'd gotten high with her friends. Her desire to own that garden had been enough for him to gift the mansion to her as a belated wedding present.

Colette had spent the weekend there perhaps once a month during the early years of their marriage. Then, as her modeling career had fizzled in her late thirties, her stays had grown more frequent. Her time had been spent gardening and painting. She had asked Rez visit only with her invitation. It had been her private lair...an escape from the Parisian bustle.

He'd been fine with that request. Colette had been a particular woman; he'd catered to her needs. Besides, his design work had always kept him busy. There had been many days when he'd only seen his wife as he'd arrived home to kiss her goodnight. They'd grown distant in later years. Yes, he could have set his own work schedule and given Colette more of his time. But he had not. And the reason for it niggled at his faulty memory.

Had they fallen out of love?

He had to stop mulling over a woman he could never resurrect. He didn't need Colette back in his life. Cruel as the accident had been, he understood that death was final, and it happened every day—to so many. Yet Viv had been right about the reason why he'd not wanted her to touch the roses. She'd also been right that preserving them would have been what Colette most wanted.

Overall...? He was putting too much energy into fighting what wasn't a battle at all.

"*Merci*, Henri."

He got out of the limo and strolled up the walk to the house.

Time to be an adult.

Rez walked through the front door to find a green velvet sofa sitting in the foyer. On the couch sat a gorgeous woman in chinos and a tee shirt, one arm across the back of the settee, the other hand holding a goblet of wine. A wine bottle and another goblet sat on the floor by her feet.

"What is this?"

"Coral approved me purchasing new furniture for the garden. It was part of my contract. But I suppose I should have asked you... I'm sorry."

"Not to worry. I honor the contract you have with Coral. But why is it in the foyer and not in the conservatory?"

"The one delivery man who could speak a meager amount of English insisted they had not been paid to place the couch. Only to get it in the front door. I offered him more money and he tutted at me and said it was lunchtime." She swallowed a gulp of wine. Shrugged. "You could use some furniture out here, I suppose..."

Rez chuckled and sat next to her. He poured himself a glass, and then kissed her cheek. "You like to make lemon cake with lemons?"

"I think you're going for lemonade with that one."

Rez bounced on the cushions. "Comfy. Very big."

"And heavy," she said. "I can't even lift an end without worrying about hurting my back. I was going to call a furniture mover, but I've gone beyond my patience with the free translation app on my phone. And Harley, who can speak French, is incommunicado. Would you mind calling for me?"

"Those movers should have taken it into the garden. I will have words with them."

"I like that. Forceful. Manly." She gave his biceps a squeeze. "So...you're home early?"

"Yes, and I want to talk to you about last night."

"Oh?"

"I'm sorry. I shouldn't have walked out on our conversation like that."

"Apologies are not necessary. I understand. I've no right to tell you what your wife may or may not have approved."

"No, you don't. And I still wish the roses to remain untouched. For now. Let me sit on it a few more days and then we'll see if I change my mind."

She clasped his hand. "You can take all the time you need. I've enough work with the rest of the garden right now. And I promise I am taking great care with all of it."

"I know that you are." He turned to face her.

"So you're not mad at me?"

"I find it impossible to remain angry with the strange and beautiful nymph who lives in my garden."

Her eyebrow lifted. "Go on."

"I desire you, Viviane. And, while I don't feel like it's cheating on a dead woman, it's something new for me. I trust you. You understand what I'm going through. Impossible to believe that you can be here, right now, when I need someone like you the most."

"Do you believe in fate? Destiny? Soul mates?"

"Never given it much thought."

"Well, I have, and I've never believed in soul mates. I believe that people can love more than one person romantically in their lifetime. One person does not have to be your *one*."

"I'm with you on that."

Because he'd never felt Colette had been his soul mate— rather his wife, his lover. Friends, of course. However, there had been something about their relationship... It was so frustrating that he could not remember! The truth about him and Colette had been torn from his memory the night of the accident.

Viv stretched out a leg and tilted back her head. Her sleek body teased him. Gorgeous, relaxed, luscious in its simpleness.

He wasn't sure what he wanted to happen right now. Talking? Kissing? Sex? Still felt too soon for that. But not for touch and connection. Feeling Viv's body heat against his aroused him. He was so ready to kiss this woman.

"Eighteen freckles," he whispered as he moved to kiss the tip of her nose, then each of her cheeks. "You make me feel eighteen again, Viv."

She set down her goblet and then performed a slide of her leg along his hip and thigh that directed him to follow her. They landed horizontally on the spacious sofa. And his long-lost teenager knew exactly what to do.

"I haven't made out on a couch in forever," she said as he kissed along her jaw and down her neck. "Mmm... I like that."

Anything she liked he was eager to continue. Licking her soft skin, he devoured the vibrant greenness, the nymph's alluring perfume. The feel of her breasts under his palms made him rock-hard. The undulation of her body beneath his coaxed him in for a deeper kiss. He wanted to fall into her. Get lost.

And yet she gently broke the kiss and bracketed his face with her hands. "I'm not quite ready for…you know…"

"Do I know?"

"Sex…"

Rez snickered. "Are you asking me or telling me?"

"Telling *and* asking?"

He nodded. "I'm not ready, either. But I want you, Viv."

"You do?"

"I'm distracted by thoughts of you at work."

"I like being a distraction. Kiss me again. And whatever you do…don't move your hands."

His hands which were on her breasts? He did appreciate a woman who knew what she wanted.

The garden was coming along nicely. And that was amazing, considering she was doing it all by herself. With encouragement from Harley. Her social media was attracting followers. The Plant Whisperer logo Harley had created featured a vector image of a pair of pink pursed lips next to a plant. It was sexy and cute at the same time. Harley had also reported a sudden uptick in her book sales. So word was getting out.

The moving team had arrived first thing this morning, and now the green velvet sofa sat at the back of the conservatory in the round gathering area. Oh, that sofa… Viv could not think of it as anything but the make-out sofa now. What a way to break in new furniture!

Unable to find a tarp or any plastic to protect it from dirt, she had tossed the extra blanket she'd found in her closet over it. It would serve as protection until she was done with the dirt-flinging process.

Now, sitting on the floor before the sofa, she worked on her business plan over a light lunch of a ham and goat cheese croissant and the Orangina she had come to love, despite its sugar content.

She could afford an assistant—probably hired hourly at each location she worked at rather than salaried, because then she'd have to pay travel expenses—and still bring in a profit. The more jobs she completed, the better her resume would look and the more she could charge. Then there was the issue of supplies. She'd had to purchase a set of clippers, and would always need pots, dirt, wiring, mulch, et cetera. The supply room here had three-quarters of the things she required, but future jobs might not have anything.

The landscaping business she and Brian had built together had been considered elite, and they'd serviced million-dollar homes in the Minneapolis suburbs. Together, they had garnered awards and honors for their work. Now it was simply a matter of rebuilding a client base. In Europe. It would be a lot of hard work and would rely on word of mouth. And excellent marketing. She loved a challenge.

Viv set aside the business plan and leaned back on her palms. The tessellated tile floor in the conservatory featured indigo, moss, and cream colors, with an iridescent tile fitted in here and there to provide a startling gleam. She went and sat beneath a fern she'd trimmed to half its original width and height. It was still almost four feet tall, and though it had been less than a week since its trim it had already straightened and unfurled.

Straight and unfurled… That was how she felt when she was with Rez. Her shoulders lifted, her neck straightened—everything inside her that had curled and withered following Brian's death began to reach out, open, and seek. It was an empowering feeling.

When taking this offer in Paris she'd counted on a path to a new job. But romance…?

"The sun on your face makes you beam like a golden idol."

Startled by Rez's voice, Viv looked up. Clad in what she could only guess was a designer business suit worth a few mortgage payments, he also wore a black shirt and tie beneath the deep blue coat, which granted him a stylish, elegant figure. He exuded calm confidence. And so much sex appeal.

"You're home early," she said.

Had that sounded like a spouse complaining? Old habits and all that jazz?

"I've a quick trip to Versailles this afternoon. Henri picks me up in ten minutes."

"How can a trip to Versailles ever be quick? That place is amazing."

"So you've been there?"

"Not yet. I've only seen photos of it in books. But I hope to work it in as a weekend trip."

"If I didn't have this meeting I'd take you along. Perhaps soon, though?"

"I'd like that. So, what sort of business does a jeweler have at Versailles?"

"Le Beau will be part of a Christmas exhibit that will feature the royal jewels and other Parisian designers. I want to create a new piece, so a consultation with the exhibit planners is necessary. It'll be donated for a charitable cause."

"That's generous. You really love designing jewelry," she said, knowing it was true.

"It is a passion."

"Did you ever design anything for your wife?"

"Many pieces. She favored black diamonds." He smiled as he shoved his hands in his front pockets. "I must admit, until I met you, I would dodge any questions or conversations regarding my wife. But you make it seem not so dreadful to summon her memory."

"I'll take that as a good thing. Memory can be a wondrous way to heal the soul. So you'll be home late?"

Again, did she sound like a spouse?

Watch it, Viv, you're not the man's keeper. Or his wife.
But did she want to be?
Nah. Not...yet.

"After dinner, for sure. Please don't wait up for me."

"I won't. I intend to walk this evening. Take in the city lights."

"Be sure to visit the Fifth. It's an interesting assortment of entertainment at night. There's tango dancing down by the river."

"Really? I prefer slow dances. I want to peek into Notre Dame as well. See how the reconstruction looks and if they're holding services."

"Sounds like you have the evening planned. I...uh... I have a question for you."

"Shoot."

"Would you be interested in going to a lavish party with me this Saturday?"

That was three days away. She had nothing to wear. And she could imagine how lavish it would be, especially knowing the set that Rez ran with.

"Hmm..."

"Don't refuse. Please. It's Le Beau's one-hundredth anniversary celebration. Jean-Louis has planned the entire thing. It'll be my chance to show him and all our clients that I am still capable and not a fumbling idiot who needs to be put out to pasture."

"Well, you don't need me to prove that."

"But I want you at my side."

If it was possible to unfurl even more, Viviane did so. But could she pull it off? Standing on the arm of a millionaire and convincing others that he considered her as a potential date?

"I'll take your silence as agreement," he teased.

"Rez, it's not that I don't love spending time with you.

But I'm not sure I can do the fancy ball thing. I've only packed work clothes, and—"

"Oh, I'm taking you shopping. That's part of the date."

"It is?" She wrinkled a brow.

"Yes. A fancy gown is necessary. Shoes… And if you want your hair and make-up done I'll make it happen. Let me treat you."

"A gown, eh? *And* a date for the ball?"

"I'm not sure it's a ball. More of a standing around and schmoozing while we look at pretty jewels event. A *soirée*."

"But it is a celebration of your company. You must be very proud."

"I am." Rez's phone buzzed in his pocket. "That's Henri."

He bowed to kiss her forehead and Viv reached up to pull him down for a better kiss.

"Yes, I'll be your date."

CHAPTER TEN

COLETTE HAD NEVER invited Rez along on her frequent and hours-long excursions to the high-end stores dotting the Rue de Rivoli and the Champs-élysées. And, frankly, following a woman from store to store, sitting on the sidelines while she tried on clothes, shoes, intimates, whatever, did not make his list of top ways to spend an afternoon.

On the other hand, he did enjoy taking a woman shopping for jewelry. *His* jewelry. It was all about designing the perfect piece for a woman.

He hadn't the leisure to design anything for Viv to wear this weekend—the moonstone she'd trusted him with wasn't set—but he did want to see her in some sparkles for the event. He wouldn't know what to put on her until he'd seen what she'd be wearing.

While he guessed she wouldn't be able to afford anything they would be looking at today, it pleased him to be able to treat her. Not because he wanted to woo her with expensive gifts. She wasn't a woman impressed by material things. No, he simply wanted to see her happy. Smiling. And, of course, wearing something appropriate for an event that would be filled with old money, celebrities, and a few royals.

One shop he knew that carried suitable gowns sat on the Avenue Montaigne, which Colette had frequented. He knew that because he'd gotten the bills. When he walked into the shop with Viv on his arm he got a raised eyebrow from the woman behind the counter. He suspected she knew who he was, and most certainly had known his wife.

"Monsieur Ricard."

The clerk smiled politely, and then inquired as to what he needed. Stepping back and allowing Viv to explain what she liked, including colors and styles, Rez was directed to the waiting area in a private salon.

With a tumbler of surprisingly smooth whiskey in hand, and a silver tray of pastries at his side, Rez stretched his free arm across the back of a red velvet divan and studied the chandelier. De Clerc, if he were not mistaken. He and the De Clerc family had known one another for decades. Their kids had gone to the same schools, and often vacationed together. Jean-Louis had even dated one of the De Clerc daughters for a few months one summer.

Rez enjoyed taking vacations, but he couldn't recall when he'd last done so. For he and Colette's honeymoon? Surely they'd gone elsewhere since that trip to St. Barth's? Had it been him or Colette who had been too busy to coordinate schedules? Possibly him. Workaholic was a label he embraced.

Hell. Had he been to blame for their waning emotions toward one another? Should he have tried harder? Been there for Colette.

He had been. He really had been.

So why did he feel as if he'd done something wrong?

Viv peeked out from the dressing room for the third time, dispelling his self-effacing thoughts. The first two times she'd worn a frown. Red was too bold for her, distracting from her gleaming copper-blonde hair. And white was too difficult—or that was how she'd explained it.

"Even though I've never liked the color, I think this is the one," she said now. She popped out of the room, landing on her tiptoes, arms extended. "Ta-da!"

Rez leaned forward, whiskey forgotten. She smoothed her hands down the violet lace from waist to thigh, then twirled slowly to show off the long, body-hugging gown. The bodice glinted with tiny crystals set in a damask pattern that curled and spiraled up to sheer sleeves with even finer glints. It accentuated her long, graceful neck. It revealed the tops of her luscious yet small breasts. And it did something wonderful to her overall.

Did she stand a little taller? Did her chin lift a little higher? The woman positively reigned in that gown.

Rez exhaled. "That's the one."

"You like it?" The slide of her palm across the low neckline drew his eye.

Without shoes on, she was a good head and a half shorter than him. He took her hand and spun her before him. "Gorgeous."

She shrugged and then nodded, sheepishly accepting the compliment. "It makes me feel kind of pretty…"

"Kind of? You Americans! *Kind of… Sort of…*" He pulled her to him and kissed her. Soundly. "You are gorgeous. Full stop."

Her sigh dusted his neck. She ran a palm up his sleeve. He could feel her beginning another shrug, so he stopped her need to qualify and dismiss his desire to compliment her with another kiss.

This kiss accepted no excuses. It told her she was worthy and beautiful and that he was lucky to have her in his arms. The way her body melded against his when they kissed was a sensual treat. Her breasts were snug against his chest. Her closeness made him, oh, so hard. He wanted to devour her. To rip away the expensive lace and…

Viv parted herself from the kiss and whispered, "Good, then?"

"Très bien." There would be no lace-tearing. *Yet.* "Now, let's get you some shoes."

"Oh? Shoes…" She stepped away from his hold and rubbed a palm up her opposite arm. Her wince surprised him. "Yes, shoes."

Her mind had fled this dressing room. Rez could sense her taking a memory leap. Something with which he was all too familiar.

"What's going on in that beautifully lush brain of yours, Viv?"

She squeezed her eyelids shut. Was it that painful, then?

When finally she opened her eyes, she asked, "Did I tell you my husband used to call me Cinderella?"

"No." He was familiar with the fairy tale. "Was it to do with shoes?"

"Yes. You see, I have these weirdly narrow feet. I tend to step out of high heels. Often. So whenever it would happen my husband would shake his head and say, 'Did Cinderella lose her shoe again?' He'd retrieve the shoe and then bend down to put it back on me. Then he'd look up at me like Prince Charming and I'd lose my heart to him again. It's silly, but dressy shoes make me think of…well…. It was a special thing between the two of us."

"I understand," he said. And he did.

Couples shared personal things that no others would pick up on. It created an exclusivity that further bonded them. He and Colette had… Such frustration that their *thing* had slipped from his memory.

"But I don't think it would be appropriate to go barefoot."

Viv chuckled. "Of course I won't, you silly Frenchman." She looked over his shoulder to the salesclerk, who lingered out in the showroom. "Do you have anything that would go well with this dress? I'm a size seven. Not sure what that is in European sizes."

"Of course!" The clerk sailed off to retrieve some shoes.

Rez took Viv's hand and leaned in for another quick kiss. "This is almost fun."

"Shopping for women's clothes? It's fun for me. But it's not going to be fun for you once you get a glimpse of the price tag."

"Doesn't matter."

She rolled her eyes. "Your bank account must be incredible. I've never dated a millionaire before."

"Billionaire."

"Ah—really?"

She swallowed. And he knew the subject had to change.

"That doesn't matter, either. What does matter," he said, "is that this dress made you burst out of the dressing room like a beam of sunshine. It makes you happy."

"It does."

He kissed her forehead. "Mission accomplished."

The clerk returned with a pair of violet leather heels. Simple, but elegant.

"Shall I put them on for you?" the clerk asked.

"Uh…sure."

Viviane had slipped into a state of numbness. It struck her so quickly she merely reacted, lifting one foot and then the other as the woman gently slid the shoes onto her feet while Rez watched.

She couldn't determine if they were comfortable or they pinched because her mind was spinning. Not because she'd learned Rez was super-wealthy instead of merely wealthy. She could deal with that. *Maybe.* No, right now she was thinking about a fairytale princess and the handsome prince who had loved her for twenty-five years and then been stolen from her by a vile villain named cancer.

"Agréable?" the clerk asked. "I will leave you to walk in them and consider."

"Merci."

Still in a surreal haze of memory, Viviane walked toward the floor-length mirror and paused. The shoes hugged her feet snugly. They might always fit like that. Or they might become loosened the more she walked, and then…

She fled toward the dressing room, closing the door behind her, leaving Rez on the sofa, nursing his whiskey.

Meeting her gaze in the mirror, she saw the first tear slip down her cheek. The voice from her past that she knew so well spoke to her.

"Did Cinderella step out of her shoe again? Sit, my love. There. It's perfect on you. I love you, Cinderella."

Viviane gasped out a few more tears, catching the back of her hand against her mouth. Brian had always treated her so tenderly, with genuine love. The shoe thing had been their shared moment. Even when shoes had fitted her well, she'd sometimes stepped out of one if she was in need of a hug. When she'd wanted to let Brian be the hero. The knight in shining armor who'd sweep in to save the princess.

She'd thought she'd gotten over all the dramatic emotional stuff following his death. The many days of crying. The times when memories would reduce her to tears while sitting at a stoplight. The sudden need to plunge her face against a sweater he'd worn, the one item of his clothing that she had saved. She'd never wash it. *Never.*

"Viviane?" Rez said softly from the other side of the door.

She lifted her head, swiping at a tear. "Just need a moment, please."

"Of course."

Rez was so kind. He understood her loss. He didn't push her and he never would. But what kind of crazy mess was she? Their first date had gone remarkably well. Now she intended to skip over the casual dating stage and go big by accompanying him to a *soirée*, of all things. A party where she had to be at her best. Fitting in with the wealthy and the famous.

That couldn't happen until she got her head on straight. Stopped running away when the smallest memory prodded her.

Looking down at the shoes, she decided they matched the gown perfectly. And they were comfortable. She could walk in them.

She shook her head. Who was she to attend a fancy ball at some fabulous Parisian landmark on the arm of a billionaire? That was so not in her wheelhouse.

But why not? she pleaded silently to her reflection.

She'd come to Paris to start something new. Why not an affair with a Frenchman? It was really happening. For the little time she might have in this city, why not play with the fantasy? She could do it. She had captured the Frenchman's attention. He wanted to take her to this party. The gown and shoes would make her look the part. Where was the strong, independent woman who was determined to grasp life?

I am here, she told herself, and lifted her head. Turning before the mirror, she studied herself front and sides. *I do look good. I love this color.* He had called her gorgeous. *Oh, Rez, I'm falling for you.*

She was not sure if that was good, bad, or stupid. Whatever it was, she was in for the ride.

Viv stepped out of the dressing room. Raising an arm while sliding the other hand down her hip, she embraced the sexy move. It felt…right.

"I can do this."

Rez pulled her into his arms. "Yes, you can."

The Le Beau boutique was still open when they arrived at around eight in the evening. The Champs-élysées bustled with tourists, women walking tiny dogs, men sporting thick gold chains, crews of teenagers texting as they laughed, and families walking with heads turning and cell phones recording to take it all in. A bright yellow Lamborghini parked at the curb offered a chance for tourists to sit inside for a hefty price tag.

Rez quickly showed Viv around the shop. Massive crystal chandeliers hung over only a few jewelry display counters. Beautiful salespeople dressed in black smiled and greeted Rez warmly before he led Viv off the sales floor and down a narrow hallway. They went through a private doorway, then took the stairs up to the offices and workrooms.

Rez opened a bottle of wine and poured Viv a goblet. Not your standard office refreshments. Then he left her to wait in a private viewing room while he went to the walk-in safe to retrieve a few items.

Viviane imagined Le Beau's "big bucks" clients were probably led to this same room and served wine as they perused pricey baubles and bangles. The furniture was antique Louis XV stuff, and the scent of designer perfume intoxicated her. The marble dais in the middle of the room must be for viewing the jewelry. A lighted mirror was the only thing on it.

She was excited to see what Rez would show her. He had insisted she borrow something to wear for the party, and how could she refuse?

A sip of wine confirmed that she might never again drink the cheap stuff. A girl could get used to wine that had been grown, fermented, and bottled only a hundred miles away. And the cheese here! And the walks in the beautiful parks! The entire city was walkable. Even if she lived here she might never see all there was to see.

Wouldn't that be a dream? To live in Paris? It was difficult to consider it, knowing her budget would never allow that. Yet she had knocked down the walls to her fantasy, so who was to know what other dreams might be accomplished? Fingers crossed, The Plant Whisperer business would take off and she'd be able to build a clientele in Europe. Because if not… It was home to Minnesota for this girl.

Rez returned with a black velvet tray and set it on the marble table. The glint of light on diamonds made Viviane gasp. One necklace lay on the tray. A pear-shaped diamond on a single strand. Classic and simple.

"Is that a pink diamond?" she asked.

"It is. It's elegant…not too heavy. It won't distract from your gown, and yet it will draw the eye."

Viv traced her finger over the cool, smooth diamond. The strand was made up of smaller diamonds, linked together. It was gorgeous.

"You designed this? You are so talented."

"*Merci.* That means a lot, coming from you."

"Now I understand why you don't want to walk away from this."

"This…" he tapped the necklace "…is my life. I can't imagine not designing jewelry. But this." He patted his thigh. The wounded leg. "Seems to freak Jean-Louis out."

"Your son wants you to leave Le Beau simply because of your limp? It's got to be more than that."

"I told you about the memory issues. Jean-Louis thinks I need to see a shrink."

"Oh. That's weird…"

On the other hand, she had read about people with traumatic brain injuries. It changed their lives—oftentimes dramatically. It could be difficult to deal with emotionally. Add to that the fact Rez had also lost his wife…

"And you don't want to do that?" she asked.

"Do I seem crazy to you?"

"You're not! But your son must have good reason to request such a thing of you."

"He wants to take over Le Beau. My brain injury is his excuse to do so."

"Hmm…"

She didn't want to intrude on a family battle. And with the necklace sparkling under her fingertips all she wanted was to fall into the dazzle and lose herself. On the other hand, Rez seemed mentally stable, even factoring in his grief. But she was no expert, and perhaps talking to someone about his medical condition would help.

"I'm sorry," Rez said. "It is for my son and I to discuss. Will you try this on?"

"I thought you'd never ask!"

He walked around behind her and she felt the weight of the heavy diamond land on her chest. Now, *that* was satisfying. Never had she worn diamonds—save her wedding ring set, which currently sat in a safe at home. Expensive jewels didn't appeal to her. Give her rhinestones any day.

And yet…

Viv leaned forward to inspect the necklace in the mirror. To say it dazzled like millions of stars was not exaggerating. *Wow.*

"You know," Rez said, leaning in near her shoulder, to meet her reflection in the mirror, "with this rock around your neck you won't need to stuff any in your bra for the party."

Viv laughed. "Oh, darling, I won't have a bra on that night."

He tilted his head. A brow lifted.

Whatever thoughts were going through his brain…she was all for it!

CHAPTER ELEVEN

CLAD IN THE LACY violet gown, Viv turned before the mirror, studying her backside. Still fit and trim. She had the body of a twenty-year-old. Very well, a twenty-year-old who'd been celebrating that birthday for thirty-some years, but still…

Not bad, she decided.

In fact, she felt great. The necklace Rez had loaned her had been delivered an hour earlier by a security car. Viv had been in the shower and found it on her bed when she'd come out. Opening the black velvet case had certainly been a Cinderella moment.

The pink diamond suited the dress—bigger than her thumb, it must be worth a bit. Best to be careful with it. Certainly if anything happened to it, it would come out of Rez's pocket. Though he was rich. Had billions…

She grabbed her cell phone and opened the internet browser. Then she set it down on the bed.

No, I won't snoop.

Financial status meant nothing to her. Seriously… A man could own all the fancy houses, cars, and suits in the world and still be a jerk. Rez was not a jerk.

But wow—did this diamond sparkle. She picked up the phone again.

Just a quick snoop.

Entering his name brought up a list of hits connected to Le Beau. Clicking on the image option filled the screen with Rezin Ricard's handsome mug. That man could work the tousled hair and stubble look. He always wore a suit, but had been captured in some easy poses that belied the staunch businessman and gave everyone a peek at the rebel she'd suspected lived within him. One of the photos featured him alongside a stunning woman with long dark hair and an incredible body clad in a dazzling silver gown. Her gravity-defying breasts could not be natural.

Must be his wife. Viv pressed her fingers to her lips. *Oh, my God, she is...was...a goddess. So beautiful. She must have been a model. Oh...*

Viv closed her eyes. What was she doing? Thinking she had any right to attend a fancy party, wearing an expensive gown and jewels, on the arm of a sexy billionaire who could date any woman he desired. Any young, beautiful, gorgeous woman.

She was no match for the cadre of women Rez must attract. Why was he taking *her* out tonight? It didn't make sense.

But appearance was not, and should not be, the most important thing in choosing a mate. Or a date. She and Rez had gotten to know one another and she was intrigued by the brain and the obvious creative talent behind the handsome face. And he had a sense of humor. And they'd kissed. A lot. She felt like they had become a couple. But he hadn't labeled her "girlfriend," and nor did she feel comfortable announcing to anyone that the man was her boyfriend.

And yet...

She sent another glance to the woman on his arm. Colette Ricard. She wasn't smiling. She wore one of those posed, pursed-lips looks that wouldn't cause a wrinkle. Most likely a model's conditioned reaction to the paparazzi. Rez wasn't holding her close or clasping her hand. It was as though she were the beauty on display and he wasn't allowed to muss her. What must that have been like? To do the public scene and put on a show for the cameras? Because Rez's smile wasn't all there, either. For some reason he looked distracted. Not happy.

Viv shook her head. She was imagining things. The couple had to have been married for as long as she and Brian had been if he had a son old enough to take control of the family business. Why hadn't she asked him?

Because he was still touchy about all things regarding his departed wife.

Had their relationship been loving and true? Or...something else?

"Viv?" Rez stood in the bedroom doorway. "I called your name. Are you okay?"

She tucked the phone behind her and stood. "Uh... maybe."

"You don't seem sure. Are you ready to leave—? *Wow.*"

The sight of his open-mouthed expression flooded over her skin like a warm rain. His gaze devoured her. A lift of her chin had her basking in the adoration.

"You," he said in his husky baritone, "are stunning."

Viv didn't even fight the blush this time. It felt incredible to be admired. His look made her feel worthy of the expensive gown and jewels. Of him.

"I knew that diamond drop would go well with the gown," he said.

Certainly, though, she didn't measure up to Colette Ricard.

Viv rubbed her fingers up the back of her neck.

"What is it, Viv? There's something wrong. I know you."

"Do you really?"

Rez ran his palms down her arms. Goosebumps shivered in their wake.

Touch me more, she thought. *Everywhere. And make me believe this is real.*

For the first time she noticed his suit. A deep purple, almost black, the color barely noticeable had his bowtie not been edged with purple satin. His hair wasn't so tousled and sexy as usual, now smoothed back and refined. She liked it no matter how he styled it.

Viv inhaled and closed her eyes. His usual leather tone was there, but it was topped with something sweeter—like cinnamon and maybe rum.

"Like something I could devour…"

"What?"

"Huh? Oh. Right. We were…uh…"

"Hey, I know I'm the one with the memory issues and dizziness, but are you sure you're all right to go out this evening?"

No, she wasn't. Pressing the flesh with celebrities and the moneyed elite was so out of her wheelhouse. She belonged with the plants, digging in the dirt, creating private escapes for other people.

On the other hand… Yes, she wanted to walk in on a handsome man's arm. To enjoy this beautiful gown and experience the life of the uber-rich and famous. Just for this one night. And then Cinderella would hitch a ride on a pumpkin—hopefully with both shoes still intact.

She wiggled her feet within the shoes. They fitted perfectly. But she hadn't walked in them much. Which had been her plan. She didn't want to stretch them and risk stepping out of one.

Viv inhaled courage and nodded. "I am more than all right. This dress makes me feel glamorous. The shoes are awesome. And my date is some kind of *GQ* model who smells absolutely edible."

He quirked a brow.

"It's your spicy cologne. I want to…" *Lick you.* "Well…"

Rez leaned in, nuzzling his nose along her jaw and into her hair. When his lips touched the top of her ear, Viv's entire skeletal structure went rubbery. Goosebumps again danced on her arms. And probably in her heart as well.

"I feel the same about you," he said in a husky whisper against her ear. "Whatever *'Well...'* entails, I'm all for it."

Another nuzzle, and he kissed her hair above her ear. Then her temple. Her eyebrow. He landed on her lips with the barest connection. A tease, really. For which she was thankful. She was not sure how her red lipstick would withstand anything too intense. She was not a big make-up wearer. Had never worried about kissing a man and then having to refresh her lipstick.

Oh, Viv, stop thinking and enjoy the man!

Threading her fingers through his soft, dark hair, she held him to her as they maintained a barely-there kiss. His scent seeped into her being. Their mingled breaths warmed skin and lips. Her lashes dusted his face.

He smiled against her mouth, and then broke the ethereal moment. "That lipstick…" he murmured.

"Too much?"

Oh, no. She'd thought it might be too bright, inappropriate. She would stick out like a—

"Exquisite," Rez whispered against her mouth. "It lures me. You are making promises to me, Viv, do you know that?"

"I…uh…" *Why the heck not? Relax!* "I'm not big on breaking promises."

He pulled back, his smile soft and sensual. "I'll remember that. But only make those promises to me, *oui*?"

"Deal. So," she said, "is this another date? I mean, what are you going to say when you introduce me to people tonight?"

"This is a date." He shrugged. "That you're my girlfriend?"

She twined her fingers in his. "You don't sound very sure of that."

"I'm *not* sure. This is…"

"I know." She closed her other hand over their clasped hands and looked up to his bowed gaze. "This is new for both of us." He nodded. "Let's let it go where it wants and wing it."

"That works for me. But…uh… Jean-Louis will be there. I may have to introduce you as…"

"You can call me a friend, if you think he'll be upset to see his father with a woman."

"He may…he may not be. He's aware I've tried a few dates and he didn't say anything about them. Probably because he knew they were failures. For all I know he wants his old man to get a girlfriend to keep him occupied and make him want to leave the company."

Viv clasped his hand firmly. "No arguments with your son tonight, okay? You need to be the calm, cool patriarch of Le Beau. Don't give Jean-Louis any fodder for this silly business of labeling you incapable."

"That sounds like a plan. We'll see how good I am at carrying it out. Lately when Jean-Louis and I speak it always ends in an argument."

"Then perhaps you should carry a glass of champagne with you all night."

Rez regarded her curiously.

"If you feel the need for heated words coming on—sip."

"Sip?" He chuckled. "Or maybe I should keep you to hand? I'd rather kiss your gorgeous mouth than sip champagne."

"I like the sound of that."

His next kiss was too quick. "Now, what was going on with you when I came in here? You were distracted."

Viv sighed and grabbed her phone. She showed him the screen, which was still open to the images page. "I'm sorry. I was curious about you and Le Beau so I did a search. Then I saw a photo of you with your wife. She was so beautiful."

"She was. But how did that upset you? You're the one who has been teaching me about leaning into grief and accepting it for what it is."

"It's not that. She's… I just got down on myself. Didn't think I could hold a candle to an obviously stunning model. I know I don't measure up—"

This time Rez's kiss was firm and not at all gentle. His mouth commanded hers. His fingers in her hair gripped, holding her to him. *Silence*, the kiss said. *It's only the two of us. Don't allow a ghost to be your rival.* And when Viv was finally able to think again she'd forgotten what the topic had been.

"Good," Rez said as he took her hand. "You needed that diversion. Now, I have a date with a gorgeous woman who makes silent promises with every curl of her lips. And we are going to have fun tonight. *Oui?*"

She nodded. *"Oui."*

The driver stopped before the Grand Palais, which was not far from the mansion, but if Viv had had to walk that distance in those shoes… Well, forget it!

Rez, *sans* cane, got out and offered his hand to help her out. Paparazzi milled. Camera flashes dazzled. And all the French shouts were likely commands to *Look this way!* or *Pose!* as arriving couples complied.

And—wow!—a real red carpet stretched up the stairs toward the entrance doors.

A man approached Rez and shook his hand. They seemed to know one another. The man was tall and brutish, like a brawler, and Viv could see a neck tattoo peeking out from his shirt.

Rez leaned in to say, "This is Victor. He's your security for the evening."

"My—?" Suddenly unsure, Viv touched the necklace.

The cool diamond wobbled over her skin. "Seriously? Because of the necklace?"

"It's standard. He won't bother you, but he will shadow you." His cheek brushing hers, and his back to the crowd of photographers, Rez asked, "Still okay about all this?"

"Maybe…"

"You're fiddling with that diamond like you're not okay."

She stopped. "Sorry. It must be worth tens of thousands. I'll be careful with it."

"Thousands?" Rez whistled low. "That pink diamond is worth one point five million."

Viv grasped his hand at the same time as her brain processed that information. In her peripheral vision a camera flash blinded her. And suddenly they were walking toward a clutter of clicking cameras and shouting paparazzi.

With a glance over her shoulder she saw Victor follow, hands folded before him, eyes scanning. But all she could think was—*What the heck?* She was wearing over a million dollars' worth of diamond around her neck. It was more than she'd ever see in her back account. How could Rez trust her with such an item? What if it got lost? Fell off her?

Rez paused at the doors to the palace and nodded to everyone. He waved and squeezed her hand. Viv managed a smile. Not sure how she did it. She was moving on automatic pilot, not processing anything but the blur of camera flashes.

Do not pass out.

As they walked inside the main foyer, leaving behind the rush of photographers, Viv exhaled, and this time when Rez squeezed her hand she squeezed back.

"I wish you'd told me how much this necklace is worth before you loaned it to me," she said on a chiding whisper.

They were approaching a lavish reception area decorated with white gardenias and trailing pale green strings of pearl succulents.

"Would you have worn it if I had?"

"Never!"

"Exactly. Viv, are you having some kind of—how do you say it?—a freak-out?"

"Possibly."

"Do you need me to slap you?"

"What? Are you serious? No." She laughed. "Sorry. You're right." Dropping the diamond and smoothing both palms over her hips, she straightened and lifted her chin. "Victor will always be close?"

"That's what I pay him for."

"Fine. I can do this."

"Of course you can. I never doubted you for a moment. What do you say we do this together?"

And the night began.

CHAPTER TWELVE

THE GRAND PALAIS had been built as an exhibition hall for the 1900 Universal Exposition. It combined the Baroque with Classicism in its steel framework, copious windows and glass dome. Chanel frequently held its runway shows there, under the dome. The Ricards would not have considered any other venue for this celebration.

Viv whispered to Rez as she took it all in, "It's amazing. Massive. And yet the place manages to feel intimate and warm, like a greenhouse."

"Then you should feel right at home this evening. Let's do the circuit, shall we?"

Rez kept Viv on his arm as he wandered through the glass-domed nave, greeting every face and thanking people as he recalled a piece he had made for them or the many pieces designed by Le Beau over the years and enjoyed by their families. He introduced Viv simply as Viviane Westberg.

It felt odd to have a woman at his side who was not Colette. And as he approached friends, they initially gave Rez a startled look, which then quickly segued into a smile. They all knew he'd lost his wife. Did they think it was too soon for him to have someone new in his life? Were they happy for him?

It shouldn't bother him, but anxiety was keeping him from completely relaxing. Time for more champagne.

Viv's fingers fluttered to the pink diamond often. He wished she would just own it—just for the evening. The truly dazzling thing was the woman wearing the diamond. And she was a real trooper as she stood at his side, listening to the mostly French conversation. Though he did start all his introductions in English, people naturally flowed into their native language.

It took a while to work the room, and as he collected another goblet of champagne for the two of them Viv veered him toward the displays in the center of the room. A whole room had been constructed of large drawings of his designs. Its walls reminded him of the Japanese *shoji* screens.

Viv broke from his arm to study the drawings. Rez stood proudly behind her, stunned that she'd even have an interest in them. Not once had she indicated this *soirée* was boring, but for him…? A hundred years was an awesome accomplishment. But, much as he enjoyed seeing clients, having to be "on" and schmooze was not his thing.

It had once been his thing. Or had it been Colette's milieu and he'd been at ease only by her side? Now that he considered it, he had to concede that truth. His wife had been his social crutch. Which made him realize that he could relate to Viviane's nervousness even more.

A glance to his right noted his son, dressed in a tuxedo and chatting animatedly with one of Le Beau's most faithful clients. Rez felt his anxiety rise—but then he breathed out. Because as he watched Jean-Louis he was overcome with a certain pride. Pride that his son was standing there, displaying to the world the professionalism and elegance that were the cornerstones of Le Beau. As Jean-Louis shook hands with the client, he laughed heartily. And a small turn found him acknowledging another client, whom Rez knew had flown in from Berlin specifically for this event.

Perhaps Rez had not considered how comfortable Jean-Louis was with all aspects of the company. *Mon Dieu*, he needed to sort out his life—and his issues with Jean-Louis. He had to get back to his normal self, which included being social and enjoying life. There had simply been too much upheaval lately. Le Beau and his jewelry design was the one thing that had remained consistent. He couldn't walk away from that anchor.

Viv was slowly walking along the wall of drawings. "You drew all of these?"

"Yes. Apparently Penelope let Jean-Louis into my drawings cabinet. They do look good blown up to poster-size. She's going to hang some in the shop also."

Viv turned a beaming smile at him. "They look as good as the real thing. You can catch the sparkle of the diamonds and the blood-red glint in the ruby. And I love the aquamarine. Where do you get your inspiration?"

Her compliments straightened his shoulders more than he'd thought possible. Some of his anxiety slipped away. "Everywhere. I love symmetry, nature, beauty. Sometimes the stones seem to design themselves."

"I can understand that. Same with plants. Sometimes I just follow where they want me to go."

"You are an artist as well."

"I suppose a little."

Americans and their need to downplay their accomplishments! Hadn't she mentioned something about once winning an award for her work?

"It must be satisfying to see your work worn by nearly every woman in attendance tonight," she said.

"Absolutely. I love it."

He kissed her hand. She smelled like the garden. How she managed that, he wasn't sure, but it was wild and fresh, and he wanted to kiss her deeply—right now.

"Look at that one!" She approached a drawing of an elaborate blue sapphire and diamond choker he'd designed for Colette's fortieth birthday.

Rez lifted his chin, fighting his need to turn away, to ignore anything that tugged at his memory. Yet the night of the accident was still a black hole. So he should appreciate any memory that came to him, shouldn't he?

He walked up behind Viviane and slid his hands over her hips. "I made that for Colette." Saying her name was growing easier. "She loved sapphires. The center stone is forty carats. The diamonds laddering along the stone are black. She screamed when she opened the box on the morning of her fortieth birthday."

Viv's tilted her head back onto his shoulder and Rez realized she belonged there, close to him. She didn't intrude on his memories; she helped him to own them, to embrace them. To simply allow them to exist.

"How much is it worth?" she asked.

"Eighteen million."

"Oh, dear… I can't imagine the security detail that must have surrounded *her.*"

Rez wrinkled a brow. Why did the mention of Colette and her security guard make him feel anxious suddenly? He hadn't seen the man who had so often flanked Colette when they attended events in years. He'd left Rez's employment while he'd been recuperating in the hospital.

Viv turned and looked up at him. "Sorry. Here we go… talking about our spouses again."

"It's okay." He shook off the unnerving sensation of lost memory. "But I would suggest that this *is* a party. And I do see the champagne server heading our way."

They switched their empty goblets for full ones again, and as Rez sipped he noticed someone wave across the room.

"That's a Scandinavian prince. I'm designing his fiancée's wedding set. I should speak to him."

"Of course! This is your party. I don't want to monopolize you. Leave me to finish looking at all your drawings.

I'll be fine. But please know I won't be able to keep my eyes off you."

"I love being your focus," Rez said.

She leaned in and whispered at his ear. "When I look at you, I lose all interest in what's going on around me."

He shivered as she slowly brushed her lips across his cheek. Not a kiss. Something so much more. She'd marked him. And her hush of breath burned deep into his being.

Viv placed her full champagne goblet on a passing server's tray. She had already consumed one glass, and the giddy feeling dancing in her brain was not entirely because she was living out a fantasy tonight. Time to cut herself off. Before she did something embarrassing. She had only been drunk a couple times in her life. It had never ended well.

Stopping before the final drawing, which featured a star design in the center of a tiara, she glanced around. Victor wasn't far behind. Not at all creepy in his constant surveillance, remarkably he blended into the background noise. Good guy.

Man, this place was amazing. It was all so open and airy. And it really did feel like a greenhouse. Though the sky had darkened above, the lighting dazzled like stars along the overhead steel framework.

"Lovely, yes?"

Viv turned at the sound of an obvious American accent and smiled at a young couple. The woman sported a head of dark, thick braids coiled in a beehive, while her husband's dreadlocks were corralled behind his head in a ponytail.

"These drawings are amazing," Viv said. "You two are... visiting Paris?"

"We just purchased a home in the Sixteenth," the woman excitedly announced. She offered her hand to Viv to shake. "I'm Evangeline, and this is my husband, Nestor. Nestor is a cutter for Le Beau. Just hired last year."

Viv touched the pink diamond at her throat. "You are so lucky to work with Le Beau. Their designs are beautiful."

"Nestor loves beauty," Evangeline said. "Now we want to bring that beauty into our new home. We're too excited about it all."

Viv smiled, but she noticed Nestor appeared...bored.

"The painting and the new furniture," Evangeline went on enthusiastically. "And we must find a gardener!"

"A gardener?" Viv's heart double-thumped. "I'm a gardener. I have over twenty years' experience. Do you have an established garden or are you looking to create one?"

"It's established on the terrace, but it needs much work. My goodness, we must exchange contact info. We don't move in for weeks, but I would love to learn more about what you do."

Viv gave the woman her number, and when Nestor nudged his wife toward the refreshments bar she waved the twosome off. A possible client?

"Good job, Viviane," she whispered to herself.

A sweeping glance about the room saw that Rez had moved on to another couple. He stood out in the crowd— tall, dark, the proverbial handsome prince. In fact he carried himself as if he were a king. Truly, he was the patriarch of Le Beau. She hoped his son would not succeed in forcing him away from something he loved so much. This was his element, standing amidst the beauty and elegance that he had created.

She couldn't wait to get him home and kiss him silly. He was her man. If only for the night.

At the sight of something troubling, Viv clenched her fingers. Rez's arm had reached out, his fingers grasping. The people he was speaking to didn't notice. But she knew exactly what that subtle movement meant. He was feeling unsteady.

Weaving her way through the partygoers, she smiled at

all the women and men she passed. Whatever they muttered in French about the oddball woman on the rich jeweler's arm didn't matter. There was only one opinion in this room that she cared about. And he preferred to call her strange.

As she reached Rez's side she smiled at the couple he was speaking to. Unobtrusively, she slid a hand up Rez's back. His spine melded firmly against her palm. She sensed his weight shift from foot to foot, and then to both as he found a steady stance.

"I should introduce you to my date," Rez said in English to the couple. "This is Viviane Westberg. Viviane, this is Maxine and Thierry Robalt."

Maxine bussed Viv's cheeks, then displayed the huge red rock on her middle finger. "Rezin designed this little bauble for me. Burmese ruby. Adorable, isn't it?"

"Oui." Adorable? It was as large as a gumball that surely would cause a child to choke. "Rez's designs are *incroyable*." Viv tried a bit of French.

"Très incroyable!"

They exchanged some pleasantries about the event and the displays, and then the couple wandered off. She and Rez were immediately approached by a man who observed Viviane with the cautious eye of a vulture sitting on a bare branch above a dying soul. The man had unruly dark curly hair that seemed to want to take control of his head. Blue eyes startled her with recognition. And when they dropped to take in the pink diamond his jaw tightened.

"Jean-Louis," Rez said in introduction. "This is Viviane Westberg. She's been refurbishing the garden at Colette's *tanière*."

Viv squeezed Rez's hand at the mention of his wife. She knew it took a lot for him to utter the name.

"My mother loved that garden," Jean-Louis said. His discerning gaze flickered over Viv's face, her shoulders—then back to the pink diamond. "You must do it justice."

"I will. And I am," she added.

"She is," Rez reassured. "She's not changed the layout or your mother's roses."

"The roses... *Oui*."

Jean-Louis noticeably swallowed. He lifted his chin in a Rez-like move that Viv knew indicated a staunch need not to show emotion.

"Interesting... You two are friends? To be here...together?"

Viv knew exactly what the man was angling at. Was she dating his father? Were they sleeping together? It wasn't her place to say anything, when it was Rez who must carefully guard his interactions against a son who wanted to wrest away the family company from him should he make one misstep. And that misstep had been prevented by her hand to his back.

"We are together this evening," Rez offered.

"And she's wearing the pink," Jean-Louis stated accusingly.

"She does it justice, *oui*?"

Then Rez said something in French to Jean-Louis. It didn't sound chastising or accusatory, just matter-of-fact. *Mind your own business*? Viv could hope for that...

"I wanted to share this amazing event with Viv, who is doing something wonderful for our family."

"Of course, Papa."

But Viv could see Jean-Louis wasn't buying it. Her heart dropped a notch. Rez hadn't claimed her as a girlfriend or even his date. She was a friend whom he wanted to thank for doing a job. *Ugh*. Had she expected more? Yes. But she could allow Rez that omission to his son. She'd stepped into the middle of a family battle. Best to stand as far out of the line of fire as possible.

"Are you going to stay for the DJ?" Jean-Louis asked his dad.

"The what?"

"Music, Papa. We're going to drop the lights at midnight and bring up the music. The stuffy part of the evening will come to a close."

Viv noticed Rez's jaw tighten.

"I love a rousing dance floor," she tried.

"You're not going to play that ridiculous club music?" Rez asked.

"It may be ridiculous to you, but our younger and richer clients love it. You must stay. Get a good feel for the clientele Le Beau must romance in order to remain relevant."

It seemed a heavy exhalation was all Rez could manage. Viv wanted to hold him. Reassure him. But instead she slid her hand up his back again—this time not to support him, but merely to convey *I understand.*

"Whatever you decide…" Jean-Louis turned and nodded to someone across the room. "Remember, you left the planning of this party in *my* hands. And the guests are loving it. Now, I've to make sure the set-up is ready to go. Good evening, Papa." He nodded at Viv, but said nothing to her in parting as he wandered into the crowd.

Rez turned to follow his son's leaving. Viv pressed both palms to his back. His tension was palpable even through the suit coat.

"Want to stay and dance?" she suggested.

When he turned toward her she wasn't sure if he was looking at her or fuming. At the very least she was thankful he had not started a vocal argument with Jean-Louis.

"Or we could leave now." She glanced to the big clock hanging above the balcony. "Almost midnight."

He grinned. "You know, I used to stay out until morning, dancing and drinking."

"Oh, yeah? I've never drunk much, but I can dance. I'm feeling the champagne, for sure."

"I feel as if I stay for the music it'll only drive my anxiety further into the red zone."

She clasped his hand. "I can sense that."

"You won't be upset if we leave now?"

"Why should I be? I've had the best evening. But can the CEO of Le Beau leave his own party early?"

"The CEO can do whatever he damn well pleases." He held out his arm and she took it with hers. "I've had enough schmoozing and pressing the flesh. Now I want to focus on the best part of this night. You."

Lifted by that compliment, Viv followed Rez and they made their way out of the building. It took a while. Rez politely paused to thank people and converse briefly with them when they recognized him walking by. But once they stood outside, at the top of the stairs, Viv inhaled the sweet night air, perfumed with the white gardenias.

In the background the beat of a rap song pounded through the open doorway.

"We'll dance back at the mansion," Rez said. "You like slow dancing?"

"Sounds like my speed."

As they stepped down the staircase, arm in arm, Rez pulled out his cell phone. "I'll call Henri. He's always close. We'll stop by Le Beau on the way to the mansion. I imagine you won't mind me locking up that necklace for the evening?"

"I've grown fond of it, actually. But I'm sure Victor would like to be relieved of his duties as well, so he can return to the party and dance."

Rez smirked and wandered down a few steps.

Viv suddenly let out a cry of dismay. Stopping abruptly, she lifted the purple lace skirt.

Seriously? After she'd been so careful all evening?

Stopping and holding his phone against his chest, Rez bent to study her face. "What's wrong, *mon amour*?"

She forced a smile. "You'll never believe this…"

"What? Do you want to go back inside? If you don't want to miss the dancing—"

"It's not that at all. It's just…" She turned and gestured to the violet leather shoe on the step behind her. "I've stepped out of my shoe."

"Oh." He met her gaze in the glow of the festive party lights. Then his expression smoothed, and he said more seriously, "Oh…"

Viviane's shoulders dropped. *Really? This was happening now?* She had been having a great time—hadn't given one moment of thought to her husband—and now…

"Got it." Rez patted her shoulder and directed her to sit down on the wide step covered with red carpeting. "You sit here." When she was comfortable, he retrieved the shoe and handed it to her. "This is yours. And I…" he again took out his cell phone "…am going to call Henri."

He bent to meet her gaze at eye level. For a moment she could feel his concern like a palpable squeeze to her heart. No kiss was necessary. She could read reassurance in his intense blue eyes.

"I'll leave you to it. You going to be okay?"

Shoe in hand, Viv nodded, fighting the burgeoning tears. "I am."

He stepped away, taking the last few stairs and disappearing around the corner to where the limos were parked. Victor held his post at the bottom of the staircase.

Viv clutched the violet shoe to her chest. The misplaced midnight shoe. Cinderella's folly. Suddenly, in a moment when she'd thought to be horrified by the replay of something that had been so special to her and Brian, she could only smile against the leather shoe. Rez had not offered to put on the shoe for her. Because he knew what that meant to her. He'd honored the memory of her husband so exquisitely.

As a tear spilled down her cheek, reality pierced her heart. She loved Rez for his discretion and kindness. The Prince had won this damsel's respect and trust. Now could he win her heart?

CHAPTER THIRTEEN

THE DROP-OFF AT Le Beau did not take long. Victor escorted Rez inside with the diamond necklace while Viviane waited in the car with Henri. Indeed, the security guard did intend to head back to the party for "the sick tunes," as he'd stated during the ride.

Henri drove them back to the mansion through a surprising amount of traffic that made the trip a slow go.

Rez was not so much tired as disappointed. And not even with Jean-Louis. He did understand what his son was trying to do because he wanted to move Le Beau in a new direction. What baffled Rez was that *he* felt so resistant to it. It wasn't as though he couldn't maintain the elegance and status of the company while Jean-Louis injected some new blood and new marketing. They could possibly create a new division, focused toward the bling and the hip designs that appealed to the younger set.

Was he fighting it for another reason? Sure, he hated being considered an invalid by his son. He had been laid up in bed for weeks following the accident, then had used a walker for another few weeks, and a cane for almost a year following. Now he had his good days and bad days. But mentally he was all there.

The thing was, how would he know he'd forgotten something if he didn't get any reminders of that forgotten thing?

And what of the things about his life that he couldn't remember?

Well, he sensed he and Colette had been heading in a bad direction the few years before the accident. He had loved her. Without question. But what about her? It drove him mad to think about it.

Viviane's asking about Colette's security guard had nudged at him. Boris, who had been Colette's personal guard, had left Paris after the accident. Rez had not heard from him except to be told he'd collected his final paycheck from Penelope.

But his marriage issues had nothing to do with controlling Le Beau. Had his reluctance to kowtow to Jean-Louis's suggestions got something to do with the fact that if he turned over control of the company then he'd be left with nothing? He'd lost his wife. What had he got left? He could not lose his grasp on the one last thing that meant something to him.

"We're here."

Viv's voice jarred him from his defeatist thoughts. He did now have an amazing woman in his life. That was something. That was a lot. But she wouldn't be in Paris for much longer. Did he have any right to ask her to stay? Was he ready for a commitment like that?

"You okay?" Viv asked.

Rez lifted his head. Rain spattered the window. He knew Henri, who had an umbrella, would bring it around and meet them at the passenger door.

"You seemed lost there," she said. "Didn't hear Henri the first time he asked if you wanted the umbrella."

Really? Maybe he *was* losing his grasp. "My mind was wandering. Sorry. I'm back now." He kissed the back of Viv's hand. "A lot of stuff going on tonight, eh?"

"Très bien."

He chuckled. "That means *very good* not *a lot.*"

"Oh, well, then…yes, a lot."

The door opened. Rez took the umbrella and walked Viv slowly toward the entrance gate, knowing those shoes of hers might fall off at any time. Narrow feet? Apparently so.

When he'd looked back to see her shoe on the step, and then at her face—Cinderella, heartbroken—he'd known he couldn't help her. It wasn't his place. And he didn't want it to be his place. He didn't want to spoil her husband's memory.

But he did want to be in her life. He knew that now, more than ever, especially after what she'd done for him tonight.

He entered the digital code and once inside the mansion set down the umbrella and shook off the rain from his sleeves. Viv wandered ahead, stepping out of her shoes halfway to the stairs, where she turned and spread out her arms.

"Tonight was a fantasy come to life," she announced with a spin.

Of course wearing a beautiful gown and a pink diamond would be appealing for any woman. But for him…? The fantasy of being understood and accepted was all he needed.

He crossed the room and kissed her red lips. Her body melted against his. He had forgotten what it felt like to hold a woman. To taste her mouth and receive what she wanted to give him. It had been too long. Much longer than the two years since his wife had passed. Because, yes, he and Colette had been experiencing distance—and, no, he wouldn't let those thoughts rise. Now was for enjoying Viviane.

He spun her around and Viv tugged him to a stop. "There's a light on in the conservatory. Would you mind getting me some water while I run to turn it off?"

"Sure. No champagne?"

"I've reached my limit. I'm feeling a little…"

"Drunk?"

"Relaxed… And a little disoriented. I just need to re-group."

"I'll meet you in the garden."

The chandelier cast a soft glow over the back circle of the conservatory. Viviane wandered inside, her bare feet taking the cool tiles lightly. The Paris sky was dark, but beneath the chandelier the newly pruned greenery gleamed.

She paused and closed her eyes. What a dream this night had been. And while Cinderella had peeked out for a look, the woman who had been rescued on those stairs was not that princess anymore. She was a woman who had taken a chance on a new life and who was currently flying. Everything felt perfect. So much so that she wanted to…

Slipping her cell phone from her purse, she opened the music app. Her favorite playlist? *Click.*

Tilting back her head, she swept out her arms and swayed to the music. A turn allowed her to spy Rez standing in the garden's entrance. He'd loosened his tie and his hair was now tousled the way she preferred it. Her rescuing knight in Armani armor.

She crooked her finger. "You said you wanted to dance with me?"

Setting the water bottle on the floor, he walked over and slid his hands down her hips. He studied her gaze as languorously as his hands studied her body, moving slowly over her hips and up her waist…just under her breasts. Her nipples tightened. She gasped and her entire body arched toward him. Then he took her hands in his.

A new song began, with a lone guitar plucking a bass beat. The slow tune was sung by a woman with a country twang.

"I love this one." She hugged up against Rez's body, head tilted against his shoulder. "It's called 'Girl Crush.'"

"Crushing a girl?" he asked in a wondrous soft baritone.

She laughed. "To have a crush on someone is to desire them…to moon over them."

"Ah, yes, then I have a crush, too. She is a beautiful nymph who lives in a conservatory and likes to seduce me with her cooking."

Viv's entire body took in that compliment with a frisson and a sigh. Clasping her hands against his chest, Rez bowed his head over hers. They swayed in a slow circle beneath the spectacle of crystals and foliage. This was her fantasy, away from the crowds, listening to a man's heartbeat, melding against his heat. She needed him. She wanted him. Every part of her being pleaded for him.

When the song got to the part about tasting her lips, Rez tilted up her chin and kissed her. Softly. And deeply. This was right. *They* were right.

He bowed his forehead to hers. "Thank you for what you did for me tonight, Viv."

"I didn't do anything for you."

"*Oui*, you did. I felt your hand at my back when I needed it most. I needed support and you were there for me."

Another kiss. He tasted like champagne and new beginnings.

"I want to make love with you, Viv."

Her mouth opened in surprise, yet her heart twinkled. "Me too."

He held out his hand. "Let's go to my room. I want you to see the view on this rainy midnight."

He hadn't been kidding about the view. The second-floor bedroom was massive, and one wall was all windows. Viv stood before the window, peering across the river at the Eiffel Tower. Strung with twenty thousand lights, the Iron Lady twinkled as much as Viv's heart did.

Life felt wondrous.

When Rez embraced her from behind, she tilted back

her head, inhaling leather and desire. His hand slid up from her waist to cup her breast. Mmm… She loved that he handled her as if he had every right to do so. Because he did.

He kissed along her neck, up to her earlobe. Marking her, exploring her with his warm breath and gentle kisses.

"I'm only going to ask once," he said, "and then we're not going to bring it up for the rest of the night."

"Sounds serious…but go for it."

He stepped around in front of her, kissed her hand and held it to his chest. "Are you okay with this?"

She knew what he was asking. Was she okay with *this*? *This* having sex with a man who was not her husband. Getting intimate on a whole new level. Stepping out of her shoes and into a new adventure.

Well, she'd already stepped out of her shoes…

"I am more than okay. What about you?"

He threaded his fingers through her hair. "Very okay with it."

CHAPTER FOURTEEN

THE FIRST THING Viviane saw when she opened her eyes to the morning light was the Eiffel Tower surrounded by a robin's-egg-blue sky. Add to that view the fact that she lay on sheets that must have cost a mint. That the pillow under her head was softer than a goose's butt, but still supportive. And the sheets smelled like spice and sex... Life could not get any better.

No handsome Frenchman beside her, though. She suspected Rez had wandered to the bathroom, which was a long stroll across the marble floor. The apartment she'd left back home, plopped above a shoe shop, would easily fit into this bedroom.

What a crazy dream. And she was living it! Frenchman included.

Rolling onto her side and tugging up the sheet, she closed her eyes, sinking into bliss. She had had sex. After years of self-imposed but not necessarily wanted chastity. And it had been perfect.

What made her smile, though, was that she didn't feel guilty about it. She deserved this. But she wondered if Rez felt the same way. Did he feel guilty about having sex with a new woman? She hoped not.

The man was a pretty easy read. He still carried a lot of attachment to his wife. If this had been a one-night thing for him, then she could deal with it. Maybe. She really liked

Rez. Heck, the man who had handed her her shoe last night had realized this damsel had specific memories that must not be trampled by a new knight. It had been a long time since she felt so respected, so...*seen*.

She could fall in love with Rez. Maybe she already had.

Could this affair become a real relationship? A *Why don't you spend more than a night with me and move in?* kind of thing?

It felt like an option to Viv. Of course she was high on the vibes of new sex and passion. But she was not beyond going there. Life had decided to lead her into Rez's bed last night, and she intended to continue to follow that lead.

How? That was the question. She didn't even live on the same continent as the man. And there was the dead wife. Could she compete with a ghost? Rez still showed signs of reluctance to move on from his grief. Not that she expected him never to think of his lost spouse again.

The bed was jostled beside her. Rez's hand swept along her waist and down her thigh. Strong fingers squeezed her leg and he pressed his groin against her buttocks. He nuzzled in near her shoulder. But then she felt him pull back for a few seconds.

"What's wrong?" Viv asked.

"Twelve," he said.

"Twelve?"

"Freckles on your shoulders. And so many more down... here..." He nipped her waist, and then her buttock, and then hugged her. "So, what were you thinking about that I was able to sneak up on you?"

"Where I belong," she answered without pause. She wanted to be honest with him. And they did need to know where they stood in this liaison. "Paris is not my home."

He rolled onto his back and Viv turned over to face him. His body was lean, but taut with muscle. The scar on his leg ran from hip to thigh. He'd flinched when she'd touched it last night, and she knew it was more from embarrassment than pain. No need to bother him about that. There were many other, more interesting parts of him…

Oh, baby, did he have a nice penis. Nothing about him screamed *I'm old and can't get it up.* Nor did it indicate he was aging out of his job and couldn't mentally handle the CEO position anymore.

On the other hand, if he was *not* CEO he could travel. With her.

"What happened last night?" she asked.

He turned toward her. Such inquisitive blue eyes. They matched the sky this morning.

"I mean, with us," she added. "This. The sex."

"The sex was awesome."

"It was. But was it a one-night thing or…? Well?"

He exhaled through his nose and trailed a finger along her hairline. "What do you want it to be, *mon amour*?"

"I'm not sure. You tell me what you want out of this."

"Viv, I thought we were playing it day by day?"

"We are." Dared she tell him she was considering them committing to one another? Becoming a real couple? Could she have a relationship and still create her dream job?

"Then let's keep doing that," he said.

Men. So afraid of commitment—or even simple plans! "But what about when I leave? The garden is close to completion."

"I can pay overtime."

"Are you saying you'd *pay* me to stay longer? Not sure I like the sound of that."

"I didn't mean it that way. I like what happened last night. I'd like it to happen again."

She kissed his shoulder. "Me too."

"So can we continue to play it by ear?"

It wasn't the answer she wanted. But what *did* she want to hear?

Oh, please, Viv, I adore you and I want you to stay with me forever?

Or even: *No, one night was enough. Let's go back to employer and employee.*

Either one didn't feel realistic right now. But she did like to have a plan. A destination.

The old Viviane liked plans. You're trying something new, remember?

Viv stretched an arm across Rez's chest and hugged him. "Okay. We'll do the day-by-day thing. And today is Sunday—which is my day off."

"Want to take a walk and pick up some croissants? Or...?"

"Or?"

"We could make love again."

"That's a tough decision."

"Really?" He genuinely looked hurt.

"Why don't we do both?"

"I do love a woman who knows what she wants."

Her heart knew what she wanted. But her logical side hadn't caught up just yet.

A private park a block from the mansion hugged the Seine. Rez set his cane to one side of the wooden bench. He and Viv had purchased *crêpes* from a vendor. The sweet treats oozed with bananas and chocolate hazelnut spread. He hadn't had one of these since his teen years. He'd forgotten how indulgent they were. And messy.

Viv finished hers in record time, then sprang up to look over the river.

The day was perfect. Their relationship felt fresh, vital, and open to so much opportunity. It was like beginning a new design on paper. The drawing stage was the most exciting because anything could happen.

He'd done it! He'd dove in this time and hadn't fled

when the date had got to the part where he'd had to kiss the woman. He'd taken her home and they'd had crazy good sex. No doubt about it—he and Viv were a sexual match.

And thinking about it… He hadn't forgotten anything about Viv. Not even the smallest detail—like the name of that weird destructive plant, or her scent, or even that she held conversations with cats. Interesting… It was as if his brain had decided she was important to remember.

But she wasn't in Paris forever. And while he'd dodged her question about what they were doing earlier, he did have to face the fact she wouldn't be around for much longer. Dare he risk his heart for a short-lived fling? What if he wanted her to stay longer? He could set her up in an apartment close to his place… If her business goal succeeded— and he suspected it would; she was smart—she could travel and then return home to him.

He couldn't tell her about that idea. She'd be offended. Convinced he wanted to pay for her to stay in his life. If he was honest with himself, it sounded suspiciously like he wanted to keep her as a mistress. And that was not what he wanted, either. Yet he did want her near. Always.

Viv's non-judgmental presence gave him renewed confidence. Her hand at his back had been the most affirming thing he'd gotten from a woman. Ever. He and Viv related on terms that were new to him. Not so superficial as he and Colette, but deep. They could simply be near one another without talking and be comfortable. Like now.

Yet would she be content with a man who intended to remain where he was? In Paris. Working every day at his passion. Her job description seemed to require that she live a nomadic life. That part of her didn't fit with him. Certainly, he did enjoy traveling. But…hmm… Did Viv's adventurous dream mean this could only be a fling?

No, what they had begun was surely something more. Was he willing to relinquish some of his control at Le Beau in order to gain time with her? That was what must happen if he wanted this relationship to work. And he wanted to make the effort to show her he was ready to…well, to *love* her.

Viv returned to the bench, excitedly telling him about the anchored barges that lined the shore. She tilted her head onto his shoulder. *Bateaux Mouches* filled with tourists floated by on the silvery river's waves. Butterflies stitched the air. And somewhere a duck quacked.

Rez had not felt so free and relaxed in a long time. And he liked this feeling.

Monday morning felt full of possibilities. Until. Sitting behind his desk, Rez noticed the pink slip of paper that must have been placed there by Penelope. Contact information for a psychiatrist in the Ninth.

A note was scribbled on the bottom:

Jean-Louis wants you to call this doctor. He uses a brain scan technique that is innovative. Worth a try?

Crumpling the paper, Rez made to toss it. But at the last moment, he did not. Flattening the paper on the desk, he exhaled. So Jean-Louis was having Penelope do his dirty work now?

He needed to have it out with his son, once and for all. It was what a father would do. Set his boundaries. State his purpose and expectations. Teach his son through his own example.

But was his current example really the correct one?

Blowing out a breath, Rez tilted back his head and closed his eyes. He wasn't sure anymore. He'd once thought he had it all: a loving wife, a family, and a luxury jewelry empire. And yet was it all just a façade? Was the one hundred and ten percent he put into Le Beau really worth it?

The answer had stepped into his life recently. She'd literally popped out from under a plant and smiled up at him.

"Viviane..." he whispered. Just saying her name changed his mood.

CHAPTER FIFTEEN

IT WAS COMING TOGETHER! The conservatory would soon be completed. Viv had programmed a watering schedule into the computer system in the supply room. With the sprinkler system automated—provided Rez hired someone to fill the water tanks—the garden would almost take care of itself.

Of course a monthly visit from a gardener would keep it in tiptop shape…

The idea that she might make return visits to her clients was not to be ignored. It would generate more income and ensure her creations were well kept, and if any problems or questions arose she'd be able to go over them with the garden owners.

She texted a note to Harley to add that service to her price list.

Sitting on the floor, with her list of things remaining to do before her, she leaned back on her elbows and took in the glass ceiling panels. They needed a good wash. *But I am not climbing a ladder with a wash rag and vinegar spray.* A window washer must be hired.

Next on the list was to give the tile floor a scrub. And the chandelier suspended above the circle would provide a good day of cleaning. That could be automatically lowered, but she was saving it for last.

Dancing beneath that chandelier with Rez had been a dream come true. And then making love with him… Cinderella truly had stepped out of her shoes and begun a new life.

Stretching back her arms, she felt her knuckles hit the leg of an old painted table. The pale blue paint was peeling. The roses climbing the legs and dancing across the tiny front drawer were delicate and detailed. It didn't look like an antique. Had Rez mentioned his wife had liked to paint? If Colette had painted it Viv could not move it from this room, nor even think to refinish it. It would be fine tucked next to the couch.

She recalled Rez had hinted that he and his wife had been at odds before she had died. For what reason? Viv's mind raced with scenarios. She landed instantly on an affair. But what woman in her right mind would sneak behind Rez's back and have an affair? Rez was kind, funny and handsome and…

Her shoulders slumped. Well… She had been married twenty-five years. She'd loved Brian. Still did. But if she were honest, although their relationship had started out as passionate and fiery, as the years passed it had morphed into different things. Friendship. Companionship. Sometimes dislike. Yes, they'd had their fights, like any married couple. But they had always kissed and made up. Sometimes not for days, but still… And yet over the last decade she'd noticed the frequency of sex had decreased and their love had become more based on companionship than passion. She wouldn't have traded it for anything, nor even considered seeking passion elsewhere. It was simply how their love had grown.

The last years of Brian's life had broken him. He'd been in so much pain. He'd gone from a healthy, muscled man to a frail shell of his former self who'd eventually needed a wheelchair. Viv would ask if he was in pain. He'd say he was not, but his grimace had told the truth.

Tears welled in her eyes. "I wish it could have been easier for you," she whispered.

Closing her eyes, she inhaled deeply. Just a moment for memory. Loving a strong, wonderful man for twenty-five years had truly been a gift. She had been lucky. Yet luck had once again deemed it right to surprise her with another immensely talented charming man.

And she had thought she'd never have a chance at attracting a lover into her life while here in Paris...

Her phone buzzed and Viv jumped. She mined the phone from under her discarded gardening gloves. Her friend Kiara had texted.

Possible Venice job for you. Indoor garden. Needs everything. Fast. Owner selling. Interested?

Did she even have to ask?
Viv texted back an enthusiastic yes.

Viv teased her fork through the olive oil bubbles in the balsamic vinegar that Rez had taught her was the best for dipping torn pieces of baguette. She'd wandered by a shop selling roasted chickens and the smell had decided her on a simple evening meal. Chicken, steamed *haricots verts* and bread. And lots of wine.

If someone squinted when they were looking at her they might think she was turning into a real Parisian. *Ha!* Her love language had certainly gotten a workout lately. Because, yes, she was falling for Rezin Ricard. Now, how to be sure the ghost of his wife wouldn't interfere in him seeking his own happiness...?

She set her fork aside and sipped the wine—Rez's favorite. "Is it okay if I ask you a few things about your marriage?"

He chewed slowly, then nodded. "It is fair. We are...in

something here." His smile hinted at their sensual secrets. "You want to know what I am like in a relationship?"

"Maybe. Sort of. Well… We both have pasts. I can honestly say I was happily married. Brian and I were friends first, lovers second. And I can also say that I don't feel as though I'm cheating on him, or his memory, by having this relationship with you. Life goes on. We move forward."

"We do. Some faster than others. But I am at about your speed."

She smiled at that. He was still a few steps behind her. "What was your relationship with your wife like? You said she was a model? Did she travel? Were you together all the time?"

Rez leaned back in his chair, settling with a sigh. She sensed his reluctance, but also a slow percolation regarding his need to speak. The man was reactionary, but he'd learned to check his anger around her. Something she appreciated.

"She did travel a lot for her work," he said. "But the last decade she wasn't modeling often. I have always worked out of the office on the Champs-élysées. But I traveled at least once a month to see clients or to go diamond-buying with Jean-Louis. Colette and I were friends and lovers. We were…" He blew out a breath. "Perhaps not so close the last few years. Not enemies. Only the usual marital arguments. It was just…"

Wincing inside, Viv wondered if she should have tabled her question. "It's okay," she said. "I shouldn't be nosey."

"I want to be honest with you, Viviane. But I have not said this to anyone. Ever."

She waited.

He studied his hand on the table. And then, "I believe Colette was having *une liaison*. It was never confirmed. But the…er…intimacy between the two of us had changed enough to make me suspect. I'm not sure I ever asked her."

"You're not sure?"

He shrugged. "One of the things my memory has locked away from me…"

"Oh. I understand."

If the accident had messed with his memory, then she suspected it was the worst things to recall that might have been locked away. Who would want to remember his wife was being unfaithful to him? On the other hand, wouldn't he like to know?

That must be the reason he still couldn't let go of Colette. Not completely. He had unanswered questions.

"I am a faithful man," he said, leaning forward on his elbows. "If you choose to remain in my life I will treat you with respect and never look at another."

"If I choose?"

"Everyone has a choice about who they keep in their life, Viv."

"I'm here. Right now." She lifted her goblet in a toast.

But he didn't answer by lifting his glass. "Right now. But when the garden is complete? What next?"

He wanted to know the answer to the very question she was trying to get answered. So the best she could give him was the truth. "A friend texted me this morning. She's a Realtor…selling a home in Venice. It's got an empty conservatory that needs a complete makeover."

"Venice is a beautiful city. Are you going to take the job?"

It was what she wanted. It was the next step in her plan to making this job work for her. But if Rez asked her to stay she knew that she would.

"I'd like to. I have a few days to make up my mind. I never make a step without thinking it through completely."

Now he lifted his goblet. "Did you think it through about me? I recall you plunged right into a kiss."

Yes, and what a plunge… No regrets. No matter how things turned out.

Really, Viv?

Fine. She would have some regrets!

"You are my leap," she finally said.

"How did that go?"

"I'm still falling." Viv smiled at him over another sip of wine.

"I'll catch you. Promise."

"I know that you will."

And he'd do it without stepping on her memories. She should show him the same respect. Whatever he'd had with Colette, she would let it be. It wasn't her place to butt in.

"So how was your day at work? You mentioned you're designing something for that prince?"

"A wedding set. It's a study in attempting to take his horrendously blingy idea and make it classy. But I won't tell him that. He'll be happy with the final product."

"Who wouldn't? To have Rezin Ricard design your wedding set? What a dream!"

"You sound like a fan."

"I wore that diamond necklace. I think I've dreamt about it since. I've never been a diamond girl, but that big pink stone changed my mind."

"It's good to be flexible. And…"

He heaved out a sigh and Viv sensed their flirtation had ended.

"And I've been flexible today, too. I made an appointment to see a psychiatrist that Jean-Louis selected."

"Oh, Rez, how does that make you feel?"

"Honestly? I'm trying not to be so rigid. Maybe this doc will have something new to say. Apparently he utilizes a brain scan and has a unique rehabilitation program."

"Sounds encouraging."

Rez reached for her hand and kissed it. "There's one thing, though."

She clasped her hand over theirs. "Yes?"

"I'm…apprehensive about the appointment. I have such awful memories of the weeks and months following the accident. Of those horrible days spent in the hospital, interacting with doctors when my brain was not functioning at top performance. So I'm…nervous." He rubbed his jaw. "Would you…come along with me?"

"Of course I will."

He'd asked for help. Viv would gladly be there with a hand to his back again.

CHAPTER SIXTEEN

An HOUR LATER, they'd finished off the bottle of wine and pulled on their clothes after impromptu sex in the garden. There was just something about that sexy velvet piece of furniture… Now they snuggled there on the sofa, wrapped in the blanket, heads tilted back to take in the Parisian night.

Rez brushed the hair from Viv's face. "I like it when you're mussed."

"That's my go-to look. I work hard to achieve such disarray."

She laughed and tucked her head against his shoulder. It had been a while since she had laughed so freely. Forgotten her woes and the insistent need to work for a meager wage simply to exist. Life had taken a drastic turn because she had dared to dive in. She never wanted to surface.

"I like what you've done in here. It looks completely different. You're a nurturer, Viv."

"I've never been called that before, but I'll take it. You didn't have too many dead plants in here, but so many were stretching toward the light. I had to prune them back. If you hire a gardener to come in once a month and check in on things, it should stay in shape."

"I'll add that to my list. Or I could hire you?"

"I have decided to add that to my *à la carte* list. Return visits."

"Sign me up. That is, if you'll be in the city."

She met his gaze and knew exactly what he was thinking about. The long-distance relationship thing. Probably wouldn't work out. Maybe it would? But there were ways to make it easier for the two of them. If they both agreed they wanted to continue with this relationship.

"I'll go where the jobs take me," she said. "But I may also consider where my heart wishes me to land. Although Paris is out of the question, rent-wise."

"If you charge your clients appropriately you'll be able to afford a *pied-à-terre* in no time."

No mention of her staying with him. Had she expected him to make that offer? She wasn't sure. It felt fast. And yet they felt so right.

"You saved that wobbly little table?" Rez asked.

"Yes, it's pretty." She stood and picked up the table. Setting it beside the sofa, she tapped the crackled paint. "Did your wife paint it?"

"I'm not sure. Possibly? Those do resemble roses."

"Oh, yes—probably those roses in the corner that I absolutely have not touched."

He smirked. "It's a good business model to do as the client requests."

He pulled the table closer, and one of the legs caught on a floor tile. The table toppled. Rez swore and lunged to catch it, but wasn't fast enough. The drawer jarred open and out spilled a cell phone. One of the older flip-type models. Viv had seen them for sale at the tourist shops. Cheap and disposable.

"What the…?" Rez picked up the phone.

Had the phone belonged to Colette? It did not look like a phone such a woman would have been seen touching. It probably didn't even have a color screen. It must belong to someone else. Maybe a maid, or someone who had tended the garden before it had been forgotten and left to grow wild?

Suddenly Rez's face tightened, his jaw pulsing as he

studied the item. Did he recognize it as Colette's? It could mean something terrible. Or it could be nothing more than a spare phone.

Rez hissed something in French and pressed the phone against his chest. Viv took the statement to be meaningful, for he'd closed his eyes in reverence.

"I...uh..." She didn't know what to do right now. A hand against his back didn't feel right.

"I will need to be alone." Rez stood and marched out of the garden, taking the phone along with him.

Viv swallowed. What had just happened? Was the phone Colette's? He had mentioned something about believing his wife had an affair. Oh, heck. Things had just gone south.

Rez limped into the bedroom, kicking the door closed behind him. He made it to the bed. Dropping the cell phone, he fell to his knees before the mattress and bowed his head.

Memory flooded his brain. He and Colette in the car that fateful night. They had been arguing... Rain had been beating the car's exterior... Colette had been an excellent driver, and she'd slowed on the dark country road as they'd journeyed back to Paris from Vaux-le-Vicomte, where they'd attended a dinner hosted by one of his clients. Rez, ever the one who needed to be in control, had clutched the armrest to keep himself from asking if he should drive. They would be fine. He trusted Colette's driving.

But he hadn't trusted *her*.

Not after what he had found...

"How's the garden?" he'd asked tightly.

Colette flashed a glance at him. Pursed her lips. Focused on the road. "It's lovely, *mon cher*. As always. Why do you ask?"

"Just thinking about...gardens." The rain pounded the windows.

"You never ask about the mansion…what I do there. I am surprised you care."

"It's your *tanière*. Whatever you've asked from me, I've given to you. I've respected your need to have an escape from me."

"Rezin! It is not an escape from you. You know I like to paint and garden. I do not desire escape—ever. I live for socializing. Why do you think I look forward to the occasional dinner party so much?"

"You were distracted the entire night," he stated through a tense jaw.

He'd heard the phone call earlier, when Colette had slipped away from the outdoor party and moved behind a hedgerow. He never jumped to conclusions. But she'd been gone longer than felt right.

Before he could stop himself, he asked, "Are you having a liaison?"

"What?" She looked to him.

He gestured to her to keep her attention on the road. She gripped the steering wheel. Her entire profile tightened.

"I heard you on the phone."

He looked away from her. The rain began to dissipate. *Merci à Dieu.*

"Kissing." It had been the sound of an air-kiss. But no simple kiss of greeting had ever been accompanied by a sultry moan.

"Rez."

"I *heard*, Colette."

She pouted. He didn't expect to see tears. She wasn't that kind of drama queen. Always in control. Always sure of everything she felt she was owed, deserved, or had earned.

When she shrugged, Rez's heart took a dive. He crushed his eyelids tightly shut.

"Well," she started, in the light tone that she assumed

when she tried to believe her own lies, "it is what all French-women do. *Oui?* It is nothing, Rezin. A folly."

"Nothing?"

His heart pounded his ribcage, confirming what he'd not wanted to be confirmed after finding the phone in the little table she kept in her garden when he'd gone looking for her. She had been unfaithful. After thirty years of marriage. Or had it been longer than that? *Merde.*

"Unless you are in an eighteenth-century costume drama, it is not 'nothing,' Colette. All Frenchwomen? Is that your excuse? I thought you loved me?"

"I do! I just require—change. You know?"

Yes, she liked to change—her hairstyle, her fashion choices, the colors on the walls and even her breasts. But love? His love for Colette had been unwavering.

"Our love has gotten…" she searched for the word "…quieter. I wanted to find the fire again. Something louder."

Louder? What the hell was she talking about? It was bad enough that his heart was cleaving in two.

The car swerved.

Rez reached for the wheel.

Bright lights from an oncoming car blinded him.

Colette twisted the wheel and screamed.

The wheels barreled over rough terrain. A forest paralleled one side of them. He couldn't be sure which way they had gone off course. But the other car had not hit them. *Whew!*

Just when Rez felt he might gain control of the wheel, the world had jerked to a halt. Colette's scream was the last sound he heard before the windshield shattered. Then an excruciating pain cut through his leg. He blacked out.

Now, Rez clenched the counterpane. This was the first time he'd remembered that night since coming round in the hospital. Remembered that moment when the fight had culminated and Colette had lost control of the vehicle.

The crash replayed in slow motion in his memory. In reality, it had probably been two seconds from the car going off the road to the front end hitting a boulder and flipping over, only to be literally speared by a tree. The thick branch had pushed through the car's metal frame—and Rez's left leg. He'd been pinned inside the vehicle.

Colette, who had not been wearing a seatbelt, had been thrown through the windshield, her body slammed onto a bed of boulders. The doctors had told him she had died instantly from massive head trauma.

He crushed the cell phone in his grip.

He'd thought to move forward. Come to terms with the cruel trick life had played on him. And yet *he* was to blame for the accident. He should have died, too.

Rez slammed the phone onto the floor. The hard plastic shell didn't break. He swore, and kicked the thing across the floor. It wedged under the closed door.

Pressing his thumb under his brow, he closed his eyes, cautioning himself against the dizzy spell that threatened. It was not something he could control. Slapping his hands to the floor, he felt the world begin to spin, very much as it had in the car with Colette…

CHAPTER SEVENTEEN

REZ CAME TO on the floor. He'd not fallen asleep. A dizzy spell had knocked him flat. A bad one this time.

He sat up and swore. Then looked around to make sure no one had witnessed his collapse. Immediately following the accident he'd gone down like that about once or twice every few months. His doctor had suggested it was a condition of his brain injury and that he would have to learn to live with it.

He *was* living with it. It wasn't that he was incapable. He simply had moments when his body didn't want to be upright. So he went horizontal. A few moments later he got up and went on with life. But try explaining that to a son who wanted to send his father to a psychiatrist. Though he knew Jean-Louis was only showing concern. And perhaps his son wasn't so desperate to toss out his father and sit in the CEO's chair.

Leaning his elbows on the bed, he caught his head in his hands. Was he being too adamant in refusing Jean-Louis's desire to jump in and handle the company? Should his son not be allowed to make some mistakes while he learned? Rez had been younger than Jean-Louis when he had taken over—in his twenties. Of course Jean-Louis could do the job. It was just the designing of jewelry that was Rez's life's work. It gave him joy. It was his *raison d'être*.

At the very least he'd made a concession with the psychiatrist appointment. He expected little from it. But perhaps Jean-Louis would see he was trying.

Wandering into the bathroom, he flicked on the faucet. Leaning over the sink, he splashed his face with cold water.

Back in the bedroom he noticed the phone on the floor. Incredible that something so small had been the catalyst for a devastating memory. Colette had been unfaithful to him. And that phone was proof of it. Could it have been with her security guard, Boris? Likely. But he had no desire to charge it to see whom she had called or how often.

He left it there, disgusted with his reaction to it.

Heading down the stairs and into the kitchen, he glanced toward the conservatory. The door was open. Was Viv in there?

He slammed down a couple electrolyte tablets and grabbed a bottle of water from the fridge. He couldn't hide from Viv. He didn't want to. Going to her felt…not desperate, but rather like seeking solace. And yet what would he tell Viv now? That he had distracted his wife so that the accident had happened? Had taken her life and destroyed his, as well as his son's? Perhaps he did need to lie on a psychiatrist's couch and have his brain examined.

Rez wandered through the foyer to the open garden doors. Viv was not inside. He took in the newly ordered foliage with a changed perspective. Viv's handiwork had breathed life into Colette's ghost. Viv's husband haunted her with music; Colette haunted Rez with this garden.

He glanced to the overhead windows, scanning across the curved roof until he spied the cracked glass. He'd have to call in a glazier to take care of that. And to check the rest of the panes, to ensure no others were in need of repair. He must maintain the value of this house. Because it was time to let it go. To finally sweep away Colette's memory. Or rather, to tuck it away. He couldn't excise her from his heart. She was Jean-Louis's mother.

Rez sighed, shoved his hands in his pockets, and wandered over to the roses. There were no blooms, and they were overgrown and ugly. He remembered Colette bringing home a bouquet after a weekend retreat here. The frothy blooms had perfumed the bedroom. It was a scent he'd never cared for, but it had made Colette purr in delight. Because they reminded her of chats with her lover? *Had* it been the security guard as he'd suspected?

Swearing, Rez gripped a branch. He wrenched at it, uprooting it from the dry earth. Tossing it aside, he grabbed another branch. Yanked and tossed. Anger seethed from his pores. All Frenchwomen took lovers. That was what Colette had said. As if she had expected he wouldn't mind her infidelity.

A thorn ripped his palm. Rez swore again and pulled harder, unearthing a whole plant and tossing it aside. A scatter of brown stalks lay around him. Dirt dusted his shoes. His hands bled. He hadn't felt the thorns. The pain in his heart was the only thing that tortured him now.

"Rez? I heard you shout— Oh." Viv raced over to him and grabbed his hands. "Oh, no, Rez…"

He tugged away from her and stepped back, putting up a palm for distance. "She had a liaison. She told me that night of the accident. *Merde!*"

He stepped over to the sofa and let his body land, elbows catching on his knees. When Viviane disappeared for a few moments he immediately wanted her back. By his side.

Don't abandon me. You are my breath now.

And then she kneeled before him, a wet towel in her hands. She dabbed at his palms, her touch gentle but firm. He bowed his head to hers. Safe with her. Loved.

"I'd suspected for a while," he whispered. "We fought. The argument distracted her. She lost control of the car and it veered off the road. It was my fault."

"No," Viv insisted softly. "You couldn't have known what would happen."

"I tried to get hold of the steering wheel."

"You did. You're a good man, Rez. It was an accident."

Viv kissed his palm. He didn't know what he had done to deserve this woman in his life. She was good. Perhaps too good for him. Would he make her want to seek attention elsewhere as he had with Colette?

"The phone jarred my memory." He blew out a breath. "You are too kind to me, Viviane."

"I care about you." Taking both his hands in hers, she gently kissed the knuckles, then turned them to study the cuts. "Just some minor cuts. But I should see if you have some antiseptic."

"Do you have gloves?"

"No… I suppose I should have thought about being sterile—"

"Gardening gloves. I'm not leaving this room until those roses are gone."

"Oh." She nodded. "There are some in the supply room. A couple pairs. I'll help you!" she called as she wandered to the back of the conservatory.

Rez studied his bleeding palms. It was a small price to pay for unearthing a haunting pain.

Viv kissed Rez's shoulder, then down his bare back. No freckles that she could find. And when she touched the scar on his leg he allowed it. They had made love. Now their bodies were lax and perspiring. A full moon shone across the bed. The twinkling Eiffel Tower had become their voyeur.

Yet she wasn't troubled by Rez's quietness. Poor man. He'd just remembered his wife had had an affair. Colette was no longer in the picture, and it might seem as though it shouldn't matter anymore. But Viv wasn't stupid. It mattered. Could this new knowledge derail their future? What *was* their future?

"You okay?" she asked.

"I am when I make love with you."

"Me too. But I mean about…you know…earlier. Remembering things."

He turned onto his back and she nestled her head on his chest, where dark hairs tickled her cheek.

"I've felt there was something I was missing," he said. "Something dark. Now I know what that was. It's big, but also I feel relief. Does that sound strange to you?"

"If it's how you feel, then it's your truth." She kissed his chest, then rested her chin on her hand to look at him. "I have to say something, but I don't want you to think I'm saying it to manipulate you or gloss over your pain."

"What is it?"

"I care about you. I love you. You've come to mean the world to me. And when you're hurt, it hurts my heart as well."

"Thank you. And you mean so much to me. It feels as though you are in my life for a reason. You understand me. It's easy to be with you."

"Same."

He hadn't said he loved her. Selfish of her to expect such a confession after what he'd just remembered about his wife.

"You're changing me, Viv."

"Is that good, bad, or strange?"

He chuckled. "Kind of…sort of…good."

Viv stared up at the giant crystal chandelier. It looked as though a century of dust had gathered on the elaborate structure. Dusting and cleaning it would take a good day.

Rez hadn't said he loved her. Would he ever? Or was there no future for them? Had she jumped in too deep?

Maybe it was time to step back, take a wider view and see what she'd really gotten into. If it was anything at all. The man was obviously haunted by his wife and her indiscretions. Was it too late to pull some armor around her heart?

"Viviane!"

Startled by the familiar female voice, Viv spun and caught her best friend in her arms. "Kiara? What—? I…"

Heck, she hadn't seen Kiara in person for over a year. Viv tightened the hug and lifted her friend and spun her around.

When they parted, Kiara held out Viv's arms. "You look so good. The Paris air certainly does you well. Your cheeks glow. And look at your hair! It's grown half a foot since we last saw one another."

"Well, you look the same. Slim, tanned, sexy, put together, and worth a million bucks."

Kiara waggled her shoulders proudly. "That's around five million now. I just sold a chateau west of Caen to the former NHL player Bear Bradford. My commission was insane."

"Oh, my God. We need to gossip. I want to hear it all. But why are you here? I don't understand."

"Didn't your lover boy tell you? He's put this place up for sale. He wants me to sell it. I was in Marseilles, working another sale, so I flew in immediately. It seemed urgent."

"It did?"

"Yes."

Kiara didn't pick up on Viv's annoyance as she strode across the tiled floor. She'd always been a fan of a body-hugging dress, and the bright red of the one she wore was her color. And those shoes had red heels. She really was living the dream.

"Look what you've done to this garden!" Kiara exclaimed. "I saw the 'before' photos of it. This is going to be a huge selling point. Besides the fact this is a fabulous mansion set riverside in Paris. Oh, Viv!"

Viviane couldn't find the same enthusiasm as her friend.

Rez had put the mansion up for sale? But she wasn't finished with the garden's refurbishment. And—and why would he sell such a lovely property? Didn't his son use it? And his mother-in-law? Had it something to do with him remembering his wife's affair?

Viv clasped a hand over her thudding heart. Pulling up the rose bushes hadn't been enough for him. He must have decided to excise Colette's ghost in the most extreme manner possible. And in the process would he also excise Viv from his life?

"What's going on in your brain?" Kiara twirled a finger before Viv's face. "You don't look happy, sweetie. Did I say something wrong? You didn't know about the sale?"

Viv shook her head. "I need to talk to Rez about this."

She started toward the doors. But then she remembered that her friend, whom she hadn't seen in forever, was here, and they needed to do girlfriend things…and chat…and…

"I won't be long! You have some things to do, yes?"

Kiara shrugged. "Yes, I need to go through the whole place. Should take the afternoon."

"Great. Help yourself to food in the kitchen. We can go out to eat later and catch up."

"You sure you're all right?"

"I'm not sure. That's why I need to talk to Rez. I'll be back soon. I'm so glad you're here!"

"I fly out tonight, so…" Kiara snapped her fingers. "Make it quick."

"I will!"

CHAPTER EIGHTEEN

PENELOPE, LE BEAU'S perky red-headed receptionist, with apple cheeks and long lashes, remembered Viv from the party. When she explained that Rez had left early because his penthouse was finished, she happily provided Viv with the address.

He'd not told her that his home was finished. Penelope had made it sound as though it had been for days. So why had he still been living at the mansion?

Where was Rez's head lately? Had it to do with his injury? His crash into memory after discovering the phone? Now she was really worried about him.

Unless…

Unless he was purposely avoiding her. He had good reason to. There was the whole learning about his wife having an affair thing—but still… That had nothing to do with Viviane. Had he suddenly decided he didn't want a relationship with her?

Speed-walking across a bridge to the Left Bank, Viviane wandered the streets in the Sixth Arrondissement, using the small guidebook that she'd picked up at a bookstore during one of her morning jaunts. The Saint-Germain-des-Prés neighborhood was old money, or so the guidebook stated. The tourist-crowded streets were lined with art galleries, restaurants, mature trees, and brick-fronted buildings.

The front of Rez's building boasted a gorgeous iridescent-tiled design, highlighted here and there with deep indigo tiles. A little modern, a touch Moroccan, it reminded her of the conservatory floor. When she pressed the bell for the top floor, Rez immediately buzzed her in without asking who it was. He stood in the open doorway, waiting, as she topped the stairs.

"Were you expecting me?" she asked as she walked toward him.

"Yes and no. I suspect Mademoiselle Kirk has arrived at the mansion?"

"She has." She stopped before him, taking him in. No shoes, a loose pair of faded jeans. Casual black tee shirt and tousled hair. He looked so un-businesslike, and not at all the image of the CEO of a billion-dollar jewelry company. "Are you okay?"

"Come inside."

That wasn't an answer.

Steeling herself for some heavy insight into Rez's memory vault, Viv crossed the threshold. The penthouse was airy and bright, with high ceilings and a glass roof that curved up from the wall and halfway across the ceiling. The walls were brick and rough timber. The floors wide herringbone. And everywhere there was leather furniture and black metal touches. A total man cave, but with the elan of taste.

"They knocked out a wall here," Rez said as he wandered into the kitchen and grabbed a bottle of wine. "It is nice to have the entire area open now."

"It's gorgeous. Modern. Exactly what I expected your style to be."

"Not like some centuries-old mansion?" He handed her the bottle. "Sip?"

Had he been drinking all morning? Or was he employing the "sip" plan to avoid discussion? She wasn't in the mood to pussyfoot around the difficult stuff today.

"Rez, why didn't you tell me your penthouse was complete? That…that you're staying here again?"

"I…uh…sorry. I just needed a place to sort my thoughts today. It wasn't meant to be disrespectful to you."

"Oh. Well, I can appreciate that. Of course you need some space."

"I do—"

"But you can't sell the mansion. It means something to you. And doesn't your son have memories there?"

"So we're going right there? I should expect nothing less from you." He countered that with a brief smile. "Viv, when I found that phone I remembered the one thing that should have stayed forgotten."

"I'm so sorry."

"It's too much, Viviane. I can't keep that place anymore. I need to move on."

Though she wanted to argue, she knew she didn't have any right to question Rez's relationship with his wife. Or what he did to try to erase those memories. But it still didn't feel right to get rid of such a beautiful home. A home his mother-in-law surely loved. Did Coral know about her daughter's infidelity?

But, even more so, Viv wasn't ready to give up on her dream.

"I'm not finished with the garden," she said quietly.

"You'll finish. You said you'd only a few days remaining?"

"Yes. But Kiara said the mansion would go in a day."

"Most likely. She's a hot seller. But it'll take time to— what do they call it?—stage the place?"

Viviane sighed. Maybe a day at the most. That mansion was perfection. Save for the garden—which, if she hurried, could be viewer-ready in a few days. The final photos wouldn't be nearly as perfect as she'd hoped, though.

Heck, this wasn't cataclysmic to her dream. It was just

a little setback. She should not overreact. Yet it felt deeper. Like an attack on her very being. When she had done nothing wrong!

"I'm sorry, Rez."

"Thank you. Now…" His heavy sigh did not warrant good news. "I still need some space today. Please…?"

Yikes. He didn't want her around. This was bigger than a setback.

"Sure, I get it."

Not completely. Don't push me away!

"I want to spend some time with Kiara before she has to fly out," she told him. "Can I pick up something for you to eat and drop it off?"

"No, I'm fine." He wandered toward the windows, hands in his pockets, back to her.

He was not fine. But it did not feel like her place to step in and try to make things better. Something held Viv back from taking a firm stance about being there for him. Could it be the ghost of his cheating wife? Could Rez ever trust another woman?

Oh, this was not good.

"I'll see you tomorrow, then. Stop by or give me a call." She walked to the door, waiting for his response, but he didn't give her one.

Viv left with her heart pounding and tears rolling down her cheeks. The man was hurting. And she'd done everything she could to help with that. Now it was up to him, and things would happen at his own pace.

Unfortunately, that pace didn't mesh with hers. Or the time she'd allotted for staying in Paris. If she were to move forward with her dream job that meant moving on to another client, perhaps in another country. Far from Rez. They didn't have the luxury right now to take a day away from one another. They really needed to get straight what their intentions for this relationship were. If they even wanted to remain a couple now, with this new information about his wife.

But she would never force him. This was more than grief; it was anger and betrayal. So she must be patient.

Once back at the mansion, Viv deposited the cheese, baguettes and sliced meats she'd picked up along the way onto the counter. Pouring two goblets of wine, she then went in search of her friend.

"Kiara!"

"Behind you!"

Viv spun, and her friend rushed to catch one goblet before wine sloshed over the rim.

"I was in the library," Kiara said, and sipped. "Ooh, this is nice. You've never been a big wine drinker before."

Viv shrugged. "It's the new me. Rez introduced me to this stuff and I can't get enough."

"I like the new you. She's still as beautiful and smart as the old Viv, but this version..." Kiara made a show of looking her up and down "...seems more frisky. Open."

"Sweetie, I've taken a French lover," Viv said with aplomb. Though it felt forced. "That's about as frisky as it gets."

Kiara hooked an arm in Viv's and steered her toward the conservatory. "Tell me everything. My flight doesn't leave until nine, so we've got time."

Hours later, after gossip, girl confessions, and unabashed consumption of meats and cheese, the two women sat on the sofa, heads back and legs stretched out. Kiara's Louboutins sat on the floor, discarded for comfort.

Viviane felt no jealousy at all when comparing them with her chinos, blouse and sandals. She had something that made her feel like she owned the world.

"Rez is perfect, Kiara. But there's the long-distance

thing I worry about. And, well, should I even try to make it work?"

Kiara sat up abruptly and gave her a discerning onceover. "Why would you think otherwise?"

Yes—why? Was she already making up reasons not to fall to pieces should she and Rez not work out? Forming a protective armor about her heart? Possibly.

"Kiara, I've been out of the dating loop for over twenty-five years. I did find a keeper, but… I don't know. Maybe I should play the field? See what else is out there."

"Seriously? Do you *want* to do that?"

No, no, and definitely no. Only a fool would walk away from a man who felt like a perfect match. As close to perfect as could happen.

Viv sighed. "Dating *is* a lot of work. And I do love Rez."

"Then that's your answer."

"But does he love me? He's having a tough go of it right now. I'm not so sure I landed in his life at the right time for him to start over. I thought we were really connecting, but then his grief punched him with some awful memories. Selling this place is a reaction to that. I don't think he should sell. It means something to his family. But he's only just remembered that his wife had an affair and that's why he's getting rid of this place—because it used to be hers."

"Viv, dear, why do you need him to keep it?"

Interesting question. Why, indeed? She had no right to influence Rez's personal decisions. And this place *had* been his cheating wife's hideaway.

On the other hand… "His son uses it. And his mother-in-law. There must be a good reason Coral wanted the garden refurbished. In memory of her daughter?"

"Yes, that was her intention," Kiara said thoughtfully.

"If Rez can't be here, he should at least allow his family to enjoy the place."

"You mustn't convince him to keep it," Kiara pleaded.

"Why not?"

"Because then I'll lose a huge commission!"

"I'm sorry. It's…complicated."

Kiara tilted her head onto Viv's shoulder. They shared the blanket between them.

"Is it hard to move on after being married to Brian for so long?"

"Yes, and no. I mean, I don't feel guilty. But I'm not sure if I should feel guilty for *not* feeling guilty. Brian is gone. Longing for him to be alive or continuing to mourn is not going to bring him back. I'm ready, Kiara. And it feels damn good to have the attention of another man. Rez makes me feel sexy. And you know I would never call myself old—fifty is the new thirty, don't you know?—but I really do love the attention."

"You are not old. I can only hope to have such luminous skin and hair when I'm your age."

"When you're *my* age? Don't make me sound decrepit, Kiara. You're turning forty this year."

"Ixnay on the ortyfay. I intend to remain eternally thirty-nine."

"Join the club."

Her friend tilted the last drops of wine into their glasses, then tapped the air with the empty bottle. "Here's to love! Be it true, new, or rocky."

"You're toasting love? Well, well, well… That makes me wonder if you have a new boyfriend!"

Kiara sighed. "Too busy. All I can manage is a hookup here and there. Benetto in Naples is a dream. We eat. We have sex. I can slip out in the morning without having a conversation. It's optimal."

"You've *never* been so poor on relationships. What's up?"

"Like I said. I'm too busy. And…well, you know… What does a relationship really have to offer me?"

Kiara had found out a few years earlier that she wasn't able to have children. She had always wanted a big family with lots of kids. Viv remembered that evening how her friend had cried over the devastating news, and how she'd moved out of her boyfriend's home that same evening, never to see him again. Kiara hadn't the heart to tell him the truth about their split. It was an extremely touchy subject for Kiara.

As for what a relationship could offer a woman…?

"Good sex?" she tried.

"Most of the time it's good," Kiara agreed. "So how is it with Rezin? I love that name. And he is so sexy. Tall, dark, and handsome. And a millionaire?"

"Billionaire."

"Nice! You found the perfect man."

"I was thinking much the same. Now? How to keep him?"

The twosome laughed and finished their wine before calling Kiara a cab for the airport.

CHAPTER NINETEEN

TRACKING A MORNING beam of sunshine through the garden to the supply room, Viv flicked the switch to move the chandelier. The electronic mechanism slowly lowered the heavy extravagance until the bottommost crystal dangled about six inches from the ground. Washcloths, a lemon and vinegar solution, and bucket of warm water for cleaning it sat ready. The dust was thick, and a fingernail test determined it was caked on as hard as paint.

This was going to require elbow grease.

"Should have gone for a walk first," she muttered as she circled the huge creation, deciding where to begin. She'd take a break after a few hours, and head out for coffee and a pastry.

It had been sad to wake in bed alone. Rez hadn't texted or called.

But Viv would not dwell on his absence. Not for a while, at least. She figured she could distract herself from worrying about their relationship for at least an hour or two with intense cleaning. After that, all bets were off.

She bent to retrieve a dusting cloth, and when she stood bumped into the chandelier. It wobbled. The sound of something cracking alerted her. Had she broken a crystal?

When a sudden slice of heat seared her shoulder she let out a yelp and grabbed her shoulder. Her fingers came away with blood on them. Viviane winced at the pain. She stepped away from the chandelier and saw shattered glass on the floor. Those thin shards could have only come from…

She looked up. The cracked glass pane had fallen out. Another small triangle of glass dangled from the iron frame. It could fall at any moment.

She jumped back—and into the arms of Rez. Spinning to face him, she let out another yelp.

"Viv, I heard you scream. What the—? You're bleeding."

"I didn't scream. It was a minor outburst."

"Why are you bleeding? Did you cut yourself on the chandelier?"

"No, the broken ceiling glass fell. I think it got joggled loose when I bumped the chandelier." She tapped her shoulder. "Is it bad?"

He swore as he pushed up the back of her tee shirt to study the damage. "There's a lot of blood. You don't feel that? It could be deep. I'll call SOS Médecins."

"SOS?"

"They do house calls. Faster than the emergency room. On the other hand…" He swore again. "I don't know. The ER might have the best equipment to deal with this if it *is* serious."

"Hospitals freak me out. What are you doing here, anyway? Maybe some iodine and I'll be fine."

"Henri is waiting out front," he said urgently. "He can get us there quickly. Is that the only place you were hurt? Are you okay? Viv?"

The last thing she heard was her name. Then the world went black.

Rez paced beside the emergency room bed on which Viviane lay. He'd carried her to the car following her faint in the conservatory. The physician here had foregone stitches. The long surface cut had just required taping shut with skin closure strips. Viv would be fine, but they would not release her until the doctor on call signed her off. She dozed right now, in and out of sleep. The chemist had provided a pill to relax her while they had been prepping the wound.

This was his fault. If he'd called the glazier when he'd been thinking to do so this accident would have never happened. *Mon Dieu*, yet another woman damaged by his indifference. Colette had said the fire had left their relationship. Was this too much fire for he and Viviane?

His watch buzzed. He checked the notification. A ten a.m. meeting with the Prince. It was important he be there to finalize the wedding set design. He knew Henri could drive him to Le Beau in less than twenty minutes if they left now. He also knew that if he were late Penelope knew where he kept the hard copy design file and could access it, hand it over to Jean-Louis.

Rez leaned over Viv. She smiled wearily and her eyelids fluttered. He kissed her forehead, her cheek, and her nose, where those six freckles danced as she wrinkled it in reaction.

"How do you feel?" he asked.

"I'll be fine." She lay on her side. The hospital gown exposed the place where the wound ran from the top of her shoulder to mid-back. "You think they'll let me wear this fancy gown home?"

"I'll have Henri bring in something for you to wear." Rez texted his driver and suggested a nearby tourist shop across the river that would provide a tee shirt. "Done."

"When can I leave?"

He shrugged. "We're waiting on the official sign-off. Just relax, Viv. I'm here with you. We have all the time in the world."

A tear rolled down her cheek.

"Viv…?"

She swiped at the tear. "Sorry. So much is going on in my life. Big, heavy stuff. I lost my husband. I'm in a foreign land. I'm starting a new job that has no guarantee it will be successful. I'm never sure if my blushes are hot flashes. I found a sexy Frenchman who actually seems to enjoy my company, but he's got a dead wife to deal with. And I'm not sure if he'll choose me over her. It's a lot."

Yes, the dead wife. Who shouldn't be in the middle of this new relationship. But, strangely, she was. And, as much as he wanted to reassure Viv who his choice would be, right now she wasn't in any frame of mind to really hear him.

"It is a lot."

"But if I'm truthful, it's actually exhilarating. Scary exhilarating."

"I'm impressed."

"By what?"

"You could have gone the victim route. *Everything is terrible and it's all happening because I don't know where I'm going or what I'm doing.* But you embrace the challenge of the new. You are a strong, confident woman, Viv."

"I am," she said with surprise. "And I'm so fortunate. I'm in Paris. I have a job for the moment. And I enjoy that job. And…well, there's you. Life is really good." She closed her eyes. "Now that I think of it, why are you here? You should be at work. You can leave me. I'll be fine."

"I know you will be." He glanced toward the hallway that led to the entrance doors. When Henri arrived with the shirt, he would make his escape to Le Beau.

Or…

He sat on the chair beside her bed. For the first time, work was not the place he wanted to be. Kissing the back of Viv's hand, he smoothed his cheek along her soft, warm skin.

"This is where I want to be."

After being discharged from the emergency room, Viv slid with Rez into the back of the limo and Henri drove them to a Lebanese restaurant in the Fifth, at Rez's direction. Nestled amidst a forest of ferns and a babbling brook, they enjoyed mezze, tea, and some exotic music.

That really hit the spot. Viv had been famished. Now she felt better—if a little tired from the morning's adventure. Her new tee shirt featured a black cat with a red beret forming a smooch with its mouth. That Henri…such a joker.

"Did you take the day off to spend it with me?" she asked as they walked through the courtyard toward the mansion entrance.

"You got a problem with that?"

"Not at all. But you're thinking about work."

"I am not." He punched in the digital code and allowed her inside before him. "I called a glazier while they were fixing you up. He should be here within the hour, to fix the glass and check the entire ceiling. No working on the chandelier until he gives you the A-OK."

"Deal. I can do some groundwork the rest of the day."

"Absolutely not." Rez took Viv in his arms. "I took the day off. We're going to spend it together. Nothing fancy… just a nice afternoon enjoying one another's company."

"Nestled on the sofa in the garden?"

"I like the sound of that. Maybe some slow dancing later?"

"You do know how to romance a woman."

Before she could kiss him, he pressed a finger to her lips. "I need to apologize for my freak-out, and…and for selling the mansion. Things are tough right now. Jean-Louis is putting pressure on me. And remembering about Colette's infidelities really threw me. It was a reaction. Poorly thought out decision. But I realized one thing."

"What's that?"

Just as Rez was about to say something that she felt would be important, the mansion door swung open and in walked Jean-Louis. The man showed immediate surprise to see his father standing there with her in his arms.

Viv's discomfort manifested itself in her wiggling out of Rez's embrace.

"Papa?"

"Jean-Louis, I didn't expect you to stop by."

"I didn't expect to find you here at Maman's *tanière*. I thought the penthouse was finished? Are you…still staying here?"

Jean-Louis gave Viviane a onceover. It didn't feel like he was giving her a glowing assessment, either.

He said something in French, and Rez answered in French. It all went over Viv's head. But she did sense she was not being welcomed into this conversation. At least, not by Jean-Louis.

She stepped back, walking toward the conservatory. "I'll leave you two to talk." She gave a sheepish wave, but neither paid her any mind as they continued their discussion in rising tones and in heated French.

What she wouldn't give to understand the language. But she suspected this was the showdown Rez had dreaded.

"So she is more than just a gardener," Jean-Louis stated.

Rez had sensed Viviane backing away and leaving them. He'd almost called for her to stay, but then they'd have to speak English, and he knew Jean-Louis would scoff at that.

"Papa!"

"She's my…" Rez almost said *lover*, but the term didn't feel right for this moment. He had intended to formally introduce Viviane as his significant other to his son. Not blurt it out in the middle of an argument. "I care about her, Jean-Louis. She means something to me."

Jean-Louis thrust out an arm as he scoffed, "So that is why you missed the meeting this morning? You were in bed with your lover?"

"Watch it," Rez warned. His son had no right to speak to him in such a manner. "You may believe I am an invalid, but I still command respect as your father."

"Dad, you missed an important meeting."

"I am aware of that."

Jean-Louis's mouth dropped open.

"I saw the reminder. But when I got it I was in the emergency room with Viv. A glass panel from the conservatory fell and cut her."

"Is she okay?"

Rez knew Jean-Louis was not cruel; he simply had a focus that would eventually prove him a force at Le Beau. *Much like his father.*

And just now Rez had realized he could let go. At least some of it.

"She'll be fine. It was a long cut, but not deep. It was a good thing I did allow her to refurbish the garden. The plants had taken over, and had she not cut down most of them more than one panel may have dropped out. The entire roof could have collapsed."

"It is good to know the room has been spared. It was special to Maman. She would want the garden to be kept vital."

Rez would never tell Jean-Louis that Colette had been unfaithful. It wasn't fair when his son had no means to go to his mother to confirm such an accusation. And he would not speak ill of the dead. Jean-Louis deserved to hold his mother in high esteem.

"The Prince is pleased with the design," Jean-Louis said. "You should have been there to see the smile on his face."

"I'm sorry. I could have been there. But I… I made a choice."

"And that choice was the American woman?"

He met his son's eyes and tried to show him his sincerity. His genuine need to simply be understood by him. As Viv understood him. That was the most intimate thing he could imagine between two people: an innate understanding. All he asked of Jean-Louis was that he not judge him. That he allowed him to walk through his life and make his mistakes and learn as he went.

But his son suffered, too. And sometimes Rez forgot that.

"How are you, Jean-Louis?"

His son tilted his gaze down. His shoulders slumped.

"I don't ask enough. We're both so busy with work. We tend to act more as office mates than father and son at times. That's wrong. And I'm so sorry. You lost your mother. It's difficult."

Jean-Louis nodded. "I miss her."

Taking his son into his arms, Rez hugged him. And when he thought to pull away, instead he pressed him closer. They had never been a demonstrative family. That was stupid. A man should hug his son more often. Because it was only he and Jean-Louis now. They must be there for one another. And he'd not been attentive enough over the past few years.

"I should have done better," he said over his son's shoulder. "Talked to you. Been there for you when you were grieving for your mother. I'm sorry."

When he pulled away, his son's eyes were watering with tears. He nodded. So much like his father. Staunch. Proud. Always there to do what had to be done. He'd taken the reins of Le Beau while Rez had been recuperating. He'd proved himself at a time when he should have been allowed to step back and grieve. *He does have what it takes.*

"She lives in this house," Jean-Louis said. "Her memory…"

Rez winced and stepped back. There was no easy way to breach the next topic. "I must let you know that I've decided to put the mansion up for sale."

"What?"

"Jean-Louis, it's for the best."

"What best? Papa, I just told you how much this place means to me. I come here sometimes. Just to…to sit in the garden. To remember her."

And Rez had had the audacity to think his son retreated here to escape his wife. That their marriage was in trouble. He really had been more disconnected from his son than he'd realized.

"And Grandmère uses it."

"I… I need to do this, son."

But *did* he? He'd not taken Jean-Louis's feelings into consideration during that moment when he'd torn those rose bushes from the ground out of rage over Colette's *liaison*. In that moment he'd not wanted another thing to do with this house. This memory trap.

And yet he'd surfaced from that rage. Viv had been there to help him understand that he could move beyond it—and he was, and he manifested his own anger. If he chose to react differently, then life would proceed differently.

Jean-Louis stood there, one hand propped on the newel post at the bottom of the marble staircase, imploring him with a look on his face that Rez had not seen since his son was a child. A lost look that silently asked, *Why would you say that, Papa? I know what makes me happy. What makes me feel loved.*

"Sorry." Rez splayed a hand before him. "I wasn't taking you and Coral using the place into consideration." Perhaps there was a way they could both be happy? "I won't sell the house if you stop badgering me about leaving Le Beau. I will remain CEO of Le Beau. You can do that, *oui*?"

"Papa…" Jean-Louis shook his head. "I will not bargain for my mother's memory."

That had been the wrong thing to suggest. He should have negotiated…given Jean-Louis more responsibility? Yes.

"It's not like that—"

"It feels exactly like that. Listen." Jean-Louis raked his fingers through his hair. A habit of frustration. "I need to be more clear with you. You seem to think that I want to boot you from the company completely."

"Don't you?"

"Of course not! You just need to take some time. You missed an important meeting this morning. You've missed many in the past few years. You need to do some healing, Papa."

"And what about you?"

"I speak of what I know! When I was able to, after your return to Le Beau, I took time away from work. You know that. My wife insists we take a spa every other weekend, and it has been good for me. For my heart. You must do the same. To heal."

"I am! I have. Can't you see? I rarely use the cane now. I work long days and the clients are always beyond satisfied with my work. You know no one creates Le Beau pieces like I do, Jean-Louis."

"You are a master. Le Beau would not be Le Beau without your talent, your designs. I'm talking about healing your head."

"I made an appointment with that doctor you told Penelope to give me the number for."

"You did? Papa, that's…" Jean-Louis bowed his head. He seemed on the verge of tears. Then he nodded and lifted a smile to Rez. "That makes me happy. This doctor is cutting edge. I've researched him. He's top of his field. He's not the stuffy kind that makes you sit on a couch and talk about your childhood."

"I'd do anything for you, *mon fils*. If this will make you happy, I'll go see what this doc has to say. Couch or not."

"I think he can help you. I want to see you happy, Papa. And, *oui*, I know Le Beau makes you happy. I don't want to push you out. I want to assume the CEO position because I think it's time I learned. But, as well, I can take on the paperwork. The office stuff that you now sometimes struggle with. I don't want you to leave. I want you to continue to design and create for Le Beau. I simply want to take some of the load from you. And, really, I won't let any of it happen until you agree to take a vacation."

"A what?"

"Exactly! You don't even know what that word means. Papa, when was the last time you took a break from work that wasn't imposed on you because you were in the hospital? Go to Greece! For a few weeks. Just…take the gardener with you. I saw her supporting you at the ball. She's… good for you."

Rez wanted to shout at his son for suggesting such a thing, and in the next second he wanted to embrace him for his cognizance. "I'm not sure. This is…"

"It's a lot to consider. But, trust me, I'm not trying to be rid of you."

Rez heaved out a sigh. And with that breath his balance faltered. He reached to grasp the newel post, but instead his son grabbed his arm and assisted him as Rez's body went backward. He landed sitting on the step. Now there was no denying he wasn't one hundred percent fit. That he never would be. It was a forever reminder of a horrible day. The day his heart had been broken twice.

"Let me think about this," Rez said.

"Of course. Are you okay?"

He nodded.

"Then I'll leave you to think. Whatever you do, do not list this house until we've talked again."

"I won't. I promise."

Jean-Louis left without another word.

He hadn't made a fuss about Rez's balance issue. It was a kindness that clutched at Rez's heart. He bowed his head into his hands and realized that this was exactly how Viv must have felt when he had handed her the shoe and left her alone. Given her space to come to terms with erratic reality.

Emotions prodded at him to give it all up, surrender, go off and live as a hermit. But Rez shook his head. No, he wasn't a quitter. And he couldn't rightfully wrest this house from under his son's feet as if it was a dirty rug that needed to be tossed out. That would be one more emotional crime against him.

It was time to heal their relationship. And perhaps letting go of some control was the catalyst to that healing.

"Did Jean-Louis leave?" Viv asked softly.

He hadn't heard her approach. Her bare feet were in sight from his bowed-head position. And, if he was seeing correctly, he was pretty sure freckles danced on them just as they did her cheeks and nose.

"He's given me a lot to think about," Rez said.

Viviane sat beside him, tilting her head onto his shoulder. He liked how comfortable she had become with him. He knew he was not making a mistake with her.

"He was angry about me missing the meeting. I told him you were at the emergency room."

"Yes, but I wish you'd told me you had a meeting. I would have been fine on my own."

"I know you would have been. But I made a choice, Viv. And I chose you. I love you. You mean more to me than…"

His work? Had his tattered heart begun to repair? Had it already allowed Viv inside in a way that made him never want her to leave?

"I'm going to pause on the sale right now. I need a few days to think it through."

She clasped his hand. "If that is what you need to do, then I'll support whatever decision you make."

"When will the garden be complete?"

"I need to clean the chandelier. And dig in the English roses that I've purchased to replace the…er…the ones we took out. Then I want to bring in a professional photographer, so I have photos for my portfolio."

"I don't think you'll have any problem making The Plant Whisperer a reality. You do wonderful work, Viv."

"Thank you, but it's snagging the clients that will be the challenge."

"Not if I recommend you to my friends."

"You would do that?"

"Of course. I've seen your work. And I never recommend something that I don't believe is quality."

"How did I get so lucky to meet you?"

"Strangely, it was through my mother-in-law. And I need to call her as well."

"She's reachable?"

"She has been for a few days."

Viv looked up at him with surprise.

He shrugged. "I wasn't going to ruin a good thing."

CHAPTER TWENTY

THE NEXT MORNING Rez kissed Viv goodbye while she lay in bed. He told her he was leaving for work but would be back early for his appointment. He walked out quietly, and she rolled over within the soft sheets to face the Eiffel Tower. What a view. What a man. What a life she could have here in Paris.

Was it even possible?

Certainly, she had started something with Rez. She loved him, and he'd told her he loved her. *"I chose you."* But where would it go from here? Did it have staying power? Was she ready to settle into another long-term relationship?

Yes, she wanted Rez. She wanted Paris. She wanted it all.

But *could* she do this? She did have that prospect in Venice. And after that job Rez had said he'd recommend her to his friends.

How many people could he know with indoor gardens in need of work?

Knowing his financial status, and the set he ran with, probably many. And they were the kind of clientele she sought. If she did a few more jobs, and those clients passed on a good word to *their* friends, this could work.

While her core giddied with the excitement of what might lie before her, that pesky no-nonsense busybody who lived within her said, *Whoa, don't rush ahead. This might be a complete disaster. The Venice job could fall through. The man could break it off.*

And then Viv would be left homeless. In a foreign country. Broken-hearted.

Closing her eyes, she mentally slashed at the busybody with a sword. Then she wondered what sort of crystal she should stick in her bra that would keep her positive. And then she laughed. She didn't need crystals. She was a strong woman, as Rez had said. She could do this.

Maybe...

All things were worth a try. And she was good at putting in the effort. So it was time to act as if she were already doing it. Time to get to work!

Down in the conservatory, Viv inspected the ceiling. The broken glass pane had been replaced yesterday. The glazier had said the rest of the glass was in good order. Now all that remained was to clean the chandelier and plant the English roses.

As she gathered the cleaning spray and a wash rag, her phone rang. "Kiara! Where are you?"

"Berlin. I got a call from Monsieur Ricard. I'm so bummed."

"Why?"

"He didn't tell you? He's not going to list the mansion. There goes my commission!"

"Oh, I'm so sorry, Kiara. He did tell me, but I'd forgotten about it."

"He said he'd pay me for my time. He certainly didn't have to, but he's already wired a sweet payment into my account. That man is delicious, Viv. Are you going to hold tight to him?"

"As tight as I can."

"Really? Can you make it work?"

"I'd like to. Depends on what he wants."

"Why can't it be what *you* want? If you want the man, tell him!"

Kiara had a point. She was creating a new Viviane West-berg. A worldly, independent, reputable gardening expert. Could that woman get—and keep—her man? When she'd initially arrived in Paris she'd laughed at the idea of snagging a Frenchman. And now…?

"What are you thinking about?" Kiara asked.

"I'm thinking about going for it."

"Yes! Keep me posted."

"I will. So, what's going on in Berlin?"

"It's a stopover. In two days I'm headed to Switzerland. You'll never believe it, but Bowen James is listing his chateau."

"Bowen? Isn't that the guy…?"

"Yes, he's the guy."

"Are you sure this is the right thing to do? Just for a commission, Kiara?"

Her friend sighed. "I want to see him again. I… I owe him an explanation. I mean, I loved him, Viv."

"You did. Well, be careful. And call me if you need anything."

"I will. Oh! I'm sending you the info on that Venetian palazzo. There's been a change in plans from the owner. She's leaving tonight because of a family emergency. Which means you need to fly out immediately to go through everything with her. Can you do that? The flight to Venice is less than a couple hours."

"I can *so* do that. I'll look up flights right now. Send me her address and the details you have. Thank you, Kiara. I owe you so much."

"You owe me nothing. You are the best friend I've ever had. Seeing you happy again is all I need." Kiara kissed the phone. "Love you. Bye!"

Rez clicked off after a call from Jean-Louis. His son's excitement had burst through the conversation. He'd thought about telling his dad in person, but he'd had to call as soon as he and his wife were walking out from the clinic. They were having a baby!

Thrilled at the news, Rez tucked a small jewelry box in his suit pocket and headed down the hallway at work. He nodded to Penelope.

"I'm going to be a *grandpère*. Exciting, *oui*?"

"Yes! I'm so happy for Jean-Louis and his wife. And you! Are you leaving for lunch?"

"I have some things to take care of this afternoon. I don't have anything on my schedule." *Except an appointment with the shrink*. He paused, holding the door handle. "Penelope, do you think Jean-Louis would make a good CEO of Le Beau?"

Her answer was immediate. "I know he would. He's smart, quick to learn, and he knows the business. Just like his dad."

"You're on Team Jean-Louis, Penelope."

"I'm on Team Ricard. I know you feel like Jean-Louis taking your place would be pushing you out. But, Monsieur Ricard, it would be like having two great minds at the top. You'd have less paperwork. Which you know you hate. And you'd have more time to design."

"I'm still going to get you a shirt that says *Team Jean-Louis*." He winked at her. "*Bonjour*, Penelope. See you tomorrow morning."

News of a grandchild made him float. By the time Rez stood before the mansion door he realized he'd walked the whole way from the office. And he hadn't once felt pain in his leg. This was what happiness felt like.

But when he opened the door his mood dropped. Viviane stood in the foyer. With a suitcase.

Rez's heart took a dive. Suddenly his leg hurt like hell.

"Oh, Rez! I wasn't sure I'd see you before leaving."

"Where are you going?"

"Venice. I told you about the job there."

"But you're not finished here."

And she'd agreed to go with him to the doctor this afternoon. It had taken every ounce of his pride to ask her to accompany him. He couldn't fathom doing it alone.

"I just talked to Kiara. The seller of the Venice place needs to see me this afternoon, before she leaves. This will be my only chance to win the job."

"Were you intending to simply leave if I hadn't come home?"

"Oh, Rez, this is a quick trip. One day in and then out. I'm told the flight is only two hours."

"But you've packed all your things?"

She gripped the suitcase handle. "Yes. I…uh… You've gone above and beyond with your kindness in letting me stay here. And the job is almost complete, so I figured… Well… I didn't want to push."

Rez wanted to shout *Push!* But he couldn't find the word. He couldn't speak. She was leaving. As if he didn't matter to her.

"My flight leaves at two, so I'll have to get to the airport soon. I need to call a cab."

"No, Henri will drive you. He'll have you there in half an hour. Viv."

He swallowed. What to say? She was following her dream, and it was leading her to Venice. The woman was independent and smart, and she knew what she was doing. He couldn't stand in her way. He might never be able to give her what she needed. He could financially, but she would never accept that. It was a guilt-free, open heart that Viv required from him.

He pressed a palm over his heart. The square box in his pocket reminded him. Damn it, he'd wanted this to be a special gift. One he'd give to her and then…

And then what? He couldn't ask her now. Could he?

"Will you call Henri?" she asked. "I would love to take you up on the offer."

"Of course." Rez texted Henri. The driver replied that he'd be out front in ten minutes. "So, you're leaving?"

"Please don't give me that puppy dog face. I'll be back late tonight. Or maybe tomorrow morning. I'll just have to see how long it takes. Then I'll finish the conservatory. Promise. Look at me! Jet-setting across Europe to build my business."

The last thing he wanted to do was deflate her excitement.

"I'm proud of you. And I hope you'll return." *To me.* "I can go to the doctor by myself."

"Huh?" She started walking toward the door. "Oh, no, Rez, I completely forgot! The appointment with the psychiatrist." She dropped the suitcase handle. "That's tomorrow afternoon, surely?"

He shook his head. "This afternoon. Don't worry about it. I can do it on my own." He puffed up his chest. It didn't feel right, but he wouldn't show her that she'd let him down. "This is important to you. And, like you said, Venice is a quick trip. I'll see you soon, *oui*?"

The woman he loved was walking away from him. She'd packed her bags, already prepared for the next job. Rez wanted to throw himself in front of her and tell her to stay. They had begun something. One day away from her would feel like forever. Could they survive a long-distance relationship?

"Oh, I can't go. I promised you."

"I insist you go to Venice, Viv. This is your dream job. I can see the doctor by myself. I am a big boy."

"You are. But…" She sighed. "Are you sure?"

No. "Of course I am. Now, go. Henri is always early."

She kissed him quickly. Too quickly. "I'll call you as soon as I get back. Okay?"

"Of course."

As she walked toward the parked limo, Rez whispered, "Come back to me."

And his heart, which had recently begun to stitch itself back together, fissured again.

That had been the single cruelest thing she had ever done to a man. Leaving him standing in an open doorway. Dashing off without so much as an *I love you*. And she had forgotten about her promise to accompany him to the doctor.

Oh, Viv, what a terrible person you are!

She considered telling Henri to turn around. But Venice, and her future, pleaded for her to continue forward. Could their new love survive long distance? She hoped so. This was going to be a test.

A test in which Rez had already answered one question incorrectly. Standing there with her packed bags, she'd hoped he might suggest she stay with him at the penthouse when she returned to Paris. He hadn't. So that meant he wasn't prepared to make that offer to her.

Would he ever?

If he wasn't ready to commit, she had to be prepared to move forward with her original plan. Build her business. Travel the world. Live out of a suitcase from job to job. She could do that. But her heart screamed that it had found a place—a person—it wanted to be close to. Always.

Once at the airport, Viv headed to the ticket counter and waited in line.

Despite the lack of invitation to stay at the penthouse, the disappointment in Rez's eyes when she'd dismissed him for her own needs tugged at her heart. This Venice job was important. But was it more important than keeping a promise to the man with whom she had fallen in love?

The line moved forward ahead of her.

Viv turned and scanned through the window where cabs were dropping people off for departure.

'I chose you.'

He had chosen her over his work. That meant something. And now it was her turn to make a choice.

After a long shower, Rez sat on the edge of the bed with a towel wrapped about his hips. The doctor's appointment was in an hour. He glanced at his phone. Viv hadn't called. She was probably on the plane right now. It was good that she'd gotten the job offer. She needed to go and confirm that job. He wouldn't stand in her way.

But that meant he had to go to the doctor by himself. He'd spent days, weeks, months going to doctors following the accident. Always by himself. Nervous. Unsure. It had put him out of his comfort zone, and that loss of control had messed with him. Sometimes he'd glance to his side to see if he might find Colette sitting there. Someone, *anyone* to support him while he navigated the cruel and confusing world of the medical system.

"It's why you need control," he muttered aloud.

Realizing that hurt his heart. A heart that had been tattered, damaged, and torn apart over the past years. A heart he could not fix by standing firm at Le Beau. Being CEO meant nothing to him if his heart wasn't whole.

Viv had made him feel as though he could be whole.

And now he was alone again.

Once dressed, he headed down to the foyer. Henri waited outside. Limping to the door, Rez looked at the cane sitting in the umbrella stand.

"Hell."

He grabbed the cane and hobbled outside to the waiting limo. Opening the door, he slid into the back seat and—

"Viv?"

She plunged into his arms and kissed him. "You're not going to the doctor alone."

"But— No, I can't allow you to ruin your chance with the job— Are you sure?"

"I've never been more sure of something in my life. I'll catch the next flight out, after you've been to the doc. I may catch the owner in time—I may not. But to imagine you sitting with the doctor by yourself…? If there's one thing I learned in those years of accompanying my husband to the oncologist it's that patients need advocates. Someone to sit beside them and listen. Because you may think you hear it all, but you're going to be in patient mode—nervous and anxious. I'll be there to take notes and make sure all your questions get answered. Deal?"

"I love you."

He kissed her, and she pulled him into the deepest most comforting hug he had ever gotten.

The moment the visit was finished, Rez grabbed Viv's hand and rushed her outside to the waiting limo. *Sans* cane! He guided her into the back seat and told Henri to race to the airport. They arrived twenty minutes before the four o'clock flight was due to leave.

She kissed him quickly and promised to be back in the morning.

He couldn't imagine spending a night alone without her snuggled against his body. He waved as she raced inside the airport and Henri pulled away from the curb.

The doctor's visit had been unique and interesting, and he had actually walked out of the office with hope. The doctor, who was indeed a psychiatrist, had initially put Rez through a brain scan. He'd then gone over those digital scans with Rez and Viv. Viv had not let go of his hand. And she had asked some important questions he'd not even considered. Her strength had become his own.

According to the doctor, there were some things Rez could do to actually mend his damaged brain. The first things, among many, were nutrition and meditation! He'd been sent home with a protocol to follow for the next three months before he would return for another scan to see if improvements had been made.

If the things the doctor had suggested could create clearer thinking and defeat the dizzy spells Rez was on board. And Viv had been excited to help him.

Now he hoped she would be in his life long enough to see him improve.

CHAPTER TWENTY-ONE

DURING THE RIDE from Charles de Gaulle, Viviane watched the red taillights buzz by. Henri had been waiting curbside to pick her up. Even though it was close to midnight. She appreciated the darkness, because she had been tearful since leaving Italy.

Viv had landed at the Venetian airport around six p.m. It had taken her too long to navigate the Italian signage and finally hail a cab to the dock, where Rez had reserved a water taxi for her. She'd frantically knocked on the seller's house just as the front door had opened. The homeowner, a gorgeous woman in her eighties, with silver hair and stunning fashion sense, had frowned at her.

Viv had been late and the owner had had to catch her own water taxi. There had been no time to show her the garden. And really…? Had Viv actually expected to be hired after showing up so late?

Viv had apologized and thought about explaining, but she knew better. It had been her choice to stay with Rez and accompany him to the doctor. She'd known there was a chance she might lose the job.

What really made her feel awful was that Kiara had done this for her as a favor, and she had blown it. She'd texted Kiara with apologies before flying back to Paris. Kiara still hadn't replied.

Blowing out a shivering breath, Viv settled against the

seat. It had been a long day. Beginning with the excitement over the chance of nabbing another job, then the struggle about whether or not to actually leave Rez behind to visit the doctor on his own. The decision to go with him had felt so right as she'd sat there, holding Rez's hand, listening to the doctor's hopeful diagnosis. Then had come the rush to the airport and the disaster in Venice. She'd cried silently most of the flight back to Paris. Because she'd failed.

Before leaving Venice, she had texted Rez about her loss. She'd told him she wanted to spend the night in a hotel. That distance felt necessary. Crying in front of him was not what a strong, smart woman would do. Although she hadn't confessed that in the text.

He'd texted back telling her not to worry and that he'd send Henri to pick her up. A hotel room would be waiting for her. His kindness had spurred the tears again. Yet to think of not seeing him tonight brought on even more tears.

Would she get any job now? Sure, it had been only this one job she'd lost. And Rez had offered to help. But who was she to think she could grow an international gardening business without clients or any sort of visibility? She was just an American woman who had jumped into a fantasy. No one in Europe knew about her silly book or the experience she had. No one was going to be excited to hire her. She was a nobody. One amongst many, surely, who might already have a corner on the indoor garden business.

"What have I done?"

More tears flowed as she circulated through the same thoughts over and over. What a fool she had been…

She tugged out her phone and contemplated texting Rez. She knew he would do anything for her. But it didn't feel right asking for what she really needed. A hug. A kiss to make it all better. And really the French lover was all a fantasy, too. It wasn't meant to be. It couldn't be. Not without any means to support herself so she could remain in Paris and be near that lover.

Time to return to Minnesota and lick her wounds.

But she couldn't do that until she'd finished what she'd started. There were minor fix-ups and some staging to do in the mansion's garden. And photos to be taken.

"Henri, take me to the mansion," she said.

Tucking her phone back in her purse, she closed her eyes and cried more silent tears until Henri announced they had arrived at the mansion.

Walking into the cool, dark foyer, Viviane dropped her suitcase by the door. Moonlight beamed in, forming a direct line to the conservatory. She stepped out of her shoes and padded into the garden.

Inhaling the fresh verdancy overwhelmed her.

Rushing to the sofa, Viv landed on it as tears spilled down her cheeks.

Rez quietly strode toward the conservatory. Henri had called him from the limo, informing him of Viv's changed plans. Rez had considered allowing her the peace to simply be alone tonight. But despite her wanting him to believe she needed to be away from the mansion to get out of his way, he couldn't let it end like that. He had been waiting in the hotel room for her. To simply be there for her.

The American woman's style of wearing her heart on her sleeve and asking tough questions, barging in where most dared not emotionally tread, had worn off on him.

Smiling to think how she had changed him, he wandered into the conservatory. She was sitting on the sofa, sniffling. When he got close, she startled and looked to him.

"Rez? I said I wanted to be alone tonight."

"I know what you said. But you really don't want to be alone."

She swallowed back tears, but couldn't stop a few from

rolling down her cheeks. "I don't. But… How did you know…? Henri?"

"He looks out for me. And obviously you. I was waiting at the hotel for you."

"You were?"

"I didn't think you really wanted to be alone. But I don't understand why you returned here if you had intended to stay away?"

"I've been a bit scattered lately. Sorry. But I have to finish this project. I just need to pull myself together and— There's sweeping and polishing, and I need to check the new roses—"

"That can wait until morning. I understand why you came looking for me at my penthouse. Because you couldn't stay away from me."

She wobbled her head and admitted, "Yes."

"I know that, because that's how I feel now. I cannot dream of letting you handle this alone. I love you, Viv. I want to be here for you."

She exhaled. "The job…"

"There will be other jobs."

She shook her head. "I doubt it. I'm a failure! But I guess I got what I deserved after I was so mean to you."

"Mean?" He sat beside her and pulled her against him. He brushed aside the hair from her forehead.

"Yes, mean. I left you to go to the doctor all alone," she said.

"But you came back for me."

"Sure, but only after I got hit with guilt at the airport. I had to return. I love you."

He tilted his forehead to hers. Her gaze glinted in the light from the chandelier. "And I had to be here for you. I love you."

With nothing more to say, Viviane melted against him.

His arms wrapped about her, stealing away worry and disappointment.

They understood one another.

His hand sliding up her back, Rez held on to the one thing that meant the world to him. Yes, even more than Le Beau. Because he couldn't be happy creating diamond necklaces for other women if he did not have the love and support of this woman. Their mouths met, and he inhaled her want and desire and was goaded deeper into the kiss. Their tongues danced. Their bodies belonged against one another. Supporting without commanding.

"I'm going to have to leave you more often," Viv said when they'd parted. "I felt that one."

"Where did you feel it?"

"Everywhere. If you want to have sex right now, I am so ready." She tugged at his shirt. *"Oui?"*

"Oui."

Lying entangled with Viv on the sofa, their clothes strewn on the floor and a cashmere blanket flung across them, Rez tilted his head against hers. Her breathing was heavy and deep. He loved it when she orgasmed. She let out a bold, moaning cry every time. No faking for this woman. She was as real and as open as a person could be.

"I love it when you come." He kissed her cheek and she curled against him, tucking her head against his shoulder.

She laughed. "You give a girl good reason to bellow, let me tell you that. Whew!"

"I want to hear your joy as often as possible."

"I'd like that, too. But…" She sighed, and he felt her mood drop as her body tensed. "When I'm done with your garden, that's it."

"Venice was a letdown, but that doesn't mean you'll never get another job. You shouldn't give up on building a client list."

"I don't want to. I won't. But I don't know how long it will take me to secure another job. Rez, who's going to hire a no-name American woman to create an indoor garden for them when there's probably tons of gardeners who've already staked their claim in Europe? I may have to go home to Minnesota."

"That can't happen, Viv. I love you. I want you in my life. I thought you were intent on the nomadic life? That's what this dream job would entail, *oui*?"

"It does. And will. Oh, Rez, I realize now that it could take some time to establish The Plant Whisperer. But my bank account needs it to happen faster. I really do want to give our relationship a go. But how can we make that happen? I don't think long-distance relationships work."

"Have you ever tried one?"

"No, but…"

"Hell, if you pursuing your dream means I have to boost my frequent flier miles, then so be it."

"You would do that for me?"

"I would."

"Thank you. But, again, my future is uncertain right now."

"I told you I'd recommend you to my friends."

"Sure, and I'd love that. But how many friends do you know who have indoor gardens that actually need work? They probably already have a regular gardener."

He shrugged. "I'll make some calls today. And if you need to stay in Paris a while, you can stay at the penthouse with me."

"That doesn't sound like a long-term invite."

"It can be."

"Rez." She sat up, pressing a palm to his chest. "I do want us to be an 'us,' but I also don't want to rush things. I don't want to force a moving in together situation for either of us. I know you're offering out of kindness, and, yes, you want me in your life, but are you really prepared to have me stay with you? Long term?"

"Honestly? I am. You've made me realize it's time to give up on the guilt. It hasn't gotten me anywhere. Time to move on. For real. And in the process of moving on I have fallen deeply in love with you, and I know it would make me happy to have you by my side all the time. But I also know that if you're working in other locations for weeks at a time it might give us time to ease into the permanent thing. *Oui?*"

"I do like the sound of that. My home base here?"

He nodded. "You've got talent, Viv. Don't sell yourself short. With the right marketing, and word of mouth, your business will grow. Just take it slowly. I will support you. Promise."

"Very well, but there's one more thing. Are you sure you can handle having a relationship with a woman who doesn't even speak your language?"

He chuckled. "*Mon amour*, you will learn."

"I honestly won't. I've tried. French does not stick to my brain cells."

Rez kissed her, rolling her onto her back and crushing his length along hers as he did so. Mmm… He was already hard again. He rocked against her, murmuring something in French.

"Fine," she confessed. "I think I know exactly what you said."

"*Très bien.*" He kissed her breasts, then leaned on his elbows. "The language will not be an issue. But I also have one more thing. You should know that I'm turning the reins of Le Beau over to Jean-Louis."

"Really? Are you sure? Le Beau means so much to you."

"Jean-Louis can handle it. He will learn because I will teach him. He's got a plan that'll slowly ease him into the position over the next year. And I won't have as much paperwork or meetings. It's win-win."

"Are you just saying that?"

"No, I mean it."

"Wow. I'm proud of you. And you'll still work there? Get to design beautiful necklaces and rings?"

"I would never walk away from what makes my heart sing."

She kissed him. "I know the change will be right for you. And with the protocol the doctor gave you, things might really start looking up."

"They already have. I have you. And that is what matters most to me. I almost forgot." He grabbed his suit jacket and fished out a small box from the inner pocket. "I finished it."

She opened the box and pulled out a silver chain. On it dangled the moonstone she had purchased, set into filigreed silver. Set above the white stone was a smaller, deep red stone.

"Garnet?"

"Yes. You said moonstone reminded you of Paris."

"Yes, and that garnet was for love."

"Exactly. But also the garnet reminds me of you, Viv. Earthy, sensual, and sexy. I hope you don't mind that I added it."

"Not at all. This is so much more pretty than I imagined it could be. Put it on me."

He secured the necklace behind her neck and the weight of it landed above her breasts. Viviane pressed a palm over it.

Rez leaned down and kissed her cheek. "This means there is someone in Paris who loves you. Who wants you to move in with him. Let's have fun with one another. Let's be lovers. Have sex whenever we want to. Eat at all hours of the day. Dash off to exotic locations. Jean-Louis wants me to take a vacation."

"How do you feel about that?"

He shrugged. "More good than bad. But relinquishing control over Le Beau will be a scary adventure for me, much as your future will be for you."

"We'll be there for one another."

"Deal. Do you want to go to Greece for a few weeks and forget about the world and have sex all the time?"

"Yes," Viv said without thought.

Because she didn't need to think about it. She was diving in deep with this man.

And life had never felt more promising.

EPILOGUE

A week later...

VIV'S PHONE RANG but she ignored it. The water was as impossibly blue as Rez's eyes. They sat on a private beach on a Greek island, sipping retsina, making love, and talking about anything and everything except their jobs.

Rez nudged her and handed her the phone. "It's an American number. You should take it."

Reluctantly, she did, wiping the sand from the phone while Rez began to kiss down her bare stomach. She whispered, "Wait until after this call before doing that."

With a groan, he rolled over and shaded his eyes from the sun with a hand.

Viv answered the call. It was Evangeline, the woman she'd spoken to at the Le Beau *soirée*. She and Nestor had moved into their Sixteenth Arrondissement home and were desperate for the terrace garden to be put in order. As well, they wanted her to teach them how to care for the plants. Was she available?

She glanced to Rez and their eyes met. His expression brightened as he seemed to hook onto the giddy feeling that was dancing through her system. He leaned over to kiss her on the head.

"I am," she finally said. To Rez—and their future—but also to her prospective client.

She heard the woman shout enthusiastically and tell someone The Plant Whisperer would do it.

The Plant Whisperer had done it.

Viviane had taken a leap into a new and wonderful future. And there was no looking back now.

* * * * *

AUTHOR NOTE

IN REGARD TO Rez's traumatic brain injury, during my research I discovered a doctor who'd created a unique approach, not just inviting the patient to sit on a couch and talk about his issues, but rather to scan the brain and see what was really going on inside his damaged brain.

I did not want to detail too much in the story. Every patient is different, and I am not a doctor. Nor would I ever suggest what the best treatment might be for any particular individual. But if you're interested check out the psychiatrist Daniel Amen for more information on his breakthrough therapy.

COMING SOON!

We really hope you enjoyed reading this book.
If you're looking for more romance, be sure to
head to the shops when new books are
available on

Thursday 5th
January

To see which titles are coming soon, please visit

millsandboon.co.uk/nextmonth

MILLS & BOON®

Coming next month

CONSEQUENCE OF THEIR DUBAI NIGHT
Nina Milne

Perhaps he should refuse to see her, but that would be rude. Stella must have some reason for being here. Only one way to find out. 'Send her in,' he said.

To his own irritation he could feel the thump of his heart against his ribs, as anticipation churned inside him. Then there was a perfunctory knock on the door, Mariella pushed the door open and ushered Stella in, nodded at Max and retreated.

He rose to his feet, actually glad that his desk separated them, gave him a barrier to absorb the impact of seeing her.

She tugged the scarf off her head and pushed the sunglasses atop her blonde hair in an impatient gesture and for a long moment they stood staring at each other. Stella looked different, every bit as beautiful but there was something he couldn't put his finger on, a subtle change. Her blue eyes held a certain something he couldn't decipher, the gloss of her hair held an extra lustre. But what hadn't changed was the instant charge, the magnetic pull of attraction, the urge to take up where they left off.

Her blonde hair was pulled back and then caught in a clip, tendrils escaping to frame her face. Blue eyes studied his face, as if she too was drinking him in, eyes that were shadowed with a trepidation that had been absent in Dubai.

'Stella. This is unexpected.'

'Yes.' Her lips twisted up into a smile that held wryness. 'I saw the article about your first date.' The article had come out two days ago, headlined with 'Spotted in the Wild – CEO Max Durante and heiress Dora Fitzgerald. Is it a date? The notoriously single CEO of InScreen certainly looked smitten as the possible couple … blah blah.'

'And I'm not here to make trouble.'

'Then why are you here?' He saw her hands curl into fists as though she were digging her nails into her palms, saw her shoulders pull back as she took a step backwards as if in preparation to turn and run and a sense of foreboding trickled through him.

'I'm pregnant.' There was a moment where the penny failed to drop where he could only look at her in bewilderment and she continued. 'With your baby.'

Continue reading
CONSEQUENCE OF THEIR DUBAI NIGHT
Nina Milne

Available next month
www.millsandboon.co.uk

MILLS & BOON

THE HEART OF ROMANCE

A ROMANCE FOR EVERY READER

MODERN

Prepare to be swept off your feet by sophisticated, sexy and seductive heroes, in some of the world's most glamourous and romantic locations, where power and passion collide.

HISTORICAL

Escape with historical heroes from time gone by. Whether your passion is for wicked Regency Rakes, muscled Vikings or rugged Highlanders, awaken the romance of the past.

MEDICAL

Set your pulse racing with dedicated, delectable doctors in the high-pressure world of medicine, where emotions run high and passion, comfort and love are the best medicine.

True Love

Celebrate true love with tender stories of heartfelt romance, from the rush of falling in love to the joy a new baby can bring, and a focus on the emotional heart of a relationship.

Desire

Indulge in secrets and scandal, intense drama and plenty of sizzling hot action with powerful and passionate heroes who have it all: wealth, status, good looks…everything but the right woman.

HEROES

Experience all the excitement of a gripping thriller, with an intense romance at its heart. Resourceful, true-to-life women and strong, fearless men face danger and desire - a killer combination!

To see which titles are coming soon, please visit

millsandboon.co.uk/nextmonth